ALWAYS LOOK TWICE

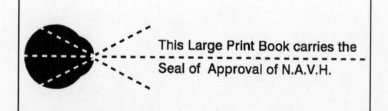

This Large Print Book carries the
Seal of Approval of N.A.V.H.

UNCOMMON JUSTICE, BOOK 2

ALWAYS LOOK TWICE

ELIZABETH GODDARD

THORNDIKE PRESS

A part of Gale, a Cengage Company

GALE
A Cengage Company

Farmington Hills, Mich • San Francisco • New York • Waterville, Maine
Meriden, Conn • Mason, Ohio • Chicago

Copyright © 2019 by Elizabeth Goddard.
Scripture quotations are from the New American Standard Bible®
(NASB), copyright © 1960, 1962, 1963, 1968, 1971, 1972, 1973, 1975,
1977, 1995 by The Lockman Foundation. Used by permission.
www.Lockman.org
Thorndike Press, a part of Gale, a Cengage Company.

Thorndike Press® Large Print Christian Romance.
The text of this Large Print edition is unabridged.
Other aspects of the book may vary from the original edition.
Set in 16 pt. Plantin.

LIBRARY OF CONGRESS CIP DATA ON FILE.
CATALOGUING IN PUBLICATION FOR THIS BOOK
IS AVAILABLE FROM THE LIBRARY OF CONGRESS

ISBN-13: 978-1-4328-6988-5 (hardcover alk. paper)

Published in 2019 by arrangement with Revell Books, a division of
Baker Publishing Group

Printed in Mexico
1 2 3 4 5 6 7 23 22 21 20 19

To my youngest, Andrew —
always remember that you're a blessing
from God, and a mighty man of God.
No matter the battles you've endured,
God is always with you. His love for
you is relentless, unfathomable, and
unshakable.

The name of the LORD
is a strong tower;
The righteous runs into it and is safe.
Proverbs 18:10 NASB

CHAPTER ONE

Few places in this world are more dangerous than home.

John Muir

Monday, 7:35 P.M.
Bridger-Teton National Forest, Wyoming

Harper Reynolds inched forward, hoping
she hadn't made a mistake in coming there.

After she positioned her camera on the
tripod, she zoomed in closer with her long
telephoto lens. Taking in those big brown
eyes, she captured the images of a grizzly
bear foraging for berries near the Grayback
River below, a good eighty yards from her.
A hundred yards would have been better.
The bear was aware of her presence — he'd
lifted his head and noticed her at the same
moment she'd seen him on her approach to
the river. Then he'd gone back to his searching, and she'd set up her tripod on a rise to
look bigger and be safer if distance wasn't

enough.

Maybe she was still too near, but she wanted to get even closer. That's what her teleconverter was for. She could get up close and personal with him without putting herself in danger. In fact, if it weren't for the trees, she could be several hundred yards away and still get great shots.

Through her camera lens, she balanced the massive creature with other elements — the river, trees, and boulders — as pure joy surged through her. The river was the perfect background and allowed her to include depth.

Raw vigor exuded from the bear's rippling muscles as he moved. Never in her life had she been this close. A rush of adrenaline — the thrill-seeker's kind — coursed through her. She wanted others to look at the images and feel the same nervous energy she felt being so close to this enormous and dangerous creature.

The sound of the rushing river anchored her, igniting childhood memories of this very spot, and mingled with the bear's grunts as he searched for food. She imagined he was happy too. She drew in the scent of pine needles and caught a whiff of the sulfurous stink from the geysers at nearby Yellowstone. Then she clicked on more images of the beast, taking in his hundreds of pounds of muscle and power.

Finger hovering over the button, she paused. Only a few more images and she would have to switch out the memory card.

No deleting images for her. She'd learned the hard way that inconsistencies in the metadata could cause all the images to be questioned and ultimately disallowed by the court. Except these weren't the kind of images for which she had to ignore the artistic rules of composition to focus solely on establishing location, evidence, position.

She gave herself a mental shake. It had been a year. Why was that coming back to her at this moment? No violent scenes, her therapist had said. And definitely no more crime scenes. She'd agreed.

Now she took pictures of nature. Peaceful. Serene. No blood or death.

The sun sank lower, forcing her to adjust for diminished lighting. She focused on the bear's eyes. Hoped for some interesting activity or behavior. She wasn't afraid. She'd brought her bear mace, after all.

And I know how to use it.

Still, she shouldn't push her luck and stay too long.

Tracking the bear as he lumbered along the riverbank, she swiveled the camera to the left on the tripod. She thought she had finally gotten the hang of panning after all the pictures she'd taken. Except the bear moved again and this time behind a large boulder, completely out of view.

She glanced around. Should she reposition the camera to get more shots?

Her cell buzzed in her pocket.

What? She got a signal out here? Emily was probably texting to see why she wasn't back yet. Her sister could have come along on the hike, but she'd claimed she needed to work on her latest mystery novel. Harper grinned. Partially true, but Emily was also nursing blisters and sore limbs from their recent hikes.

Harper reached for her phone, but a flash of bright pink caught her attention. She peered through the lens and panned the camera to search across the river.

Maybe a hundred yards out she spotted a woman.

Her arms flailed as she tore along the brush, bursting through the thick foliage. Her mouth hung open. Was she screaming? If so, the rushing river drowned out the sound from this distance.

Harper's heart pounded. She peered through the lens and zoomed in closer. Took pictures.

The woman's face twisted with pure terror, then she glanced over her shoulder at something. What was she running from?

Harper panned again to follow the woman. She snapped pictures. She should call 9-1-1, just in case. She couldn't stand by and do nothing while someone was in danger. With her free hand she reached for her cell in her pocket and tugged it out. She peered through the lens again. With a sharp intake of breath, she caught sight of a man with a rifle looking through his scope from at least four hundred yards away. Harper couldn't be sure he was actually watching the woman or had ill intent.

Regardless, she fingered 9-1-1. The call wouldn't go through. No signal now. She shifted the camera back to the woman. Magnified the image.

The woman's eyes widened — that final look of horror. Then . . . a blank stare.

Harper's heart seized as the woman collapsed face-first onto the grassy earth.

A crack split the air as it echoed across the river, finally reaching Harper's ears.

And Harper turned to stone, becoming one with a nearby boulder. She wanted to turn and run. Like she had in the past. She wanted to flee from the crime committed in front of her.

But no. This time, she had to be strong. She had to do what she should have done long ago.

Stay. Watch. Be the witness this woman needed.

Get live-action proof, not evidence gathered after the fact.

She focused her camera on the killer, taking a kill shot of her own. His face would be plastered everywhere. He wouldn't, couldn't, get away with this.

With his face still pressed against the weapon, he peered through the scope, his camouflage ball cap pulled low and shadows covering the only part of his exposed, wrinkled face. She took one last picture before she ran out of room on the memory card.

She should delete the photos of the bear, but she was trained otherwise — and if these photos were needed as evidence, best to follow protocol. With trembling hands, Harper slipped the memory card out of the camera and inserted the new card.

Pulse racing, she quickly repositioned the camera on the tripod and panned to find him again. He was moving in now, hiking toward his kill with his face still pressed against the weapon.

Frustration boiled to the surface. She

couldn't get a good, clean shot of the murderer. Still, she'd fill the camera with his image. She'd commit every detail to memory.

She wouldn't turn and run in fear and be the reason justice wasn't served.

Come on, come on. Take off that cap. Lower the rifle. Something. I need something.

Then he suddenly stopped. Wouldn't he go check his victim? Make sure he'd killed her?

But no. He remained in position. Still. Cold.

A hunter.

What was he waiting for?

He shifted the rifle on his shoulder and angled it.

The bear had drawn his attention. Harper had forgotten about the grizzly. That it hadn't run off with the report of the rifle surprised her. Would the killer shoot the bear now?

Run, bear!

She wanted to scream at the animal. Tell it to flee. Her hands slicked against the camera. Against the cell phone as she repeatedly tried to call out for help. Get a signal. Something.

The bear turned away from the river as if responding to her silent pleas and headed

15

into the woods.

A chill crept up her legs, spread around her midsection, and inched over her back. The wind shifted. A sensation she'd experienced before swept over her — she was in mortal danger.

She took one more picture, but it wouldn't be enough to nail this murderer. Harper waited. She'd give him a few more moments to reveal himself, and then she'd commit his image to memory.

But he lifted the scope from the bear as if searching for something else. The rifle traveled upward. Higher and higher until . . .

Until the barrel was trained on her. He was looking right at her! He peered at her through his scope. She saw one crinkled eye beneath the shadows.

He saw her. The murderer was watching her.

Heart pounding, her mind raced. A bullet could blast through her now, and she'd never know what hit her.

Fear rooted her feet in the soil like an old oak tree. She was going to die. Right here. Right now. That's what she got for trying to do the right thing. For trying to stay and see it through. To be the witness she hadn't been before.

Move. Your. Feet.

Run!

But the pictures!

Grabbing her camera, she yanked it from the tripod, exposing herself like an idiot. She pulled her foot from the ground and took one step back. Instead of running, she dropped to her knees and inched over behind a boulder. She had to calm her breathing.

From there, she peered around the rock, looking through her camera again. The large lens was unwieldly without the tripod. She couldn't see the killer. Her shaky hands didn't make it any easier to search. It was no use. She wouldn't get another chance to photograph him. Regardless, she had to get out of there. Had he gotten a good look at her? He could shoot her from this far away, couldn't he?

Harper crept across the pine needles until she was well into the thick of the forest. She crawled until the trees were close together and much too dense for him to find her even with his scope. She hoped. Then she scrambled to her feet and ran. Harper was running again. Like before. Nothing had changed or would ever change.

Heart pounding, Harper could see the hiking trail through the trees. Only a little farther.

Her foot caught on a branch hidden in a tuft of needles and she pitched forward. She was powerless to stop her fall. A scream erupted as momentum propelled her toward the jagged edge of a boulder. Pain ignited when she hit the rock, and her camera slipped from her fingers and clattered as it tumbled into a deep gully.

Coming here had been a mistake, after all.

CHAPTER TWO

Monday, 7:43 P.M.
Bridger-Teton National Forest, Wyoming

The report of a rifle echoing off some distant mountain hadn't given Heath Mc-Kade pause. Not in Wyoming, supposedly the most heavily armed state in the country, where people kept guns not so much for protection against two-legged creatures — but four. Protection and hunting.

No. It wasn't the gunfire that gave him pause, but the scream that resounded mere moments before. That scream had been awfully close to where he'd brought a group of Emerald M guests on horseback from their backcountry camp in the wilderness area. Still, in these mountains, sounds could travel for miles.

He did a quick head count of his guests who hiked up from the Grayback River where they'd been enjoying the scenery before getting back on their horses. This

19

group was late heading back to the camp because two teenage boys had taken off on their own, and Heath had searched for them and hauled them back. As the founder of Emerald M Guest Ranch as well as their trail guide, he was responsible for keeping them safe. Easy enough when they followed the rules.

Frustration simmered in his veins, but he tempered it with a layer of patience that was already running too thin.

Quickly, he mounted his horse, Boots. Settled in the saddle, Heath cranked his head to listen for any other sounds — screams or otherwise — that might give him a better idea which direction to search.

No one else reacted as if they'd heard something out of place, but they'd been down by the river, which had probably drowned out the scream. He reined Boots around to head up the trail.

"Where're you going?" Leroy called after him, emerging from the group of campers gathering around some horses.

"I heard a scream. I need to check it out."

"You think you're going to find someone in three million acres?"

Heath slowed Boots and glanced back at Leroy. Heath counted on him to pick up the slack.

"Nope," Heath said. "But if she's close and I can find her, I will. You go on ahead. I'll contact you if I need your help." Heath held up the radio.

Leroy Miller had twenty years on Heath, a lot of ranching experience, and was only now wrapping his skills around guest ranching — herding tourists around the back-country — since Heath had hired him five months ago.

"Sure thing." The uncertain look in Leroy's eyes told Heath the older man thought Heath was hearing things. Maybe he was. He hadn't been the same since he'd been shot nine months ago by someone he trusted.

"Heath, let me do it while you take care of your campers."

He urged Boots up the trail, leaving Leroy standing there. "No, I'll handle it."

He had no time to waste talking about it. Leroy was persistent. Not a bad trait, but Heath had no patience or time for this. He'd already taken too long if he was going to be any help.

Leroy would have his hands full with these riders. He had to get them on their horses and back to base camp before it got too dark. And Pete Langford couldn't help because he'd already gone ahead to check on the camp.

But Heath couldn't leave without investigating, and he would catch up to them.

In the distance, he faintly heard the man call, "Be careful. I don't want to have to come looking for you!"

Heath directed Boots to quicken the pace. He figured he'd look along the hiking trail. People usually stuck to those. Someone might have taken a tumble and it would be getting dark once the sun started setting behind the mountains. Easier to find them now. He hoped that was all that had happened and whoever had screamed had picked herself up and kept walking.

Except the scream echoing in his mind curdled in his gut. With his Remington pump-action shotgun in the saddle scabbard, he palmed his handgun, his .44 Magnum, for a potential short-range battle. He hoped it wouldn't come to that. He'd already had enough to last him a lifetime, but he would never go unprepared.

Mentally or physically.

"Come on, Boots." He directed the horse up the trail for half a mile, then ran into a hiker's trail that circled Red Rock Hill and led him to a fork in the road. He could continue on the horseback riding trail, but he and the campers had come from there.

He chose the hiker's trail instead.

The rangers didn't appreciate horses on the hiking trails, but this might be an emergency and it was taking far too long to respond.

Heath the hero, coming to save the day. Right. He could have sent Leroy to search, but the man didn't know the area nearly as well as Heath, who'd grown up exploring Bridger-Teton National Forest. Spent his childhood hiking in the Gros Ventre Wilderness.

He urged Boots up the steeper way and kept his eyes out for anyone who could have fallen off the trail. He wished he could have brought Rufus and Timber, who could have sniffed someone out, but this particular region wasn't dog friendly.

"Help . . ."

"Whoa," he said to Boots. The call for help was so faint he was surprised he'd heard it. "Who's there?"

Quickly, he slid from the horse. Boots lifted his head high, his tail too, and snorted. Stomped the ground. Could he sense someone was hurt?

"Easy, boy." Though the horse was highly trained, Heath loosely tied him to a whitebark pine.

Heath swept his gaze over the darkening

forest near the edge of the trail where it sloped downward toward the Grayback River that was pebbled with boulders and roots bursting from the ground. He could see how someone could trip and then slide down along the pine needles.

He took slow and easy steps as he made his way down. "I'm here to help. Anybody there?"

The hair on his neck stood on end. A low growl rumbled too close for comfort and crawled over him. Every warning his father had ever given him flitted through his mind at the same instant.

"Keep the length of a football field away from bears. Hike in groups. Make lots of noise. Back away. Never run. Leave the area immediately and give the bear more space."

Maybe the bear hadn't seen him, and he could back away. Then again, maybe the beast was looking right at him.

He remained perfectly still except to angle his head to see.

CHAPTER THREE

Big, dark eyes stared back at him through the trees, a mere twenty yards away. Too close for comfort. Seven hundred and fifty pounds of flesh and fur rose up on its hind legs. Roared. Teeth seemed to glow in the darkening forest.

A challenge.

If the grizzly decided to charge, this would be over fast. Still, the charge could be a bluff. If Heath had to shoot, he'd better be quick about it.

Be bear aware!

Heath knew the rules.

Had memorized the rule book. Could recite every rule backward as well as forward. Rules meant nothing if you didn't follow them. He hadn't brought his bear spray. Though touted as the answer, it didn't work every time. It had its limits. Instead, he'd brought a gun to this battle. Besides, he'd been too focused on the scream. And then the barely audible call for help.

The bear had probably been down at the river fishing. Maybe the shot and the scream had agitated him long before Heath had stepped into his life.

Heart pounding, Heath palmed the Magnum — a pistol loaded with heavy bullets for such an occasion — but it would be a shame to have to shoot. It wasn't the bear's fault that Heath had startled him.

Maybe he could fix this.

Lifting his arms, he spoke in even tones as he backed away slowly, adding a few more yards. He had to keep putting distance between them while he let the beast know he wasn't dinner. "You don't want to eat me or kill me. No. That would send the rangers after you. You'd be relocated away from your bear friends and family. But more likely, you'd be killed."

In all his years living in Wyoming, he'd never come face-to-face with a grizzly. He'd seen them foraging off in the distance, sure, but he'd never been this close. Rangers usually let the public — wilderness guides in particular — know when a grizzly had been spotted in an area. But mostly, everyone was warned — this was grizzly country. Be aware. Be on alert.

Now if Heath could back away and out of

sight and the bear went along his own path, Heath could get back to his business.

His heel caught on a fallen branch and he tripped. Fell on his rear. The bear lumbered forward. Not quite a charge, but still intimidating since the grizzly was so close and could be on top of Heath in seconds.

Panic seized Heath's limbs. He gripped the pistol, fingered the trigger, and prepared to shoot to kill the beast in self-defense.

"Wait!" A woman stepped into view next to Heath.

"Are you crazy?" he asked. "Get back!"

With both arms extended, she pointed her canister of bear spray and started spraying. The mist shot out and formed a cloud. She had nerves of steel to face a grizzly. Heath kept his weapon aimed at the creature in case the spray didn't work. It wasn't a guarantee, especially if the bear was angry.

When the animal was ten feet away and closing in on them, the spray hit its face and eyes.

The woman remained where she stood, her limbs visibly shaking. He was surprised she could keep her aim. The spray would soon run out.

Heath continued to aim his gun as he slowly got to his feet and stood next to her. Two humans facing the bear could deter it.

The beast moaned. Grunted. Pawed at its face and eyes.

"This might only make him madder than a hornet and meaner than a whole nest." He kept his voice low.

"What should we do now?"

"Slowly back away."

The grizzly rubbed his face in the pine needles.

"The cannister's instructions say the effects of the spray should last a few minutes," she said, a significant tremble in her voice.

"Do you want to wait around and see?" Heath started up the hill. It was best to recede and put distance between them. Let the bear get back to his life. Heath shouldn't have turned his back on the bear, but the terrain was too rough and that had already gotten him in trouble when he'd tripped.

He felt like such an idiot.

When he realized she hadn't joined him, he backtracked and took her hand, urging her up the hill and back to the trail. He found Boots — still agitated — tethered where he had left him. The horse's earlier jitters made sense now.

Heath turned to the woman and took her in for the first time. Blood streamed down her forehead on the right side, and she was unsteady on her feet. He'd been on her left

28

side when she'd sprayed the bear, and since the woods were darker than the open trail, he hadn't seen the blood. His heart rate finally evened out, and his head cleared.

Then it hit him. The scream. "You were the one who screamed earlier? Called for help?"

"Yes. I screamed. But I think someone else screamed too. There's a guy with a rifle out there. He shot someone. I . . . I witnessed a murder."

Heath's heart jumped right back to his throat. He hoped he hadn't heard correctly. "Wait, you witnessed a murder? Are you sure?"

"Yes. A man shot a woman. It was the rifle shot that disturbed the bear. Now can we get out of here? I need to tell the sheriff."

Her words left him shell-shocked. "Are you sure she's dead?"

"Yes."

Heath eyed the forest. He thought of the gunfire he'd heard. "Where did this happen?"

"Across the river."

So he couldn't check the woman to see if she was still alive. And since it happened across the river, they weren't in imminent danger. He breathed a little easier. He would radio ahead for Leroy or Pete to contact the sheriff's department. Heath wasn't on duty at the moment, but even if he was, others needed to get to the scene. Find the body. Secure evidence. Look for the shooter.

He returned his attention to the injured woman in front of him. "I need to stop that bleeding." The scent of blood could draw the bear from miles away, and he was much too close as it was. Fortunately, Heath's saddlebag contained all the essentials. There was the old adage "If a horse could get hurt, he would." Quickly he removed the first aid kit. "I'm going to stop the bleeding for now, then we'll clean it up at the camp. This might hurt a little when I put pressure on it."

He opened the saddlebag and pulled out bear spray. He grumbled and squeezed it, then put it aside for some gauze and an elastic bandage and went to work. She winced as he wrapped the bandage around her head and over the wound. Did he know her? He didn't think he'd seen her around. Probably a visitor to the region. Still, her red hair reminded him of a childhood friend.

"There. That will hold it for a while." Then she needed a doctor. No doubt about it.

He gestured for her to get on Boots. She shook her head and stepped back. "I can't ride."

Compassion flooded him. That and a sense of urgency. Twigs snapped. Grunts and eerie groans grew louder. This bear might be too ornery for his own good. Heath had hoped the beast would take another path and they wouldn't run into him again. He still felt like such an idiot. If anyone should have been prepared to face a bear, it should have been Heath. Instead, this slender woman stood up to a grizzly on his behalf.

"We need to get out of here now," he said. "You don't have to know how to ride. Let me help you up. Put your foot in the stirrup and lift your leg over."

Boots was over fifteen hands and feisty, so probably intimidating to her, even though she'd stood up to a grizzly bear.

She frowned but did as he asked, placing her foot in the stirrup. He grabbed her waist to guide her the rest of the way. "You're a pro."

Good thing she was slight, and Boots was big. The horse could handle their combined weight, but Heath didn't make a habit of riding double. He considered this an emergency, and it was only for a short distance down the trail.

Pro or not, she had a nasty cut on her head. Probably needed stitches. He eyed the saddle. He could probably ride with her, but that would be much too close. "I'm going to ride behind the saddle, but my arms will be around you, okay?"

She nodded. Her adrenaline was probably crashing. Definitely an emergency. He climbed on behind the saddle. "Let's get you out of here and fixed up." He was concerned she could have other injuries from the bear. She was lucky to be alive.

"Come on, Boots." Heath radioed ahead to the camp and got ahold of Leroy. "Call the sheriff. Someone's witnessed a murder." He gave Leroy the general location about where to search for a body. Maybe they could find the shooter before he got away, but it was doubtful. The Bridger-Teton National Forest encompassed over three million acres. They wouldn't make it to the crime scene before dark. Maybe not even before the rain started.

As for his transporting her down the mountain, dusk would afford them some light for another hour or so, but darkness came fast in these woods. He urged the horse down the trail that grew hazardous with the fading light. A trail in the dark was definitely not optimal, but he could use a flashlight if needed. Boots was sure-footed either way and could handle this.

Heath kept his arms around the woman as he held on to the reins, and he could feel her body tremble. He hoped she was only getting chilled because the evening was cooling, but he was concerned she would go into shock.

Come on, Boots. The stallion seemed to sense the urgency and quickened his pace down the trail.

"It's going to be all right. I'm glad I heard you scream and came to investigate," he said. "Thank you, by the way, for saving the bear."

"Excuse me? I thought I saved *you* from the bear."

"Oh, that." He cleared his throat. He hadn't meant to sound as if he didn't appreciate her effort, but the truth was that he would have shot the grizzly once he knew for certain it was a threat. The bear could have been bluffing, but it was a risk to wait and see. By spraying the bear, she saved it. But now that he thought about it, she'd stepped boldly out in front of him to save them both. "Thanks for saving my life with the bear spray."

Thanks for not asking why I didn't have my

own in hand.

"You don't think the bear will follow us?"

"Nah. He's long gone." He hoped. He needed to warn Leroy and his campers about the grizzly in the area, and to be careful. They always packed away food in bear boxes. He'd give his friend Ranger Dan Hinckley a call to notify him he'd run into an aggressive bear.

The shooter was another matter altogether. Concern for his guests churned in his gut. Packing up and heading back to Emerald M this late would be too treacherous. But one thing at a time.

On the trail, Heath focused on guiding them back to the horse path and then the spot by the river where he'd brought his horseback-riding campers. They were gone now, as Heath had hoped. Leroy had rounded the campers up and started them on their way to the base camp in the wilderness, where they would stay one more night.

As for Heath, he would let Boots take them back to camp. The horse knew the way as well as Heath.

Other than their discussion about her saving him from the bear, they traveled in silence. Heath focused on the trail through the darkening woods, concern for her and for his horse taking up his thoughts, while the woman kept to herself. Just as well. He didn't have the bandwidth for a conversation. He hoped she didn't feel awkward with his arms around her to guide Boots, but it couldn't be avoided.

At the base camp, Heath slid from Boots first, then assisted her down. Her face still caked in blood, she eyed the backcountry camp — tents, tables, and big flames roaring in the fire pit, while he looked at her head. The bandage appeared to have put enough pressure on the cut to stop the bleeding. Hopefully she hadn't lost much blood.

She studied his face, then her eyes grew wide. "Heath?"

The way she said his name, the earlier familiarity he'd sensed rushed through his brain. It couldn't be her.

"Heath McKade?"

"Yes. That's me." He looked into those golden amber eyes and remembered. He'd been too distracted to fully comprehend it earlier.

"You don't remember me?" she asked.

"Harper . . . Harper Larrabee." He struggled to believe it was actually her.

"It's Reynolds now. Mom changed our names when we moved."

His mind rushed back to those rough

grade-school years. He took in her thick red hair, long, pretty face, and slender feminine form. She wasn't the twelve-year-old girl he'd known. Even with glasses and braces, she'd been a pretty girl then and was now a beautiful woman. They'd been best friends. She'd been there through the worst time in his life. Then her family moved away suddenly after her father died. He wanted to reach out, grip her arms, hug or something, but he thought better of it.

Instead, he said, "You've grown up." *Brilliant, Heath.*

"I can't believe it was you who came to investigate. Though I guess it does make sense. This is Heath McKade country." Her smile was tenuous. "You came riding in like a knight on a horse, only wearing a Stetson."

He hadn't meant to give her the impression he was a hero. He refused to let her words bolster him. She was injured, and he focused on that.

"Let me change that bandage and clean up the wound." Even a minor head injury could bleed profusely, but she still needed professional medical attention. "Then we'll head to town to get that looked at by a professional. You can talk to the sheriff there too. If Leroy did as I asked, then the sheriff will have sent deputies to look for the woman and the shooter. Go ahead inside the big tent there."

She did as he asked and took a seat at a long picnic table. He positioned a bright lantern so he could see better. Then he sat down next to her and unwrapped the bandage. He could hardly believe Harper Larrabee was there. Wait — Reynolds. Harper Reynolds. Weird to think they'd been so close once, but with so much time gone by since he'd seen her, they were almost strangers now.

She reached up to touch her head and winced. "Is it bad?"

"Doesn't it hurt?"

She nodded. "It throbs, but it's the least of my worries."

He didn't know why, but he took her hand then. "The bear could have done a lot worse. You're safe now."

"Oh, this?" She gestured to her head. "The bear didn't do this."

Leroy entered the tent. "Heath, what's going on? I started to radio again. What's this about a murder?"

Her gaze jerked to Leroy.

Leroy eyed her. "I'm sorry, Ms. . . ."

"Harper. Call me Harper." She swayed in her seat.

37

Leroy held out his hand as if he thought she would fall over. Heath did the same. "Get me the medical kit," Heath said.

"Sure thing." Leroy turned to rush away.

"Oh, and Leroy, we ran into a grizzly. He's agitated. Let's make sure everyone stays alert to that fact." Harper's bleeding head didn't help matters and could attract the animal. "We should get ahold of Ranger Hinckley and let him know what's going on with the bear and the shooter. You contacted the sheriff, didn't you?"

"Yes. I didn't have a lot of information, but they're sending deputies. Contacted rangers in the area too. I'll get right on warning them about the bear though." Leroy exited the tent.

"If this wasn't the bear, then what happened?"

"I fell and hit my head."

"Where else are you hurt?"

She probably didn't have any idea how nasty of a gash her injury was. Heath didn't have the heart to tell her or scare her more.

Leroy came back with the first aid kit and a blanket, which he wrapped across Harper's shoulders. Food sizzled on the fire pit outside. He wasn't sure that was such a good idea. The smells could draw the bear. "Let Pete know to keep an eye out. Get the

38

food put away as soon as possible."

"Uh, he's not here."

Heath swung around to stare at Leroy. "What?"

"He wasn't here when we got to the camp."

"Well, call him. Radio him. Get him back here. We need the hands."

Heath returned his attention to Harper and wiped around the wound. "We really need to get you to a hospital, but that's a bit of a drive. I thought I'd clean it up first, but . . ." He hesitated.

"It's that bad, huh?"

"Did you lose consciousness?"

"No. I was only dazed. Everything was fuzzy. I called for help, but I hadn't really thought someone would hear me and come to help. It was more of a cry of desperation."

He paused to look at her eyes, and in them he saw the person he remembered — the girl he'd known so well was still there inside, despite the years of life between them. She'd been so important to him then. Helped him through a tragedy. She'd been his lifeline — he could return the favor, if nothing else.

"Don't worry. I'll get you down the mountain to the clinic. How did you get to the trail?"

"I parked at the trailhead."

"Mind if we take your vehicle? We packed all the way up to this camp, so I'd have to go all the way to my ranch to get a vehicle. Or we could call for help. Get a ranger here to take you down."

Leroy stuck his head through the tent opening. "Pete's back."

"Thanks. Warn him about the bear and the shooter, but I don't want anyone to panic. Make sure the horses are safe too." Heath rewrapped her head, his own hands shaking now. Maybe he should have Pete and Leroy go ahead and help the guests pack up the camp. Or have them head back to the ranch and they could come back tomorrow for the camp.

"I can drive," Harper said. "I'm fine. You don't need to worry about me. You have your hands full already." She pulled the blanket tighter and stood up as if she would walk out of the tent and follow the dark trail to her vehicle alone, then hesitated. Was she afraid of the bear? The shooter? Her legs still shaking, she lifted the tent opening. Beyond the camp, the woods had turned to complete darkness as dusk had drawn to an end and night had settled on the Bridger-Teton National Forest.

That look on her face. Fear. Pure fear. He

40

thought of those he'd known in his life who'd had that same look. Women who'd been stalked or abused or traumatized in some way. Harper was one of those — she'd been terrified and grief-stricken after her father was murdered. And then her family moved.

He hadn't seen her again until today.

"I don't think you should drive yourself anywhere. I'll drive."

Harper was turning pale. Despite his efforts to rewrap the wound, blood oozed down her forehead again. She reached up to touch the gash, then examined her blood-covered fingers. She swayed as though dizzy, then her body went limp. Heath caught her before she hit the hard ground.

CHAPTER FOUR

Dressed in a white lab coat, Dr. Lacy Jacob, a fifty-something woman with a few gray roots sprouting in her shiny brown hair, hovered over Harper's head. "Now, hold still. You're going to be just fine."

A sharp pain stabbed her. "I thought I wasn't supposed to feel anything."

"You're not. We'll give you some more anesthetic." She eyed the nurse named Jesse James.

Like the outlaw, he'd told her. Jesse grabbed a syringe and injected more pain-killing anesthetic into her head near the wound.

"*Now* you shouldn't feel a thing," Dr. Jacob said. "Try not to think about it so much. Tell me what happened. How'd you get this nasty gash?"

Harper squeezed her eyes shut. "I fell and

42

hit a rock."

As the doctor continued to close the wound, Harper thought back to the moments leading up to that. After the shooter killed the woman, he found Harper through his rifle scope. Pain spiked through her again, bringing her back to the present.

Tears surged. She reached up to swipe them away only to be blocked by Dr. Jacob's arms.

The doctor eyed her suspiciously. "Oh, now I'm almost done, hon." She backed away and looked at her handiwork. "You'll need to come back in a week or so and I'll look at removing them. These aren't dissolvable. I wanted to minimize the scar."

Minimize the scar? She'd have a scar. "A week?" She and Emily had planned to start home to St. Louis tomorrow, after they drove by the house where they used to live.

"My sister!" She'd completely forgotten about Emily. Harper sat up and threw her legs over the bed. "I have to call her. She's going to be worried sick."

Where was her cell? Oh . . . she'd dropped it when she was scrambling away from certain death.

"Hold on." The doctor urged her back onto the bed. "You need to take it easy for a few minutes. I'll be back in to check on you." Dr. Jacob left the room.

Harper directed her words to the nurse. "I need to call my sister. Can I borrow a phone?"

"We'll see what we can do," Jesse said as he prepared a syringe.

"What's that for? You're not giving me something to relax me, are you?"

He chuckled. "This is a tetanus shot, dear."

She was getting a tetanus shot and stitches while a murderer was out there. Someone had been killed tonight.

Her pulse jumped. Where was the sheriff? Heath had called him on the way to the hospital. Told him what Harper had said. The sheriff was supposed to meet them there so she could tell him what she'd witnessed.

The images rushed over her like the Grayback River rushing over the Canyon Falls.

She'd been photographing the grizzly. Pure unadulterated nature. Then she'd witnessed a murder. She'd taken a yearlong sabbatical from her job as a crime scene photographer per her therapist's suggestion, and what happened? She took live-action shots of a murder as it occurred. The sheriff would want to know how Harper knew the woman was dead. Lifeless eyes. Had she

44

caught that part on her camera? She'd tried to be proficient as she captured the scene, but everything happened so fast, and she'd been both horrified and scared to death.

That woman. She was so young. Had her whole life ahead of her. Harper would never forget her eyes.

She started shaking. She might never stop.

Nurse Jesse handed her a landline handset.

Harper stared at it. "What's this?"

"You said you needed a phone."

"Right. Oh no. I can't call her with this. Her number is in my cell, and I lost that. I don't have her number in my head." Harper looked from the phone to Jesse.

"I get that. These days, who remembers numbers anymore? Sheriff can help you contact your sister as soon as he gets here. Doc Jacob wants you to sit right there until then."

She shook her head and slid from the bed until her feet touched the ground. "I need to head back to the camp before Emily calls a search party on me. She probably already has."

"Harper?"

She peered around Jesse at the familiar form standing in the doorway. Heath Mc-Kade. Once upon a time she'd known this man. Or rather, she'd known this man when he was a boy, and had known him well. It was weird and awkward to be in this situation with him. He sure looked nothing like the kid he'd once been. He had been scrawny even at twelve — gangly then too — but she'd still thought he was cute. He'd had a certain way he smiled . . .

And just like then, Heath grinned at her now, as though he would take all her troubles away. She knew that was for her benefit. That was the Heath she remembered. And that smile. She could never forget that. Or the fort he'd shown her where he would hide.

She remembered the trauma he'd been through, then she'd gone through her own. Had his experience changed him forever like Harper's had changed her? She wouldn't wish that on anyone, but how could one escape the deep scars left from childhood devastation? Still, time hadn't stopped, and life had moved on.

And here they were. No longer kids. Heath was definitely anything but scrawny. His mussed, dark brown hair shagged near the edge of his collar, and his eyes were still the most brilliant blue. His face had filled out, and he had a strong jaw that he left scruffy. He certainly hadn't had whiskers as a twelve-year-old.

They'd been best friends at one time — finding a connection to each other they hadn't been able to find with anyone else. But now . . .

For all practical purposes, the man was a stranger to her, wasn't he?

He stepped fully into the room. "Harper."

She blinked. "Sorry. I was thinking."

Honestly, she'd thought he'd dropped her at the small-town emergency room and left. Funny how glad she was to see a familiar face — well, not so familiar anymore.

His square jaw worked back and forth as his brow furrowed with concern. "Everything all right?"

"My sister Emily. I need to let her know that I'm okay." She reached for the stitches, but Jesse caught her hand.

He shook his head gently. "Don't touch. I still need to put a bandage over the wound."

"Where is she staying?" Heath asked. "We can let the rangers know. Either they or a deputy can find her."

"Okay, that'll work, but it's still going to freak her out." Harper sat back on the edge of the bed. "Where's the sheriff? I need to speak to him and make sure someone is out there looking for the man who killed the woman in the woods. I should have done

47

more. I tried to call 9-1-1, but I couldn't get a signal. Instead of staying I . . . I ran." Grief tried to overcome her, but she held it back. Later, when she was alone, she could fall apart.

Heath crossed his arms, which seemed to make his shoulders broader. "You won't have to wait long for the sheriff. He's already in the hospital questioning someone else. He's coming to talk to you next."

"One of those mailbox bombs hurt someone this time," Jesse said. "I think the sheriff's talking to him before we send him on to St. John's in Jackson. Different county. Different sheriff."

Heath stepped closer and sucked the oxygen out of her personal space. "Someone is already out there looking where you said you witnessed the crime. And you did everything you could, Harper. Don't beat yourself up."

She wished this had been a nightmare. "Emily will be —"

"Don't you worry, Harper," Heath said. "I got this. What was the name of the campground?"

"Granite Ridge. Our site is registered to Emily Reynolds."

Heath got on his cell, his eyes never leaving hers.

Did he have a wife? His marital status didn't matter one way or another. Harper was curious, that was all.

"I need to assist with other patients. I'll be back to check on you." Jesse smiled and stepped from the room, but Dr. Jacob returned.

She pulled out a small flashlight and shined it in Harper's eyes, moving the light to the left and the right.

"Is everything okay?" Harper asked.

"Seems to be." Dr. Jacob turned off the flashlight.

Harper blinked a few times, relieved to be rid of the bright light in her eyes.

Cell phone to his ear, Heath glanced her way, winked, and exited the room, leaving her with the impression he was taking care of her. Though she was grateful to have someone in her corner, she didn't need his help. "Why would he bring me all the way in and stick around?" Harper hadn't meant to say the words out loud.

"That Heath McKade is a good man." Dr. Jacob entered information into a computer. "You should be glad he stayed. Tell me again. You said you didn't lose consciousness, right?"

"No." As far as she remembered. "I was dizzy and disoriented." Terrified. Admittedly, Harper had been confused. Maybe she had lost consciousness, but she didn't think so.

After she'd fallen and hit her head, she grappled with the pain for a few moments. Her camera clattered into the gully next to her — Harper could have easily fallen down there too. Instead, her camera had left her behind. And where was her cell phone?

Then she saw blood on her hands. Blood everywhere. Fear choked her. Had she been shot? Waves of dizziness kept her anchored.

The blood and pain blurred her eyes so that she couldn't see. Using her arm, she wiped her eyes, and finally, she got up and tried to find her way back to the trail but somehow got turned around.

When she heard someone coming, desperation compelled her to call for help. But then she realized her mistake. What if the shooter had crossed the river to find her? She then hid for a few moments and watched the man get off his horse. She had to make sure he had come to help. Finally, she decided the man in the Stetson wasn't the shooter. He couldn't have so quickly changed his attire and made it to where she was. And Heath — though she hadn't known it was him at the time — had that protective demeanor. Harper decided to make herself known when the grizzly she'd been photographing moments before approached the man who'd come to help. She couldn't simply stand idly by while a bear tore him to shreds, so she'd intervened.

Now Heath appeared in the doorway again. Her breath caught as if she were surprised all over again that this man was Heath McKade — her childhood friend. So many bittersweet memories that she'd long forgotten came drifting back, along with that terrible goodbye she'd offered him without explanation after her father was killed. Murdered.

Behind Heath a formidable man in a uniform entered, whom she assumed was Sheriff Taggart.

Heath approached her. "I called the campground offices and found someone to notify your sister that you're okay and will be back soon."

Soon was a relative term.

The sheriff stepped forward and offered a surprisingly warm but serious smile. "I'm Sheriff Taggart. Tell me more about this murder you claim to have witnessed."

Claim to have witnessed? Law enforcement speak.

"Not only did I witness it, I took pictures."

That news didn't change his facial expression, but he tugged out a pad and pen. "I'm going to need details. I already sent deputies and my investigator out to the general area, but so far they haven't found anything. We can get a better look at the crime scene tomorrow."

Harper frowned, thinking of all those deputies stepping on any evidence that might have been left behind. Still, how could they avoid it when they needed to search the area for the woman's body?

"Primarily, we're looking for a body tonight, though honestly, I hope we find a woman who is still alive. I'll need to see the pictures too."

Harper held on to a fragment of hope too. Then again, she'd seen her eyes. Lifeless eyes couldn't be mistaken.

"I . . . I, uh, lost the camera."

He arched a brow. Ah, so the sheriff could show surprise. Maybe even displeasure. "We can get it back. Tell me where you lost it so I can send someone to collect it and secure the scene."

"No, wait. I have a memory card in my pocket." A thrill shot through her. She'd all but forgotten. "I had to switch them out in the middle of taking pictures of the crime." Harper felt around in her jeans' pockets.

Where is it? "Excuse me while I find it."

She stood from the bed and dug deep in all her pockets. No. It couldn't be gone. How could she have lost it? Both Sheriff Taggart and Heath watched her. "I could've sworn I stuck it in my pocket. But I was trying to call 9-1-1 and take pictures, and I guess I dropped it instead of sticking it in my pocket." Shame flooded her. "But the memory card is out there somewhere with the camera." She looked to Heath. She was familiar with the trail from her childhood, but it had been so long since she'd walked it. "Tell him where the bear attacked you."

Heath shared details about the trail and the area, sounding far more familiar with the region.

"Why were you in the area?" Sheriff Taggart asked.

Harper cleared her throat to explain. "I was on my way back from Yellowstone. Back to the campground. I stopped when I saw the trailhead. It reminded me of my father." Harper pursed her lips, wishing she hadn't brought him up, but now that she had, she might as well finish. "We used to hike that trail years ago. Would sometimes fish at the river from the other side — where the woman was shot. And it just happened a grizzly bear was down by the river. I've been hoping for a chance to photograph one."

For months now. "So where Heath explained he ran into the bear, the murder happened across the Grayback River from that point. I was using my zoom lens to get close shots of her face. She was terrified. She knew he was hunting her."

And now he could hunt me.

Her only consolation? He had to figure out who she was and find her first. Still, the doctor's words drifted back to her. *"You're going to be just fine."*

Even though the doctor had patched her up, Harper was not going to be just fine.

CHAPTER FIVE

For some reason he would never understand, Heath always ended up assisting someone in the direst of circumstances. Maybe that was the simple matter of him answering the call. Maybe his Green Beret training and the motto — *de oppresso liber*, to free the oppressed — kicked in, and he was obligated to respond.

Or more recently, his role as a reserve deputy added that extra assurance that he would step up to the task. While that remained the right thing to do, Heath still doubted he was the right person to do it.

Every time he tried to fix what was broken or to help people, things only got worse.

He should leave Harper while things were good. He didn't have to stay with her. He wasn't on duty now, but he could hardly stand back and watch from the sidelines. She'd appeared surprised that he'd stayed at the hospital with her. He'd done his duty as a Good Samaritan. Heard her call for help and brought her down the mountain and all the way to the hospital. He'd even made sure Sheriff Taggart was informed and talked to Harper. Heath could walk right out of this room and Harper Reynolds would be the sheriff's problem.

Unless Heath was called in to assist as a deputy.

He hoped Taggart wouldn't need help with Harper now. Heath had other matters that needed his attention. The Emerald M Guest Ranch campers trusted their guide to provide a unique wilderness experience and get them home safely. Sure, Leroy and Pete could manage things, but it was best if Heath returned as soon as possible. He was usually only needed by the sheriff for special events or local emergencies or natural disasters, like the supervolcano at Yellowstone erupting. Yeah. Usually only special events.

As he listened to her story — the details she hadn't shared earlier — he wasn't sure why he was staying. Except that wasn't true at all. He knew exactly why he was here.

He knew this woman. Or had known her when she was a girl.

And the girl turned woman kept him riveted to her story. He'd always thought she had the most beautiful eyes. He didn't like to see them filled with the horror of what she'd seen. To her credit, she did a good job holding back the tears that tried to break through her words.

Harper pressed her hand against her midsection. "He peered through his scope and aimed his rifle. I saw her drop before I heard the sound of gunfire."

Her hands shifted from her stomach to cover her eyes.

Heath willed himself to stay put. He wanted to comfort her, but he didn't know her well enough. Not anymore. So what if he'd held her in his arms when she'd passed out? That didn't mean he could do it again or that his act of compassion would bring her comfort.

"Ms. Reynolds, can you be sure that he shot the woman? Or that she fell due to a gunshot wound? Or that she was even dead?"

She dropped her hands, her eyes now rimmed with red. "What do you mean? You don't believe me?"

"My deputies will find a body if one exists, or find an injured woman. Maybe someone with a gunshot wound. But you were taking these pictures from a distance. I think you believe you saw a murder. But at that distance, even with a camera, you could be mistaken."

"You don't understand. I had a 600mm telephoto lens with a teleconverter. That means I can get a closeup shot from a distance. Even without my camera, Sheriff, I saw the woman running. I know what I saw. Then I zoomed in to get a closer look."

He nodded and jotted more notes. "The pictures you took will help."

"Make sure they look for the memory card in addition to the camera," she said.

"Heath," Sheriff Taggart said, "please stick with her while I make a phone call. I'll be right back."

Heath should have already walked out. Not because he was a coldhearted jerk, but because she needed someone else. Someone who wasn't him.

Except he couldn't leave because his boots were cemented to the floor. She'd sucked him right into her world, telling a story that held him captive and made him feel the terror with her as if he had been there too. He sensed that behind Harper's pretty face was someone who'd been on a tumultuous journey since leaving the area. There was an inner strength to her. Beyond that, she was physically strong and had the toned muscles of someone who'd hiked many miles.

She definitely had more than one story to tell.

And he realized they were still kindred spirits. Definitely not what he had expected to find tonight when he took Boots up the mountain trail. Still, Heath didn't have it in him to be there with her on a more personal level, and somehow he needed to cut the connection before it was too late.

The way she looked up at him now, Harper already had the wrong idea about him. She stared at him as if she would accept his help. That gave him the nudge he needed to step away. Literally. He pressed his back against the farthest wall in the small space. Folded his arms across his chest. At the very least, he would keep his distance, emotionally. Heath had gone into bad situations thinking he could make things right but had failed people he cared about. He wouldn't add her to that list. As soon as he could, he'd extricate himself.

Sheriff Taggart stepped back into the room, apparently finished with his phone call. "All right, Ms. Reynolds. Heath explained that you're staying at Granite Ridge Campground. Please stay in the area so I can contact you with more questions."

If Harper was the only witness to the crime, then at some point her testimony could be needed too, especially if they couldn't retrieve her camera.

"I haven't finished my story yet. I haven't told you everything," Harper said.

"Well, what is it?"

Her big eyes went from the sheriff to Heath.

"The killer saw me witness his crime. He stared right at me through his scope while I took his picture."

The meaning behind her words knocked into him. Heath thought his heart had stopped.

The killer could try to find and target Harper next.

Taggart scribbled more notes on his pad. His cell phone chimed, and he excused himself again.

Heath held up a finger, letting her know that he was leaving too but would return. He followed the sheriff down the hall and waited for the man to finish his phone conversation. When Taggart ended the call, Heath cornered him.

"Don't you think she's in danger?" Heath asked. "She witnessed a crime. He could target her."

"The shooter was across the river, three or four hundred yards away, at least, and in the trees, part of the woods. This is tourist season. She's a tourist. Even if he got a good look at her face, chances are that he doesn't know who she is or where to find her. If we learn differently, then we'll act accordingly." Taggart leaned closer. "I've had two deputies resign over the last six months."

"You're saying you don't have the manpower to keep your only witness safe. Isn't a situation like this the reason you talked me into being a reserve deputy?" But the man hadn't called on Heath for much more than providing security at the county fair, though he'd had to go through the same rigorous training as full-time deputy sheriffs.

"I don't know that she's in danger, McKade. We'll take it as it comes. I'm considering putting you on investigating the mailbox bombs. Find those kids and stop them before somebody else gets hurt. Before someone gets seriously injured."

Heath scraped a hand through his hair. What was happening to his town? Wyoming had a low population and supposedly a low crime rate. "Why do you think it's kids?"

"The first bomb — Reece Keaton saw three teenagers running away from her mailbox, that's why. She couldn't give me a solid description of the boys. They took off into the woods around dusk. Sure, they're kids, but these days anyone can learn how to make a bomb from the internet."

Heath nodded. As good a reason as any to start searching for the boys. "As for Harper, let's hope she's not in danger, then."

Taggart cocked a thick brow. "But you'll watch out for her if needed."

"Uh . . . no . . . I didn't mean me." Considering his past, he wasn't the guy for that particular job.

"We'll see. It depends on the state's response if I decide to call for outside resources. In the meantime, you can deliver her back to her campsite."

CHAPTER SIX

Silence enveloped the cab of Harper's Dodge Ram as Heath drove it back to Granite Ridge Campground. Deputy Herring, a young guy with freckles and a baby face, followed in a county SUV to give Heath a ride back from the campground.

Harper glanced at the dashboard digital clock.

Nearly midnight thirty.

The Ram followed the ring of light on the road. Otherwise darkness pressed in on all sides. Harper barely registered the drive or even Heath's presence next to her. Images of the day's horrific events clicked across her brain like snapshots, and she couldn't shutter them out of her mind.

How many crimes would she witness in this life before it was over?

Harper leaned her head against the headrest. Dr. Jacob said the painkillers would make her drowsy, yet even considering the pills combined with exhaustion, Harper couldn't fall asleep or shut off her brain.

All she wanted to do right now was curl into a ball on a bed piled high with quilted blankets.

The crunch of gravel jarred her, and she opened her eyes. Heath steered around the small circular parking drive allotted to each camping spot. Lights were on in the camper. Emily had poured her heart and soul into renovating the vintage Airstream.

"Nice," Heath said.

She had no energy for words and opened the door. By the time Harper had climbed out, Emily was standing in the camper doorway, a blanket wrapped around her shoulders. Emily had to have been holding herself back from flying out of the camper and demanding answers. Harper suspected the county vehicle behind the Ram was keeping her glued to the Airstream at the moment.

A flashlight beamed through the woodsy campground. Someone probably heading to the facilities. Heath got out and stood between the Ram and the county vehicle. Before heading to the Airstream, Harper paused and glanced his way.

She wasn't sure what to do or say next. This all felt so awkward. "Thanks for everything. It was good to see you again." Running into him tonight after so many years and the manner in which their paths had collided surprised her. Still, their friendship had been all drama at the end. So it made some kind of weird sense that meeting him again would start with drama too. She couldn't help but wonder if she'd see him again. Or if she even wanted to.

"You're welcome, and it was good to see you too." Heath tossed her the keys. "Be sure to lock up and watch out for grizzlies."

Was that almost a grin? She'd prefer to see the full-on smile, but she couldn't offer a big smile herself.

Deputy Herring waited in the vehicle. Harper gave a small wave, then turned her back on the two and walked toward Emily. A figure holding a flashlight downward emerged from the shadows and into the light. Mr. Stein, the guy who ran the campground.

"Oh, hey there." What was he doing here? "I'm sorry if we're disturbing the campers."

"Don't worry about it," he said. "I came over to see if everything is all right."

Emily smiled. "Mr. Stein was the one who

delivered the news that you were at the hospital and someone would bring you home."

"You can call me Ken." He shined the light up and down Harper as though to get a better look, then nodded. "I see you're all in one piece, with some tape to hold you together. I'll leave you ladies to your business. If you need some more help" — he looked at Emily — "let me know."

He disappeared into the darkness, his flashlight guiding his path.

Harper stepped into the camper and released a long exhale. "I never thought I'd be so glad to be back."

Hands trembling, Harper closed and locked the door, then peered through the mini blinds and watched the county vehicle roll slowly through the campground to the exit. "What was the campground guy talking about?"

"Oh, I had some trouble opening the door, that's all. These old things. Maybe I should replace the door entirely. He showed me a trick to get it open. But who cares about that?" Emily took two short steps in the small space and hugged Harper. "I was so worried when you didn't come back!"

Emily released Harper and lifted her hand as though she would touch Harper's bandages but dropped her hand to her side instead. "Oh, Harper. What happened?"

"It's only a few stitches, that's all."

"A few stitches? I feel so bad that I didn't go with you. I should have gone."

"Don't be ridiculous. You had a deadline. Did you make it?"

"Barely."

"I doubt any of what happened tonight would have turned out differently." In fact, Emily could have been hurt — or worse, the killer could have seen her too.

Harper went to the pullout sofa bed.

"No. You're sleeping on the real bed tonight. It's your turn anyway," Emily said.

With no energy to argue, Harper dragged herself to the small bedroom and dropped onto the bed.

"Aren't you going to tell me anything?" Emily asked.

"I'm drugged and exhausted, but I'll try. I was running and fell and hit my head. I yelled for help and then Heath McKade came to my aid, but a grizzly bear almost attacked him. No one was hurt. I sprayed the bear and we got away. Heath took me to get the stitches."

"Wait. *The* Heath McKade? The guy you were so close to growing up? That you secretly had a crush on?"

"What? I didn't have a crush on him. He was my best friend."

Emily gave an exaggerated pout.

"Em . . . you were older. Dating. You were too cool for me anyway. Don't take that the wrong way. I looked up to you and wanted to be like you."

"I'm sorry if I made you feel that I was too cool to be your best friend," Emily said. "I didn't mean to."

"It's okay."

"But seriously, Heath?" Emily's eyes widened. "I can't believe he was the guy."

"Yep. He rode up on a horse like a knight in shining armor, only wearing a Stetson." She might have actually told him that too. She hoped he hadn't thought she was flirting.

"Wow. Well, what did he say? He remembers you, doesn't he?"

"Sure. It took him a minute. It's not like we instantly recognized each other after more than twenty years." Harper shifted on the bed and pulled the covers over her, the memories of the evening gone wrong gripping her again. "Emily, there's a lot more I need to tell you."

At Harper's serious tone, Emily eased onto the edge of the bed. "What is it? You're scaring me."

There was no easy way to tell her. "I witnessed a murder."

A few seconds ticked by as Emily absorbed her words. "My first thought was to say you're joking, considering I write murder mysteries. But I can see you're not. What happened?"

Harper shared the morbid story with her crime-writing sister. She wished this would be the last time she had to relive the events, at least for a few days, but she knew the sheriff's office investigator would have more questions. With exhaustion and grief rippling through her, Harper pressed her face into her hands.

"Oh, sis, I'm so, so sorry. After everything you've been through already, I don't understand why this had to happen."

Harper closed her eyes and listened to her sister's soft sniffles — her tears on Harper's behalf.

"You don't deserve this. You don't deserve any of what's happened to you."

The room grew so quiet that Harper thought Emily had left her to sleep, but she heard another sniffle. Harper opened her eyes to study Emily. She hated seeing her sister upset.

"I know we were supposed to head home tomorrow," Harper said, "but the sheriff asked me to stay a few more days in case he has questions. As soon as possible, I want to go home." Maybe after all these months, she would see the therapist again. She'd been close to feeling like she'd had a breakthrough, but then a murder happened right before her eyes.

"Okay, but let's not forget to look at the old house before we leave. I've been thinking about that for months."

Oh, great. "I don't want to see it now. I can't. Not after what happened today."

That house was already sullied by a murder — the murder Harper had witnessed as a child. Her father's. Then her mother whisked them away to Missouri to start over, even changing their surname.

Emily scrutinized her. The move had probably been hardest on her — she'd left friends behind. A boyfriend. She'd been popular in school. Harper had left Heath behind. And yeah, maybe Emily was right. Maybe she'd had a little bit of a crush — but they'd only been twelve going on twenty-one.

"Sure, I understand." Emily touched Harper's arm and rubbed, attempting to comfort her. Well, it wasn't going to work. She didn't want to be comforted. "Get some sleep."

Her sister slipped out of the small room and shut the door.

Now Harper hoped she could actually sleep.

Instead, the murdered woman's eyes haunted her. The woman's fear. The realization that she was about to die at the hands of a killer, no matter her efforts to escape. Harper felt the woman's terror to her core. She hadn't turned away from the horror, from the blood — everything she'd wanted to escape over the last year — no. She'd taken the right images.

The victim.

The murderer and the scene as a whole.

Then she'd kept watching through the zoomed lens to take in as much as she could. She'd committed to memory an image of the victim, with her dark hair pulled into a ponytail and her bright pink T-shirt and khaki cargo pants. The hunter dressed for tracking backcountry big game.

Oddly, the homicide survivor's guilt that she'd worked hard to free herself from had raged back to life. Once again, she had survived while someone else died. She'd been on the sidelines and there'd been nothing she could do but watch — but that was far more than she'd done in the past when she'd chosen to run and hide.

This time she hadn't looked away. She'd seen the man who committed the crime. Taken a picture of him. Though with a rifle covering half his face and the shadow from his cap hiding the other half, the picture would do no good. In the end, she ran away. With his high-power scope and long-distance rifle, he could have shot her, so she had no choice.

Still, if she had stayed, maybe she could have gotten a better look at him. Watched him make his way to a vehicle. Something.

But the victim? Harper couldn't get her face out of her head, and maybe this time she shouldn't.

"Wake up."

Harper opened her eyes and found Emily standing over her. Morning light filtered through the mini blinds. So she'd slept, after all.

"There's someone here," Emily whispered.

Harper sat up on her elbows, waiting for the details. "Well? Who is it?"

"It's a deputy. He needs to speak to you."

Was it Heath? He'd mentioned being a reserve deputy.

Harper groaned. She was already in sweats and only had to slip on a hoodie. She finger-combed her hair, then met him at the door.

It wasn't Heath. Funny that she was disappointed.

"Deputy Herring, what can I do for you?"

"We can't find a body. I'm going to need you to come with me."

CHAPTER SEVEN

Tuesday, 9:00 A.M.
Emerald M Guest Ranch

After pouring himself a cup of coffee, Heath stared through the kitchen window at the canvas awash with green — acres and acres of evergreens spread before him. Beyond the hue of green and off in the distance, grays and blues stretched toward the sky. The mountains were hazy due to smoke that had drifted down from a big fire in Montana.

Heath tried to remember that he was a fortunate man to have this view, but life had a way of pulling him in too many directions.

He hadn't stopped thinking about Harper and his run-in with her last night, or the fact that she'd witnessed a murder.

Concern for her, as well as the victim's family, weighed on him. Heath reminded himself that Harper wasn't his business and he needed to keep his distance. The best thing he could do was pray for her. He needed to clear his mind long enough to take care of his guest ranching business.

While sifting through the mail that had come while he'd been gone at the backcountry camp — only a four-night stay this time — he went over his mental checklist.

All his guests were safely back and getting ready to head to their respective home states this morning. A whole new set of guests would arrive this afternoon, with more trickling in the rest of the week. Hired help would clean out and restock the cabins before the new guests arrived.

Then one particular piece of mail drew his attention. He opened the small package to find a framed photograph of his brother and his new wife. Mr. and Mrs. Austin McKade. They could have emailed or texted a picture, but Willow wanted to make it special since Heath hadn't been able to attend the wedding. And how could he when they'd eloped in Hawaii? Good for them.

Easier that way, Austin had said. Willow wouldn't miss her grandfather as much. Heath got that.

He set the framed photo on the counter for now. It could go right next to the picture Charlie had sent from Texas, where she was now thriving. He couldn't be happier for her, after all they'd been through together.

Next he lifted an envelope from the state medical examiner. His father's toxicology report. His hands shook as he opened the envelope, then slid the pages out.

The results confused him. Five years ago, his father had died in a head-on collision that had taken the lives of a senator and his family. His father had been blamed for driving while intoxicated, but a few months ago someone who should know the truth had told Heath that Dad hadn't been drunk.

Paws clicked across the floor as Timber approached and whined. The old dog plopped down next to Heath's feet.

He patted the dog's head, then studied the paper. According to this report, his father *had* been drunk. What was the truth? That was something Heath intended to find out. On the one hand, he could go even further in fixing the damage done by his father. On the other hand, dredging up the accident could do more harm than good.

Boots clomped on the front porch. Leroy or Pete? Heath dumped his tepid coffee into the sink and poured a fresh, hot cup. He'd better get his fill of caffeine before the day got busy.

When he turned around, he was startled by Leroy standing in the kitchen. He had taken off his boots and slipped into the kitchen without Heath realizing it. Leroy's mother had trained him well. But this was Heath's home, and he would good and well wear his boots where he pleased. Right. He peered down at his own mismatched socks.

"You heard anything more about that murder last night?" Leroy got some coffee too.

"Nothing yet."

"Seems like being a deputy would mean you were privy to that kind of information."

Heath frowned at Leroy. "If I was privy to it, that wouldn't necessarily mean you were."

Leroy chuckled. "I didn't mean to pry. Word is going to get out about the murder sooner or later. Besides, I thought you knew that girl who witnessed it happen. Seems like the Heath that I've heard about would be all over this."

Yeah. Well. Maybe the old Heath had learned his lesson. This was the new Heath. The Heath who knew he couldn't always be the hero. The Heath who knew his limitations.

"Only if they need me, and they'll contact me if they do." There. That should keep Leroy quiet.

What was Harper even doing in Wyoming?

He'd never even asked. He'd thought she was something special two decades ago, and he had a feeling she'd grown into something even more special. But she looked haunted. It was the same look she'd had in her eyes after her father was murdered. And the same grief when she came to say goodbye and tell him her mother was moving them. He'd had the feeling then that Harper and her family were running scared.

Heath had been too wrapped up in his own misery — and Harper, she'd been the one to help him through it. Now he should be the one to help her through this. But it was probably better for her if he didn't.

He let his thoughts shift from Harper to the crime she'd witnessed.

What that poor woman went through being chased and hunted like an animal brought his fury boiling to the surface. To think that Harper had witnessed everything and the killer knew it disturbed Heath to his core.

"Looks like they need you." Leroy's words brought Heath back to the moment.

Chugging the rest of his coffee, he eyed Leroy over the rim. "Why's that?"

"A county vehicle is heading up the drive."

"Will you go see why they're here?"

"Nah, I think we both know the sheriff or

one of his deputies wants to talk to you. I have a feeling you're getting dragged into this murder business whether you like it or not. You'll do the right thing." Leroy left the kitchen, probably in search of his mother, Evelyn. He lived in a cabin on the property, but Evelyn had a room in the main house.

Heath sort of adopted Evelyn as his grandmother a few years ago after he had hired her to help around the house while he focused on getting the guest ranch up and running. She was like family to him. So when Leroy needed a job, Heath hired him to help with the ranch. Leroy thought of himself as the voice of reason, offering what he considered sage advice. The jury was still out. Evelyn offered more of that for Heath, if he ever needed to talk through his issues.

Heath found his boots and opened the door as Deputy Randall Cook was about to knock. "Can I help you?"

"Sheriff sent me to get you. We need you to confirm exactly where you were last night when you helped Ms. Reynolds."

"Why didn't you just call?"

"We did. You might try answering your phone."

He'd left it charging on his dresser.

"Does he want my help in an official capacity?" If he did, then Heath should change into a uniform, which he didn't rightly feel worthy to wear.

"Yes. But you don't need to waste time. Come in plain clothes."

Heath grabbed a light jacket, though the day would warm up too fast, slipped on his boots, and clomped onto the porch, shutting the door behind him. "What can you tell me?"

"There's no evidence of a crime, much less a murder."

CHAPTER EIGHT

"This is where it happened." She eyed the drop-off. "And look down there. See, that's where I took pictures of the grizzly bear. I set up near that boulder by the gully. The bear was by the river. Across the river, that's where the crime happened." And where, a lifetime ago, she and Dad had gone fishing on the Grayback River. Now the murder overshadowed those memories.

Harper carefully led Sheriff Taggart and his investigator, Detective Moffett, closer to where she had been when she'd taken the pictures.

She hesitated. "I don't want to destroy evidence. You do plan to collect evidence, don't you? I mean, in case the guy came over here to look for me." As soon as she said the words, she regretted them.

Taggart eyed her. "We know what we're

doing, even here in the country. Moffett will collect it — that is, if she finds any."

Harper wasn't sure she liked the suspicion in his tone. Add to that, Moffett was taking pictures with the camera on her cell, not a high-quality camera that would be used by a serious crime scene photographer. Harper pursed her lips before she said something else she'd regret.

"Nature has already taken care of evidence." Detective Moffett gestured at the ground where rain had formed rivulets that left pine needles, leaves, and debris behind on its path to the river. "Even if it hadn't rained, the pine needle carpet wouldn't reveal footprints easily. So far, I haven't seen any. Yours, McKade's, or the killer's. But we'll keep looking."

Harper didn't want to be critical of their methods — then again, if they hadn't found a body or evidence of a crime, then maybe they weren't looking hard enough. She wanted to suggest they bring in the state and use those additional resources, but she didn't want to further antagonize the sheriff, who already seemed irritated. Maybe it was more that he believed her but wasn't uncovering the required clues to confirm her story.

She wished Emily had come with her today, but she and Emily had agreed they should leave as soon as the sheriff said they could go. So Emily stayed behind to do some prep work. She was very particular about her vintage Airstream that way. And Harper didn't want to spend one minute longer here than necessary.

"Right next to this boulder is where I stood to look through the camera after I positioned it on the tripod."

Detective Moffett angled her head. "You used a tripod here?" She was referring to the steep incline.

Harper shrugged. "This was an extreme situation, but I've had a lot of practice, and it was worth it to get the bear."

"Do you have any idea how dangerous it is to get that close to a grizzly?"

"I wasn't close. This isn't close. The bear was way down there. At least eighty yards away." Harper pointed.

"Still too close. You should keep at least a hundred yards away if possible."

"The gully prevented me from putting that much distance between us. I couldn't have gotten the shot a hundred yards away." Unless she'd been on the other side of the river. Her heart palpitated at the thought. Who knew if she could even have seen the murder from there? But it was more likely she would have been a victim too.

Sheriff Taggart stared across the river. "You say the camera was pointed toward the bear down there. Your camera was focused on the bear. Tell me how you took pictures of a murder across the river."

"I saw something. A flash of color. So I panned the camera — moved it until I saw the woman across the river. That's where it happened." She pointed straight across. "See where the woods open up to the meadow at that stack of rocks? I zoomed in to get a real close look."

Taggart angled his head. "You're sure about that? We were just there."

A lump grew in her throat. "Yes. I'm sure. Have you considered the possibility that he disposed . . ." She couldn't finish the words.

"I've considered the possibility that he got rid of the body, yes. You weren't able to witness what happened next because you say he spotted you and you ran."

"Yes. I was afraid he would shoot me too. I was able to grab the camera. I knew the pictures I had taken would be important, but in scrambling to get away I stumbled, fell, and hit my head. That's when I dropped the camera." Harper slumped at the confession. They already knew about the camera, but the failure grated.

His gaze flicked to the bandaged wound

on her head. "Are you taking the painkillers this morning?"

Was he accusing her of not remembering where the crime happened because of being drugged? "No. I didn't take them. I won't lie, the wound hurts and I wish I had." The painkiller she'd taken last night had worn off sometime early this morning. Should she simply speak her mind? "I'd like to go over to the other side to see for myself where it happened. If you've already looked, I want to look for myself. I don't see any yellow tape cordoning off the scene yet, so will you take me there?"

"We've secured the area across the river. No one is coming or going until further notice." He scraped a hand across his jaw. He seemed young for a sheriff, at least in Harper's limited experience. Sharp brown eyes stared back at her. "Ms. Reynolds."

"Please call me Harper. I'm not big on formalities."

"Ms. Reynolds, if I don't find a body or evidence of a crime, I'll open a file and keep it open, but without anything to go on, there's nothing more I can do."

"But you have the pictures from my camera."

Detective Moffett stepped up, her form

inflexible. "I'm afraid that's another dead end."

"What do you mean?"

"We've already looked here and only wanted you to confirm we were looking in the right place since we didn't recover the camera, the phone, or the memory card."

"You're telling me that someone climbed down to look for my camera and it wasn't there?"

Moffett nodded.

Harper stared at the woman for a few long seconds, her heart in her throat. Deputy Herring had failed to mention that on the drive there. Maybe he didn't know. Or maybe they wanted to see her reaction to that news.

Harper turned and retraced her steps. "This is where I was when I fell and dropped the camera." And she would get it now too. She started making the climb and slipped, barely catching herself on a rock that stopped her fall. Her stomach clenched. This would be a hard, rocky descent.

"Ms. Reynolds, Harper, please come back up here," Sheriff Taggart called down after her. "We've already looked down there. I told you. And you hit your head last night. I don't need you getting hurt again, and on my watch."

"I'm going to find my camera. The proof you need." Her hands shook. This turn of events had surprised her. The sheriff was having doubts about the murder she witnessed. Doubts about her.

Well, she would prove she was telling the truth.

"Oh, for the love of Pete!" Taggart scrambled down after her.

Arms crossed, Detective Moffett supervised from above like a petite drill sergeant.

Harper continued down, using patches of foliage or jutting rocks for leverage. "I would have gone after it last night, but . . ."

Now wasn't the time to add in that she'd been confused and disoriented. She never should have left her camera. Honestly, with the gash in her head, the bear, and Heath, she'd all but forgotten about it until she'd told the sheriff last night. In the back of her mind, she'd hoped to go back for it and believed it would remain where it had fallen. She hadn't considered the rain or the possibility that someone would take it.

Finally, she hopped to the bottom. Last night's rain had washed a ton of debris into the gulley. Had it also washed her camera out to the river? For some reason, she didn't think it had fallen all the way to the bottom. And in that case, she should have seen it on her way down. The deputy who searched earlier would have found it already.

She looked at her path down. The rocks, trees, bushes. No camera. The camera, with the big telephoto lens and the tripod, all gone. That was going to cost her in multiple ways.

"What happened to it?" Harper eased to sit on the edge of a boulder. Was she going crazy? Losing her mind?

I know what I saw.

She'd been thinking about how she didn't want to photograph blood and crime and violence again, and then she'd seen him.

A killer.

A murderer.

That woman brutally hunted and shot.

That couldn't have been a figment of her imagination brought on by past traumas.

Unshed tears surged in her eyes. She'd better pull herself together or the good sheriff would think she was crazy and had imagined it all, or was pulling a stunt and wasting his time.

She and Emily had planned to head home as soon as the sheriff said she was fine to leave, and she'd been hoping that would be today or tomorrow, after he found the crime scene. She'd told him everything she could. But things were turning out much differently than expected. How could she leave if he wasn't even convinced a crime had taken place there?

If no one believed Harper, then who would solve the murder? Harper thought about the woman. In her mind, she could see the woman's eyes pleading for help from her unmarked grave in the Wyoming wilderness.

Justice hadn't been served for Harper's father either. "The woman, she should have been reported missing by now."

Sheriff Taggart frowned again as if he feared Harper would send him on a wild goose chase. If he'd called her old boss, he might already know about her mental health issues. He lifted his palms and approached her slowly. Yep. He thought she was unstable.

She'd have to prove otherwise.

"I want to meet with a sketch artist. I can describe the victim for you."

CHAPTER NINE

Tuesday, 9:59 A.M.
Bridger-Teton National Forest

The sun shone harsh and bright on the trail by midmorning and Heath paused to remove his Stetson. He wiped his brow. He found the spot easily enough, though dusk had set in when he'd ridden Boots up the trail to search. But he was on foot today.

He pressed his hand over the familiar throb in his side. He'd received a gunshot wound last fall, and though it had fully healed, he could still feel the pain. The doctor had explained that his experience was psychological. In other words, the pain was all in his head. He could definitely believe that. With each throb, the experience flashed in his mind.

He'd already been through tragedy in his life, and he'd had plenty of stressful experiences during his time overseas as a Green Beret — so why was it that this one event had stayed with him? Changed him?

Left him doubting himself.

He pushed the doubts aside for now.

"This is it. I tethered Boots to that twisted pine to the left. I made my way down where the trail slopes to the river right here."

"This is the spot then. Ms. Reynolds led us here earlier. Rangers identified that trench for us. Called it Draper's Gully."

He glanced at Cook. "I thought Taggart was going to meet us."

Deputy Cook shrugged. "He was supposed to, but looks like he's over there now." He lifted his chin, gesturing across the river.

Heath couldn't see them and made his way down a bit, then recognized the Bridger County Sheriff uniforms as well as the park ranger uniforms. The red-haired woman must be Harper. The other small woman was a brunette. Detective Moffett. She didn't wear a uniform. He'd been on the receiving end of her interrogation skills last fall when they'd needed to unravel the thick tangle of murders, deception, and betrayal spanning two decades.

Someone held a leash for what he would guess was a search dog.

Heath figured they'd already had the dogs out looking for the body last night, searching for a criminal on the run, but they'd come up empty-handed. Today they needed to confirm the location.

Cook followed him down. "He's beginning to doubt her story, especially since there is no camera so there are no pictures. What do you think? You were there."

"I didn't see the murder. I only faced off with the grizzly and Harper showed up with the bear spray."

"But what do you think about her story? What's your impression of her?"

Heath didn't like Cook's insinuation. "I think she's telling the truth. Why would she make this up?"

"It could be that she believes her story, but it never happened. She *did* bump her head, you know."

He'd heard of amnesia, but could a person remember events that never happened?

"My Aunt Johnida experienced that. She had memories of stuff that never happened. It's called . . . wait . . . it's on the end of my tongue." The deputy snapped his fingers. Tilted his head. "Confabulation. That's it. When someone gets a brain injury, they can have false memories."

"She doesn't have a traumatic brain injury." He didn't think. Had Dr. Jacob looked into that? He couldn't remember if Harper had gotten an MRI last night while he waited or if she would need to go into Jackson for that. Maybe Dr. Jacob had scheduled one for her. Harper hadn't said.

Since Heath wasn't a medical professional, he didn't want to have this conversation and say the wrong thing, considering the deputy had asked his opinion. His opinion shouldn't count one iota.

Only the facts mattered.

He thought back to everything that had happened. Again. Not like he hadn't relived the incident in his mind a hundred times already. He believed Harper was telling the truth about what she saw. If he was wrong about that, and she had false memories — that would mean a woman hadn't been murdered. That would be for the best.

But it would also mean Harper had some significant issues to deal with.

"Let's look around here and then you can take me across the river," Heath said.

"That'll take a half hour or more. They might be gone by then. Besides, they already looked here."

"Still. I want to look around myself and see what's what." The rain had come down hard, but the tree canopy would have sheltered the area from the full torrent.

He found the boulder next to the gully, the position that matched Harper's description of where she'd been standing when she took her photographs. Whatever evidence the rain hadn't washed away, he hoped Detective Moffett had collected and documented earlier.

Across the river, maybe Moffett would find specks of blood where the body had fallen. Taggart was claiming that so far there was no evidence of a crime. How could that be if someone shot and killed a woman? Even if it had rained last night, and from the looks of it, harder here than in town.

Heath returned his attention to what had happened on this side of the river.

Harper said the shooter had seen her. Heath imagined Harper looking on, watching the crime through her telephoto lens and seeing the murderer look at her through his scope. She panicked. He could definitely see that happening. He gazed upward and could see how if someone was in a hurry and scared, it would be easy for them to stumble and hit their head. Somewhere between that boulder where she'd taken her pictures and the trail, she'd lost her camera.

He glanced down the gaping gully and saw nothing but rocks, broken limbs, and pine needles. Then something shiny wedged under a fallen branch caught his attention. He slid down the incline and peered under the branch.

A cell phone. Harper's? Or someone else's? He was surprised those gathering evidence hadn't found the cell. Then again, a person would have to be standing at the right location with the sun shining in that specific position for the reflection to be seen. So he was at the right place at the right time.

He looked up and spotted Cook searching near the edge of the gully but closer to the trail. "Hey, Cook, get down here."

The deputy scrambled to the edge. "What have you got? The camera?"

"A cell phone. I don't have evidence bags. I'll let you handle it." The rain could have ruined the cell and it might be useless to them.

Heath moved out of the way so Deputy Cook could take care of the possible evidence. The deputy snapped a few pictures while Heath turned his attention to the gully, which was washed out from decades of runoff. Branches lay broken. Rock scuffed along the ridge. Someone had gone down into the gully today. The deputies had indeed searched for the camera. But had they also searched for footprints — someone who could have gotten to the camera first? If the killer had watched with his scope for any length of time, he might have seen her drop the camera. He also would have seen her fall and hit her head. He might have made his way across the river so he could get a better shot at Harper.

And found her camera instead. And dropped his cell phone in the process.

Heath lowered himself to sit on a flat boulder and dragged in a breath of mountain air. He listened to the roaring Grayback River echoing off the slope, the encounter with the grizzly still fresh in his mind.

If the killer had Harper's camera, then he could destroy the pictures. The evidence. Or use those same pictures or other identifying information found on the camera to find her. Taggart's suggestion that she wasn't in danger was way off.

CHAPTER TEN

Tuesday, 10:36 A.M.
Crime Scene on the Grayback River
Harper's head throbbed, and the sun blazed down on her until she thought she would be baked alive. Maybe that's because she sat on a flat rock — the perfect baking stone — avoiding the grassy meadow, now muddied. She watched Detective Moffett and other deputies comb the area, along with a US Forest Service ranger and a Wyoming Game and Fish Department agent. Multiple agencies and nothing but her word to go on. Multiple people trampling whatever evidence might have remained.

The sheriff had asked Harper for her assistance in pinpointing exactly where the woman who was shot had exited the woods — but he hadn't allowed her to walk anywhere near the actual scene. She'd had to pinpoint from a distance. His mood wasn't too friendly, because right now, Harper couldn't prove that anything she said had taken place.

Add to that, she knew that the person who called to report the murder was often considered a suspect. Most murders were committed by people who knew the victim. In this case, she didn't know the victim or the murderer. She only knew she wasn't guilty.

But without those pictures — if they found the body — Harper could be considered a suspect.

Her presence could contaminate the crime scene.

Unbelievable.

She didn't think Sheriff Taggart actually believed she was a killer. He seemed to lean more toward thinking she was unstable, but he had to work things by the book in his search for the truth.

She'd wanted to tell him, "Well, make up your mind, already. Am I unstable or am I a suspect?"

But Harper knew when to keep her mouth shut. Usually.

And if she put herself in his shoes, she could understand. She showed up with a gash in her head and reported that a woman had been murdered. For all the sheriff knew, she had fought with the woman and made her way to the other side of the river, where she called for help.

The sheriff had insisted that Deputy Herring return her to the campground. She'd argued and he'd relented and let her wait there. Deputy Herring was supposed to stay with her. Watch out for her. Watch over her. Guard her. Instead, he drifted closer to those with like minds and stood near the river discussing the weather or the murder or both.

Buffalo droppings and divots of grass scattered the area. In addition to a rainstorm, a herd of buffalo had taken up residence in the area long enough to destroy more evidence — any proof that a man had murdered a woman was gone.

There could be a fine blade of grass hanging onto blood, clinging to DNA, calling out for someone, anyone willing to search. But she understood that the elements had destroyed too much. The search area was too vast.

If they found the body, the atmosphere would change. Additional resources would be called in to search the crime scene. Right now, they had a witness but no evidence. No body. Sheriff Taggart might not even know the best way to go forward.

Her heart rate spiked as frustration

pumped through her veins.

He did this. The shooter knew how to cover his tracks. He herded the buffalo over to the river. The beasts remained grazing in the meadow right over the hill.

Despite wanting to escape blood and murder, Harper couldn't let this go. He wasn't going to get away with it. She would remind the sheriff she wanted to meet with a sketch artist. She didn't need the pictures from her camera. She'd committed everything to memory. At the very least, the murdered woman would be identified.

Closing her eyes, she saw the woman's terror-stricken face. A sob rose up and she might have released it, except someone was coming.

Footsteps drew near. Taggart? Moffett? She wasn't ready to talk to either.

Someone sat down next to her on the other half of the flat rock. Harper opened her eyes.

Heath McKade.

She was happy to see him.

He propped his knees up and dangled his arms over them.

"What are you doing here?" she asked.

The Stetson shaded his face. "The sheriff brought me in."

Harper released a slow breath. "I

shouldn't have left without retrieving my camera last night." She squeezed her eyes shut and forced back the tears. "They don't believe me."

"So I heard."

Harper feared asking Heath, but she wanted — no, needed — someone to believe her. Though she didn't know why, it would mean a lot if that person was Heath Mc-Kade, her childhood friend. He'd been such a tough boy on the outside, trying to remain strong for his brothers. For his mother, until the accident that killed her. The accident for which he blamed himself. He appeared to have gotten over that and Harper couldn't be prouder of what he'd become.

Everyone seemed to respect him. Though she didn't know Heath the adult, she could easily understand why he was respected. And there was something about his presence that made her feel that he could be trusted. Right now, he was exactly the kind of person she needed. It didn't hurt that she'd known him years ago and, if she closed her eyes, she could almost imagine that Heath McKade the kid sat next to her.

She looked him in the eyes. Though he squinted, one bright blue eye returned her gaze. Dare she? Her heart stumbled around. "I'm almost afraid to ask you, but I need to know. Do *you* believe me?"

He stared at her long and hard, then dropped his head. Pain slipped across her chest. Harper averted her gaze to watch the river, where Detective Moffett was crouching. Had she found something? She stood again as if she'd lost interest. Archie, the guy with the cadaver dog named Darla, approached the investigator. They huddled in deep discussion. Maybe Harper had imagined the murder, after all, and she had squandered their time. She was impressed with how much effort they had already put into it based on her words alone.

"Harper." Heath's tone was gentle.

Something about the way he said her name made her feel warm inside. She turned her face back to his, not wanting to hear his words, his answer to her question.

Both bright blue eyes stared at her now, taking her in. "I believe you."

She huffed out a laugh. "What you mean is that you think I believe I saw what happened, but it never happened. This is all due to my head injury. I heard one of the deputies talking. I know what they're thinking."

He tugged his Stetson off, ran a hand through his thick hair, then stuck it back on his head. His picture could go on a magazine cover.

"No, that's not what I mean. I believe you witnessed a murder."

"Why? Why would you take my word for it when there's nothing here? Not even a speck of blood."

"What? Are you starting to doubt yourself now?"

She grimaced. She couldn't give in or let them persuade her. "No. I saw what I saw. But please tell me why you believe me."

"Because I heard a woman's terrified scream. I also heard the gunfire that came after the scream. It's the whole reason I went looking, and then I found you. I heard you call for help, but you ended up saving me from a bear."

"Well, did you tell the sheriff?"

"Yes. Like your words, my words won't count for a whole lot without other evidence. The sheriff could reason that the scream I heard and the gunfire were unrelated to each other or to the crime you witnessed. Sounds can echo from miles around in these mountains."

"Thank you for putting it that way. The crime I witnessed rather than the crime I *claimed* to have witnessed."

"Honestly, Harper, I would believe you anyway."

103

Her breath hitched a little at the way he looked at her, and she knew without a doubt he would have believed her even if he hadn't heard a scream or gunfire. She didn't understand why. Still, she'd needed to hear those words from him.

"You're the only one," she said.

"I'll talk to Taggart and Moffett. I carry an ounce of persuasion in this county."

"There's still a problem if they can't find evidence." Harper wanted to search more. There had to be something. A hair. A speck of blood. A piece of torn clothing.

Looking out over the flowing Grayback River, Heath leaned back on one hand and sighed. "There's that, yes. Taggart won't be inclined to call in any additional help from the surrounding counties or the state unless he has a solid reason. He wants to find the truth, Harper, don't worry. But that means that right now all possibilities are on the table."

She understood what he meant — including the possibility that the crime never happened. Still, she found reassurance in his words that the sheriff wanted to find the truth.

Heath had made her feel better. "As for finding evidence," she said, "maybe I can help him with that."

"How's that?"

"I was a crime scene photographer."

"Is that so?"

"I realize that Taggart probably won't let me be involved. But from my point of view, I need to prove what I saw." And just how would she do that?

"How'd you end up becoming a forensic photographer?"

"I . . ." Memories blew through her. "Remember when my dad was killed? Murdered?"

"That, I do. I couldn't be more sorry, Harper. I never got to tell you. Not really."

"No. Because Mom took us away. She let me tell you we were leaving, at least. Let me see you one more time. I . . ."

"You don't have to tell me."

Her chest grew tight. *I want to.* It's what she might have told him years ago if she'd had the chance. Still, the words caught in her throat. She couldn't tell him everything. Not at the moment. "They never caught the guy. That's why I decided to go into evidence photography, so I could help put criminals away. Be part of that process."

There was more to it, and in his eyes, she saw that he understood. But this would have to be good enough for now.

"Because you're a survivor, Harper. You've

always been strong."

Her shoulders drooped. Heath had no idea what he was saying. He couldn't truly understand what she'd been through. "Yeah. I'm always the survivor."

"What do you mean?"

Taggart approached. Though Harper appreciated that Heath listened to her story, she was glad she didn't have to tell him the rest. He would think she was pathetic and weak. And right now, she needed him, the sheriff, Detective Moffett, and whoever else was investigating this case to believe that she had her act together. That she was strong. Someone needed justice. There was a killer on the loose.

Heath stood and offered his hand. She didn't need it but took it anyway and stood.

The sheriff opened his mouth to speak, but Heath interrupted him. "Taggart, I believe Harper's story, and I'm worried that the killer has her camera. He might be able to identify her that way."

"We haven't established that a crime happened here."

"You have to admit that there could have been a murder committed here last night and the buffalo destroyed the evidence. The killer could have driven the herd to the river to cover his tracks. Am I right?"

Heath standing up for Harper was the re-assurance she needed.

"We'll continue to search for evidence for now," Sheriff Taggart said. "I'll call in some resources and expand the search area and include underwater sonar. Though, if he threw her body into the river, she could have been washed downriver. In the mean-time, if a woman was murdered last night, then like you said Ms. Reynolds, someone could have reported her missing by now. We'll check into that and see if anyone matches your description."

Thank you. Harper sucked in a breath. "I'm happy to meet with a forensic artist too."

"Those are our next steps. And there's something else. I'd like for you to see the doctor again, Ms. Reynolds. Let's make sure you don't have a brain injury, too, that could somehow interfere with your memo-ries of the event. And for my part, I've opened a case file. Let's hope it goes some-where." He leveled his gaze at her. "Do we have a deal?"

His request surprised her. "Fine."

"Now, I have a bomb investigation to get back to. Wyatt Hayes opened his mailbox this morning and an explosion put him in the hospital too. Stupid kids. This has gone too far. Four kayakers are also missing."

"What about Harper?" Heath asked. "The killer could target her because she witnessed the murder."

A chill crawled over Harper. She wanted to go home. To leave this place. But now she realized she needed to stay and make sure that the woman's murderer was brought to justice. Running away this time would destroy her. She knew that to her marrow.

"McKade. We've been over this. Ms. Reynolds is a tourist here, passing through. I'm not convinced she's in any danger. Unless she knows the murderer." Taggart directed his next words to Harper. "Did you recognize the murderer? Do you believe he knows you or can identify you?"

"I can't exactly say that I'm in danger. But that doesn't change the fact that a murderer is out there somewhere." Harper took in the area around them. To her right was the vast meadow and to her left the woods opened up to the river. Beyond the woods and meadow, a cliff rose to meet rolling hills and mountains.

He could be watching her through his high-powered scope.

CHAPTER ELEVEN

At this distance, the judge could safely watch. Nobody was carrying one of those long telephoto lenses. They couldn't even hear his ragged coughing, which nearly got the best of him this time. The sickness was spreading, taking over his body, despite that he'd taken advantage of everything medical science had to offer.

He needed more time to complete his task, and this woman could cost him. Grinding his molars, he lifted the scope and peered through. The scope extended his vision far behind the hill where he was propped. Below him, the evergreens spread before the meadow and cliff where the buffalo grazed and past the ridge overlooking the area where he'd killed the woman.

At least he was getting good use out of the scope and optics that cost more than his rifle — an expensive hobby he'd taken up to fill the void.

In the scope, he could easily view Sheriff Taggart and his good-old-boy crew. Rangers and that wildlife agent jerk, Kramer. From this vantage point, he could watch them all day long and they'd never know.

He dialed in the scope and focused on the woman who'd watched him with her camera last night. Crazy bad luck, that. He'd done his best to erase the evidence. These local yokels wouldn't find a thing.

He hadn't wanted to kill the hikers, who were honeymooners, but they had stumbled on things they shouldn't have. He tied them up and kept them fed and hydrated. He also learned that they were expected to be away for a while on their hiking excursion — what kind of honeymoon was that, anyway? — and nobody would be looking for them for another four days at the very least.

And then it could be another day or so before anyone realized they were missing.

He had plenty of time to finish his business and get out of Dodge before the couple was found safe and sound.

But then the man had to go and be a hero. Sacrificed himself to free his wife.

She'd escaped.

The judge had no choice but to hunt her down. Had no choice but to shoot to kill.

The last thing he needed was the law

traipsing around these woods. Maybe he should have left them the bodies and then they'd only be looking for a killer. But this way, it would take them much longer to sort things out. Nothing to go on except for one lone witness.

At least the sheriff's department was distracted with finding a body and the shooter. Their attention would be divided.

Divide and conquer had always been a winning strategy.

CHAPTER TWELVE

Wednesday, 9:33 A.M.
Bridger County Sheriff's Office

Sheriff Taggart hadn't answered Heath's calls. Detective Moffett either. He wanted to know what was going on with the murder investigation. Heath was worried about Harper. He'd come in to see the sheriff in person.

At the kitchen in the county offices, Heath poured congealed coffee into a mug and then poured it right back out into the sink. He wished someone around here knew how to make a decent cup of coffee. *I guess that's going to have to be me.*

Might as well make it while he waited on Taggart to give him the time of day.

Maybe he was only a reserve deputy and didn't rank for his own cubbyhole with a desk, but he had all the same powers as a full-time paid deputy — same training too. The only difference was that Heath didn't work full-time and wasn't paid for hours he was required to work. Honestly, he liked it this way. He could assist when needed, and his attention could remain focused on the ranch. It was the best of both worlds.

He would need to keep reminding himself of that.

He stood back and waited for the coffee to brew. The sheriff still hadn't assigned him the mailbox investigation yet. That made him antsy. He needed to be working on something in the department if he wanted to find out more about what was going on with Harper's case.

All he needed was five minutes of Taggart's time to get things moving.

He thought the sheriff would have the courtesy to give him that. Then again, the guy was busier than usual. Wyoming wasn't a state filled with too much crime. Horse abuse, lost hikers, road closures. But in the last year, this region of the state had faced a few challenges.

A murder two nights ago, and now another mailbox bomb. Taggart had been appointed to serve as sheriff last year and would soon face elections. He needed to prove himself capable of the job. He didn't want to call in the US Postal Inspection Service or the FBI to find some foolish kids who needed redirection. Heath wouldn't want to be in Taggart's shoes.

"Heath?" Jasmine Dylan, one of the office assistants, stuck her head through the kitchen door. "Sheriff says you can go on back to his office."

Without his coffee, he walked through while she waited for him and then leaned in.

"He's not in a good mood," she said.

"No, I wouldn't think so."

She ushered him into Taggart's office.

The sheriff stared at his computer but spared Heath a glance. "You have three minutes, McKade."

Maybe this was the worst possible time for Heath to bring it up. It certainly wouldn't get Taggart's full attention. And in light of recent developments, it wasn't important, but he was using this as his excuse to see the sheriff. Heath hesitated. How did he make this concise?

"Well? You're down to two minutes and thirty seconds."

Heath thrust the toxicology report in front of Taggart. "This."

"What is it?"

"Before he died, the last sheriff told me that my father wasn't drunk. The accident

114

that killed the senator's family wasn't his fault."

Taggart rose slowly and stared at the report.

"At first I was denied the report," Heath said. "Which makes no sense. I threatened with a lawyer. I had been planning to try again since I'm a deputy now, but then I got this in the mail. It confirms that he was drunk and conflicts with what I was told."

Taggart's brow furrowed. "What are you asking me to do with this?"

"I want to know how and why my father took the blame for that accident. I don't think he was drunk. I think someone doctored this report. I want an investigation into this."

"Can I ask you why it's so important now? Since your dad died, you've created the Emerald M Guest Ranch. People have forgotten your father's legacy of drunkenness. But you could be dragging it all out again. Do you really want that?"

Why was Taggart stalling? Heath liked the guy and didn't want to believe he was involved or had anything to hide. But then again, he once made the mistake of trusting too much and received a bullet in the gut. Heath leaned in and pressed his fists against Taggart's desk. "I want to know why my father took the blame. I'm trying to do the right thing by bringing this to your attention."

"Did you ever stop to think that the person who shot you and then told you this information thought you were dying and wanted to ease your mind about your father, so he lied to you?"

"To ease his own conscience." Heath had been trying to find and save a friend when he'd been shot and left for dead. "I've considered that, yes. But I can't let it go. I'm letting you know that I'm digging into this — officially or unofficially, take your pick. Did I make a mistake in coming to you with this because you might not like what I find?"

"Are you threatening me, McKade?"

Heath eased back and crossed his arms. "No. I'm giving you the facts."

The sheriff eyed him as if he considered that he might have made a mistake in coming to Heath to ask him to be a reserve deputy. Which brought to mind his question — why hadn't Taggart called him into action? He had wanted Heath full-time, but Heath's heart was in his ranch. Taggart had needed his help and now he wasn't using it.

The sheriff lifted the report and read it again. Then he looked up at Heath. "I know you have trust issues, and I know why. But I'm asking you to trust me on this. Let me do it. I'll see what I can find out. But I'm going to need you to be patient."

"Why do you want to do it? Seems like it's beneath you. Why not send a deputy — that would be me — to look into things?"

"You're too close to it, that's why. If you don't like what I find out, then you can investigate. Are we good?"

Heath crossed his arms. Could he trust Taggart with this? He'd had his back on numerous occasions. He couldn't hold everyone else responsible for one man's actions. "For now, we're good. Don't make me wait too long for answers."

"While I'd like to jump right on this, we have mailboxes to safeguard. Kayakers to find. Oh yeah, and there's a killer out there, if Ms. Reynolds can be believed."

"Oh, come on. What does she have to do to convince you?"

"It's not about her convincing me. We can't do anything without information. Once we've finished a thorough search today, if there are no clues to follow, no evidence of the crime, then I'll leave the file open. That's all I can do." Taggart scratched his jaw. "Listen, Heath, we've been through a lot together. You should know that I did some checking into her background. I called the PD in St. Louis to see if they could give me any information. This is confidential. Between you and me. I shouldn't tell you this, but Harper Reynolds has PTSD. Survivor's guilt. More specifically, homicide survivor's guilt."

"I'm always the survivor."

"If you called the PD in St. Louis, then you know she was a crime scene photographer. PTSD is not unusual for police officers, first responders, or crime scene photographers. Those who deal with acts of violence. So what's the big deal?"

Taggart shrugged. "She took an indefinite medical leave."

"None of this means she didn't witness a murder."

"I'm not so sure about that. The PTSD could cause her to have hallucinations. Maybe what she thinks she saw wasn't real. I'm telling you this to warn you that you shouldn't get tangled up in it."

Heath had thought the same thing, but then Taggart called him to the scene, and now he couldn't walk away like he'd intended. "I'm disappointed in you, Taggart, for not believing her."

"I was told that she was the best they'd had, but then she had to take a medical

118

leave because she couldn't handle the sight of blood or documenting the evidence left behind by violent crimes. Imagine that, McKade. A crime scene photographer who can't do her job. Now here she is in my county and she comes up with a story about a murder. Here in Jackson Hole, we arrest people for DUI or abusing animals. That kind of thing." He blew out a long breath. "We don't see a lot of murders. I'm trying to give her the benefit of the doubt, but you can see my struggle."

"Not a lot of murders, huh? Marilee Clemmons comes to mind. I could name a few others if you'd like." Heath and his family had almost been murdered in the fall. Then there was the man who killed three people in the park last year. But he wouldn't bring that up. "We could have a killer out there, Sheriff. You don't want to be the man who didn't listen to a witness and let him get away."

Taggart studied Heath for a few seconds, then said, "Point taken." Someone knocked on the sheriff's office door, then opened it without waiting. Jasmine eyed Heath, then spoke to Taggart. "I got that information you were waiting for."

Sheriff Taggart stood. "You've gone over your three minutes anyway, McKade. I'm

119

going to call you up to assist soon. Today probably. I haven't decided where to put you. But this is fair warning. Get your Emerald M business in order." Taggart headed out the door as though he'd leave Heath standing in his office.

Instead, Heath followed him out. He wanted to ask about the sketch artist for Harper. Taggart quickly got involved in a heated discussion with Jasmine and Meghan, the IT girl, as they marched down the hall, and Heath was on his own. He felt like he was the only one on Harper's side. For all their sakes, he sure hoped evidence came to light soon.

After what Harper had been through, he hated that she'd had to witness a murder. She had to be feeling alone in all this.

He wished he could figure out a way to reassure her.

When they were kids, he'd been the one who was alone. He was alone in shielding his younger brothers as much as possible from their angry father and his parents' broken marriage. He was alone in defending his mother. He hadn't protected her at all, and she died because of him. And the man his father became after that — sometimes Heath thought he was responsible for creating that monster.

CHAPTER THIRTEEN

Wednesday, 9:47 A.M.
Bridger-Teton National Forest

At home, it was time to take a closer look at the items he'd collected. The judge browsed the few images he'd found on the woman's camera. Images of a hunter. The photographs had been taken by a deft hand and an exceptional eye. A professional. Not a portrait photographer. No. Not that for her. Nature, maybe — for nature enthusiast websites or magazines.

She'd caught him as he moved in on his kill. He'd been smart to wear that cap and keep the rifle close.

Even with her exceptional photography skills, he wasn't identifiable.

But this was a memory card with few photos. Did she have another one on which she'd captured more images of him and the woman he'd shot? One thing he did know — she'd seen enough to drag law enforcement out to search.

She was a distraction to him because he'd had to make sure she didn't have a leg to stand on. No body. No evidence. No charges. He'd evaded the law long enough to know how it worked.

He shifted his focus back to the map spread out on the table.

This . . . this deserved his full attention. It would be his legacy. He had to carry it out before it was too late. He had a feeling this time would be different.

Decades ago, he'd come close to getting caught, but instead he holed up here in Jackson Hole, not far from where his great-great bank-robbing grandpa had hid out in the "hole-in-the-wall" — where all the outlaws had come to hide in the Big Horn Mountains of Wyoming over a century ago.

A historical museum in downtown Grayback had relics and articles about the Old West on display. There was even a mention of his outlaw ancestor. His great-great died — and with a chest full of bullets, of course — making a name for himself, but not before he fathered a child. And the rest was history, as they say. But it was all a complete fabrication to sensationalize the story. In truth, the outlaw had died years later from consumption. Tuberculosis. He'd had a family. All that money he'd stolen hadn't done him any good.

Another laborious cough racked through the judge, a raucous sound that felt like a spike driving through his whole body. Like his great-great grandpa, the judge didn't have his health either, but he didn't care about the money.

CHAPTER FOURTEEN

Wednesday, 11:02 A.M.
Granite Ridge Campground

Heath stood outside the old Airstream camper made to look shiny and new. He cleared his throat and calmed his erratically beating heart, then knocked on the door, hoping to see Harper. He held the package he'd brought behind his back. Even without evidence, he believed her story. At this moment he didn't care. He wanted to see her.

But would she be there? Though her Dodge Ram was parked next to the RV, she could be out somewhere enjoying nature.

On a beautiful day like this, he would typically be outside himself. Hiking a trail. Riding a horse. Fishing. That would be the case if this were a *normal* beautiful day. After witnessing a murder, Harper was frazzled. Heath understood her struggle better after what she'd told him yesterday and what Taggart had shared today. He should take

Taggart's advice and avoid getting wrapped up in her situation. But this was Harper, and deep down Heath knew that he was already there.

Movement in the camper let him know someone was home.

The door cracked open. "Yes?"

It wasn't Harper. Her sister? "My name is Heath McKade. I'm here to see Harper." He still hid the package behind his back.

"She's sleeping."

The door was opened enough for Harper to peer over the woman's shoulder. "Heath? What are you doing here?"

"Is that how you're going to greet me every time you see me?" As if there would be more times.

"Are you here on sheriff business?"

"No. I'm here as an old friend stopping by to see how you're doing."

She opened the door wide. "Come on in."

He took three steps up into the cool air of the beautifully renovated camper. Wood floors, fresh cream-colored paint, modern cabinets and amenities, along with travel-themed decor. A Scripture plaque with a Bible verse hung on the wall as well. "The name of the Lord is a strong tower; The righteous runs into it and is safe. Proverbs 18:10."

"This is my sister. Emily, you remember Heath McKade. He's the man who found and rescued me, on his big stallion no less." Harper's eyes flicked to the package he'd given up on hiding until the right moment, then back to his face. Her smile was warm but not as brilliant as he'd seen in the past. Her laugh from years ago suddenly echoed in his head.

"I remember you." Emily smiled and pushed a strand of her bobbed brown hair behind her ears. "You're all grown up now though. Are you married?"

"Emily!" Harper glared at her sister.

"I'm not married." He returned her smile with a grin of his own. But he wasn't flirting. Or was he? "Did she tell you that she saved me from a bear?"

Emily, who he remembered was about three years older than Harper, admired him from head to toe. He wasn't sure he appreciated her open approval. "She might have mentioned you. Something about saving a guy wearing a cowboy hat."

"Oh, yep." Heath removed his hat and scraped his hand through his hat hair. "Pardon my manners."

Emily smiled. "You can keep the hat on if you like."

"My hair's that bad, huh?"

"It's not bad, no." Emily winked. "Of course I remember you, Heath. Make yourself at home. Looks like you came bearing gifts."

He wasn't ready to unveil that yet and shoved the package behind him. *I'm an idiot.* He needed to redirect the conversation and turned his attention to the renovated camper. "It's beautiful."

"You like the place?" Emily asked. "I got it for a steal. I spent, what, two years on the inside."

"I'm impressed."

"I'm glad to hear it." Emily moved to the kitchen. "Something to drink?"

Harper grabbed her sister's arm. "Can you take a walk around the campground and give me a few minutes, please?"

Emily chuckled. "Oh, I get it."

Harper whispered something in her ear, then pushed her sister gently out the door. Emily waved with a knowing smile. Heath wasn't exactly sure what Emily thought she knew, except he got the feeling she might have been flirting with him. Maybe she thought Harper had claimed him. What had he gotten himself into? He felt ridiculous now, considering his purchase. He could be over-the-top sometimes.

He returned his attention to Harper.

Though she was tan and healthy like someone who spent a lot of time outdoors, her face had a pale shade to it due to her injury. Still, she was beautiful. Strong. Intelligent. Everything good he knew of the girl she had been bloomed in the woman she was now.

Her cheeks colored. Had he been staring? He'd done more than that. He'd been admiring her.

He cleared his throat. Gestured to her stitches. "When do you get those out?"

She reached up and gently touched the injury. "Oh, these old things? In a few days or so. Then I'll have to deal with a scar, though Dr. Jacob assured me it would be minimal. Emily says I can get bangs to cover it if it's too bad."

The way she plopped into the plush chair, he thought she might cry. "It won't be that bad. You have beautiful hair, and your sister's right. If needed, you could easily cover it right up with bangs. But it won't change how beautiful you are." *Just stop talking, Heath.*

Her golden amber eyes stared at him. "I know you didn't come here to tell me that I'm . . . That my scar won't be that bad."

No, he hadn't. He let his gaze roam the camper. "Mind if I sit down?"

"Please do. I should have offered."

He cleared his throat. "So, um . . . how are you doing? Really?"

"I have a headache. I haven't taken the painkillers in case Sheriff Taggart needs something from me. I don't want him to accuse me of being overmedicated."

"Understandable."

"Nor have I called to schedule an appointment with the doctor like he asked."

Heath didn't want to talk about all that. He toyed with the rim of his hat. Might as well get to the reason for his visit. Or at least one of the reasons he'd come other than he wanted to see her and make sure she was all right. He handed her the package. "This is for you."

Her eyes flashed with wariness. Not the reaction he'd hoped for.

"What is it?" she asked.

"Why don't you open it and find out?" Too late for him to back out now. *Heath McKade, what were you thinking?*

She reached for the package, then held it as if trying to guess what was inside. But she didn't open it. "Heath, I don't understand what you're doing here. You don't owe me anything, certainly not . . ." Curiosity must have gotten the best of her, because she ripped it open. Her eyes widened and she gasped. Now that was the kind of reaction he'd been going for.

"A camera?" She held on to it like she treasured it, then suddenly thrust it toward him. "And not any camera. Thank you, but I can't accept this. I know how much it costs. It's too expensive."

"You saved my life."

"You don't believe that."

"I don't know what would have happened. I didn't react like I had always imagined I would if I ever encountered a grizzly." Heath refused the package, leaned forward, and clasped his hands. "Look, I know it might seem over-the-top, but you lost your camera. You were hurt. Got stitches. Witnessed a murder, so I . . ."

"Thank you." Her voice was soft and accepting. "I shouldn't accept it, but —" Tears pooled in her eyes, but she kept them at bay. She moved from the chair and pecked his cheek, then sat back down. A blush rose in hers again. "I don't know what to say." She stared at the camera as if she were second-guessing her decision to keep it.

"You might as well keep it. I can't return it. I lost the receipt." Somewhere in the cab of his truck. "Besides, I have a ginormous telephoto lens in the truck to go with it." Maybe a tripod, but he wouldn't tell her that yet. He hadn't known what he was doing in picking out the camera equipment, but the guy at the camera shop had been happy to help Heath empty his bank account.

"I'm surprised you were able to find this."

"Oh, come on, this is tourist country. People bring high-powered cameras to capture the scenery that's unlike anywhere else on earth. That and the wildlife. They forget their cameras or lose them or break them, and then they go buy another one in one of the many shops in Jackson or Grayback."

"The most expensive place in the world to buy them," she said.

Um, yeah.

Harper opened the box and pulled out the camera. She removed the lens cap, and before he could stop her, she snapped a picture of him. "Now, wait a minute."

She laughed. He loved the sound — he'd made her happy and that warmed his heart.

"I'm surprised it had enough charge to do that. This is great. Maybe I can go back out there and look for evidence myself, though now that rain, the buffalo, and too many humans probably completely destroyed it, that would be a waste of *my* time. There must be something else I can do."

"You don't need to investigate, Harper.

Let law enforcement do their job." Heath had a feeling where this conversation was leading, so he directed it to his other reason for coming. "Back at the river you said something that has been bothering me. You told me that you're always the survivor. What did you mean by that?"

Her incredulous laugh caught him off guard. "And here I thought I'd gotten out of telling you."

"My apologies. I'm overstepping. You don't have to tell me."

She pursed her lips. "I don't like to talk about it. And why, now, do I find myself wanting to share it all with you? Maybe because I haven't seen my therapist in a good, long while. You have that quality about you, Heath, you know that?"

"What? Now don't call me a therapist." She was the one with that quality. She had been there for him after his mother's death. A death he felt responsible for. And Harper had been only a child at that time.

"Since you believe me, or at least you told me you do, maybe you deserve to know who it is that you're believing. So I'll tell you, Heath McKade. Seeing so many gruesome and violent crimes had started to weigh on me. Then I took photographs of a scene that reminded me of what I'd been through as a kid when my dad was murdered, of how I hid away instead of being the witness he needed. I started having nightmares. Flashbacks. I was out of sorts. I saw the department therapist. I guess my past traumatic experience made what I was going through that much worse. He told me I was experiencing homicide survivor's guilt. That unresolved past loss had triggered grief and depression." Harper shook her head as though disappointed in herself and looked at him. "I guess I haven't resolved my past. I needed emotional healing, so he suggested I take time off. Take nature pictures. Well, here I am. See what happened?"

After hearing the guilt and shame in her tone, Heath hung his head. "You're a survivor, Harper. That's nothing to feel guilty about."

"So I've been told by my other therapist. The last thing I want to do is to make it all about me."

Great. He wasn't making any headway. "You didn't look away this time. You took those pictures. You looked at the killer. You watched him . . ." Commit the murder.

"A lot of good it did. I couldn't do anything to help her. I took pictures and lost them. But she's still dead. He's still out there somewhere and might get away with murder."

"I understand what you're going through."

"How can you understand?"

"I've been through some bad things too, remember?" Heath couldn't bring himself to relive what had happened. This wasn't about him, and he didn't want her to feel his pain all over again when she had so much of her own. "And I do understand that even in taking those pictures, witnessing a woman's murder, somehow you feel guilty about surviving. About being the one to walk away."

Harper covered her face. Oh no. Had he upset her? She dropped her hands, her expression somber, transparent. "I was wrong. You *do* understand."

He held her gaze and felt that connection with her again. He hadn't come here to find a way into her life. He'd been trying to help. If only he wasn't always driven to fix what was broken, as if he actually could. Because at the same time, he wanted to protect himself and others from what happened when he tried and failed.

He couldn't have it both ways.

Too late. He admitted he shouldn't have come back to talk to Harper. But he'd justified his actions easily enough. Oh yeah. He had justified his actions all the way to the camera store, where he'd gone overboard with his need for a reason to see her. He wanted to give back somehow. He hadn't been given the chance to help her through her father's murder.

Why had he thought he should be the one to give Harper solace? "I should probably get going."

Hurt flashed over her features and then it was gone. She took his hat and tucked it back on his head. She was close enough that he thought she might give him another peck, but she backed away. "Thanks for coming by, Heath."

"What are you going to do?"

She shrugged. "If the sheriff isn't going to take me seriously, then I will have to figure this out on my own."

"I don't want you doing that, Harper. It's too dangerous."

"Well, it's a good thing you don't have any say in it, even if you did get me a new camera."

She was right. She didn't owe him a say in her life. He hadn't really owed her anything — they had saved each other. "I'll get the rest of the equipment from the truck."

If only Heath could believe the danger was over.

CHAPTER FIFTEEN

Harper peeked through the mini blinds to watch Heath the Cowboy march to his big truck with dual wheels in the back.

His jeans and shirt fit nicely. He hadn't smelled of horses like he had at the river. Instead, she'd caught the scent of soap and musky cologne. He'd been clean-shaven as well. While those scents lingered in the camper, she closed her eyes and drew them in. Broad-shouldered and thoughtful, he filled her mind. His goodness filtered through to a part of her heart, though she had tried to guard it.

She knew to always steer clear of letting herself grow attached. She was much too shattered, too broken already, and couldn't afford to risk losing someone. Besides, Heath was loyal and trustworthy, and he deserved someone he could count on. Harper wasn't that person.

Why Heath had triggered these thoughts

she wasn't sure — except the man, this person from her past, had somehow quickly curled around her heart as though he would soften it and step right into her life.

Why couldn't she follow her own advice to steer clear? She'd accepted the camera, telephoto lens, and tripod. Her mother would have given her a lecture. Shame filled her.

She thought about the reasons he'd given for getting her a new camera. An expensive new camera. She shouldn't have accepted it. But Heath was such a good guy, and Harper had the strong sense that refusing his gift would have been the wrong thing to do. It would have hurt him. The last thing she wanted to do was hurt Heath McKade.

A big cowboy with a big heart who gave big gifts.

She'd hurt him once before when she'd been forced to leave with only a goodbye. They'd had a bond then.

A murder had broken it. Time and distance had sealed the break.

Strange that a murder had brought them back together.

And that drew her back to her question. What was the real reason Heath had given her a new camera?

The reasons he had offered were good,

but nobody was that thoughtful anymore. It couldn't be that Heath wanted to pursue a relationship with her, could it? Sure, they'd been best friends long ago, but that couldn't possibly translate into something romantic years later.

Even if it could, she wasn't staying in Wyoming. Eventually, she would go back to Missouri. If he showed up again bearing gifts, she'd have to make it clear she wasn't interested, even if she hurt him.

The camera rested on the small table, accusing her.

Another glimpse through the mini blinds confirmed that he'd left. Emily was nowhere to be seen, but Harper could trust that her sister had been watching for him to leave and would be back soon. Emily had seemed especially cheerful earlier. Harper suspected that Emily was trying to lift Harper's mood.

And that meant Harper needed to avoid her for now. So she went to the bedroom and closed the door. She hated sleeping the day away, but she'd been through a lot and was dealing with the pain. She made sure the room was nice and dark before climbing into bed.

Emily would have questions, and Harper didn't have answers. She would try to persuade Harper it was time to head home as soon as the sheriff released her to go.

But the woman . . . her eyes . . .

God, please let him find something to corroborate my story.

Harper couldn't think straight. Maybe Emily was right. She'd sleep on it, then decide — that is, if her mind would let her rest.

Witnessing her father's murder had left her with flashbacks. Nightmares. Insomnia. Childhood trauma victims often dreamed about death. Like she'd told Heath — the grief of the past stood in the way of her healing.

Hence the reason she'd snapped at her captain — on multiple occasions — and that was that. He put her on medical leave.

But what was she supposed to do with her time? Sit home and fold in on herself? Fortunately, her therapist suggested she focus on photographing something other than crime scenes, such as nature, so she decided on national parks instead. She figured after enough time and many images later, she'd be ready to see the park closest to the place where she'd grown up — where the tragedy had occurred. So she left Yellowstone and Grand Teton for last.

As for the old house where she and Emily had grown up, seeing that was on Emily's list. Her sister had spent time and money renovating the old Airstream and could work from anywhere, so the pieces fell into place and off they went on an adventure. Their last stop before heading to Missouri — to see the old house — Harper could live without that.

After all, she'd witnessed a murder there and had nightmares about the place.

She'd been sleeping better these last few months as they traveled, but the murder across the river had fired all her insomnia neurons.

And the guilt had reared its ugly head again.

She rolled over and tried to get comfortable.

"You're a survivor, Harper. That's nothing to feel guilty about." Heath's words drifted back to her.

He was right. She should stop feeling guilty and do something this time about the murder she witnessed.

Chapter Sixteen

Wednesday, 12:15 P.M.
Granite Ridge Campground

A knock came at the camper door.

Where was Emily? Harper groused, then got out of bed to answer the door. Harper's heart jumped.

"Detective Moffett?"

"Ms. Reynolds." The detective peered up at her, all serious as usual. All official business.

"Call me Harper, please." Should she invite the detective in? Nah. "I hope you've discovered some evidence of the crime."

"Not yet. I've arranged for you to meet with a forensic artist. She's one of our deputies at the county office. I would have called, but I don't have your number."

The detective probably hoped she would be invited in. She wanted to see inside the camper because she remained skeptical of Harper. "As it turns out, I don't have a phone right now." She needed to get a new one next time she went to town. It was funny that Heath had gotten her a camera, but she still didn't have a cell.

"Right. We have your phone, actually. It's not in working condition, so you'd probably need to get a new one anyway while we hold on to it in case we need it for evidence. As for today, if you can come in with me, the artist will have time to work with you this afternoon."

Moffett's words surprised Harper. She had doubted the investigators would follow through with her request. "Sure. I need to change into something besides sweats. Has anyone reported a missing mother or sister or friend?"

"No."

"Okay. Give me a few minutes to change."

Moffett nodded. "I'll wait in my vehicle."

Harper shut the door and headed to her closet, closing the bedroom door behind her. This could be the break they needed.

"Harper?" Emily banged the RV door shut. "There's a deputy outside. What's she doing there?"

The pocket door to the bedroom slid open.

"I'll be meeting with a forensic artist today. Detective Moffett came to pick me up." Harper searched the small closet for something decent to wear. If only she could grab a quick shower too, but that would take too long with the deputy waiting. She wished, too, that she'd cleaned up before Heath had surprised her.

Emily sank to the bed. "That's good. Yeah, I guess that's good. I had kind of hoped we could go home tomorrow. Maybe after you meet with the artist we can finish getting ready."

She hadn't told Emily that going back to Missouri wasn't an option yet, at least for Harper.

"Look, Em . . ."

"I hate it when you call me that. You only call me that when you know I won't like what you're going to say."

"That's not true. I call you that for other reasons too. I call you that as a term of endearment. Because I love you. That's beside the point. I have to stay. I'm not going anywhere until I know this murder is solved."

"What?"

"I know you're disappointed. But you're a writer. Seems to me you'd want to see this investigation through too. But if you really want to go home, I think you should go, and I'll stay. I don't want to be the one to keep you here. You've been the best sister to come with me on this trip."

"Yeah, see how well that turned out. I bailed on you when I should have been with you."

"You had a deadline. I understood. I'm the one who made the mistake — hiking that trail alone." Business-casual slacks and shirt in hand, she sat next to her sister. "I think now it's time I cope with my issues on my own." Though she had been advised repeatedly to seek support from family and friends.

But enough was enough. She'd spent a year avoiding everything that reminded her of violent crime. Supposedly that would help her gain control over the flashbacks and nightmares. Push away the guilt that consumed her and impeded her ability to function as a normal person. She sighed.

"By sticking around here? Why?"

"Come on, I think you know why. Dad's killer wasn't caught. I think it's time I stop running from the bad that happens in this world — the bad that happened to me — and face what's happening now head-on. But more importantly, I need to stick around to make sure justice is served for that woman who was killed out there. The way things are going, I'm not sure the

144

sheriff is going to see this through. He's skeptical of me, for one thing. And that doesn't sit well with me." Harper shrugged. "More than that, I can't be that woman anymore. I can't be the person who lives and does nothing when someone else dies."

"You've always felt guilty for living, which is ridiculous!"

"Is it?" How did she bring this up without dredging up the pain? How much Emily's words still hurt her was sobering. "Maybe it's not about that anymore. You once told me that if I had been brave and looked to see who had shot Dad, that the man would have been caught." Harper pursed her lips, feeling the wound open up and pain surge in her throat. She didn't want to drive a wedge between her and Emily after they'd come so far. "So I would think you, of all people, would understand my need to stay until it's over."

Emily said nothing. Seconds ticked by. "I . . . I never should have said that. It was stupid and I'm sorry. We were kids. I was hurt over Dad. But hearing you say all this, I understand. It tells me that you're better now. That taking the time off was good for you. But, Harper, even if you're better, even though you feel like this time you can make it right by sticking around, you don't *have* to stay. The sheriff isn't asking you to do this. Once he has the picture of the woman, he'll probably tell you to go home. Besides, where are you going to live? *How* will you live?"

"Wow, really? I could live here in this, your vintage camper" — she offered Emily a pleading smile — "at least for a while. I have a few funds left, and if I run out I can get a job."

"Doing what?"

"What I do best. Taking pictures. I noticed Detective Moffett, the investigator, took a few, but I wasn't impressed. I could do better." And with those words, Harper realized that finally, she actually missed her job as a crime scene photographer. That she was eager to get back into it if the opportunity arose.

Emily scoffed. "You really think a sheriff who believes you're lying about a crime, either that or you've lost your mind, is going to hire you as his crime scene photographer?"

Harper refused to let Emily's words hurt. She hadn't meant them like that. "I have to try. Take the truck and head home, if you want."

"I don't go with you one day and look at the trouble that happens. No. I can't leave you alone again, especially not here in this campground surrounded by strangers coming and going. Ken is nice, but he's only one person and he isn't here all the time."

"Who?"

"Ken. Mr. Stein. The guy at the campground office. Fixed the lock on the door? Hello?"

"Fine." Harper brushed her hair, then pulled it into a ponytail. "Stay if you want, but I'm not making you."

"One month."

"Four." She hoped it wouldn't take that long, but crimes weren't solved as quickly as they were on TV. If it went longer, she'd renegotiate.

"Two."

"Three."

"Two and a half."

"Three months, Emily."

"And if the killer isn't caught by then?"

"We'll figure it out." Harper slid across the bed and hugged her sister. "It's going to be all right."

It felt good to reassure Emily for once. She'd been lost in her own morbid memories for so long. When was the last time she had comforted anyone?

"Can I make one more request?" her sister asked. "Can we move the camper into town?

I saw they had some campgrounds there. I'd like to be closer to civilization."

Harper laughed. "I think that's a great idea. While I'm gone, why don't you try to find a place and make a reservation, though you know that might be kind of hard this time of year."

A knock came at the door again. Detective Moffett was growing impatient. "Would you mind telling the detective I'll drive myself in? There's no reason for her to wait."

Emily nodded and disappeared. Harper quickly dressed as she listened to Emily giving the detective the news. Then Emily stepped back into the room.

"There could be cancellations at one of the campgrounds," Emily said. "Or you could see if the sheriff's department could help you. I mean, you witnessed a murder, remember?"

Now Harper understood Emily's true reasons for wanting to move closer to town. Emily wrote murder mysteries and had murder on her mind a lot. She was afraid for both their lives. Maybe Harper was wrong to stay and see this through if Emily insisted on staying with her. She'd lost Dad. Mom had died from a heart attack three years ago.

I can't lose Emily too . . .

Chapter Seventeen

Wednesday, 2:46 P.M.
Emerald M Guest Ranch

"You're spending an awful lot of time brushing down that horse."

Evelyn.

Heath looked up but continued to brush. "You don't usually come out to the barn."

"I don't usually have a reason, but you weren't answering your cell. Text or otherwise."

He stopped brushing and stood tall. "Something wrong? I thought the next group of guests were enjoying themselves."

"They are. At least Leroy told me. But he said you were MIA. That stands for missing in action."

Heath chuckled. "I know what it means."

"I don't think you know what *he* means. Usually you introduce yourself to the guests when they arrive."

He put away the brush. "You didn't hike

all the way down here to tell me that."

"Maybe not, but it's a good excuse."

"Come on. I'll walk you back to the house." He led Boots out of the barn and freed him to graze the small enclosed pasture.

Evelyn followed.

Heath had a feeling he was about to get a lecture. "So what's on your mind?"

"I came to ask you how the girl is. Leroy told me what happened yesterday. That you had to go look at a crime scene. Everything all right?"

"As far as I know, the girl's fine. Her name is Harper, by the way."

"Oh, so you're on a first-name basis already."

"We went through a lot together in a few hours." How much should he tell Evelyn? If he told her everything, she might get the wrong idea. But there was no point in trying to hide the truth from her. She would find out eventually and make even more of the fact that he hadn't told her up front. "We were friends in grade school."

"Ooh. So it's like that." Evelyn walked by his side as they hiked toward the house.

"Not like that. No. We were best friends. We both struggled with family issues and leaned on each other. Trusted each other.

There was never anything more than that."
Sure, Heath had thought Harper was pretty and dreamed that one day she might be his girlfriend, but most of the time he had too much else going on to think those dreams would ever come true. She'd been his lifeline and at that time in his life that was all that mattered.

Together they clomped up the steps to the porch.

"Are you going to see her again?"

What was with the questions? "I doubt it. She probably isn't staying since she is a tourist passing through. The sheriff's department and the forest rangers are handling the investigation." Or not. There wasn't any evidence and no leads they could follow.

But he *had* gone to see her today. Bought her a camera. And not only a camera but accessories to go with it. He rubbed a hand down his face. What had he been thinking?

"You're part of the sheriff's department."

"Only on the rare occasion that I'm needed and for a few obligatory volunteer hours a month." Sheriff Taggart hadn't contacted him about working like he said he would. Maybe he was so busy, he didn't have time to make the call. All the more reason he needed Heath. He wasn't sure why it bothered him so much.

"I'm worried about you, Heath. I think of you like a grandson. I appreciate you giving Leroy a job. We're like family."

Hadn't he been thinking the same thing? He took her hand and patted it. "No need to worry about me. I've got everything to be grateful for." A guest ranch with a beautiful view. Great employees who cared.

She pointed her finger at him. "But you're still missing something. I can see it in your eyes. You know what you're missing."

He shook his head. He had no intention of getting into this with her. She could never understand. He shoved his hand into his pocket and yanked out his truck keys. "I need to get going."

"I care about you, Heath. I don't like to overstep, but you need someone who has the right to overstep."

"Looks like you're doing a fine job of that." He grinned.

She gave him a friendly smack on the arm. "You know what I mean. Someone who is your real family. Someone to love you and for you to love back. Your brother found someone. You see how happy he is now. That could be you too. What about Lori Somerall? She runs a guest ranch too. I've seen her coming around now and then. I see the way she looks at you. She's a beautiful

152

woman. Smart and strong too. More importantly, she loves God. Why don't you ask her out?"

Evelyn the matchmaker, he did not need.

"Tell me something, will you?" He furrowed his brow and stared off at the ducks landing on the lake. "What in the world brought this on? Why are you hammering on me to find someone now?"

"You haven't been the same since Austin was here with Willow."

"If you recall, I was shot and left for dead." Admittedly, he hadn't been the same since then. The familiar ache in his side erupted. Yep. The doctor was right. It was all in his head.

"That would be enough, I agree, but it's more than that. You need someone. You're special, Heath. Look at it this way. A beautiful woman out there is missing the chance to be loved by you. Please don't deprive her of that."

He choked at her words. "You've got it all wrong. Got *me* all wrong. Every time I try to fix something, things go from bad to worse." All the more reason to stay away from Harper.

"That's not true. Look what you've done with this ranch."

"I'm talking people. I'm not who you

think. People I've tried to help have died. Or gotten hurt. I . . . I'm not the guy you're describing."

"Heath McKade. Don't say that about yourself. You're a hero. The only real hero I know in person."

He moved to make his escape. He couldn't bear to hear this from her. Not now.

She grabbed his arm and held him in place. "Now you listen to me." Evelyn stuck her finger in his face. "God looks at the intent of the heart. Not the outcome. You think that when those firefighters and police officers went into the World Trade Center and it came crumbling down, that they aren't considered heroes? Of course they are! It's not the outcome, Heath. It's the fact that they tried. It's that *you* try. It's your heart that matters."

Tell that to my dead mother. But he couldn't say the words. Because . . . he desperately wanted to believe Evelyn's.

"All that to say, you need to let the good Lord give you someone special, to have and to hold. To love and, yes, protect. Will you do that, Heath?"

An explosive boom resounded, rattling the windows of the house. He feared they would break, so he grabbed Evelyn to steady her and shield her. They exchanged a look of horror.

"What on earth?" she asked.

"Stay here." Heath jumped from the porch, then ran around the house to the woods. Flames rose from a structure that used to be a guest cabin.

CHAPTER EIGHTEEN

Wednesday, 3:02 P.M.
Grayback, Wyoming

In the parking lot across the street from the county sheriff's office, the judge sat in his vehicle with the window down, even though the temperature was in the high eighties. These days, he got chilled too easily.

He glanced at his watch and frowned.

The photographer had once again interrupted his plans.

He'd spotted her entering the county sheriff's building — up to no good, she was. But not for much longer. His chuckle morphed into a hacking cough.

He would have to speed up his timeline again because of her. He was glad he'd stopped the chemo. He'd been sicker with the treatments than he'd ever been on his own, and his body would lose to the tumors either way. Why had the cancer suddenly decided to spread?

The disease made it hard to keep his edge. He needed to stay strong for what was to come.

He was off the hook unless that woman met with a sketch artist. She might not have her camera, but anyone with an eye like hers would remember the details. She would remember the woman.

The question was — had she seen him behind his cap and rifle? The photographs she'd taken said she hadn't gotten a good look at him. Still, how long had she been watching him?

All this peripheral business messed with his plans. He didn't have time to waste on this, yet he couldn't afford to ignore it. The verdict? He'd have to take out the one witness to this crime.

CHAPTER NINETEEN

Wednesday, 3:11 P.M.
Bridger County Sheriff's Office

Harper found herself relaxing in Laura Kemp's presence. The forensic artist was easygoing and made her feel comfortable — an important aspect of the artist's job. Detective Moffett had assured Harper that Laura had a real knack for creating composite drawings and was excited to have a reason to use her skills. The young woman had made Harper feel at ease during the interview process while she undoubtedly looked for signs of deception.

Though Harper knew what she'd seen and was able to describe the victim in detail, which made Laura's job easier, she worried she would come off as edgy. That was never a good thing. Harper shouldn't feel nervous, but if she blew this, Sheriff Taggart wouldn't take her seriously. This was her chance to prove what she'd seen.

If Harper failed, the murdered woman's case might not get solved.

On the wall behind Laura, a large map of the Jackson Hole area gave her something to look at. She took a deep breath and focused on the map. Describing the woman had brought back the horror and fear. "Her eyes. I can't forget the terror in them."

"I know it was a traumatizing experience. I'll have you out of here soon. You've been great to work with, by the way." Laura focused on the image she created.

The artist didn't ask more questions because Harper had described everything she could remember about both the victim and the murderer. From Harper's description, Laura had created a composite sketch of a man holding up a high-powered rifle. The rifle and the hunter's cap had obscured his features. In the sketch, he could be anyone. Still, he'd had deep crow's feet around his eyes, so she knew he was older.

Concentrating, Laura furrowed her brow, the *scratch-scratch* of her pencil on paper the only sound. "I hear you used to be a crime scene photographer."

Harper was surprised that Laura hadn't brought that up during the rapport or interview phase of the session.

"Yep. I'm taking a year off." Harper had

no intention of going into the reasons why. Best to redirect. "So how did you get into forensic art?"

Laura grinned and shrugged. "I'm artistic. Already worked for the department, so they sent me to some classes and here I am. I don't get to do this often. We don't usually get these kinds of crimes here."

"Thank you for that."

Laura glanced up from her work. "For what?"

"The way you said it, it sounds like you believe I witnessed a murder."

"Of course I believe you. You know what you saw and have great attention to detail."

"It's my understanding that witnesses or victims will remember maybe four facial features. I tried to commit them to memory — but that could be distorted."

"And that's okay. My job is to present an image that allows for distortion. In other words, more like a caricature — people are more likely to recognize that than they are an exact image."

"Like one produced on a computer."

"Exactly." Laura looked up from the drawing. "See what you think." She showed Harper the sketch.

Harper took in the composite drawing and saw the victim she'd described. "I wasn't expecting you to get the eyes."

"You were good with details. I'm sorry for the woman, and sorry you had to go through this experience. At the same time, I'm glad this person had someone watching. Someone like you to take in all the details of the crime, the victim, and the shooter. Someone who could help find her murderer. If you think this is right, I'll turn this over to the sheriff. Maybe no one knows she's missing yet. We could also be on the lookout for the shooter, though he looks like most of the hunters around here. Except this isn't big game hunting season."

Deputy Herring opened the door and stuck his head in. "You done here? There's been an incident at the Emerald M Ranch."

Emerald M Ranch. Harper's heart jumped to her throat. She hoped nothing had happened to Heath.

Laura glanced at Harper. "Yes. We were finishing up."

The deputy nodded, then shut the door.

"If you don't have any other business with Detective Moffett," Laura said, "you're probably good to go. I suspect her attention has been drawn elsewhere for the moment."

Harper touched Laura's arm. "Please, I know the guy who owns the Emerald M. Heath helped me at the river after I'd fallen.

161

What's happened at his ranch?"

"Let me see what I can find out. Wait here." Laura disappeared, taking the pictures she'd drawn with her.

Harper paced the small room.

When Laura stepped back inside, her features were pinched. "I'm not sure if this information is correct. It sounds like a mistake. But I'm told there was an explosion."

Harper gasped as she struggled to comprehend the words. "An explosion, as in a bomb? I heard something about mailbox bombs. Is anyone hurt?"

The forensic artist frowned. "I don't know the details. You could wait around if you want, but you look exhausted and you've been through an ordeal yourself. Go home and get some rest. You can check back with us later and maybe someone will know more."

Or call Heath. Except she didn't have a cell yet. She would remedy that first thing.

Harper nodded and grabbed her purse. "I'd like to get a copy of those images, please."

A few minutes later, Laura returned with a large envelope containing the copies. "Thanks again for coming in. Your help will be invaluable to the department in catching this guy. I'm happy to see you out."

"Sure." Harper followed her down the hallway. "Is there a phone I could use before I leave?"

Laura showed Harper to her small office. "Here, use mine. I'll give you some privacy."

Harper stared at the landline phone and was grateful she'd taken a moment to memorize Emily's cell number. She hoped Emily was in a spot where she got reception.

Emily answered.

"Hey, it's me. I'm surprised you answered."

"Oh, thank goodness it's you. The caller ID said Bridger County Sheriff. Scared me. I'm sitting in the perfect spot for a signal because I was just on the cell. I got us a campground in town! They didn't tell you? One of the deputies worked some magic for us because of our situation."

Sounded like Emily had worked some of her own magic.

"I'm glad to hear it. I'm headed back to you soon." She decided to wait to tell Emily about the explosion at Heath's ranch.

"Good. I'll see you soon."

Harper ended the call. She would try one more time to learn more about the explosion and Heath. She found Laura in the hallway. The deputy had geared up and was exiting the sheriff's office.

"Laura, wait. Have you heard anything yet? Do you know if Heath is okay?"

Deputy Herring stepped up next to Laura. "Heath made the call for an ambulance," he said. "He's okay, but I hear someone's hurt. We're headed that way now."

Both deputies' expressions remained grim as they exited the offices.

Heath is okay . . .

She let the news sink in and calm her heart. But her concern for the person injured remained.

Copies in hand, Harper followed them out the doors and headed to her truck. She stopped off to get a cheap burner phone, then headed out of town and back toward Granite Ridge Campground, though she really wanted to drive straight over to the Emerald M Ranch.

Law enforcement would be all over that place, and she probably wouldn't be allowed anywhere near it. What had happened? Even if she showed up there, she couldn't do anything to help Heath, though she wanted to offer the same comfort to him that he had offered to her.

Maybe . . . maybe even help gather evidence. She couldn't believe she would even consider it — she hadn't wanted to take photographs documenting acts of violence again. But two nights ago was a turning point for her. She admitted what she'd known all along — she could never truly get away from crime. Humanity lived in a fallen world. There was no getting around that. The nightmares and flashbacks and the memories of crime scenes she'd processed would keep her in this prison. Only God could help her out. If only she would let him.

Please, please, God, help me so I can help others. Help me let go of the anguish, the pain and suffering, and give it to you.

She momentarily squeezed her eyes shut.

The vehicle bounced as she steered onto the shoulder. She corrected her course and turned her thoughts back to Heath. If only she could help him somehow. But there was nothing she could do. Except pray. And it had been so long since she'd prayed. Would God even hear her? Would he listen to her prayers for Heath, for anyone who was in the line of fire?

CHAPTER TWENTY

Wednesday, 10:32 P.M.
Granite Ridge Campground

Harper tossed and turned in bed. She and Emily had spent the rest of the afternoon prepping the Airstream, doing laundry, and getting ready to leave early in the morning to head to the campground closer to Grayback. The list to get the RV ready for travel was long and detailed, and they always completed the tasks the night before. Rain was expected in the morning, so it was even better that they had prepared to leave tonight. Everything had been done, including raising the stabilizers — but the trailer was hitched to the truck, so it should be fine for them to sleep in.

All they had to do in the morning was raise the steps to the Airstream, then get in the truck and drive off. That is, if Harper could get out of bed. All that heavy lifting

— the hitch wasn't light — had her back aching.

Her heart was in pain too. She hadn't been able to stop thinking about Heath. She'd been told he was okay, but what exactly did that mean? And someone had needed an ambulance. Worry had chased her all day and night.

Funny to think that their paths had once again crossed — more like collided — and he'd inserted himself into her life. She'd accepted a gift from him — his way of comforting her. Offering reassurance. She reached over and pressed a hand over the camera on the small side table. But she deluded herself into thinking she was part of his world. She wasn't anymore. Not really. She should stop worrying about him. She had enough issues of her own.

Except.

Heath . . .

His face and broad shoulders came to mind. The way he smelled and walked and talked. The way he made her feel. He'd left one of his business cards, with his cell phone number on it, in the camera case. It read: HEATH MCKADE, PROPRIETOR, EMERALD M GUEST RANCH. She'd already plugged the number into her new phone, along with Emily's. She could call him, but she wouldn't. He would be wrapped up in dealing with the incident at his ranch.

Was he really okay? What happened? How could she find out? She'd tried calling the sheriff's department like Laura had suggested, but of course that got her nowhere.

Before they unplugged, she and Emily had watched the local news, but Harper didn't learn anything new about what happened at the Emerald M Ranch. No names were released. At least she'd seen for herself that Heath was okay when the newscast showed him talking to reporters.

Images of Mom, along with Heath, swirled around in her mind.

Harper had been too young to remember much, or maybe she had been too wrapped up in her silly little-girl things. But she could clearly remember her mother sitting at the kitchen table, her hair hanging down over her face as she cried. Her hands shook as the nightly news broadcast talked about a horrific bombing.

While Harper wanted the sheriff's office to get on top of what happened at the ranch, she worried that the woman's murder she'd witnessed would not be given priority.

An image of the shooter's scope looking straight at her came to mind. Harper shuddered.

168

While she wanted the man to be caught and brought to justice, she didn't hold out much hope for that. In her experience, the bad guys didn't get caught that often. And if he couldn't get caught, then she hoped he had left the area for good and would receive his just reward elsewhere.

Would she ever sleep?

CHAPTER TWENTY-ONE

Thursday, 12:31 A.M.
Granite Ridge Campground

Harper's bed jerked. Bumped. Vibrated. She stirred awake. Confusion rocked through her.

What in the world? She sat up on her elbows.

We're moving? Emily, why didn't you wait for me? She would much rather be in the truck riding than in the RV. Maybe Emily thought she needed the rest.

A scream from the other end of the RV alerted her. Emily wasn't in the truck driving. Harper climbed from the bed and steadied herself against the wall as the camper rocked back and forth. She slid the pocket door open and remained in the doorframe for stability.

The camper bounced, and she fell forward. On the floor, Harper pushed to her knees. She looked up in the dark camper,

170

grateful they had secured all the contents in the cabinets last night. All except the coffeepot. Something slid across the counter and crashed to the floor. The coffee pot?

"Emily! Where are you? Are you okay?"

"What's happening?" Emily was on the floor too. She switched on a flashlight and crawled toward Harper.

"We're moving. Our camper is moving!" Harper struggled to wrap her mind around it. "Someone's driving the truck!"

"But why?"

How? Who? "I don't know that, but it doesn't matter. We have to get out." She fought to gain her footing and finally stood.

The driver was going much too fast. Harper made her way to the door. "It's moving fast, so we have to be careful jumping out."

Whoever had stolen their truck — camper included — would have to slow down at some point. Stop signs. Traffic lights. Corners. Something. And that's when Harper and Emily would be ready to act.

Except the door handle wouldn't budge. Was it stuck? "Oh no."

"Harper? What is it?" Terror edged Emily's voice.

"The door won't open. I don't know if it's jammed or someone locked it from the outside."

"Someone can do that?"

"I don't know. Didn't you say it got stuck the other day and Mr. Stein fixed it?"

"I thought he fixed it." Emily gasped for breath. "Okay, so plan B. The emergency escape window. We practiced this, remember?"

"No. We talked about it. But we never actually took that swan dive from the sofa through the window." Or tried to slip one foot up and over and through the window while the other balanced on the furniture. She wasn't 100 percent sure she could get her hips through that small window — the downside of going vintage.

"But we practiced taking the screen off, opening the window, and closing it again." Emily's voice had grown excited. Or frantic.

Harper almost laughed, but the camper swerved hard to the left and she hit the counter, her face slamming into a cabinet. Pain lanced through her. What happened to Emily? The flashlight beam had gone out.

"Are you okay?" Harper asked

"No. Let's get out of here."

Harper held on to anything she could find as she made her way toward the window. Whoever was driving was intentionally making it hard for them to move around.

And if he or she had somehow locked the

door, what about the escape window over the sofa? Had they intentionally blocked that too?

Acid crept into her throat.

"We need to call for help," Emily said.

Okay. Deep breath. This wasn't a fire. They wouldn't burn to death or suck in noxious gases and die. They could think this through calmly.

"I'll go for the phones." They were charging in the kitchen. "You make your way to the window and get it open."

The camper continued to sway back and forth on the road. Harper thought she might have gotten her swaying camper legs when the camper hit a bump and she suddenly bolted into the air, knocking her head on the ceiling. Someone screamed.

Was that her or Emily? She didn't care. She reached for the cell phones and yanked them from the chargers. "Got the phones. How are you doing on the window?"

"I can't find the latch."

They had to get out of there before the driver killed them. Would that be an accident? Or on purpose?

Granite Ridge Campground was located at the top of a granite ridge.

Emily grunted. "It won't budge."

Harper thrust her cell into her pocket.

"Let me help you. You call 9-1-1 while I try. Maybe you'll get a signal."

As the RV moved and swayed, Harper tried to open the window as she balanced on the sofa Emily had rolled out to a bed. If only she had something she could use to smash through it. Then. The latch moved. They laughed in unison as if they were out of trouble.

Not yet.

Emily's voice trembled as she spoke into the phone. "Granite Ridge Campground. Yes. Someone's driving away with my camper with me in it! I can't get out!"

The camper whipped to the right, jarring Harper's hold. Emily screamed as they both slammed against the opposite wall. Something clattered.

"Em, are you okay?"

"I'm alive. And I want to stay that way. But I dropped the phone."

This was an abduction or a murder in progress. No way Harper could let either of those things come to pass. Moonlight broke through the clouds. She shared a look with Emily. They were going to get out of this together.

Harper crawled onto the sofa bed and finished opening the window. "We can do this. We can fit through." They had to. They couldn't wait for someone to come to their rescue.

Why hadn't someone stopped this maniac by now? A park ranger? Anyone? Someone should have noticed the dangerous driving.

Fear corded her neck and tightened. Maybe she and Emily couldn't make it. The driver was going fast enough that the fall out of the camper could kill them.

Emily held on with one hand and swiped at her furious tears with the other. "I don't understand why this is happening."

"We're getting out of here. Don't think about why it's happening right now." She thrust her head out the window and held on. She took in the view.

And sucked in a breath.

Harper pulled her head back in to look at her sister.

"What's the driver doing?" Emily asked. "Where are they taking us? I have a bad feeling. I mean a worse feeling. I think I'm going to throw up."

Nausea roiled in Harper's gut too. The driver was steering the camper along the switchbacks on a curvy mountain road. The most treacherous part. It wasn't easily traversed, even in the daytime while driving slowly.

Others had died there before.

She and Emily, they wouldn't be the first.

"We have to get out. Now!" Harper urged her sister forward toward the window. "You have to go feet first. You don't want to land on your head."

The road dipped. It might already be too late. Harper had a feeling the driver had already jumped from the truck and was letting momentum carry the vehicle and camper forward toward the deadly cliff's edge. Was there any hope they could survive the drop from this camper?

"Go, Emily. I'll hold your arms. I won't drop you, I promise. If you can't do this, then we're both going to die."

Emily climbed through the window, legs first. When she was halfway through, Harper grabbed her arms. The camper bounced up and Harper lost her grip. Emily disappeared from the window.

"Emily!"

Oh, Lord, please let her be okay. Let her survive this!

Harper climbed through the opening and positioned herself to drop from the window. Her sweats caught on the latch. *No, no, no . . .*

Squeezing her eyes shut, she prayed hard and shoved, ripping the sweats. Though she had planned to hang from the window and let herself drop, the camper bounced again, and Harper fell. She tried to roll when she hit the hard ground, pebbles cutting into her skin, asphalt scraping and gouging her.

The camper bounced violently as it tumbled over the cliff. Metal clanked and crashed.

She was hyperventilating.

She was alive.

But she wasn't so sure nothing was broken. Every bone in her body ached. Her head pounded. Had her head wound ripped open? She'd be bruised all over, but nothing mattered except Emily.

"Emily!"

Harper crawled until she found her. "Emily," she whispered.

Sirens resounded in the distance. Good. Emily's call to 9-1-1 had been taken seriously.

Emily lay sprawled on the side of the road. Unmoving.

"Emily!" Tears spilled down Harper's cheeks as she reached for her sister. Her hands shook as she looked for signs of life. Breath. A pulse. Something. Then she found a pulse. "Oh, thank God."

Harper wasn't sure what to do. She wanted to cradle her sister's head while she waited for help, but she was afraid to move her. Instead, she rested her palms on Emily's face. "It's going to be okay, Em. You're going to make it."

She grabbed her cell from her pocket and called 9-1-1. After she explained the situation and their approximate location, the dispatcher informed Harper that EMTs and deputies had already been sent out with the first call and she wanted Harper to remain on the line until help arrived.

But that help was going to take far too long.

"Please tell them to hurry. I don't know. Send a helicopter or something. My sister is badly hurt. I . . . I have to go."

Her trembling fingers struggled to end the call, then find Heath's stored number. She was grateful she'd put his number in her new phone. He lived out here somewhere close. Law enforcement might even still be at his ranch, given the explosion.

"Oh, Heath, please answer."

The call went to voice mail. Her voice shaking, she did her best to leave a coherent message, but she couldn't count on him getting it in time.

Harper took in her surroundings as she remained with Emily.

Had the driver gone over with the truck? Or was she right to believe that he had jumped out while slowing down at that last switchback, knowing the slope alone would carry the truck and camper right over? He might have fled the scene.

Or he could still be out there, watching.

CHAPTER TWENTY-TWO

Thursday, 1:39 A.M.
Granite Ridge Viewpoint

Grief-stricken and furious over the explosion that had taken out one of his cabins, Heath hadn't been able to sleep. He'd gone out to look at the stars, but the clouds blocked them, allowing only occasional glimpses of moonlight. He'd walked the perimeter where crime scene tape cordoned off a portion of his ranch. The fire chief suspected the explosion had been caused deliberately and was not the result of a leaky propane tank. The state lab out of Cheyenne would process the evidence. If the kids Taggart suspected of bombing mailboxes had suddenly ramped up their game for some insane reason no one could fathom — a cabin on a secluded ranch? — then they would receive the full wrath of the law. Taggart was furious.

Not nearly as angry as Heath.

Emerald M Ranch was in the news, but not for any reason Heath wanted.

As a result of the damage and the continued threat, until they knew more about who was behind the explosion, Heath had sent all his guests away and refunded their money. Leroy was in the ICU at St. John's in Jackson.

Heath — to his regret — hadn't seen Harper's call until he had gotten back to his room where he'd left his cell.

Nothing else had mattered except getting to her.

Now he stood on the road leading to Granite Ridge Campground, searching for Harper. Law enforcement and emergency vehicle lights still flashed. The ambulance caught his attention. Nearby, he spotted Harper wrapped in a blanket, her red hair spilling over.

His heart might come right out of his chest.

From where he approached on the far side of the sheriff's department vehicles, the scene appeared surreal. Harper's cry for help — for him to answer his phone — played repeatedly in his mind. Torture. Pure torture.

Someone was on a gurney and EMTs rolled it into the back of the ambulance.

Oh . . . Please, God . . .

He'd arrived much too late to help Harper. To save her from whatever had happened here.

He weaved his way through the ample law enforcement presence.

Two deputies from neighboring Hoback County stepped in his path and warned him away. He showed them his deputy credentials. He wasn't on duty and hadn't dressed the part. Instead, he had showed up in jeans, a T-shirt, and his Stetson. Heath's gaze found Harper again. Stunned, bruised, and beaten, she stared at the gurney as it rolled away. He could have heaved right there.

Then, as if sensing someone watching, Harper snapped out of her shock and her eyes searched the gathering of rangers, highway patrol, and deputies. Her eyes found him. For a good, long moment he held her gaze. Unwavering. Unable to see anything else.

He willed her to understand the depth of his concern, then forced away his own pain. He had to shove the images of the tragedy at the ranch far from his mind. He couldn't function otherwise. Then he compelled his legs to move again, one step at a time, and started toward her. He picked up speed and momentum.

The next thing he knew, Harper had flung herself at him, pressed her warm, trembling form against him. He had no choice but to wrap his arms around her. No other desire, really. He held her, comforted her, and wished he was able to end her pain.

She finally eased from him — he would have held her as long as she needed — and he gently gripped her arms. "Harper." He struggled to say more as he took her in. *Are you okay?* He wouldn't ask the ridiculous question. Finally, he found his voice. "I'm so sorry about everything. I'm sorry I didn't answer my cell. I didn't have it with me. I got here as soon as I could."

Why had she called him? Maybe because the ranch was close and she was in trouble. But he'd failed to hear her call for help. Still, the way her eyes searched his, he knew her need went much deeper, and he knew why she'd called.

Deep in his soul, he knew that she had needed someone she could count on, and she had hoped he would be that someone. On that point he had failed, but he was there now.

She hiccupped and swiped at her nose. Her pretty amber eyes shimmered in the moonlight. Harper had been through entirely too much trauma in her life. More than anyone should have to bear.

"I . . . I thought you lived close. That you could help us before he . . ."

He nudged her chin up. "Before he what, Harper? What happened here? Who are we talking about?" Had he been right to think she could be in danger?

"Emily and I got the camper ready to move into town. We always prep the night before. About an hour ago, I woke up and the camper was moving. Someone was driving the truck and pulling the camper. At first, I thought Emily had decided to get going and hadn't woken me up. Then I heard her scream and knew she was in the camper too. We couldn't get the door opened. With that killer still out there, I thought . . . I thought someone was abducting us to hurt us or kill us."

Harper turned her face to the cliff's edge. Heath realized he saw no camper. No Dodge Ram.

"You mean . . ." His gut clenched as his mind grappled to comprehend. "How did you escape?"

"We climbed out the window, but he had made it nearly impossible the way he steered. Then he steered the truck and camper to fly over the cliff. He must have

184

jumped out before the vehicles went over. We barely made it out." Tears choked her words. "I was helping Emily through the window, but I dropped her. She's unconscious."

Heath fought for the right words but came up empty. He wrapped his arm around her shoulder like a friend or a big brother might, though he felt far differently about her. *I'm here now.* That wasn't nearly enough.

Together they watched the ambulance turn onto the road and speed away, lights flashing, siren wailing.

"Emily." She gasped. "I have to get to the hospital. They're taking her to Jackson. I thought they would let me ride with her."

And Heath thought maybe she should be in an ambulance herself. Had she refused treatment because of Emily? "I'll take you."

"Are you sure? I don't want to be a burden. I know you have your own trouble to deal with. I could get one of the deputies on duty to take me."

He arched a brow, letting her know what he thought of her rejection.

Her shoulders sagged. Relief? "Thank you. I appreciate your helping me again. I hope I haven't caused you too much trouble."

"Harper, you and I go way back. Call me anytime." *What are you doing, Heath?*

He guided her over to his truck.

Once they were inside the cab and buckled, he drove them to the hospital. Quiet filled the cab, but it wasn't awkward. No, not that so much, but he would have preferred awkwardness to the gloom of apprehension.

She stared out the window, her thoughts much too far away, so he reached over and grabbed her hand, then squeezed. "She's going to make it. She's going to be all right. They know how to take care of people in Jackson." Grayback's small hospital, more like an acute clinic, wouldn't do for Emily, whose injuries would best be treated at the area trauma hospital, St. John's Medical Center, in Jackson.

"She wanted to leave as soon as the sheriff gave me the go ahead, but I convinced her to stay. The truth is we never should have come back here."

"Don't blame yourself. Emily wouldn't want that. You don't do either of you any good by taking that kind of burden on. You didn't do anything wrong." He should listen to his own words. He continued to blame himself for so much. "Can I ask why you decided to stay?"

"I wanted to make sure the woman's murderer is found. I was afraid the sheriff wouldn't take my story seriously, especially now with the explosion . . . Heath, I'm so sorry. I didn't even think to ask you about that. I wanted to call you when I heard. I wanted to come to the ranch. But I —"

"It's okay, it's okay. You were almost killed, Harper. That had to be terrifying for you. I'm glad you were able to climb out the window. I'm sure that was no easy task."

"Especially with the way he was driving."

"You said 'he.' Did you actually see him?"

"No. I didn't have time to think about anything but getting out. I can't help but think it's the same man who saw me with his rifle scope. He knows I witnessed his crime."

Heath nodded. His thinking exactly. He hoped they were wrong. But if they were right, then the big question was, how had he found Harper?

"Now, please tell me what happened at the ranch?" she asked. "I heard someone was in the hospital."

"Leroy. One of my employees you met at the wilderness camp. I could blame myself for that if I thought about it too long."

"You can't blame yourself," she said.

"And neither can you."

"I thought Wyoming was supposed to have

187

a low crime rate. What is happening around here?"

"I wish I knew. Sheriff Taggart has his hands full."

Heath was glad the sheriff had called in the state regarding the explosion at his ranch. Other agencies could end up involved too. Still, he hoped it wouldn't come to that. He hoped it wasn't some kind of crime wave and was more an isolated incident. Taggart even held on to the possibility that the explosion was a fluke, and that an actual bomb wasn't involved, though the fire chief thought it was deliberate. But the state would decide.

"And that's exactly why I have to stay. I want to help him find the woman's killer. And whoever attacked us tonight."

"I have to advise against that, Harper. Maybe as soon as Emily is able to travel, you should head home. Be safe somewhere away from the dangers of Wyoming." If only he could laugh at those last words. He needed to convince her to leave, but part of him — the insanely selfish part — wanted her to stay. He'd made a connection with her — an emotional one he'd tried to avoid, but he needed to be strong enough to cut that link with her before they both ended up hurt.

"I've spent too much time running away from the villains in my mind. I witnessed her murder. I saw her terror-stricken face. The fear and then death in her eyes." She shuddered. "I don't know why, Heath, but I'm compelled to stay and see things through. Maybe the sheriff will let me help."

Heath didn't see that happening. "So if the camper is at the bottom of Granite Ridge, where's your new camera?"

"You *would* have to ask."

"Ah, I figured. Well, that's the least of your worries. I'll get you another one."

"Look, I appreciate the camera, and I'm more than sorry that once again it's at the bottom of a . . ." Her words trailed off.

"I'm sorry. I shouldn't have brought it up," he said.

Harper and Emily could have ended up at the bottom of the ridge with the camper. He'd smelled the smoke when he arrived and suspected the vehicle and camper were charred by this point.

"What I mean to say is that it's not necessary for you to get me a replacement camera, though your offer is sweet, very sweet."

Did he want to come across as sweet? Nothing he could say at this particular moment would help. Besides, if he wanted to get her a new camera, he would good and well do it without asking permission.

They drove in silence for a while. Harper had to be worried about her sister. "Let's pray for your sister. Is that okay with you?"

"I don't mind, no. I've *been* praying. I don't understand why any of it has happened."

He remembered that she had offered to pray for him after his mother died. He had let her, but his heart hadn't been in it. He had been mad at God and himself. But knowing that she was still a praying woman warmed him through and through.

Together, they prayed for everyone who'd been hurt today. And for the murder investigation to be solved. For the missing woman's family.

Evelyn's words came back to him. *"You need to let the good Lord give you someone special, to have and to hold. To love and, yes, protect. Will you do that, Heath?"*

Those were the words she'd said right before the explosion that sent her son to the hospital. Heath hadn't had the chance to reply. He wasn't sure now what his answer would be. He hadn't exactly stood in God's way, had he? But he'd stood in his own way. His current *modus operandi* should be to keep his distance from the Lori Someralls and Harper Reynoldses of the world.

But for the first time in a long time, he wanted to be free of the burden that kept him believing he had to keep his distance. And Harper was the reason. Maybe because of their childhood friendship he still felt like he could open up and be himself with her.

Maybe he should listen to Evelyn.

Except Harper had no plans to stay long-term. He squeezed the steering wheel until his knuckles ached.

This wasn't the time or the place to even think about that kind of relationship. She'd almost been killed. Her sister was injured. Leroy was in the ICU. What was the matter with him? Irritated, he bulldozed those crazy thoughts far away as he pulled up to the hospital entrance.

Harper turned to him. "I can't thank you enough, Heath."

"I'm dropping you off here, but I'll be inside soon. I want to see Emily with you, and also check in on Leroy."

"I know I called you tonight. I was desperate, and I appreciate everything. But I feel like I've been far too much trouble for you already. You have so much to worry about with what happened at the ranch." She leaned in close enough to give him a warm peck on the cheek again, like she'd done before, then she opened the door. "You take care of yourself."

What a nice way to say goodbye. That's what he got for letting himself believe something could be there — a chance for love, maybe. With a woman who, despite having been his best friend when they were twelve, for all practical purposes was a stranger. *Get a grip, man.*

CHAPTER TWENTY-THREE

Thursday, 3:24 A.M.
St. John Medical Center

In the hospital waiting room, Harper sat hunched in an anything-but-comfortable chair, her mind reeling as she waited for what seemed like a lifetime for news on Emily. The pain from her head wound throbbed back to life and now she had additional bruises and scratches to contend with. But she ignored them.

Emily was in trouble.

Harper prayed the hardest she'd ever prayed and sipped from a cup of the worst coffee she'd ever tasted. Vending-machine coffee.

You're all I have, Emily . . .

When Dr. Drew, her therapist, suggested she take time to photograph something else entirely, she and Emily started out on this trip. A healing trip.

The irony was that she ended the trip —

on their last day — photographing a murder. And now Emily was hurt because of it.

She wanted to rail at herself for running away, but Heath McKade's face came to mind. His words floated through her heart and mind — confirming, reassuring, and soothing.

"You didn't look away this time. You took those pictures. You looked at the killer. You watched him . . ."

Commit the murder. He hadn't said those words out loud, but she knew that's what he had meant.

She refused to let the tears fall and instead tried to take what he'd said to heart. Maybe he was right. Maybe she had changed. She sure hoped so, because she had made the decision to stick around. She'd told Heath she wanted to help find the woman's killer. Those had been bold words, bolder than she truly felt inside. But somehow Heath had understood. She could see it in his eyes. So when he assured her that she'd done the right thing, it was like he was reaching into her brokenness and pushing the pieces a little closer together.

She'd tried to do that for him twice — after his mother left him and his brothers and then again after she died in the fire.

Now Harper wished she hadn't pushed

him away tonight. She'd been the one to call him and ask for help. She'd justified that call with the fact that her survival, Emily's survival, might depend on him living close enough to help, but part of her had wanted to reach out to someone familiar.

Not anyone. Who was she kidding? She had wanted Heath, when she shouldn't have.

And then what had she done? She'd cut him off, though gently. She'd seen it in his eyes — he understood that she hadn't wanted to see him again. That hurt her too. Something about Heath had gotten to her.

Instinctively, she knew he was someone she could fall for, but she'd made a habit of keeping her distance to avoid entanglements.

A nurse approached. "Ms. Reynolds?"

Harper almost spilled her coffee as she shot from the chair. "My sister . . . is she all right?"

"She's in a room now. You can see her. Follow me."

That wasn't exactly an answer, but Harper would take it. It was something. Her sister was alive. She had survived. She had a room. Harper followed the nurse to Emily's room and almost crumbled to the floor when she walked in and saw her lying on the hospital bed.

Was she asleep? Or was she still unconscious? Tubes connecting to three bags of fluid ran from her arm. Monitors were hooked up. Heart and oxygen. A blood pressure cuff expanded and tightened on her arm.

A white-coated woman turned to her. "Are you Ms. Reynolds?"

"Yes. I'm Harper, Emily's sister." Her gut twisted into a tight knot.

"I'm Dr. Malus. Your sister is in a coma. We did a CT scan to rule out a subdural hematoma."

"Excuse me, a what?"

"Bleeding on the brain."

"Oh." Harper found herself sitting. "Is she going to be okay? What's her prognosis?"

"She's alive. She's breathing on her own. For now, we monitor her. We run tests. We wait for her to wake up."

"And how long will that be?" Harper held her breath, held herself together as she took in the doctor's words. The movement of her mouth.

"Twelve hours. Twelve months. We can't know for sure."

Harper couldn't look at the doctor anymore. She stared at her sister. Eventually, Dr. Malus left her alone with Emily.

Harper had refused to cry while she waited. But as soon as she was alone, right on cue, her vision blurred. She couldn't have held back the tears if she wanted to now.

She would let herself feel the pain and get it over with. "Oh, Em . . . I'm so, so sorry."

She wasn't sure how many minutes passed before she was able to move her feet — put one foot in front of the other — and step closer until she could touch her sister's hand. She pressed her fingertips to Emily's skin.

"Em," she whispered. "I don't know if you can hear me. I don't know. I pray you can. I've heard it's possible. Please wake up. Please come back to me. I'll spend the rest of my life telling you how sorry I am that all this happened, though I know you'd grow tired of hearing it. Please. You're all I have." Thinking about Emily's condition in that way seemed completely selfish.

"I'm going to make sure the sheriff gets the person behind this." At the very least, she'd stay on top of Taggart's investigation. Make sure he saw it through. If necessary, she'd offer her assistance and hope he would take it. Anything less would be running away again. Emily wouldn't get justice, and Harper couldn't fail Emily.

One thing she knew — without help, she couldn't find out who had attacked them tonight.

Harper needed someone who held sway in this community as well as with the sheriff.

She knew just the person. If only she hadn't pushed him away.

At some point — minutes or hours later, she didn't know — Harper realized she'd fallen asleep in a chair close to Emily. She wanted to pray but had no more words. God knew, didn't he?

Except for the monitors, the room was silent.

Sterile and lonely.

Heath had prayed for her sister in his truck. She thought back to his rich voice and heartfelt words of faith. Someone at his ranch had been injured. And Harper had acted like such a jerk. She hadn't even asked him about the injuries before she'd told Heath goodbye. Thinking of Heath made the room seem less lonely, which made no sense.

Harper eased from the seat, her bruises aching and scrapes burning. A paramedic had put a few bandages here and there, but she'd refused more than that. She wasn't that hurt. No. Emily had taken the worst of it all.

She kissed Emily on the cheek. Gently ran her hand over her sister's forehead, avoiding the obvious knot. If only she hadn't dropped Emily, but would that have made a difference?

"I need to see a friend, Em. I need to go pay my respects. I need to see Heath. You've always liked him, remember?" *And so have I.*

He might have left already, but at the very least she could find out how Leroy was doing.

"I'll be back, Em, I promise."

Like she'd promised not to drop her. Harper turned to exit the room.

Detective Moffett blocked her way. "We need to talk."

CHAPTER TWENTY-FOUR

Thursday, 4:07 A.M.
St. John Medical Center

Arms crossed, Heath stood in the far corner of Leroy's hospital room, his insides in a tangle. The anguish might eventually overwhelm him, and he wasn't sure how to stop it. Fury at what had happened to the cabin could carry him a long way, but now he felt deflated in the worst possible way.

Head bowed, Evelyn sat in the only comfortable chair in the room. He wished she were sleeping, getting the rest she needed, but he knew her well enough to know she was praying for her only son. A guy who'd been down on his luck. Why had Heath thought his offer of a job could lift the man out of the low place he'd fallen? Another case of Heath trying to fix something. See how things turned out?

He and Leroy had become friends, and yeah, sure, he'd even thought of the man as

200

family like he thought of Evelyn. The family he'd been missing.

He hadn't realized how much he missed his brothers until Austin had shown up. He regretted not trying to convince Austin and Willow to live in the valley — she seemed to love the surroundings. It wasn't like she couldn't conduct her business from anywhere, but apparently, she had an assistant — Dana Cooper — with whom she was close. Heath understood that, but he'd been disappointed all the same. As for Austin, Heath had seen that look in his eyes — he missed Grayback and his home, despite all the ugliness they'd endured. He missed Wyoming.

And why shouldn't he miss all the raw, wild nature surrounding the Emerald M? At least Heath had reconnected with Austin, but he still had another brother out there unaccounted for. He'd tried to contact Liam too many times to count and hadn't heard back from him. Maybe he never would.

Exhausted, Heath scraped a hand down his face. He should focus on Leroy.

"You don't have to stay, Heath." Evelyn slowly lifted her head. "I know you have a business to run."

"Had, Evelyn." He pushed off the wall and

approached her, then crouched down to look at her. With her red-rimmed eyes and frazzled hair, she looked like she had aged ten years. "*Had* is the operative word."

She snatched his hand, surprising him with her strength. "You listen to me. You still have a business. Only one cabin was destroyed. You're going to recover, so don't you even think about it any other way."

How many people would believe it was safe to stay at the Emerald M Ranch now? *Why my ranch, God?* "All the guests are gone. I've canceled new arrivals for the next two weeks at least, until we find out what's going on. I'm . . . so sorry."

She squeezed his hand again. "Please stop. It's not your fault. He's going to be okay. My Leroy is going to be all right. You wait and see."

Given that he was in the ICU, Heath wasn't so sure. He wished he had the woman's faith — because she was hanging on with all she had. While Leroy's injuries were terrible, they could have been so much worse. Heath shuddered to think of it. He rose and paced the small space. Evelyn probably wished she could have some time alone to think and pray instead of having to encourage Heath. He'd been selfish to stay, but at the same time, he wanted her to know how much he cared.

"Would you like me to take you home so you can get some rest? I'll bring you right back whenever you need, I promise."

"No, thank you. I'm not ready to leave his side yet."

Restlessness surged inside. He needed to do something about this. What, he didn't know yet. "I should get going, then. His wife and kids are coming up, right?"

"His ex-wife could show up. Maybe. The kids live in other states and travel for their jobs too. Not to mention, they're not so close to their father."

Heath didn't understand that. Leroy seemed like a good, honest man. Heath would have treasured a man like Leroy as a father. But it wasn't his business. "Let me know if you need anything at all. I'm here for you."

"Remember what we were talking about when . . ."

"You need to let the good Lord give you someone special, to have and to hold."

"I'm not sure." He really should get going.

"That young lady. Harper. She had some trouble last night too."

Heath had given Evelyn a summary of the situation. Her son was in critical condition, and yet she'd thought to ask about Harper.

"Yes."

"How is she?"

"Her sister was unconscious when they brought her to the hospital. Harper came out of it in better condition. With bruises and scrapes." To add to the stitches in her head.

"I'm so sorry. Please tell her that I'll be praying for her and her sister. What's her name?"

"Emily is the sister. But what makes you think I'll see her to give her your message?"

"You're neighborly that way, Heath. The woman was in a terrible accident, so you need to check on her."

Harper wasn't his neighbor, for one thing. He didn't have the heart to tell Evelyn that Harper didn't want Heath to check on her. He was glad he hadn't told Evelyn about the camera he'd bought for her.

"Okay, I'll check in and give her your message. But after that, my focus is going to be on finding out what happened. And if it was deliberate, who's responsible."

Heath exited the room and headed down the hallway. As he neared the waiting area next to the elevators, he spotted Harper leaning against the wall as if she were watching and waiting for him. At first his heart warmed a little too much. Had Harper come to see him, and her sudden goodbye hadn't been the brush-off he'd thought? Or was Emily in the ICU too?

Harper's eyes lit up as she stepped toward him. "Heath." She closed the distance. "How is he?"

"Leroy's in bad shape, but he's strong and the doctors believe he'll pull through." He hoped so for Evelyn's sake, if not his own. He glanced at the stitches. She had too many bruises and scrapes to count. "How are you holding up?"

She definitely looked as if she needed rest. "I'm okay, but Emily is in a coma." Tears glistened in her eyes.

He wanted to take her hand and squeeze it again like he'd done in the truck, but he refrained. "I'm supposed to give you a message from Evelyn — she's Leroy's mother. She said she would be praying for you and your sister."

"Oh?" Harper's eyes teared up a little more, then she stood taller and blinked the tears away as if for good. "That's so sweet of her when she has her own troubles."

Heath nodded, unsure where to take the conversation next. He let his gaze roam the hallway instead of lingering on her incredible eyes. He was glad she'd come to ask about Leroy, but by the look on her face, there was more to her visit.

"I know I'm keeping you from something and I apologize for that, but . . . can we talk?"

"Of course."

"I know you have a lot going on with the incident at the ranch, and I wouldn't take you away from that —"

"Harper. Please tell me what this is about." The atrocities of the night were beginning to wear on him, and that deep ache in his side from the gunshot wound, along with the sheer fury, was building up again. He wasn't sure he should subject Harper to that side of him.

"I shouldn't ask you this. I hate it, but I don't know who else to turn to. I need your help. I want to go down to the ravine where the camper fell. I'm sure they'll be processing the scene soon. Maybe even call in the state. But I don't trust anyone else with my life. Emily's life. I'm going to take pictures. But I need someone of your position in the community with me or else Taggart won't believe me even if I show him the evidence. Especially if I find something his investigator missed."

Whoa. What? Her words stunned him. "What's this all about? Someone tried to kill you tonight. I think we both know who that could be. You're the only witness to his crime — a murder. In fact, maybe Sheriff Taggart should even put you in protective custody."

When her features twisted up, she pressed her hands over her face. Hiding her anguish? Then, finally, she dropped them.

Heath braced himself. "What's going on, Harper?"

"The deputy investigator — Detective Moffett — she claims someone witnessed me driving tonight. The witness said I was the one to get in and drive off in the middle of the night. We barely escaped with our lives. I told the detective I wasn't driving. Why would I do that? I brought up the 9-1-1 call that Emily made. Detective Moffett said that was more incriminating than anything because Emily didn't mention me. She only said someone was driving away with the camper and she was locked inside. The detective asked me to stay in town in case she had more questions. I can't tell what she's thinking. If she believes me or not. But Heath, if I can't prove otherwise, they could potentially arrest me. Emily's in a coma, so she can't tell them what really happened. She can't tell them that I wasn't driving!"

Heath absorbed her words, struggling to believe them. What else could this day bring? They weren't going to arrest her. Taggart wouldn't go that far. Would he? "I don't think Sheriff Taggart will allow you to visit the crime scene and take pictures if there's any suspicion, even if I ask nicely." He fisted his hands. Harper was the victim here. Couldn't Taggart see that?

"I'm not asking you to convince him."

CHAPTER TWENTY-FIVE

Heath studied her, almost as if gauging her value — was she worth the risk and his time? She had to be wrong. The Heath she knew wouldn't think in those terms. He was the kind of person who figured out a way to assist someone in need, and that was one of the reasons she'd come to ask for his help. Harper could almost cower under the pensive stare of his intense blue eyes, but she couldn't afford to back down.

She took in his rough appearance that was so different from when he'd shown up at the camper to give her a camera. With his scruffy jaw and shaggy hair, he could easily be the hero in an epic fantasy — brooding, dejected look and all. She hadn't missed that his eyes had been haunted when he came out of Leroy's room but had brightened slightly when he saw her.

Her breath had caught in her throat. Heath had been glad to see her, and now that she thought about it, being near him brought the reassurance she craved.

Harper focused back on the reason she had sought him out. She loathed sounding so needy. Perhaps even fragile. She definitely didn't want this strong deputy/cowboy to think she was weak.

He crossed his arms and shifted his attention to the floor. Harper hoped she was reading him wrong, but his reaction deflated her, and her shoulders sagged. "Look, I would never ask this of you if it weren't for the fact that Emily is in a coma, and I trust you. You appear to have earned a lot of respect in this town." Her trust in him went far beyond that, but she kept that to herself. "You're a deputy too. I know I'm asking a lot. I wouldn't want to hurt your reputation."

His arms still crossed, he pressed a hand over his mouth as if to suppress a grin, then dropped it. "Is that what you think?"

"I don't know what to think. Maybe it was a mistake to ask." The courage she'd worked up started slipping away, and if she didn't snatch it back, it would be completely out of reach. Gone forever.

And . . . there, just like that, her courage fled.

She took a step back, then another. "I

shouldn't have bothered you."

He gently caught her wrist. "Where are you going? I haven't even given you my answer yet."

"I can see what you're thinking."

"You can read my mind, can you?"

"Heath, please, tell me. Did I overstep to ask you for help? What are you thinking?"

"How strong and brave you are to face this head-on. I would think you would be looking at the fastest way out of town — taking Emily with you — or talking to the sheriff about protective custody."

"Are we talking about the same sheriff? The one who thinks I drove the camper over a cliff?"

"We don't know what Taggart thinks. We should talk to him. Gauge his reaction to you gathering evidence."

"In my experience, it's better to act and then ask forgiveness."

His eyes smiled. "I'll have to remember that about you. So that's what you're asking, then — for me to go with you and gather evidence, and then we'll share the good news with Taggart."

"Yes. Please go with me."

"Heath?" A woman's voice spoke softly from behind.

He whipped around. "Evelyn. Is everything okay?"

Tired eyes took Harper in. "I'm Evelyn Miller. You must be —"

"Harper Reynolds." Exhaustion rolled through her. She only had so much energy left and needed that confirmation from Heath.

"How is your sister?" Sincere concern filled the woman's eyes.

"She's hanging in there. And your son?"

Doubt flitted across her face, then determination replaced it. "He's a survivor. He'll be fine. God is watching out for us." Evelyn turned her aged gaze on Heath. "I hope I didn't interrupt anything."

"Not at all." Love and respect poured from Heath — he obviously adored this woman. "Are you ready for me to take you home?"

Despite her somber features, she smiled slightly. "Yes. I changed my mind. I need to be fresh for when Leroy wakes up." Evelyn reached across the distance and grabbed Harper's hand. "And you, dear. I heard about your camper. You'll stay with us, then."

It wasn't a question. Harper didn't know what to say. She hadn't even thought about where she would stay.

Heath chuckled. "Evelyn sees a need, and

she doesn't bother asking. You'll get used to it."

Would Harper be around long enough to get used to it?

"I can see you hadn't thought that far ahead." Evelyn leaned against the wall for support.

Heath reacted quickly and placed his arm around her shoulder but looked at Harper. "I should get her back to the Emerald M Ranch. You're welcome to come along. Welcome to stay at the main house. There's plenty of law enforcement presence at the ranch right now. I can't think of a safer place for you."

Harper followed Evelyn and Heath down the hallway. Should she stay with them? They were strangers, really, and yet the thought of sleeping in a warm bed and a house filled with love on a ranch that would have law enforcement officers close by compelled her to consider it.

Evelyn stopped and turned to look at Harper. "For your sister's sake, you need the rest. I thought I would stay here all night with Leroy, but if he wakes up and I'm haggard, that won't help either of us."

Evelyn had given her the small nudge she needed. "I have to check in on my sister before I leave. Is that all right?"

"Sure," Heath said. "I'll pull my truck around to the entrance and wait for you there."

Heath and Evelyn started walking again, and Harper headed toward her sister's room.

"I won't be long. I promise," she called over her shoulder.

"And Harper," Heath said.

She paused and turned. Heath watched her.

"We'll talk about your request later." He dipped his chin, then continued ushering Evelyn away.

So Heath was actually considering helping her process the crime scene.

Maybe the bump on her head had messed with her thoughts. She'd agreed to an MRI but hadn't taken care of that yet. Had she lost her mind to think she could or should process that scene, especially since she would do it after everyone else had finished with it? Maybe she should simply ask the sheriff if she could be present while it was processed. What could be the harm in that? Whatever his answer, she definitely wanted to find the person who'd tried to kill her and Emily.

Heath and Evelyn took the elevator, and Harper headed down the hallway to the other side of ICU to Emily's room. She'd promised to come back, and now she would tell her unconscious sister that she would be staying at the Emerald M Ranch. She hadn't had the heart to turn down Evelyn Miller, or Heath for that matter.

With the way he cared about people, he was definitely one of a kind. Harper knew that from experience, and she was taking advantage of his generosity and kindness. She needed to see this through, but was she wrong to invite Heath to stay in her life through this storm? Especially when he had troubles of his own?

At the end of the hallway, she took a left. Her heart contracted at the sight of a figure standing at the last door on the left. Her sister's room. She pushed herself to move faster. A deputy stood like a sentinel outside Emily's door.

Oh, thank God. Taggart was taking this seriously and had sent someone — albeit a Teton County deputy — to guard Emily. Why hadn't Harper thought of that?

"I'm so glad you're here." She smiled up at him as she made to enter the room.

"Sorry, ma'am. Nobody's allowed in."

"I'm her sister. It's okay."

"Nobody's allowed in her room except for medical staff."

CHAPTER TWENTY-SIX

Thursday, 5:17 A.M.
Emerald M Guest Ranch

Finally. Heath steered toward the arch carved out of one solid piece of pine. The words *Emerald M Ranch* burned into the wood had never been so welcoming. While an expected sense of rightness would normally settle over him, dread rose up, preventing it. The despair he'd driven away by renovating the place, and that he'd kept at bay for so long, was closing in on his world again.

Still, he welcomed the sight of his home — his ranch — as it came into view.

Dawn peeked over the mountains as Heath steered his truck toward the arch. At least he would soon be liberated from the longest drive of his life.

Evelyn and Harper had both remained silent on the drive from Jackson, where they had both left a loved one behind. Eventu-

216

ally, Evelyn started softly snoring in the back seat. The woman needed her rest, then she would go back to the hospital to be there for Leroy. Her son wasn't the only person Heath was worried about. Even though Leroy was in the ICU, Heath couldn't help himself — he was more worried about Harper at this moment. She stared out the window and he suspected she still had that glazed-over look. She wasn't connecting.

He knew she would pull herself together, but her words kept replaying in his mind.

"They won't let me see my sister."

As soon as they got settled at the main house, he would call Moffett or Taggart. This was all some kind of crazy.

One problem after another. He squeezed the steering wheel. There was no way Harper sent that truck and camper over the cliff. The so-called witness was wrong. Or lying. Had they thought of that?

He slowly approached the arch, intending to drive through, only to be stopped by law enforcement. Wyoming Highway Patrol — the de facto state police. He had better allow Heath onto his ranch.

He jumped out of the truck. "Hi. How are you doing?"

"Sir, no one's allowed on the premises.

It's a crime scene."

"I'm Heath McKade, proprietor of these premises. Last I knew, only one cabin had exploded. I hadn't realized they had concluded it was an actual bomb or that the main house was also deemed a crime scene. I need to get home."

"I'm not saying it was a bomb. Let's see your driver's license. I have to vet everyone, you understand."

Heath pulled out his wallet and flipped it open to reveal his Wyoming driver's license and sheriff's department credentials.

"So you're with the state," Heath said. It was a statement and not a question. He hoped the man would elaborate.

"Yes, sir. And you're a deputy. I'm Lester Vernon, by the way."

"Nice to meet you. Have they figured out anything? What happened? Who's responsible?"

"I'm only the grunt called in to keep the vermin out of the fortress."

Heath cocked a brow as he looked at the ladies watching from the cab of his truck. "You do realize that three million acres of wilderness and national forest surround this ranch. If someone wanted in, they probably wouldn't come through the front gate."

Vernon half grinned. "I'll agree, it's a

problem. Who's in the truck with you?"

"Evelyn Miller and Harper Reynolds. They're staying at the main house with me."

"Are you sure you want to stay here, considering the suspicious activity?"

He rubbed his chin. "No. I'm not entirely sure, but it's been a long night, and looks to be an even longer day."

"I understand. Go ahead and pass."

Heath climbed back in to face two sets of wide eyes staring back at him.

"What's happening?" Evelyn asked.

"Nothing to worry about. They don't want anyone here who shouldn't be here." The sheriff didn't have the resources for this and the state would assist in processing the cabin. He would think Taggart would let him know what was going on, call him in to work even, except it was his ranch, so he probably needed to remain hands-off. Who knew who else would show up? The bomb squad out of Cody? The ATF — the Bureau of Alcohol, Tobacco, Firearms and Explosives? This could turn into a twisted tangle of law enforcement barbed wire at his ranch.

Heath glanced at Harper, who watched Vernon as Heath steered by him. Was she having second thoughts about staying here? He wished he could have shown her the renovated Emerald M before all the ugliness had stolen its beauty. A lot of photographers stayed at the Emerald M for all the splendor of nature they could catch on camera. He had a feeling she would have loved the place. Except, well, she had already gotten her fill of nature, he supposed, and a big heaping dose of violence to soil the beauty.

As he neared the main house, the truck tires crunched over the gravel drive. His rustic-looking two-story log cabin came into view. When Harper had seen it as a kid, the wraparound porch hadn't actually wrapped all the way around. Heath had added on quite a bit. Would she remember what the old house had looked like — before and after the fire that had taken his mother? Beyond the cabin was the pasture and horse barn, and a small lake for the guests to fish if they didn't want to hike into the wilderness and fish on one of the many rivers and streams in the Gros Ventre Wilderness. A measure of pride swelled. He wanted her to see and appreciate what he'd done.

County and state vehicles came into view deeper in the woods near the destroyed cabin. Their presence disfigured his haven. Heath's stomach sickened at the sight of the blackened foliage. The cabin — or what was left of it — was just out of his line of sight.

Thank goodness none of his guests had been hurt. Bad enough Leroy had been injured.

He didn't get it. Who had done this and why? The fact that he even asked the question told him that, deep inside, he leaned toward agreeing with the fire chief that the explosion was a deliberate act of violence against his ranch. Against him.

He parked the truck, turned off the ignition, and then climbed out to assist Evelyn. She was strong, but he was worried about her current state of mind and the fact that she was exhausted. He eased her out.

She patted his arm. "You're treating me like an old lady, Heath." She chuckled. "But thank you. You've always been a gentleman."

"All in a day's work," he said.

She leaned closer and whispered, "I'll show Harper to one of the guest rooms, Heath. Then you can show her around the place so she can make herself at home."

"Sounds good. I'll take you back up to the hospital when you're ready."

"I can see you're eager to find out what's going on. So as soon as you can, you go talk to the sheriff. Whoever you can find. Maybe it's time for you to put on your deputy uniform."

Harper came around Heath's truck, hugging herself, her golden eyes wide.

She still wore the sweats and hoodie she'd been in when he'd answered her call for help last night. They were dirty and torn. He still needed to discuss what she planned to do. But he had a better idea. He would talk to Taggart and end this nonsense. She wasn't a criminal.

He offered a soft grin for her sake, though anger boiled inside at what had happened to his ranch. What was still happening to Harper.

"It's going to be okay," he said. "Go with Evelyn. Get some rest. We have plenty of room. She can find you some clean clothes too. I'll show you the renovations as soon as you're ready."

"I can't thank you enough" — Harper looked at Evelyn then too — "both of you, for your generosity."

"Think nothing of it." Evelyn, gracious woman that she was, draped her arm around Harper and guided her onto the wraparound porch and into the house.

God had smiled down on him the day he'd hired Evelyn. She'd been the voice of wisdom and could cook the meanest lasagna. He left the house behind him and marched toward what looked like too much chaos here on his property.

The peace and serenity were ruined. Destroyed. Who would have believed this could ever happen here? He spotted Taggart and hiked over to the sheriff.

Heath had to approach this right if he wanted to stay on Taggart's good side to get information about what was going on here and also defend Harper.

"Hey, Taggart." Heath crossed his arms and looked at what was left of the cabin. A man and woman walked around with gloved hands and evidence bags, taking photographs. "What do we know?"

Taggart gestured to the two people searching through the remains of the cabin. "We know the fire chief cleared the cabin for the state to come in. Other agencies are undecided if their involvement is required. I'll keep my hands in it no matter what. This is my county and my people." He didn't say more for a while. Heath waited, understanding Taggart liked time to process what he would say next. Heath wasn't disappointed.

"I thought it was those kids," Taggart said. "The mailboxes."

"You're thinking this definitely was a bomb."

"What else could have happened? My gut

tells me the mailboxes and this explosion weren't done by the same person. But I can't figure out why someone would bomb your ranch. Target a specific cabin. We'll need to get information on who had planned to stay there. See if they were the specific target. Seems like there'd be an easier way to take someone out. Other than targeting a guest, do you have any ideas?"

"You know I don't."

"I'm not sure you should even stay here at the ranch until this is resolved."

"That could take a long time. I need to rebuild the cabin. Clean up. Rebuild the Emerald M's reputation. I'll have to put the horses somewhere else too. I'm losing money every day someone isn't renting those cabins." He took a step toward the charred debris.

Taggart pulled him back. "I need your help, Heath."

Acid burned in his gut. "When you convinced me to sign on as a reserve deputy, this wasn't what I thought I'd be doing."

"Trust me. This isn't what I had in mind when I agreed to be sheriff. We don't get to pick and choose. That said, I know you didn't mean it that way. I can understand you're a little uncertain after what you've been through — but it's because of what you've been through that you understand we need more people like you. So get your act together. I'm not saying I want you on this bomb thing. Actually, it would be best if you stayed out of the way where it concerns your ranch. For all I know, the state or feds could end up turning the tables on you. Say you were responsible. You needed the insurance. Took the mailbox bombing idea and ran with it."

Heath's stomach clenched. Twisted into a knot he'd never untangle.

He thought of Harper — the anguish she must have felt when the detective suspected her. "You can't be serious."

"Anything's possible at this moment."

"Me. A suspect." He ground his molars. "I have put everything into this ranch. Why would I destroy even one cabin? Destroy the reputation I've fought to build? What do you think, Taggart? I want to hear what you truly think about me."

"We both know that anything is possible. That said, I don't believe you had anything to do with it or I wouldn't be telling you I need your help — get your deputy uniform on and let's go to work."

"And what about Harper? Do you think she tried to kill her sister last night? That she would be so crazy that she would try to kill them both by driving off a cliff?"

"Look, Heath. It doesn't matter what I think. The facts are what matters. If she's innocent, we'll know soon enough." A sheriff's department vehicle steered through the entryway.

Heath tore his gaze from the charred remains of the cabin and watched the vehicle. It turned away and headed for the main house.

His jaw dropped. Before he thought to close it, he looked at Taggart and realization dawned. Someone had informed Taggart that Harper had left the hospital and was with Heath. They would take her in for questioning, or worse, like she feared — arrest her.

At least Taggart understood he couldn't ask Heath to do that. He'd flat out refuse.

He wanted to throttle Taggart right then and there.

"She's the victim in this!"

CHAPTER TWENTY-SEVEN

Thursday, 6:30 A.M.
Emerald M Guest Ranch
In the more-than-adequate bathroom, Harper wiped away the condensation on the mirror to study her reflection, which still looked haggard even after a long, hot shower.

Oh . . .

She wished she hadn't looked. No wonder Heath kept watching her at the hospital.

At least her stitches remained intact. At least she had a place to stay. A good place where she felt safe. Though she was beyond frustrated that she hadn't been allowed to see her sister, she was grateful that Emily was safe and guarded.

Soon enough, the sheriff would learn she shouldn't be a suspect.

She would have to bide her time.

In the meantime, the murderer was still out there in the area or he'd fled the region, fearing capture. What a joke. Nobody was even looking for him yet.

At this rate, she would never get dressed, so Harper pushed the thoughts aside. Evelyn was so sweet. The woman was distraught over her son, yet she had found time to assist Harper. She'd brought her some clothes. A knit peach top and nice jeans. A few items accidentally left behind by Willow, Heath's sister-in-law.

Evelyn reassured Harper that Willow wouldn't mind, but the woman was a lot taller than Harper. She slipped into the clothes but had to cuff the jeans. After dressing, she tried to make herself as presentable as possible, but with all the bruises and scratches, she wasn't sure it was worth the effort. She intended to crawl into that woods-themed quilt-covered bed and sleep for a while. The only problem was, she had the feeling nightmares and flashbacks would keep her awake.

Evelyn's and Heath's generosity and kindness might be the force that cracked open her strong and determined façade. She was trying to stay strong, especially for Emily, but she really wanted to crumble. Curl into a ball somewhere. Not give up, not completely. But she needed time to grieve and to fight the dark depression that threatened to close in on her. Maybe a few hours in that bed would be enough, but she didn't think so.

Before she tried the bed, she wanted to grab something to drink from the kitchen. Her mouth was parched.

She reached for the door and heard a light knock, then someone said, "Harper?"

Tension lurking in Heath's tone set her on edge. She eased the door open and took in his guarded demeanor. "Is everything okay?"

He tried to smile but failed and seemed to struggle for words.

Her heart pitched. "Did something happen to Emily?"

That strong wall she'd built around herself was about to collapse.

"No. Detective Moffett is here."

She searched his face, looking for some hint as to why. "It's not good news."

"She didn't tell me why she's here. My guess is to ask questions." Heath stepped aside as if he would walk her to her interrogation.

This can't be happening.

God, please don't let her take me into town to the sheriff's department for more questioning. I already told the detective everything at the hospital.

Taking a few long breaths, she mentally prepared herself to face the detective.

Stay calm. It's going to be all right. You didn't commit a crime. Answer the detective's questions and let her discover you're innocent. You're the victim.

Before they could leave the hallway and enter the great room, Heath slowed and turned to face her. "It's going to be all right, Harper. Whatever happens, you're not alone in this."

He tried to reassure her, but his words only served to scare her more.

"Let's get this over with." She pressed by him and found not only Moffett but also Sheriff Taggart. The detective paced the big room. Harper had seen that stance before — Moffett was confident, resolved. She wanted to nail Harper. To charge her, if she could.

Harper mustered the last of her reserves to face the woman detective who had something to prove.

"Detective Moffett. What can I do for you?"

"We're continuing to process the crime scene at the base of Granite Ridge."

"I'm glad to hear it." She hugged herself. "Whoever did this needs to be caught."

She hated how long the cogs of law enforcement processing could delay the tracking of a criminal. A murderer, in this case.

"There were no skid marks, which means you didn't even try to stop."

"Now hold on!" Heath's voice rose as he stepped between Harper and the detective.

"It's all right, Heath." She pressed a hand on his arm and urged him back to her side. Moffett hadn't given her the Miranda warning, which she should only do if Harper was both under arrest and also being interrogated. Had the detective gotten ahead of herself? "I wasn't driving, Detective. So it wasn't me who drove through the guardrail. Do you plan to charge me? Do I need a lawyer?"

Taggart's cell rang, and he tugged it out before slipping to another part of the room to talk.

"No," Heath said, his arms crossed. "There isn't enough evidence here."

"Yet."

The sheriff approached and lowered his cell. "Harper, your sister is awake."

A few seconds ticked by as Harper absorbed his words. Relief swelled in her heart.

"Oh, thank God." She covered her face to hide her tears of joy and turned right into Heath's broad chest, lingering there a few moments until she could get her composure.

Then she stepped away and gave him a tenuous smile. A silent thank-you for his support. For standing up for her. Since he was a deputy, would his actions cost him?

"Is she all right?" Heath asked.

Harper had been so exuberant about hearing Emily was awake, she hadn't thought about the possibility of other complications.

"Well enough to speak to the deputy guarding her against another attempt on her life —"

"You mean by me. That's why he wouldn't let me see Emily."

Taggart gave a subtle nod. "That, and I wanted someone to interview her before you had a chance to speak with her. She corroborated your story. Said you were both locked in the camper and someone with malicious intentions drove off. You both had to escape through the emergency window, which is how she received the traumatic blow to her head."

"I need to see her. Are you done with me? Are you ready to look for the person behind this?"

Detective Moffett appeared relieved, which surprised Harper. She thought the detective had been too eager to charge her with this crime. "For what it's worth, I'm glad you're innocent. I was simply doing my job."

"No hard feelings. But now you can focus on finding the *actual* killer?"

The detective frowned.

Incredulity rolled through Harper.

"Sheriff Taggart." Strong and intimidating, Heath's voice boomed through the great room. "I agree with Harper that we need to start looking for the real criminal behind this. Harper is the only witness to that shooting, and last night's incident appears to be an attempt on her life. You must see that by now."

"I've been following all the leads, Mc-Kade."

"The wrong leads, if you ask me."

Taggart glared at Heath. "Since Ms. Reynolds has been targeted, I'm going to assign you to stay with her, McKade. Her and her sister. You're their security while she remains here and in danger." Then he turned his gaze on her. "You're free to head home to Missouri, Ms. Reynolds, if you so choose. I'm happy to contact law enforcement there on your behalf for protection services, if needed. But while you're here, McKade will stick with you."

Heath stiffened. His reaction surprised Harper. "I think we need to talk about that first. Maybe a safe house would be in order."

"Sure, we can talk, but you have your marching orders. Ms. Reynolds, I'm sorry for the undue stress my department put you under, but I hope you understand our reasons."

Harper eyed the sheriff. "By way of an apology, how would you feel about letting me process the scene from last night — after it's been officially processed, that is?"

"I don't know what you think you'll gain by that."

Harper didn't allow the sheriff's or detective's intimidating postures to affect her next words. She had to bulldoze her way through if she was going to get anywhere. "Another set of eyes won't hurt your efforts. I can help catch the man I witnessed murdering a woman, if you'll let me."

"That's not going to happen."

CHAPTER TWENTY-EIGHT

"Uh . . . Sheriff. Can I talk to you a minute?" Heath asked.

Harper watched him. Did she hope he would persuade the sheriff to let her help with the investigation? He'd do what he could on that, but he had an entirely different reason for speaking to Taggart.

"I need to get back," Detective Moffett said. She let herself out the door.

Harper remained where she stood. Heath had meant to talk to the sheriff in private. "Is she free to go, Sheriff?"

The sheriff nodded. "I've already told her she is."

"Good. Make yourself at home, Harper. Get some rest. I'll be back soon." Heath ushered the sheriff out the door and onto the porch. He eyed the door. Maybe this was still too close. He didn't want Harper to listen in on the conversation. "Let's walk back to the cabin."

They stepped off the porch and started hiking. Taggart would need to head this direction anyway since his vehicle was parked near the cordoned-off area.

"Spit it out, McKade."

"You assigned me to keep Harper safe. I can do anything you ask me, but I'm not the right man for that particular assignment."

Taggart stopped and fisted his hands on his hips. "Is that so? And why not?"

Where did he even start? He was a deputy, for crying out loud. Sharing with Taggart all his perceived weaknesses or about how he thought he was such a screw-up wasn't something the man wanted or needed to hear. But here went nothing. "I don't have a great track record when it comes to protecting people."

Taggart arched a brow. "You're talking about what happened a few months ago when you were shot."

Heath's attempt at helping, fixing what was wrong, always seemed to be the catalyst that caused the incident he meant to prevent.

Every time. "Assign me the mailboxes like you said earlier."

"Not with the bombing of your cabin. Those incidents could be related. As for protecting Harper, you're the best man for the job, Heath." Taggart took a step closer and squeezed Heath's shoulder. "I don't know how many times I've seen you put yourself in the line of fire for the sake of others."

"And you know how it all turned out."

Taggart nodded, his expression somber. "That doesn't matter. What matters is that you're a hero, Heath. Willing to put your life on the line for someone else — whether you know them or not. And in this case, I can tell that she matters to you. If anyone is going to keep her safe, it's you. So you see, there's nobody better."

The sheriff gave one last hearty squeeze, then hiked off and left Heath standing there, grappling with his words.

Then he realized he'd all but forgotten about convincing Taggart to let Harper look at the camper and truck. He jogged to catch up to him.

Looked like he wasn't getting out of bodyguard duty. And if that was the case, then this time Heath had better get it right — he couldn't bear it if something happened to Harper on his watch. He would have to suck it up, bolster himself with a confidence he didn't feel.

Heath would protect her at all costs.
This time he couldn't fail.

CHAPTER TWENTY-NINE

Friday, 10:24 A.M.
Crime Scene at Granite Ridge

Harper hiked over to the wreckage at the bottom of Granite Ridge, her gut twisting into a thousand knots at the sight of the camper and truck, now broken lumps of blackened, crumpled metal.

Her limbs shook, but she kept moving. She had to hold it together. She couldn't collapse to her knees and sob.

Evidence photography required emotional detachment. Impartiality. But that would be impossible.

Detective Moffett and Heath hiked alongside her until they were at the scene of the accident — the crime scene — where they stood back and let Harper work, watching her every move. To Harper's surprise, the county's crime scene techs had finished up their work this morning and released the scene.

As Harper studied the wreckage, she fought the nausea building in her stomach.

God, please give me nerves of steel.

She'd wanted this, after all. It wasn't like the sheriff had hired *her.* He was simply allowing her to look for anything his investigators and techs might have missed. He had nothing to lose. Heath had been right about Taggart being a man who wanted the truth. Like her, he wanted to catch this killer and shut him down. The sooner that happened, the better for everyone.

Detective Moffett was present to make sure that any evidence Harper found wasn't contaminated or even planted — so there still remained that thread of suspicion, but she understood that this precaution was only meant to preserve Harper's findings if they were used later in a trial. Harper wondered if part of Moffett hoped Harper found nothing at all. Finding something would put the detective's and the techs' skills into question. Still, they were a small, shorthanded operation.

Harper had reservations, too many doubts about herself to count, but she ignored them. She didn't have time for that. This killer had come after her personally and had included Emily in his death plans.

Drawing in a few stabilizing breaths, Harper switched on her photographer's brain, shutting down composition mode for the time being. This wasn't artistic photography. Crime scene or evidence photographs required a different mind-set and focus.

Fortunately, one of the techs had allowed her to use the department camera, tripod, and tools.

"So what have you figured out so far?" Harper asked. "How did he lock us in? How did he get into my truck and start it?"

Moffett's eyes were hidden behind dark sunglasses. "With this old retro Airstream, blocking the door wouldn't have been hard. I can detail a list of ways if you need that, but nailing that down with this mangle of materials is going to take time."

Heath stood next to Moffett. "The truck is easy. It's an older model, so either he hot-wired it or one of you left the keys in the ignition."

"It would have been an oversight on my part. The truck is mine. Or I should say was. The Airstream was Emily's."

Moffett pursed her lips. "An awful lot of trouble, if you ask me."

As Harper listened, she took pictures of the overall scene. "What do you mean?"

"Easier ways to kill a person."

Harper didn't respond, even though retorts erupted in her brain. Yeah, he could have simply locked them inside and burned down the camper or shot them in the head.

"Not if he wanted it to look like Harper had been driving. That way it wouldn't actually look like she'd been murdered. She and Emily would have been thrown from the camper as it broke apart, and with the twisted tangle of metal, investigators would not have been able to tell whether they had been in the camper or in the truck," Heath said. "He hadn't counted on them escaping."

"But the person responsible couldn't have known for certain that the RV would break apart, so if that was the plan, it was flawed," Harper said.

Bile rose in her throat.

The conversation was distracting her from her task, so she tuned them out while she focused. Normally she would take pictures of everything before anyone else had touched anything. Or had removed even the smallest piece of evidence. She wished she knew what they had taken, if anything.

First, she started with the overview shots. Harper moved from the crumpled metal until she was a good distance away and set the Nikon D100 to capture the widest possible shots of the entire scene, including the ridge in the background. She walked around the scene and took the same wide shots from every possible angle. Done right, it could take hours, while processing a crime scene thoroughly could take days. But she would do her best with the time allotted because she might not get another chance.

"I'll need to take shots of this from the top of the ridge too, after I've taken pictures of that area."

Maybe she was pushing it and Moffett would rein her in, but she heard nothing from the detective. She took more shots to show the relation to the ridge and the surrounding area.

Then she moved in closer to take the midrange images, which normally would focus on key pieces of evidence in situ and context, but unless the techs had missed something, Harper wouldn't have anything to photograph, so forget about the closeup shots.

But she would keep looking for something missed.

Only an hour into taking the photographs and Moffett stood closer. Growing anxious? Was she trying to intimidate Harper? The sun was high in the sky, shining directly into the ravine next to the ridge. To her credit, the detective said nothing.

"The witness said I was driving."

"Another deputy is asking him for clarification," Moffett said. "It was dark. He must have gotten it wrong. So that you don't ask and insult my intelligence, yes, we have checked for fingerprints in and on the vehicle and the camper, what's left of them. We checked the footprints and tire tracks up at the campground and near the place where we suspect the perp hopped from the truck. That jump had to have hurt. You and your sister know that from experience. We're still checking the local clinics and hospitals for anyone reporting the kinds of injuries that could be sustained from a jump like that."

"Okay. Thanks." Good to know.

Harper stared at what was left of the cab. Burned. Crushed. Except part of the seat had come dislodged and rested off to the side. She knelt down and took photographs. Zoomed in. Hoped for more evidence.

"Did they already gather evidence from this seat?"

"A few hairs and fibers. Yours and your sister's probably."

Through the lens, Harper peered at one particular hair on the seat. "They missed one."

"Your hairs don't mean anything."

"No. But a long hair that isn't mine means something." She lowered the camera and looked at the detective.

Moffett stared at her. "Make your point."

"My hair isn't this bright shade of red. Someone could have been wearing an old or cheap wig to make it look like I was driving. Take all the hairs, not some of them. Since I'm not official here, would you mind collecting, documenting, and packaging the evidence? Even better, take this whole seat to the lab."

"You think that hair is a synthetic fiber?"

"I don't know. But I'm pretty sure it isn't mine." Harper studied the hair. She'd been an evidence photographer, but she'd also worked as a tech and knew how to gather the evidence and document it. "Send all the hairs to the state crime lab to see if even one of them is synthetic. There's a database of the types of wig hairs and the manufacturers. If it's synthetic, that will tell us something."

"And what if he or she wore a wig but it was made with real hair?"

"That won't help us at all." And would be impossible to track. Maybe Harper was trying too hard. "Unless the hair belongs to the perp. He could actually have long hair, for all we know. He could be a she." Harper had believed the shooter had been behind the wheel of the truck, wanting to silence her — the witness to his crime — but maybe he had a partner in crime.

Moffett blew out a breath. "I'll go ahead and have them come back and get this entire seat to the lab."

And then Harper saw it. Admiration sparked in Moffett's eyes as she removed her sunglasses.

What? Did Harper's competence surprise her?

Still, Harper didn't care all that much about impressing Moffett, even though it served to validate her effort. No. Harper cared only about what Heath thought. As she lifted her gaze to meet his, a nugget of fear lodged in her throat. Would he think anything at all? If he didn't, that might actually disappoint her.

Why did she care? She shouldn't . . .

Heath's sunglasses were resting on his head and his arms were crossed.

His grin and the respect in his eyes said it all.

CHAPTER THIRTY

Friday, 3:33 P.M.
St. John Medical Center

Just when Harper thought things were moving in the right direction . . . *Oh, Em . . .*

Dr. Malus sat on a stool near the bed. Heath leaned against the wall and crossed his arms.

An issue had been discovered.

Harper had to be strong for her sister. She held Emily's hand, grateful her sister had come out of the coma. Harper had spent all of Thursday with Emily. Then today after Harper had finished processing the crime scene, she'd come directly to the hospital. At least she could be here with Emily to hear what Dr. Malus would say.

She was so grateful she could look Emily in the eyes, though they were filled with fear. Squeezing Emily's cold hand, Harper hoped to reassure her.

Emily's head was wrapped in white tape,

so it looked like she wore a cap. At the base of her cap, electrodes protruded and twisted together, then extended over to connect with a computer that recorded brain wave activity. Harper stared at the waves on the monitor and waited for Dr. Malus's prognosis.

Dr. Malus delivered her news with kindness. "You're doing well, but we need to watch you over the weekend."

"Why?" Harper asked for the both of them.

Dr. Malus looked at Emily. "You've had a few seizures, which isn't unheard of after a head injury or in the case of a coma, but they've continued even since you've been awake. They're non-convulsive, meaning we can't see any physical signs. We considered putting you on analeptic medication for control" — Dr. Malus looked at her notes — "but this could resolve in a couple of days. Even if it does, I'd still like you to see a neurologist when you return home. In the meantime, I saw in the electronic medical records that you're supposed to be on lithium, so we're going to restart those meds."

Confused, Harper stared at Emily.

"Ana —" Emily started.

"Anti-seizure medication." Dr. Malus rose

from her stool. "Clinically speaking, you look great. You're improving. Can I answer any more questions?"

"No." Emily stared at her hands.

"Wait . . . Lithium?" Harper asked.

Tears leaked from Emily's eyes. "I didn't want to tell you." She glanced at the doctor. "Can I talk to her alone?"

She nodded. "Of course. I'm on tonight if you need anything or have more questions."

Harper waited until Dr. Malus left the room before lifting her gaze to Emily.

Heath cleared his throat. "I'll be right outside the door."

"Thanks," Harper said.

She waited for Heath to step out of the room. "Why didn't you tell me you were taking lithium?"

She and Emily hadn't been all that close until after college when they both lived near their mom until she died. They'd grown closer on this trip. They didn't keep secrets. Or at least Harper had thought they didn't. Even so, how could she have missed this?

"Mom was so focused on you after what you went through. Being there when Dad was killed. Getting you therapy. I had to deal on my own. Finally, a boyfriend persuaded me to see a counselor at school who urged me to get help — it was more serious than I thought. I've been on lithium for a few years for mild bipolar depression." Emily swiped at her cheeks. "I know we talked about staying, but as soon as I can leave, I want to get out of here. It's not like we have to pack up the Airstream."

Emily choked on the words.

A hollow ache throbbed behind Harper's ribs. "You put so much into renovating. We can do it again. We'll get another camper and start over. Okay?" Harper had no idea what she was saying, but she would say anything to get them through this. This whole time she had thought there must be something wrong with her to struggle so much with the past, but Emily had been struggling too.

It hurt that her sister hadn't confided in her, yet Harper could see that Emily had only wanted to stay strong for her. She hadn't wanted Harper to know about her struggle.

Emily nodded. "Sure, we can do that at some point. But before I leave, I want to see the old house, Harper. Like we talked about. I might never get another chance to see it. I know part of what you've gone through — the survivor's guilt — has to do with what you experienced as a child there. So I have to ask — are you good with that?

Can we at least drive by?"

Harper was still reeling from everything new she'd learned in the last half hour involving Emily. Why did Emily always press her on the house? "I would do anything for you, Emily, but . . ."

Emily's eyes glistened.

"Oh, Em, I'm sorry. You're right. It's just a stupid old house." She had no idea why Emily wanted to go back. If it were up to Harper, she would never look at it again. Still, she wanted to be there for her sister, who she'd almost lost forever.

"Thanks." Emily squeezed Harper's hand.

Harper took this moment to bring Emily up to speed on today's photographs of the camper and truck.

Harper had intended to stay in town, but now with Emily's potential neurological issues, she didn't see how she could. "We'll go home as soon as you're released."

"No."

"What?"

"You're not going anywhere. I want you to help them find who did this to us. Find who killed that woman. You have to do this. I see that now, and I'm sorry for trying to persuade you otherwise. Since you took this on, I can see how it's helping you overcome the fact you didn't face things before. This is good for you and it's the right thing to do. And besides, you have Heath the cowboy to watch over you. I won't worry about you so much. I'm so proud of you."

"You're proud of *me*?"

"For seeing this through. You're ready for what comes next."

Harper wasn't so sure she agreed with Emily, but it seemed life wasn't giving her any choices. While photographing the wreckage of the truck and camper, Harper realized she actually missed being part of the crime-solving process.

The door creaked open. Heath. "Okay if I come in now?"

Harper wouldn't tell him she had forgotten he was out there. "Sure. Sorry about that."

"No problem."

She hated leaving Emily, but her sister looked tired. "Is there anything I can get you before I go?"

"No." Emily stared at her hands, then glanced up. "Wait. You can take the clothes I had on. Burn them. Wash them. I don't know. Maybe they're not salvageable. Bring me new clothes for when they release me."

"You got it." Harper pulled the plastic bag containing Emily's clothes out of a small closet. "Okay. Anything else?"

Emily swiped at her eyes. "I'm glad I turned my book in already."

"Should I call your editor? I didn't even think of that."

"No, it's fine. Maybe bring my lap —" Emily stopped midsentence. Put her hand to her mouth. "Oh. It's gone, isn't it?"

"I'm afraid so." Harper glanced to Heath, who nodded. "But we'll get you a brand-spanking-new one. You can download from the cloud or wherever you store your files."

Emily smiled the biggest smile Harper had seen in days. "I'm so glad I have you." She glanced to Heath. "You keep her safe or I'll have to kill you."

He didn't even blink.

"In a book, Heath. She'd have to kill you in a novel. Emily's pen name is L. E. Harper. The *L* stands for Leslie, our mother. I'm not sure you would know her as an author." Harper angled her head and sent him a wry grin. "You'd have to read."

He pursed his lips. "I can read fine, thank you."

"No." She chuckled. "I mean, you'd have to read mysteries to know. You look more like a Louis L'Amour kind of guy."

Heath grinned, and the room tilted just a little.

CHAPTER THIRTY-ONE

Friday, 8:42 P.M.
Emerald M Guest Ranch

Heath stood on the porch as the evening waned and tried to ignore the black smudge on his property. But all it took was one inhale and he drew in the scent of smoke and ash. The expected rain hadn't come — and while it could hurt any remaining but undiscovered evidence, Heath wished for a torrent to wash it all away. Until then he'd have to live with the pungent odors, and the aftermath.

Finding the person responsible for bombing his cabin wasn't his only concern, and until Harper and her sister were safe and a murderer was caught, Heath would remain working in his capacity as a deputy.

He wasn't dressed in official deputy garb, but he had on his Sam Browne belt, sans the extra fifteen pounds of equipment. Right now, all he packed was his gun, so he wasn't geared up much differently than if he were working the ranch.

He felt split between his two jobs — deputy and Emerald M Ranch owner, and it wasn't supposed to be like this.

Until the state was officially done with its investigation, rebuilding the cabin had started, and Harper's safety was no longer an issue, the guest ranch would stay closed. Pete was the only one of Heath's employees who remained at the ranch. No horses. No dogs. He couldn't very well leave Timber and Rufus at the ranch with law enforcement buzzing around. Leroy wasn't there, well, because Leroy was in the hospital. Heath's other employees catered to the guests' needs and, without guests, there was no need for their help until this was over. Still, he would continue to pay them for the foreseeable future so he wouldn't lose them as employees.

He leaned against a knobby pine post with his hands in his pocket, listening to the evening sounds. Why his ranch? He'd already been questioned several times by the state and could expect more questions if the feds got involved, but he had no answers. All he had was an empty guest ranch, when this should be the busiest time of year. The time of year when he made his money.

He had a reputation to keep up. Now he'd have to rebuild even that.

Pete approached from the barn and stomped up the porch. He leaned against the opposite post. They could have been two wrought-iron cowboy statues, if anyone looked on from a distance.

"What are you going to do, Heath?"

"As soon as they release the cabin and my ranch, I'm going to rebuild. I've already spoken with Jeffers over at JH Construction. As soon as I give him the go-ahead, he'll rebuild the cabin. We'll bring the horses back and look alive."

"I'm glad to hear it."

"In the meantime, you don't have to stay here. You can go visit family. Friends. Go somewhere and be safe." And that was just it. His house wasn't exactly the safest place, considering someone had targeted one of his cabins.

Harper hadn't been there when that happened. The bomb wasn't about her.

And the law enforcement presence — the very thing he'd used to persuade her to stay and be safe — had died down.

"Nah. I'm good. I haven't exactly got anywhere to go except to my doctor. This is my home. I can keep a lookout for you too, though I didn't do such a good job on that cabin."

"Not your fault. No one saw the intruder. I'm relieved the cabin wasn't occupied at the time. How you doing anyway? You're done with chemo, aren't you?" Pete had insisted on working through it all, though in the evenings he often got nauseous. Thing was, Pete had never really told Heath what kind of cancer he had.

"Sure am."

"Good." Heath wanted to ask him about his prognosis, but he'd leave that to Pete to share when he was ready. Maybe the guy wanted to focus on one day at a time and not look at the future, especially if doctors thought he had no future. The truth was that everyone died. It was a simple matter of when and how.

Pete didn't offer more.

"Heath?" Harper's smooth voice spoke from behind.

He glanced over his shoulder. She had been standing in the door but now came all the way out of the house.

"Well, I'll let you two talk," Pete said. "I'm going to walk the perimeter. There's still a couple of state guys lingering over at the cabin remains. Maybe I'll watch them."

"Still? I would think they would be done

by now." One could hope.

"I suppose it depends on what they find," Pete said as he clomped down the steps. "They asked lots of questions. I guess they have to suspect everyone around here."

Pete disappeared around the porch.

"True." Harper stood next to Heath and jammed her hands into form-fitting jeans. She looked nice. More than nice. He'd always thought so.

She sighed.

"You sound like you have a lot on your mind and can't decide what to say."

She gave him a sidelong glance. "You always knew me so well."

Weird. He would have thought that had changed. So much had happened in each of their lives.

"I'm ready to listen." He grabbed her arm and urged her back inside. "But I'd prefer if you weren't on the porch and an easy target."

"Why do you say that? You think I'm in danger out here?"

The shooter could be a highly trained sniper. How did he speak the truth without scaring her? "He had a long-range rifle, you said. A scope to peer at you from across the river."

Harper shivered. Rubbed her arms. She

did that a lot lately.

"Listen. I'm going to keep you safe. It's going to be all right." Heath hadn't believed he was the guy to do it. He hadn't wanted the responsibility, but now as he looked at Harper, he knew he couldn't trust anyone else with the job. Harper held a special place in his heart. She always had. He could never forget her being there for him through the worst time of his life. The friendship they'd shared. The tragedy that bonded them then, and danger that tied them together now. Another deputy stood watch over her sister in the hospital until she was released, then she would stay with Heath and Harper unless she left for Missouri. If she did head home, Heath would urge Harper to leave too.

Though a big part of him didn't want her to go.

He led her to the kitchen and put on a teakettle. He'd have to remember to scoop it off the burner before it actually whistled or he would wake Evelyn, who had gone to bed early. Leroy was improving, but the situation wore her down.

"Now, can you tell me what's on your mind?"

She slid onto the bar stool and smiled. She hadn't done nearly enough of that lately. It warmed his heart to see it. "I'm not sure I'm ready to put my thoughts into words. But you'll be the first to know when I am."

Fair enough. "I have to tell you something."

"Go ahead." She crossed her arms and leaned her elbows on the counter.

"I was impressed with your crime scene photography skills. You were so focused, so on top of your game, gathering the evidence. That hair. I think Moffett admired you too."

She blushed and hung her head. Then that amazing smile again when she lifted her face. Her long red hair hung over her left shoulder. What would it be like to run his fingers through that? He busied himself getting her tea so she wouldn't somehow read his inappropriate thoughts.

"Thank you, Heath. No need to flatter me. The truth is, I don't know what to do now. So what? I found something. We don't know if it's a true lead, and I don't know what to do next."

"Why do you think you have to do something?"

"I want to help find the guy who killed her. I have to see it through this time. I don't know if I can explain why."

"I'm pretty sure things happen much

slower than what we see on television."

"Don't you think I know that?"

"Of course you do. But it's not your job to find him. Let the sheriff's department and the other agencies Taggart brings in find him. And it's my job to keep you safe. If you keep going out there, you could put yourself in danger."

"Maybe that's exactly what I need to do."

"Come again?"

"I need to put myself out there. I've been a coward for too long. It's time to be brave."

He moved around the counter and, after turning her toward him, gently squeezed her shoulders. Lifted her chin so her eyes would meet his gaze. "Harper Reynolds, you're the bravest person I know."

Heath wanted to draw her into his arms. Hold her. Comfort her. That want stemmed from a deeper place inside him. None of these thoughts were appropriate. Official duty alone should restrain him from acting on them. Fat chance. He cupped her cheek and felt its softness as she leaned in, responding to his touch.

Fire, McKade. You're playing with fire.

Her lips parted slightly as if she would say something, but she released a soft sigh instead. A furious need to kiss her stirred within him.

Evelyn's words came back to him, urging him to let God bring him someone special to love. What about his resolve, after everything he'd been through? Loving someone was too risky. Sure, Taggart had convinced him that he was the only man to protect Harper. This was Heath's chance to prove himself — to himself. But Harper deserved so much more. She deserved a better man than he had been or could ever be.

His cell buzzed, breaking the moment. Disappointment warred with relief. He glanced at the text, avoiding the look on Harper's face. He wasn't sure he wanted to see her reaction.

Lori Somerall.

Great.

"What is it?"

"A friend. I can't believe they let her up here."

He stepped away from Harper, something he absolutely didn't want to do, and headed for the front door. As soon as he stepped on the porch, he saw a white Lincoln Navigator driving up. He waited with dread in his gut. Lori stepped out and strolled toward him.

He wouldn't exactly say Lori flaunted her subtle feminine curves, but she had a way about her. A beautiful, sweet woman —

she'd lost her husband two years ago. Evelyn had brought her up to Heath several times. They were both in the guest ranch business. Yada yada.

"How did you get past the guard?" he called.

"I told him I was keeping your horses and dogs, and you wanted to see me."

Only half true. Pete had worked with Lori to transfer and board the horses and dogs, for which Heath was grateful. Despite her generosity, Heath hadn't wanted to see her, especially right now.

As if emphasizing his thoughts, Harper came up behind him. The last thing he wanted was for her to get the wrong idea. That shouldn't matter to him, but it did. Lori was interested in Heath. He had no doubt about that, but he didn't return her interest. Still, she was a fellow guest ranch owner, an active member in the community, and they were friends.

Lori stepped onto the porch and her light perfume found its mark.

"What can I do for you?" he asked.

Her smile made him uncomfortable. Maybe he was overly sensitive. The woman was simply being warm and friendly. She had told him that all Texans were that way. "You and Evelyn. Pete too. Y'all need to come stay with me. I'm worried about you staying here. It could be dangerous."

The door shut behind him. Harper had gone back inside. She probably thought Heath had something going on with Lori.

"She can come too. Anyone who's here with you is welcome at Circle S." She leaned in closer to whisper. "Now don't go telling anyone I said this, but I heard that a lot of law is about to drop down on this ranch. They're probably going to kick you to the curb anyway."

"Why would you hear that before me?" Heath said the words, but he had a pretty good idea why. Lori had a way of making people give up secrets. She might have even heard that from whoever was on guard duty at the gate.

Heath ushered Lori off the porch and into his home where he found Harper back in the kitchen making hot chocolate with water from the teakettle. He introduced the women to each other and Harper offered to make Lori hot chocolate too.

Heath left them and got on his cell to Taggart. Left a voice mail. Then called Moffett.

She answered. "Heath, I was just about to call you."

"Is there something I should know?"

"We found out who we believe could be

the victim based on Harper's sketch. Her parents reported her missing today. She was backpacking with her new husband. They were honeymooning. He's also missing. We'll need Harper to look at photographs and ID her as the woman she believes she saw."

Heath rubbed his eyes as Harper approached. "Heath, what is it?"

CHAPTER THIRTY-TWO

Saturday, 9:12 A.M.
Bridger County Sheriff's Office

The passenger seat in Heath's truck was becoming all too familiar. Harper's palms slicked. She wrapped her hand around the door grip on their approach to the Bridger County Sheriff's Office. When she'd come here to meet the sketch artist, the place had appeared calm. Everything was as it should be.

Today tension rippled through the air, with the heat already rising from the black asphalt as they made their way to the building.

Her heart had broken at the news that not one but two people were missing. Even more shattering — honeymooners. That she had possibly witnessed the new bride's demise left Harper broken and empty. The woman's parents had flown in from Nebraska last night, hoping for news of their

266

daughter. They recognized her as possibly being the woman in the sketch artist's composite. Harper had been called in to identify the victim from a photograph lineup.

Harper wanted to meet the parents. To somehow console them, but that wouldn't happen during the investigation. Sheriff Taggart would have to look closely at them. It was standard procedure to suspect the people closest to a victim because murders were most often committed by someone the victim knew. Despite her time as a crime scene photographer, Harper still couldn't fathom that truth. Would Harper also be asked to look at pictures of the father — was he the man behind the weapon? She shuddered. The sheriff would also suspect the husband. He was still missing but could have committed the crime. Waves of grief rolled through her as she struggled to believe that a family member could murder a loved one.

At the doors to the county sheriff's office, Heath ushered Harper through to find Detective Moffett waiting.

"The parents are sequestered in another room, waiting to hear the news. We have photographs of their daughter for you to look at."

"What about her father?" Harper didn't spell out her meaning for the detective.

"At this moment, he doesn't match your description of the murderer." She leaned in. "He's in a wheelchair. Has MS."

"I see."

Moffett led her to a room. Photographs were laid out on the table. Harper closed her eyes and recalled the images of the victim she had committed to memory.

Before Harper looked at the photographs, she glanced at Heath, then Moffett. "They'll want hope that she's still alive." Harper couldn't give them any. She'd seen the woman's empty eyes.

"We all do," Moffett said.

Harper steadied herself, then faced the nameless photographs lined up on the table. Many different women stared back at her. Blood rushed to her head, roared in her ears.

She ran a forefinger over the edge of one particular photograph. Those eyes — she could never forget them.

The woman in the photograph was smiling. Laughing with friends. Tears burned down Harper's cheeks.

Why had this cruelty happened?

She glanced at Moffett. "This is the woman I saw. Is it . . . Is it her?"

268

"Yes."

"Can I have her name, please?"

"Sophie Osborne. Her husband's name is Chase," Moffett said.

"And the parents?"

"Rick and Netta Batterson." Moffett studied Harper. "Anything else?"

Harper shook her head.

"Thank you for your help."

Strong but gentle hands gripped her shoulders and led her out of the room to another, more comfortable room. Heath brought her a mug of hot, steaming coffee. "I'm so sorry you had to go through this. I'm sorry for the parents."

"And now that we know for sure it was her, we also know her husband may have been murdered too." Harper shivered. "Or could it have been him who killed her? Do you happen to know how old her husband is?"

"I looked at pictures of him too. He's around Sophie's age."

"Then he didn't kill her." She'd seen part of the shooter's face. The wrinkles surrounding his eyes. "The shooter was much older. Not a young man on a honeymoon. It wasn't the husband."

"Agreed. At least that's what I gathered from Laura's composites."

The good news was that multiple agencies would now look for the two missing hikers. The bad news was that Harper was certain at least one of them was dead. She didn't hold out hope for Chase, unless he had somehow escaped and gotten lost in millions of acres and was still trying to find his way back to civilization. But with a hunter after him — someone who was familiar with the area — his chances of survival were slim.

Detective Moffett came into the room with a laptop. "I've informed the parents. We're now searching for two people. We'll ask for volunteers as well. Ms. Reynolds, are you up for it? If so, you and Deputy McKade can help with the search. The sheriff appreciates your eye for details. You've brought us this far."

Wow. The sheriff's crew had gone from being skeptical of Harper to being staunch supporters almost overnight. The detective's question surprised her, and she glanced at Heath.

He crossed his arms. "I'm not on board with it. It would be too dangerous for Harper out there."

"Sheriff says it will be fine. With a huge contingent of law enforcement out there, search dogs too, the shooter would be a fool to stick around. But Sheriff assigned Deputy

Arty Custer to go with you as a precaution. We need all the help we can get."

CHAPTER THIRTY-THREE

Saturday, 2:28 P.M.
Bridger-Teton National Forest

Flanked by Heath and Deputy Custer, Harper hiked the trail with the new camera she had bought in town. She and Emily had each gotten a new laptop as well. They were burning through their remaining funds much too quickly as they waited on the insurance to process their claims on the Airstream and truck. She hoped this would be the last time she had to spend big bucks for a while. She still needed to replace her tripod and get another telephoto lens.

As they hiked, she couldn't stop thinking about Heath. So what if he wasn't on board with her joining the search? Law enforcement needed all the able bodies they could get — and Sheriff Taggart had okayed it. Shutting down the national forest was no easy thing at the height of tourist season. Still, Heath preferred that she stay back at the ranch safe and sound until this was over. But Lori Somerall had other thoughts. She wanted them all to move to her ranch house, away from the chaos and danger.

Harper liked the woman, and in another life they could have been friends, but in this life Lori definitely had her eyes on Heath and that set Harper on edge. So she was relieved when he declined Lori's invitation. Before Lori had showed up, he had almost kissed Harper. And she had leaned into his hand, unable to resist his touch. What was the matter with her? Had this situation made her entirely too vulnerable?

She had the feeling that it wouldn't matter. She would be uncontrollably drawn to Heath in any situation. It was almost as if an invisible force that spanned time and distance had brought them together again. But Harper knew she could never be with Heath. He needed someone though — just not her.

She refocused her thoughts on the task at hand and resolved to keep them there. But that was difficult since the man in her thoughts hiked right next to her, his broad shoulders distracting her.

She stopped and guzzled water. Poured some over her head, the shocking cold a slap in the face.

"You don't want to drink too much too soon," Deputy Custer said. "Save it for later."

Right. She hiked forward and followed the deputy off the trail. He yanked out a paper search map. "We're supposed to search this region off trail for, you know, a body or anything out of the ordinary."

The sun beat down on them, deterred only by the shade they now entered along the trail. They hiked up an incline, gasping with the effort, always looking, always searching for evidence of a violent crime.

A couple of hours later, Harper broke the silence. "Sophie and her husband, Chase. They hiked for days on miles and miles of trails. What did they see, Heath? What did they come across that got Sophie killed? That sent her running from a killer? You don't think he was a poacher out hunting and didn't want them to snitch on him, do you? Is that worth a life?"

Heath shook his head. "In my opinion, nothing is worth a life. And yet lives are taken for reasons beyond me all the time."

She couldn't argue with that. "He's a psychopath. That's what I think. Nobody but a psychopath could murder a woman like that."

Deputy Custer chugged his bottle of

water. "I don't think we're going to find anything. This guy hid his tracks well or else we would have found something by now. We've covered our area. We should head back and regroup." He took a step.

Water slid from his mouth as he collapsed. Rifle fire echoed through the woods.

Chapter Thirty-Four

"Get down!" Heath shoved her to the ground, threw his body over her, and relayed the emergency on his radio, grateful that he'd donned full deputy gear, which included body armor.

Harper wore body armor and carried a weapon too. Heath had insisted, and she hadn't argued.

But none of it mattered. The body armor worked against pistol rounds but not high-velocity rifles — like what had probably taken out Arty.

He needed to shield Harper, but what about Arty? "Arty! You okay?"

He waited, covering Harper, contemplating how to get her out of there. This wasn't supposed to happen!

"Heath, can you let me up now?"

No. How was he going to keep her safe? *Oh, God, help me.*

If Harper had been the intended target,

276

the shooter had missed. The guy had missed her with his long-distance rifle, so maybe he wasn't a military-trained sniper.

"Stay down. I'm covering you," he whispered in Harper's ear. "But let's very slowly crawl over between those boulders."

"What about Arty?"

He feared the worst. "I'm going to check on him after I get you to cover."

"Heath, no. The shooter will kill you. I've seen what he can do!"

"Please do as I ask. We don't know where he is. The report sounded after the bullet hit Arty, so he's not close, but he could be moving toward us."

Heath stared at her until he saw in her eyes that she would comply. She nodded her agreement. She was his responsibility, and more than that, she was his friend and someone he cared deeply about. But he cared about Arty too, and the deputy needed his help.

He protected Harper as they inched over to hide between two boulders. Heart pounding, he pressed his back against the rock to catch his breath. "He could make his way around and catch you from a different angle. Please, stay down and hidden."

Heath hunkered to make his way over to Arty. Harper grabbed him, fear in her eyes.

"Please be careful."

The sniper hadn't fired another shot. That was good, right? Or was he merely waiting for the right moment or making his way closer? Sweat beaded along Heath's brow. He sucked in a few breaths, then crawled from tree to tree until he slid behind the trunk closest to the fallen deputy. Heath crouched down and peered around the tree.

Arty lay facedown. A bullet hole in his back.

Oh, God . . . Why?

Had he stepped in front of Harper at the wrong moment? Or exactly the right moment?

"Arty, please, say something."

Crimson blood spread out beneath him.

Heath flattened himself and crawled closer. He touched the man's carotid. Nothing. Fury boiled in Heath's gut. He didn't want to leave the man there, but he had to get Harper to safety.

He radioed again for help. "Deputy down. Shots fired." He relayed their location the best he could.

"Response team is on their way." Laura's familiar voice came through.

"I don't know if we can wait."

"Then get her out of there, Heath."

He'd completed thirteen weeks of basic

officer training at the Wyoming Law Enforcement Academy, but it was his military training that he would fall back on now. Training and experience. He found Harper crouched behind the boulder, palming her weapon. Good. She hadn't fallen apart, though he hadn't expected she would.

"Arty?"

He shook his head.

"We can't leave him."

"He'd want me to get you to safety."

"We don't know where the shooter is, Heath. How are we going to get out of here?"

Heath eyed the woods ahead of them. Hoping. Praying that the shooter wasn't making his way around to shoot them from a new position. "Let's stay low and close to the trees."

"Are you sure we shouldn't wait here for help?"

Sometimes the only choices weren't choices at all. "Yes. I'm sure." The doubt in his voice belied his confident words.

Heath fired several rounds into the ground to see if he could get a reaction.

Nothing.

"Let's go." Together, Heath and Harper held their weapons at the ready as they traversed the woods heading back in the direction from which they'd come and away from Deputy Custer. Arty. Heath couldn't let the pain of his death strangle him now.

He had to get Harper to safety. Anger at Taggart nearly blinded him. She shouldn't have been allowed to come to these woods. At least they knew the guy was still lurking in the national forest. He hadn't run.

Heath wished he had.

Whop, whop, whop . . .

A helicopter. Search and rescue? Or law enforcement? Relief whooshed through Heath. He wouldn't have to get her out of here alone.

"How do we signal them without exposing ourselves?"

Heath shouted into his radio, letting dispatch know the helicopter was right on top of them above the trees. Despite their efforts, Heath and Harper hadn't made it that far from where Arty was shot.

Two heavily armed men in tactical gear — SWAT — rappelled from the helicopter to the ground.

How determined was the shooter? Had he left the area like Heath hoped? Heath stepped from the cover of a tree and jogged over. The helicopter hovered. "Loosely judging by the trajectory of the shot, I'd say the bullet that took Arty out came from the northwest. Of course, he could have moved by now."

"We'll stick with you until the rangers get here." The officer nodded down the trail. "They'll get you to safety."

"I'd prefer if Harper got out of here in the bird."

"She could be more exposed just getting up there."

"I see your point."

Ranger Dan Hinckley hiked toward them from the south, another ranger by his side. "Thanks for coming, Dan," Heath said.

The two SWAT team members handed Heath and Harper off, then headed into the woods.

"Come on," Dan said, "let's get you out of here. Law enforcement is scouring those woods. If that shooter has any sense, he's long gone by now."

"I think you're wrong," Heath said. The shooter was still there after killing two hikers. Sheriff Taggart had requested Harper's help, believing that the shooter wasn't still in the woods. He'd made a bad call that had cost a life. The shooter had stayed behind to target Harper, even with law enforcement searching. That high-powered scope let him keep his distance in the hunt.

He was cunning. He had a purpose. A mission.

Heath had a feeling that, unless caught, the killer would leave when he was ready and not before.

Chapter Thirty-Five

Saturday, 4:52 P.M.
Bridger-Teton National Forest
Weakness trembled through the judge's limbs. It took all his strength to lay down his rifle. He gripped the armrest and eased onto the old sofa. He would have plopped down but feared his body would break. Somehow, he had to find the strength to finish this before it was too late. His left elbow still ached after the jump from the truck. She should be dead now. That should have been enough.

"Blast this cancer!"

He was hungry for the first time in a week after losing his appetite for far too long. Needed meat. Needed to hunt for sustenance, both mental and physical. He needed to feel on top of the food chain. That he was strong. That he'd show them. But the woods were crawling with searchers and he knew why.

That woman, Harper Reynolds. She'd set them on his trail.

She was messing up his plans. He didn't have time for these two failed attempts on her life.

The searchers would never find the hikers' bodies.

When he got his hands on the Reynolds woman, they would never find hers either.

CHAPTER THIRTY-SIX

Monday, 7:59 P.M.
Circle S Ranch

Harper stared out the spacious panoramic window in Lori Somerall's home. She wanted to absorb the sheer expansive beauty of the evergreens sweeping up the mountains. Capture that in her mind, if not on a camera. The tip of a familiar peak rose off in the distance between other mountains — Grand Teton. The majestic mountain was the picture of strength and beauty and reminded Harper of that Bible verse on the wall plaque in the Airstream. When she'd been a kid growing up in Jackson Hole, the mountain had always made her think of God.

Unshakable. Unmovable.

"The name of the LORD is a strong tower . . ."

If only she could feel some of that strength right now. If only she could use this view to replace the image of Arty, surprise and shock on his face, the instant before he crumpled.

It was a repeat of what had happened to Sophie.

A pang radiated through Harper.

The deputy had been wearing a vest!

Heath had explained that the kind of body armor they'd worn couldn't protect against rifle fire because of the high velocity. What had they been doing out there without ample protection?

His death is all my fault.

She knew the sheriff would feel the burden of that guilt as well, for believing Harper would be safe. And with this, she had to consider the strong possibility that Heath could be hurt next.

At least Heath was being proactive. After the second attempt on Harper's life, he had agreed that moving to Circle S ranch was best. Yesterday Lori had insisted on a small Sunday service at her home, which proved to be more comforting than Harper had expected in the aftermath of Arty's death.

An eagle swooped down as if to catch a small creature but returned to the air empty-clawed, pulling Harper's thoughts back to her surroundings.

Lori had a big, empty house like Heath's.

Evelyn moved with them, but Pete stayed behind for now, waiting for the crime scene at the cabin to be released. Then Heath could start rebuilding the cabin. He'd said that Pete would oversee the rebuild.

"Harper?" Emily came up behind her.

She turned and hugged her sister, who'd been released from the hospital earlier that afternoon. Another EEG showed great improvement over the weekend. Plus, Emily had insisted she needed to return to Missouri, so the doctor had referred her to a neurologist at home for a follow-up. Despite the strain of the last few days, Emily looked much better.

"It's so good to have you home." Except this wasn't their home. It wasn't even Heath's home. She squeezed her even tighter before finally releasing her.

The amazing rustic and spacious log cabin made her think of a villa in the Swiss Alps. The owner was a lovely blonde to complete the package.

Maybe Lori didn't have her claws in Heath yet, but Harper wouldn't be surprised if she tried. She shook off the ridiculous jealousy slithering through her.

Who cared about Lori and Heath? Emily was here with her. She was going to be okay.

Harper took a good long look at her sister,

the mystery writer. Her bobbed brown hair framed a striking face defined by high cheekbones and big brown eyes. Harper's attention drifted to the colorful display of roses and lilies on the table, a gift from Emily's friend in the publishing world. A guy friend.

While the bouquet was appropriate under the circumstances, Harper wondered if there was something more going on. "How are you feeling?"

"Much better now that I'm out of the hospital." Emily plopped down on the plush sofa and grabbed a pillow. Held it close. A tendril of fear emerged in her eyes, then it was gone. She reached for the Bible on the coffee table and flipped through until she found what she was looking for and focused on the page.

Though she'd been released, Emily had been advised she shouldn't drive until the neurologist in Missouri gave her the go-ahead. Concern over seizure activity lingered.

She forced a smile to reassure Emily. "When do you start your next book?"

Emily lifted her gaze from the Bible. "As soon as possible."

Harper waited on her to elaborate on the book, then remembered she no longer shared about her crime and mystery novels, at least while Harper was trying to recover. Instead, Emily studied her.

"I'm worried about you and this guy who is determined to hurt you," Emily said. "I know I told you to stay, but I'm not so sure that's a good idea now."

Harper sighed. "That's exactly the reason I can't go home with you now. I want you to be safe. You already ended up in the hospital. He's already hurt you once because of me. I won't let that happen again." But who would drive Emily?

Harper wrestled with indecision. What was best for her sister? Should Harper stay away or should she go home with Emily?

Her sister rubbed her eyes. "I want you to be safe. I wouldn't think the guy would follow you to Missouri if you came home with me."

Heath entered the room and hung back as if unsure if he was interrupting a private conversation.

Her expression shifting, Emily angled her head and tossed him a mischievous grin. "And if he did, maybe Heath McKade can come with you to guard you like he's doing here."

Emily was showing a bit of her old self again, which relieved Harper.

She couldn't help but think Emily should have been a romance writer instead. "I don't know about Missouri, but as long as I'm here, Heath is a fixture in my life for now."

Heath said nothing in response to her comment, but he studied her. The intensity in his eyes scared her. What was he thinking?

"I want to do what's best for you, and right now, I don't think I should go home, but I'm worried about you — who will drive you around?"

Emily's laugh was humorless. "I have no shortage of friends, and actually, I need to catch up with them after being gone for months." She looked at Harper, her expression softening. "I wouldn't trade the world for the last few months with you. I only wish things had ended differently." She reached over and squeezed Harper's hand. "Please take care of yourself. Don't do anything stupid."

Her sister's words weighed on her. Emily was actually going. And Harper was actually staying. "I promise I won't."

But neither of them would be safe until this was over.

Emily rose from the sofa. "I'm tired, so I think I'll go to bed early. I know this probably isn't the best time to bring it up, but

I'd still like to see the old house before I go. How about tomorrow? Then you can take me to the airport."

Tomorrow? Emily really was ready to head home.

Admittedly, Harper was still shaken from what had happened. Did she even want to leave this safe haven in the mountains despite her brave words — especially to see the old house? Why was Emily insisting on that? Some part of her mystery-writer brain wanted closure? She glanced at Heath, hoping he'd agree to at least a simple drive-by.

"I think that would work," Harper said.

Heath didn't answer right away. "We'll talk about it tomorrow."

His life was wrapped up in watching over her now. She wished she knew how he truly felt about that. If he hated it and wished he'd been given another assignment altogether. Or if he *liked* being with Harper.

CHAPTER THIRTY-SEVEN

When Emily disappeared down the hallway, Heath was glad Harper hadn't joined her. They needed to talk. He'd kept his composure in front of Emily and hoped he could maintain it when he and Harper were alone.

She moved to once again stare out the window.

Avoiding him?

He didn't blame her.

Strange that he had to work up the nerve to talk to her. He had a feeling he would risk making her run off to join Emily if he didn't do this right. Maybe it wasn't so much working up the nerve to approach but rather to speak the words that had been building inside. To speak his mind. He eased forward until he stood next to her. He took in the trees, the mountain peak rising above them. The spectacular wash of pink and purple.

"There's nothing quite like a mountain

sunset," he said. Okay, well, that wasn't exactly what he had planned to say.

"It's truly stunning."

His gaze drifted over, and he took in her profile. Red hair spilling over her shoulders and down her back. Soft features, a spattering of freckles — though he couldn't see those now. "Stunning is right."

"Don't you need to go get Evelyn?" she asked.

Again, he got the sense she wanted to be alone. Maybe he should give her space.

"I'm staying with you, Harper. I'm not leaving you. Besides, Evelyn called and said her granddaughter would bring her out here to Circle S. She'll be spending the night with her grandmother here."

"That's awfully generous of Lori."

"Yes." Lori was a generous woman. And she was interested, definitely interested in him. Heath would have to be blind and an idiot not to know that. It felt wrong and even misleading to be staying at her home. But with Harper in danger, Heath had accepted Lori's offer.

Still, Lori was a kind-natured woman and he'd leave it at that. He focused on Harper, a woman for whom he cared deeply. That had never gone away, even though time and distance had kept them apart.

Except a relationship with her wouldn't go anywhere because she was leaving when this was over. And even if she, by some miracle, decided to stay, Heath might care about her too much. According to his track record, people he cared about got hurt. He didn't want that for Harper. He knew that, yet she was all he could think about. "Harper . . ."

His voice was too throaty. What was the matter with him? He had to keep it under control.

Harper lifted her face to look at him. The way the low evening light filtered through the window, her amber eyes were pure molten gold. Inside, she was so strong yet vulnerable at the same time. The girl he'd trusted and admired was now the woman he couldn't stop thinking about.

"That night," she said. "That night I was there when he was killed. I can't say I saw the whole thing. If I had, his murderer would have paid for his crimes. It was dark. Momma and Emily had gone to shop for clothes for some party. I was mad at Emily and didn't want to go. Someone drove up to the house. I thought it was them, but Daddy told me to stay inside. He told me to go to my room and stay there. Then he went outside. Of course, I wasn't about to

294

stay in my room, so I snuck into Mom and Dad's room. It faced the front, and from there I listened through the window. I heard a heated exchange. Accusations, maybe. I've never remembered the words. From that angle, I could barely see Daddy's back and nothing more. A shot rang out and Daddy fell. The way he lay. His lifeless eyes. I knew he was dead. And I ran back to my room and hid under the bed." Harper rubbed her arms.

Heath wanted to take her in his arms. He wanted to say something, but then she might never tell him more. So he waited.

"I should have made my presence known and maybe the murderer would have run away instead of killing him. So not only did I not make a sound, I didn't even look at his killer. I ran away. I curled in a ball and hid. I whimpered like a coward."

"You might have been killed along with him otherwise."

Pain skirted across her features. "Or I could have gotten a look at the killer. My father's murder was never solved. No justice for him. I couldn't describe the man who killed him. I could have been in a position to see everything if I had tried harder. Maybe I could have helped solve his crime. I lived with that growing up. Detectives asked me to describe the man and I couldn't."

"That's a pretty heavy burden for a child to carry." And it seemed like she had carried the burden all the way into adulthood. He wished her mother had not moved her away. He wished he could have been there to help her through — as if he truly could have if given that opportunity.

Her gaze flicked to him for a moment, then she looked out the window again. "Well, you have the whole story now. I didn't look that night, so in photographing crime scenes, in a sense, I can never look away again. But years of photographing gruesome scene after scene, and always asking why this person? Why that person? Just like when Dad died. Why had I survived? It became too much to bear when I took that last set of evidence photographs. A child had witnessed her father's murder. It was like my life had come full circle. So I had to take a break. For almost a year, I hadn't been exposed to crime or violence until I saw him kill that woman. And now Arty too."

Oh, Harper. Grief and sorrow, along with a good measure of guilt, twisted in his gut at Arty's senseless death. But he put that all aside for now to focus on Harper. If only he knew what to say. He knew exactly what she was thinking. He saw her blaming herself for Arty's death. She believed it should have been her. Given what she'd shared of her history — there was no doubt in his mind.

But he had no words for her.

He waited for her to say more, but she was done. Instead, she stared through the window as if mesmerized. Soon they would find themselves staring at their reflections as darkness fell.

They were thirty miles from the area where Harper had witnessed the murder. Where she'd been hiking to search for the missing couple. Still, Heath wasn't sure standing next to the windows was a good idea.

He pressed a switch on the wall and shades began to lower. Definitely a fancier setup than he had. This was a more upscale kind of guest ranch. Lori had more people working for her too, but she'd kept her home to herself after her husband, Glen, had died.

"What are you doing?" Harper asked.

"Protecting you."

"I need to see the sky and the trees." She huffed and left him. He caught up with her as she headed down the stairs and out the door that led to a cozy deck outside. Maybe she wanted to be alone, but he didn't care. Her safety was his priority. She crossed her arms and stared out into the same woods.

"Are you sure you really want to expose yourself like this? We know this guy can shoot from a distance. I wouldn't go so far as to say he's a military-trained sniper, but why tempt fate?"

"I thought you said we were safe here."

"I hope we are. That said, there's no reason to take unnecessary risks."

She shrugged. "I don't like being a prisoner in the house. Please give me a few minutes, okay? He couldn't have followed us here. He can't know where we are yet, even if he eventually finds out."

Heath felt the same way. He wanted to be outdoors, riding horses. Fishing. Something. He'd love to take Harper riding as well. But he knew that wouldn't take her mind off what was bothering her. Arty's death weighed heavy on her, as it did on them all, but Harper especially took it to heart because that bullet had been meant for her.

How could he help her? He dug deep into the past, into his heart. Though he tried not to think about those days, especially his role in things, he'd go there for Harper. Heath thought about how much she'd helped him when they were kids. Having someone to confide in had been such a relief. Sure, he'd had his brothers, but they shared in his grief and he tried to shield them as much as possible.

"Remember when my mom left us?"

"Yes . . ." Her voice sounded raspy. "You were a mess. So distraught. I didn't know what to do for you. How to help you."

"But you did." He remembered that much too clearly. Her hair had been long even back then, and when she'd leaned over, it hung down like a curtain, shiny and red. He remembered that moment. She'd said, "You could ask her to come back, Heath."

Her suggestion had been a simple request. A good idea. But it had turned to ash. Literally. Heath never blamed Harper for suggesting that he should ask his mom to come back. He couldn't hold her responsible.

"When she called to check on us, I begged her to come back. Told her that I would keep her safe." What had he been thinking? He had tried to fix all that had gone wrong in his life. He had thought if he could bring his mother back, then their lives would be better. He couldn't have been more wrong. And now he'd allowed the sheriff to persuade him that he was the best person to protect Harper.

Was Taggart wrong?

Focus, man.

"So, sure, she came back. I don't think she wanted to leave in the first place, and maybe it was more about scaring some sense into Dad. He'd started drinking too much and became verbally abusive, and then he hit her."

"She came back to protect *you,* Heath. You and your brothers."

"I don't know. I'll never know now. She hadn't been home two days before the fire took the back of the house. I tried to run in to get her, but my father, the fireman, stopped me. He went in after her himself and came out empty-handed. I shouldn't have trusted him with her life."

He pulled himself out of the dark place his mind had headed and focused back on Harper in the here and now. He'd meant to help her. Not get distracted in the dark shadows of his past. Seeing Harper like this, what she was putting herself through, brought clarity to the past. He shouldn't hold himself responsible for what happened.

"Why are you so hard on yourself?" she asked.

"I could ask you the same question."

"I don't know . . . I guess I want to do more to help. Not simply document evidence after the damage has been done and someone has been hurt or murdered. I don't want to see the violence, turn in my photos, and turn away at the end of the day. But I don't know what more I can do, Heath."

"I wish I could tell you. I don't want to suggest that you put yourself in harm's way to find justice, but I understand why you feel you need to. And I'll be right here with you through it all."

He leaned over the railing next to her as they both enjoyed the colorful display of clouds reflecting the setting sun. She was close enough now that he could feel the warmth coming off her. Heath wanted to put his arm around her and comfort her, but his desire went much deeper than simple comfort.

"Heath." His name from her lips had barely been a whisper and stirred him.

He tilted his head toward her.

A breeze lifted a few strands of her red hair and swept them across her face. Her eyes were soft as she smiled at him. Then she turned to face him completely, still so near.

"Thank you, Heath. It means the world to me that you're here. I mean, I know it's your job, but I can't help but think there's more to it. Would you be here, Heath, if you weren't a deputy?"

Her eyes searched for the truth in him. He sensed she wouldn't have asked the question if she didn't already know the answer, but she wanted to hear those words from him. Sharing their deepest, darkest moments had brought them closer.

"Heath?" Her smile faltered.

Yes. Oh, yes. "Definitely, I'd be right here." The words came out much too breathy. Emotions he couldn't put into words flooded his heart and mind. Warmth thrummed in his gut. He shifted to face her and gently lifted her chin so he could look into her eyes. "There's nowhere else I'd rather be."

Her lips parted slightly. His pulse jumped. The desire to kiss her flooded his soul. Wrong time. Wrong place. Wrong, wrong, wrong. But he ignored his brain. He was only listening to his heart. Her eyes almost seemed luminescent. He saw the longing there. The same longing he felt for her. He heard her sharp intake of breath, felt the emotion pouring from her — the need.

Nothing else mattered except Harper. Her nearness.

The tenderness that had always been between them, though hidden before, now ignited. No power on earth could prevent

302

his mouth from finding hers.

Her soft lips suddenly turned eager. *Harper . . .*

He breathed in her essence. His hands stroked the thick waves of her hair. He cherished the feel of her and her willing response to him, the overpowering sensations.

Dizzy with the kiss, he struggled to ground himself, but finally he eased away enough to cup her cheeks. If only this moment could last longer.

He couldn't let her get away. He couldn't let her go.

"I wish" — he breathed the words against her lips — "I wish that when this is over, you didn't have to leave. That you could stay here in Jackson Hole." What was he doing?

Harper edged away from him as if he'd broken the spell with his words. In her eyes, he saw the hope he'd ignited — and the questions.

But Heath was the worst kind of man. He'd once again made a terrible mistake. He'd messed things up.

"I'm so sorry, Heath." Harper backed away, then rushed into the house.

Chapter Thirty-Eight

Heath slammed the glass down too hard on the counter. He would wake someone, and he definitely didn't want to talk to anyone at the moment.

Not Harper. That would be too awkward.

Not Emily. She'd ask too many questions.

Not Evelyn or her granddaughter. He didn't feel like smiling.

And he certainly didn't want to see Lori, with her warm, flirtatious grin. If anything, Heath wanted to leave the house and get some air.

He completely understood where Harper was coming from. She wanted some space. Freedom to go where she pleased without fear of getting shot or someone standing too close to her and getting shot. Or stepping wrong and getting shot — like Arty. In that, Heath could understand how she

304

might feel guilty — she was always the survivor, like she'd told him a few days ago.

He grabbed his head and pulled his hair. Why had he kissed her? They'd both wanted the kiss, that much was evident. Weren't they the perfect lonely couple of friends?

Now came the hard part. They had to figure out how to work together. Maybe he should tell Taggart he couldn't do this anymore. To find someone else.

Headlights brightened the shades he'd drawn. Now, who could that be at this hour?

A text buzzed on his cell. Taggart.

I brought someone I thought you would want to see. Are you awake?

What was Taggart up to?

That depends on who it is. Care to tell me?

He can tell you himself.

It was too late for these kinds of games. Heath was in the middle of sending another text when a knock came at the front door. He rushed to unlock it, wishing he had the choice not to. Heath cracked open the door.

He did a double take.

Liam McKade gave him a tenuous grin.

"Hello, Heath."

While he searched for words, Heath swung the door wide open. At least he could invite his brother in. A duffel bag slung over his shoulder, Liam stepped inside.

Taggart remained on the porch and waited, his appearance understandably haggard.

"You coming in too?" Heath asked.

"I'm merely the delivery boy tonight. Tomorrow bring Harper to town. I have something to show her."

"What is it?"

"This can wait. You need to play catch-up tonight."

"Taggart, are you okay?"

His features drew together. "I will be when we find him." Taggart lifted his chin — a good-night gesture — and turned to walk away.

Heath shut the door, feeling Liam's eyes on his back. He slowly turned and closed the distance. Then he embraced his brother in a bear hug. Slapped his back a few times for good measure before he released him.

Liam — the middle brother — stood taller than Heath by an inch. He'd inherited their dad's crop of light hair and dark brown eyes. Liam removed his ball cap and scraped a hand through his hair. "Sorry for dropping in on you like this."

"Not a problem." Heath studied him.

"I stopped by the ranch first. Maybe I should have called, but I wanted it to be a surprise. I had envisioned walking in, dropping my duffel bag, and proclaiming, 'Honey, I'm home,' but nobody was there. The place was locked up. That disturbed me. Then Pete found me. The only problem was that he didn't know where you were staying. He knew the horses were being stabled here."

"Why didn't you call me?"

"I wanted it to be a surprise. I . . . you know how we disagree on the phone sometimes. I didn't want things to unravel." Liam grinned. The girls had always loved that grin in school — triple dimples. Heath had been kind of jealous.

"So you called Taggart."

"Yep. Pete said he would know."

The sheriff himself had picked Liam up and brought him there. That was impressive. Maybe he didn't trust anyone else to make sure they weren't followed to the Circle S.

"Did the sheriff fill you in on the way?"

"After he decided I wasn't a suspect. I told him I'm happy to help if needed."

Heath still couldn't believe his eyes. "Let's

take this into the kitchen. We can talk in there if we keep it quiet."

Tension rolled off his brother.

Heath and Liam never got along when they were together. If they were going to be at odds, he would have preferred that he was still at the Emerald M and not here at Lori's place.

Liam eased his duffel bag off his shoulder and set it by the door. This wasn't Heath's home, so he couldn't offer Liam a room — if there was even one left — without clearing it with Lori, though he suspected Liam would be more than welcome.

"You can bunk with me tonight." Heath would sleep on the small sofa in his room.

"Sounds good."

In the kitchen, Heath offered Liam some of Lori's lemonade and had a glass himself. In his wildest dreams he never thought he'd be standing there looking at Liam. Awkward silence filled the air. Well, that and the clinking of glass as he set his lemonade on the granite counter.

Heath took in his brother's appearance. His disheveled hair. Haggard face as if he'd come from a war zone. Liam held on to the counter like he was tired to the bone and he'd fall if he let go.

"It's good to see you," Heath said.

"There's so much to catch up on. I have no idea where to start. What brings you back? Did you come up from a deep undercover assignment for some fresh air?"

Liam puffed his cheeks, then blew out a breath as if his story would take much too long. "Something like that. I got your messages. Instead of calling, I decided to show up on your doorstep."

Heath released a low chuckle. "That sounds about right. So how long will you be staying?"

"As long as you'll let me."

"What?"

"I'm not going back."

CHAPTER THIRTY-NINE

Tuesday, 1:00 P.M.
Bridger County Sheriff's Office

This was taking much too long. Harper sat in the stuffy meeting room again. Heath and his brother stood behind her against the wall, along with Sheriff Taggart, waiting for the computer tech.

At least she wasn't sitting in this room alone with Heath after the fiasco last night. At least his brother had shown up to keep him company, but if she remembered correctly, he and Liam fought a lot. By the looks of them together now, neither of them was happy.

Harper rubbed the tight muscles in her neck. She wasn't sure how much longer she could wait for an explanation as to why the sheriff had asked her to come in. Had they found Sophie's body? She didn't get the feeling it was that. Maybe a piece of evidence. Something they needed Harper to see and confirm.

Heath didn't know what was going on either. She suspected that was because he would only share the information with her. Taggart likely wanted be the one to deliver the news so he could see her reaction.

Maybe Taggart had grown tired of waiting as well because he moved to stand in front of her and crossed his arms. "A tourist found a memory card. Looked at the contents and then turned it over to us."

Her chest constricted. "You found the pictures I took."

"We don't know that yet. You tell us."

"What are we waiting for?"

He paced the small space. "The computer tech transferred the photos and will be here to pull them up in a minute."

Seconds ticked by on the wall clock.

Heath moved to stand against the opposite wall, his expression unreadable. Why had she given in to her ridiculous desire to kiss him? Because being near him drove her to do stupid things like lean closer for a kiss. Because they'd connected before as kids, and for some inexplicable reason it was as if they'd picked up where they had left off and deepened their connection.

Except given the traumatic events of her childhood, and the scenes she'd witnessed each week at her job, she knew that the worst kind of tragedy could steal a loved one away. So Harper long ago resolved she would never leave herself vulnerable to that kind of pain. Kissing him had been a huge mistake.

The door swung open.

"Sorry about that." A short-haired brunette woman, young and lively, rushed to the table.

Harper had half expected a stereotypical nerdy guy.

The girl sat next to her. "I'm Meghan."

"Nice to meet you, Meghan."

But Meghan's focus had tunneled in on the computer. She glanced at Sheriff Taggart.

"Go ahead, Meghan. Let's see what we've got. Moffett will join us soon."

Harper held her breath, uncertain of her reaction to the images, if they were hers.

Meghan typed on the keyboard and the dark screen lit up. She opened up a digital photo album.

Though Harper had braced herself, the breath whooshed from her.

"Are these your images?" the sheriff asked.

"Yes."

"I thought so. Though you aren't the only one to photograph thousands of pictures of

Yellowstone National Park, the bear and then the victim and her shooter were as you described."

"The other images are still on the camera — if only I hadn't dropped it." She averted her gaze from the images before her. In the past, she'd failed to look. This time, she'd failed to retrieve her documentation of the scene. At least they had found this card.

It was something.

It was everything.

"We learned of the missing woman and know what happened to her, thanks to your efforts," Sheriff Taggart said.

"No one could have done better," Heath added.

"We'll see if we can get someone on this to enlarge the images," Meghan said. "Find some detail to help us identify this man. Great photography, by the way. You got some great close-ups with the telephoto. Too bad about your equipment."

"Are you going to be okay?" Sheriff Taggart asked. "I know these images must bring back those traumatic moments . . . Witnessing a murder is hard."

"You're right. It's hard to see them again." Heart pounding, she kept her composure. "Will I get the pictures back? I mean, at least the thousands of images of the national parks? I've already uploaded most of them to the cloud, but those of Yellowstone haven't been transferred yet."

"We'll see what we can do," Taggart said, "but for now, these images stay with us."

"Sheriff?" Liam spoke up now.

"You're only here to observe because of your law enforcement experience. I thought we could use a fresh set of eyes on this case."

"And that's what you've got. A fresh set of eyes," Liam said. "Let's see about magnifying the images of that rifle. From this angle and the way he's positioned, I don't think we'll be able to see the serial number. But maybe there's another way to identify who made it and who bought it."

"Are you kidding me? Wyoming is hunting paradise. You'd be looking for a needle in a haystack. The possibilities are infinite. He could have bought it online or anywhere in the country and brought it with him."

"Except this guy is local." Heath sounded sure of himself.

"How do you figure?" Taggart asked.

"Someone coming in from another state to hunt? This isn't the season for that. I'd say it's more likely that he's from around here." Heath continued to study the image. "This rifle is also custom made. I mean, look at the scope alone. Long range. The scope could be worth, at a minimum, three or four thousand dollars. And the rifle. Definitely not a factory rifle. Someone spent thousands of dollars on a rifle that can take up to a year to make, it's that custom."

Liam leaned in for a closer look. "Magnify that rifle, and we'll see if there's anything else special about it. The checkering or patterns. I could check out the local custom shops. See if I can learn anything. Unless it's a ghost gun — one he made himself. Still, he could have gotten the parts locally. If this guy is a felon, he'd get it on the black market or definitely make it himself. It's a direction. A lead I can follow."

"You're not on the county payroll."

"Exactly. I'm just a guy interested in getting a rifle exactly like my friend's there."

Sheriff Taggart nodded. "I appreciate the assistance, Liam. I'll consider you a consultant on this case."

Heath smiled. Harper watched the three men. Respect for both Liam and Heath shined in Sheriff Taggart's eyes.

Then Heath looked at her. He kept his smile in place, but somehow, she knew it was for her. They were okay again, despite the attraction between them.

Her heart sang.

Not good.

CHAPTER FORTY

Tuesday, 3:35 P.M.
Bridger County Sheriff's Office

As they left the county building and headed to Heath's truck, Harper texted Emily to let her know they were coming back now.

At least the trip into Grayback had been worth it. Those images added to the slim evidence file. Now they had an actual photograph of the shooter to go on. And Liam would be proactive in canvassing local custom rifle makers.

Harper's cell chimed. Emily was calling her?

"Hey. So what happened?" her sister asked.

"Hold on." At Heath's truck, Harper waited while Heath opened the door for her. Liam got in the back and Harper into the passenger seat.

As Heath drove them out of the parking lot, Harper shared with Emily that someone

316

had found her images that showed both the victim and the shooter. Her heart ached as those images shot through her mind again. *Sophie . . .*

Somehow it hurt even more now that Harper knew the victim's name.

She squeezed her eyes shut. They were going to get this guy. She believed that to her core.

"Where are you now?" Emily asked.

"Headed your way."

"I need you to head to the old house. I'm with Lori. That's where we're going."

"What? Why?"

"I was afraid you weren't going to get out of there in time to take me to the airport. Lori offered. I was about to text you. I'll meet you there."

Harper glanced at Heath and asked him to head to her old house. He nodded and made a U-turn in the road.

That familiar dread filled Harper. Would Emily be upset if she didn't come to the house? After all, Lori had the honor of that experience now, so why should Harper have to be there too?

"I have something to tell you," Emily said.

Harper squeezed the handgrip. Something more about her health? "Well?"

"You're not going to believe this."

Harper pursed her lips and tried to be patient.

"After I finished packing, I was thinking about the house and who might live there now. Driving by is one thing, but I really wanted to see inside. I know, I'm pushing it. Who is going to give two strangers a grand tour of their home? So I looked at the public records." Emily released a heavy breath.

Harper sat taller in the passenger seat. "Em?"

"Our *uncle* owns the house."

Huh? "Our uncle?"

"Jerry. Mom told us he was gone. He was dead. So I don't know what this means."

"I don't either." Harper's palms slicked against the cell. "Don't you dare approach the house until I get there."

CHAPTER FORTY-ONE

Bridger-Teton National Forest

Heath steered his truck toward the house where Harper grew up. He wanted to ask her about her conversation with her sister, but she had taken several deep breaths. She needed to process her thoughts.

He glanced in the rearview mirror. Had Liam heard any of that conversation? Maybe not. He sat in the back seat looking contemplative.

"I'm not going back." Liam had said the words with conviction, but Heath harbored no hope that his brother would stay in the area. Regardless, he was glad to see him.

Liam caught Heath's eye. "After we do this, please take me to get my stuff and then back to the ranch. Is it all right with you if I use your extra truck until I get my own vehicle?"

"Consider it yours, Liam."

"Thanks, Heath. Just for a while though. I'll stay at the Emerald M Ranch too, if it's all the same with you," he said. "Help Pete move the horses back. He didn't look so good."

"He's been sick, but don't say anything. He doesn't like to talk about it." Heath could hardly believe the man had continued to work. "I'm sure he'd appreciate the help. As for staying at the Emerald M, I think if you're going to help solve this case, staying with us might be best."

"Whatever you think, then."

Liam had a defiant streak. He hadn't liked how Heath had taken up the slack and acted like a father figure, or rather the one in charge, as their father drowned himself in the bottle even more after their mother's death. Heath understood his father's deep sorrow and might have succumbed to his grief too, but he had brothers to take care of. That responsibility kept him sober and responsible. Strange how having three sons hadn't done the same for their father.

He reminded himself that though Liam was still his brother, he was no longer a child.

In his peripheral vision, Heath noticed Harper shaking her head.

"What's going on?" he asked.

"I can't believe this. Emily looked at public records about the house. Our *uncle* owns it." Harper was silent a few breaths, then added, "Mom told us he'd died years ago."

Heath shifted in his seat. "So you're telling me your uncle lives in that house now and you thought he was dead? You never saw him? He didn't contact your mother?"

Harper slowly shook her head. "No. If Mom was still alive, we could ask her. We could get some answers. She might have protested our trip here to begin with, knowing we would see her brother. He was much older than her, but still, I wonder what happened between them?"

"Maybe he can tell you. Sibling estrangement is not all that uncommon, Harper." Heath and his brothers had gone long periods of time without speaking. Years. He and Austin were even estranged. It wasn't the way he had wanted it, but sometimes emotions ran far too high to have a civil conversation and then the next thing he knew, time had slipped away.

He was glad Liam was back, but something was eating at his brother. Something had happened. What had driven him here and made him proclaim he wasn't going back? Did that mean back to his job? Heath hadn't gotten anything more out of him last night and wouldn't press him. He would try his best to be there for him however he needed.

Finally, Heath stopped at the end of a drive where it met the county road. The house sat fifteen yards back. Emily stepped from Lori's SUV. Heath, Liam, and Harper joined her. Lori waved from the vehicle.

"I'll hang out here, if you don't mind." Liam crossed his arms and leaned against the truck.

Heath should remain on alert, especially now that they were closer to the region in which Harper had seen the murder. "Ladies, can we make this quick?"

CHAPTER FORTY-TWO

The old house waited for them at the other end of a gravel drive that had been rutted dirt the last time Harper had seen it.

"Well, are you ready to do this?" Emily asked.

"I don't know." Harper rubbed a tension knot in her neck.

Heath stood near them, watched and waited, but said nothing.

"At least we don't have to ask a total stranger if we can come inside," Emily said. "This is Uncle Jerry. Remember?"

"No, I don't."

"Well, I do. I met him once."

"You're forgetting that he and Mom were estranged. She thought he was dead. Or lied to us about that. Maybe he was dead to *her*. Whichever it is, there has to be a reason. I'm not sure this is a good idea."

"But you agree we need to try?" Emily asked.

Harper hung her head and shrugged. "I guess we do." Being here gave her the creeps. A strange sensation had clung to her ever since Emily had mentioned visiting here months ago. She looked up and took in the house where she grew up, now dilapidated and in need of multiple coats of paint. Maybe a bulldozer was in order.

Emily started walking up the drive toward their childhood home.

Instead of joining her, Harper watched her go. Emily, the mystery writer, was looking for closure or story fodder. Which one, Harper wasn't sure. Why had their mother insisted they had no other family? It was possible Mom hadn't meant that literally. Maybe as kids they had completely misunderstood her. Still, Harper had been under the distinct impression that they had no living relatives left. She'd always assumed the house had been sold to a stranger.

"Oh, all right." Harper didn't want to do this, but she wouldn't leave her sister to go it alone. She looked at Heath, who'd been watching her and their surroundings. "Are you coming?"

"You know I am," he said. "And then when you're done here, Harper, we'll take Emily to the airport and you can say goodbye. I want to get you back to Lori's where

I know you'll be safe. Unless, of course, you've changed your mind and you're going home with Emily, which would be best. You'd be *safer* there."

What happened to his earlier sentiments about wishing she didn't have to leave when this was over? Those words had been spoken in the heat of a moment that never should have happened.

Sighing, she shook her head. She wouldn't throw that back in his face. "Come on."

She had to jog a little to catch up to Emily, who was almost to the house. With his long strides, Heath was right behind her. They passed an old red pickup parked close to the house.

Emily clomped up the porch. Up close, the old, rickety house was so much smaller than Harper remembered, as if baking in the sun for two decades had caused it to shrink. Harper made her way up the steps to stand at the door with Emily. Heath followed and remained close.

"I think a phone call first would have been better," Harper said.

"I don't have time for that. It'll be a nice surprise. You wait and see." Emily knocked.

Harper let her gaze roam the overgrown yard. The woods backed right up to the house. Memories of her young life flooded her.

Emily frowned and knocked again.

Finally, she shrugged. "I guess nobody's home."

"He could have another vehicle besides that old red pickup."

They turned and took the steps down the porch. "Since nobody's home, let's look around a bit."

"Emily, no." Harper felt like she was an adult telling a young child to behave herself.

The door creaked open from behind them. A man stood in the doorway. Thin as though wasting away. A shiny, unnatural head of hair. That couldn't be their uncle, could it?

"Can I help you?" His voice was raspy and weak to go with his wary eyes.

"Uncle Jerry?" Emily rushed forward. "I'm Emily Larrabee and this is Harper, your sister Leslie's daughters. I met you once a long time ago. Remember us?"

Harper stepped forward and smiled.

He stared for a few long seconds. "My, you girls have grown up. What brings you by?" He stepped halfway out the door, still blocking the way. No invitation to come inside.

"Mind if we come in? We'd like to catch

up on old times, that's all. We won't stay long, I promise," Emily said. "I have a plane to catch this afternoon."

Emily was trying hard to connect with a long-lost relative who didn't seem to return the feeling. For what purpose, Harper wasn't sure. After all, this guy didn't rank high enough for Mom to stay in touch. That Harper knew of. Mom had wanted to forget the place where Dad had died. But she'd forgotten a lot more.

"Or we could sit here on your porch," Emily offered.

With no chairs.

"I'm sick and not feeling like having company today. Could you come back tomorrow?"

Emily scrunched her nose. "Well, I'm heading out of town this afternoon."

"I'm sorry." He coughed. "Today isn't possible. If you could come back tomorrow, that would be better." He looked at Harper long and hard as if expecting her to reply instead of Emily, then he said, "You look like your father."

Uncertain what to say to that, especially since she saw no warmth in his eyes, Harper shrugged. "Emily's leaving, so tomorrow won't be possible."

"But you're staying," he said matter-of-factly.

She hesitated before her reply. "I don't think I can make it."

Pursing his lips, he nodded. "I hear my phone ringing. I'm sorry, but I have to go. Thanks for stopping by. If you change your mind, you're welcome to come back." He took one step inside and closed the door.

Well, that was weird. Totally weird. She had expected as much. Still, shame filled her that she hadn't been willing to agree to see him tomorrow. What was wrong with her anyway? She was surprised Emily hadn't pressed her into agreeing right then and there or changed her plans to leave. Staring at the closed door, Harper considered knocking again, but being here disturbed her too much. Besides, Uncle Jerry hadn't been overly exuberant to see them. So that was that.

Harper walked with her sister down the drive toward the parked vehicles, Heath behind them. Next to Heath's truck, Liam jammed his hands into his pockets.

She hugged her sister to her as they walked. "I'm sorry."

"You were right to begin with. I thought since he was a relative it wouldn't be awkward."

"Seriously. For me, being at this house, in this yard, is weird."

Emily chuckled through tears. "Listen, Lori is going to take me to the airport."

"What? No. We can take you."

"You know how I hate goodbyes." Emily sniffled. "Lori is heading back to Jackson today anyway. It's on her way. We already decided."

"So you're saying goodbye to me now, while we're at the creepy old house?"

Emily grinned through her tears. "It's the stuff of any good mystery novel."

Harper smiled in return. Her sister was well on her way to recovering, and Harper was going to miss her. At Lori's SUV, Harper hugged Emily good and long. "I'll be home as soon as I can."

Emily slowly released her, then opened the door and climbed into the vehicle. "You be careful."

"I'll be fine. I have this guy" — she gestured with her thumb at Heath — "and also maybe his brother to watch out for me. It's you I'm worried about. Call me as soon as you've seen that neurologist, okay?"

"Okay." Emily shut the door.

Lori had lowered her window. "Y'all don't worry, I'll take good care of her, I promise."

Harper fought the guilt. She wanted to go

with Emily. Her sister needed her, but Harper was a magnet for danger and Emily could get hurt worse than she already had been. A chill ran over her. Could the killer have followed them even to this house in the woods? She hoped he was on the run since law enforcement from every part of the state was after him.

"Come on," she said to Heath. "Let's get out of here."

Lori's Navigator headed away.

Heath and Liam were like sentinels around Harper. She wasn't exactly sure how she felt about that. It only meant both of them could be in danger. They climbed into Heath's truck and Heath started it up, then steered down the road, not far behind the Navigator.

"Wait, stop," Harper said.

Heath slowed and pulled the truck to the side of the road. "What's wrong?"

She opened the door and stepped out before he could prevent her. Then she grabbed her camera bag from the back.

Heath bounded out of the truck and ran around to stand in her way. "Harper, what are you doing?"

Liam jumped out too.

She hefted the bag over her shoulder and hiked around Heath and into the woods.

"I'm going to take pictures of the house. That way, if I ever get the crazy thought in my head that I want to see it again, or if Emily begs me to go with her, all I have to do is look at the pictures instead and then I'll remember. She'll remember."

Emily had reopened the book on this part of her life with her request to stop by the old house. Harper was relieved the book was now closed for good.

Chapter Forty-Three

Liam thought he would never get back to the ranch.

Another deputy was staying with Harper at Circle S this evening while Heath brought Liam to Emerald M so he could see the renovated house in daylight and they could get Heath's other truck for Liam to drive. Tomorrow he could start looking for information on that custom rifle.

Now that they were alone and here at the ranch house, this was it. The showdown. The moment for which they'd both been waiting. Liam could almost laugh at the image of Wyatt Earp in *Tombstone* that suddenly popped into his head. But it wasn't like they were going to battle it out literally, for which he was grateful. He would never have come back here if he didn't know that, whatever their differences, Heath wouldn't turn him away.

They were brothers.

Liam could have gone anywhere he wanted but found himself back in Grayback.

Unfortunately, he couldn't talk it out and wasn't even sure he wanted to until he and Heath were truly alone. No girlfriends from the past or the future loitering — he grinned at the thought of Heath staying in that house with Lori Somerall, who had her sights set on Heath. He wouldn't go so far as to say that Harper had set her sights on him too, but she had eyes on him, whether Heath realized it or not.

Liam's sneakers squeaked across the spacious wood floor that used to be half this size. His shoes were silenced by a big chocolate-brown rug with turquoise diamonds. Nice touch. He was glad to see the changes, but on the other hand, it reminded him how bad things had been when he lived here. He didn't think there'd even been a rug. Only torn, ratty carpet.

Mom had tried. But life had worked against her.

He peered up at the tall ceiling and rafters and western decor where nothing used to hang.

"You did it," he said. "You actually did it. You changed the face of this place. The whole feel of it." Liam crossed his arms as he strolled through the renovated house, the place he used to call home, sensing Heath's eyes on him. Watching and waiting. It wasn't like his brother ever wanted or needed Liam's approval. In fact, Heath wanted Liam to need *his* approval. He thought he had taken up the slack where their father had failed. Liam never saw it that way.

Heath blew out a long breath. Shoved his hands in his pockets. "Before he died that day, Dad told me he planned to leave everything to me and for me to do something good with it. To make up for the past."

Liam wasn't accustomed to seeing his brother appear so dejected. "Well, like I said, you've done it, then."

"When he told me that, I threw his words back in his face, Liam. I never should have been so harsh. So cruel. Four hours later, he died in that crash."

"I'll admit I was mad at him for leaving it all to you. Jealous, even. But even when you offered to sell it and split the profits among us, I rejected your offer. Austin was too riddled with guilt over Dad's accident to want part of it." Liam scratched his chin. Maybe he'd been an idiot to turn down the offer, but what was done was done. And besides, the ranch was in the right hands now. "I know why Dad did it — he knew you could make something of this place. That had been his dream. One he only succeeded in destroying. But please don't tell me you fixed it up because you felt guilty about your last words to him."

"Oh yeah. Guilt paralyzed me, at least for a while. Then I took up his request and renovated the place. Hoped to renovate myself in the process. I threw every ounce of my energy into fulfilling his request in hopes that I could somehow make up for my last words, and yes, maybe even some of the past."

"You've done more than that. You've about buried any reminders. I could almost forget how hard he was."

"That's good to hear, coming from you. It means more to me than the fact that the Emerald M now has the reputation of being one of the top guest ranches in Jackson Hole."

"And what about you? Do you feel like you renovated yourself, as you put it?" Liam grinned.

Heath's chuckle sounded forced. "Not even close."

Liam would let that comment go without digging deeper. Heath was always too hard on himself. They had time to talk about that later. Liam hoped.

"Still, it seems so empty without Dad," Heath said.

Nicer. Quieter. "Peaceful, even." Liam glanced through the window at the barn in the distance.

"I'd say that's the good part. Still, whatever his issues, his downright meanness at times, I miss him." Heath released a heavy sigh.

Liam had nothing to say to that, so he kept silent. No point in stirring angry embers of the past. Heath was allowed that sentiment. Liam wasn't ready to miss their father yet. So maybe this wouldn't be a showdown, after all.

Though he was back and thought he was ready, he realized he didn't want to talk too much about their lives there. Not yet. Time to change the subject.

"Care to tell me what's going on with you and Harper? Oh, and the woman whose house you're staying in, for that matter."

"You know why we're staying there. Nothing's going on with either woman."

"So Harper — she was your friend when you were kids." Heath cocked a brow. Surprised? Liam chuckled. "Yeah. I paid attention."

"All this time I thought you were busy with the horses. You were good with them, even as a kid."

"You remember how it was. We each had to pour ourselves into something to get us out of the house. Horses in the summer. And skiing in the winter. Brad took me, remember? His family could afford the ski lift passes. I had a friend too, only he wasn't some cute girl. Harper was cute back then. She isn't cute anymore."

Heath crossed his arms.

Liam continued walking the room. "See. I knew you liked her. She's not cute, she's a real looker. And serious. But maybe she was that serious as a kid too. So why'd you leave her with that deputy to come with me?" He wished he hadn't asked that. He knew exactly why. Maybe he wanted to hear actual words this time. Not just second-guessing what his brother was thinking.

"I'll tell you why, but you go first."

"What?"

Heath walked around the big kitchen counter. Liam ran his hand over the rich pine butcher-block countertop. *Nice.* He looked up at Heath, waiting for an answer, but he didn't need one. Still, he'd wait.

"You always were stubborn, but that's beside the point. I want to know what's bothering you."

"Oh. I thought you wanted to know why I'm back. You asked me that before."

"And you never answered."

Liam had experience controlling his emotions. Keeping the darkness that threatened at bay. Working undercover in the Drug Enforcement Administration had taken him down dark roads for which he hadn't been prepared. He shook off the shadows pressing in on him. "Let's say I needed a long break. There's nothing I can share with you anyway. Heath, I'm . . . I'm glad I had a place to come back to." Despite the darkness of his childhood here, this place now seemed like the purest, brightest light, especially compared to the people he'd had to pretend were his friends.

He released a heavy sigh he was sure must have echoed through the mountains and disturbed the neighbors for miles away. Heath peered at him. The man's concern might actually cut through the hard shell Liam had built around himself, inside and out. Heath moved around the counter and came just short of hugging Liam. Again. Instead, he clapped him on the back, and that touch of his strong hand contained a comfort that words could never express.

It was exactly what Liam needed, and he

hadn't even known.

"You stay long enough to be good and well rid of whatever forced you back."

Liam chuckled. "Nothing forced *you* back."

"Maybe not, but you . . . I know you. You wouldn't have come back otherwise. I can't say I'm not grateful that something sent you here, but it had to have been pretty bad. You're always welcome here. You know that."

"Speaking of which, how long until we can all actually come back?"

"Soon, I hope."

"And once this is over, do you think Harper will leave?"

"Probably."

"And you're going to let her walk away?"

"I have no reason to keep her here. Besides, there's a lot you don't know about me. Things that happened. I'm not marriage material."

Right.

"You look through the rest of the house. Take your time. I'm going to check on Pete."

"See you in a few minutes."

Heath flipped off the lights when he walked through the door. It was still daylight, but windows didn't let in enough light for Liam. Liam flipped on more lights.

That's better.

His cell rang. He glanced at the caller ID. That darkness wanted to follow him even here.

CHAPTER FORTY-FOUR

Wednesday, 9:43 A.M.
Circle S Ranch

Harper was alone with Deputy Naomi Thrasher, who was on protective duty in place of Heath for today. The deputy would take her to see Dr. Jacob to get the stitches out this morning. Looking through pictures that had been retrieved from the memory card, Harper studied photographs of Emily smiling next to the Airstream at Granite Ridge Campground.

Her sister texted last night that she had arrived home safely.

After so many months with Emily, it felt strange that she wasn't there now. She almost felt the same about Heath's absence. He'd needed to check on something at his ranch and didn't want her with him there.

As for Deputy Thrasher taking Heath's place for a few hours last night and then again this morning, sure, Heath probably needed a break from babysitting duty. A break from her. He also wanted to be actively involved in finding the person behind the shooting. Or the person behind the bombing.

Or both.

She understood that need completely and shouldn't have been hurt by his relief at escaping the Circle S and Harper, because she had felt the same way. They both needed space to recover from the awkwardness of being unable to continue to act on their emotions.

She'd hurt him when she brushed him off after the kiss. Shoot. She'd hurt herself. But it was for the best. They both knew that.

Then Liam's sudden appearance on the scene shifted Heath's focus — it was subtle, but she'd noticed. For all Harper had known, Liam was a regular at the Emerald M, but Heath set her straight. He hadn't seen or heard from Liam in going on five years — since their father's funeral. And while he was there now, a restlessness emanated from them both. An edginess that she hadn't seen in Heath, even with all that was going on.

Deputy Thrasher approached the table and peered over her shoulder at the pictures. "I'm told you're an exceptional crime scene

342

photographer."

Harper heard the approval in the deputy's words and it made her heart swell with satisfaction that at least while she'd been on the job, she'd done it well. Then she realized the deputy could very well know the rest of the story.

Though Harper had been dealing with psychological issues, the murder she'd captured on camera was forcing her to move past those issues out of sheer necessity.

So what if she had cowered beneath her bed as a kid when her dad was murdered? The familiar pang made her cringe, but she pushed passed it. Harper longed to be the person to find the truth — on her camera or otherwise.

I can do this. I can be that person.

She glanced up at the young deputy. "I'm not sure what else you might have heard, but thank you."

"Nice RV. I'm sorry it was destroyed." Deputy Thrasher studied the photograph. "We searched for evidence at the campsite but didn't find anything. There has to be something. I might be new, but I've come to believe there's always evidence at a scene. It's a matter of finding it."

Harper liked her. "I couldn't agree more. But even knowing that, the evidence isn't always found."

"Mr. Stein, the guy who runs the Granite Ridge Campground for the forest service, told us that no one would be allowed to camp there for a while, even after we released it. He said it would take him a few days to get over what happened to you."

"He seemed nice enough. I only met him a couple of times, but he helped Emily get into the trailer when the door got jammed." Harper clicked through more images of the campground. Hmm.

"He did?" Deputy Thrasher asked.

The tone in her voice drew Harper's attention up. "What's the look on your face? What are you thinking?"

"Your door was jammed so you couldn't get out that night." Deputy Thrasher wrote something on her pad. "We questioned him, I'm sure of it. He was the witness who saw you drive away. He thought he saw you, but now we believe that the perp had worn a wig."

"You don't think . . . You're not saying . . . No. He seemed so nice."

"Sorry, but that shooter in that picture could be anyone beyond, say, fifty, behind that hat. You know that."

Unfortunately, she did. She pressed her hand against her stomach. "I can't believe it could be him."

Thrasher got on her cell. "I'm going to ask for someone to check into his background. Find out what we know about him. Someone needs to question him again."

"Please make sure they don't go alone." Harper shut her computer and stood. Could Mr. Stein be their guy? She'd had it with being stuck there like a prisoner. She hadn't stayed behind to do nothing. "Would you mind taking me to the sheriff's office after I get these stitches out? I could hang out with Meghan and look through pictures."

"You got it. Just looking through the pictures has given us another possible lead."

After taking Harper to see Dr. Jacob to get her stitches removed, Deputy Thrasher parked her department vehicle in the parking lot of the sheriff's office.

Harper got a text at the same time as the deputy got one.

WHERE ARE YOU?

"Is yours from Heath?" Harper asked.
"Yes. I should have let him know."
"Tell him to meet us here," Harper said.
Inside the sheriff's department, Taggart approached them as they came down the

hallway. He eyed them with purpose.

Before he could speak, Deputy Thrasher said, "We need to check into Mr. Stein, who oversees Granite Ridge. He helped them unstick their door a day or two before the incident. I don't know, I thought we —"

"Go ahead and run a background on him. Do what you can from here. Stay with Harper. We got an anonymous but strong tip about another possible suspect a few hours ago. We've been investigating, but we don't have probable cause to search or arrest. I sent a couple of deputies over to bring him in voluntarily for questioning. Or see about a consent to search. We're looking for evidence to corroborate the tip. Let's see how this plays out. It could be nothing at all. But in case this is our guy, you stay here with Harper. This is the safest place for her."

CHAPTER FORTY-FIVE

Liam meandered up to Curt's Custom Rifles, which was not even a mom-and-pop establishment but a large workshop at the back of a small ranch house. Liam had already visited five out of eight custom rifle makers in the area. He had asked the same questions, but more than that, he had tried to get a sense of the maker's style and personality. The guns' purpose. The aesthetics.

Curt's was a very private establishment. Appointment only.

Liam might not be welcomed. Sheriff Taggart was probably right — this was a colossal waste of time. Still, if their perpetrator had bought his custom-made rifle in Jackson Hole, Liam would find that out. It was good old-fashioned police work. Grunt work that nobody else wanted to do.

He knocked on the door before pushing it open to step inside.

A man in his early thirties, about Liam's age, hovered over a rifle barrel secured in a lathe on a large worktable. "Can I help you?"

Good. He wasn't going to get berated for showing up without an appointment.

He thrust out his hand and the guy took it. "Name's Liam. I wanted to check out your work."

"My name's Chad." After noticing the question in Liam's eyes, he said, "Curt's my father."

Liam dropped his hand and glanced around the room, noted a display, and got that good deep-in-the-gut feeling he'd been looking for.

"You don't have an appointment."

"No. I wanted to check you out before I made one." Liam smiled, angling to get on the guy's good side.

Chad eyed a couple of stainless-steel barrels next to the lathe. "What would you like to see? I have rifles ready for purchase if you don't want to wait. And" — Chad studied him — "someone who has an appointment will be here in five minutes."

This shouldn't take that long. "What

about a rifle custom made to my specifica-
tions?"

"Let's hear it."

"Namely this." Liam pulled out his copy
of the photo of the hunter and his custom-
made rifle and stuck it on the counter. He
pushed it forward. "Is this one of yours?"

Chad adjusted his glasses. Emotion
flashed in his eyes, then was gone. "Are you
asking me to make this for you? Or are you
asking if I made this particular rifle?"

Smart man. "Did you make this rifle?"

Frowning, the man looked at the picture.
"This looks similar to what we call our
extreme long-range hunter rifle. I'm talking
twelve-hundred–plus yards. That's our
specialty. But I can't be sure that we made
it. Beyond seeing the registration code, I'd
have to take it apart."

"What about the scope? Would you have
to special order it?"

"Yes. Or someone could add that later."

Liam was glad to hear the guy wasn't going to lie to him, but he wasn't telling the
whole truth either. "But chances are since
you'd make the bullets too and would need
to test the gun's precision since the extreme
long-range rifle is your specialty, you would
need the scope to do that."

"Are you a cop or something?" Chad

arched a brow.

A loaded question. "I'm searching for the man who killed two hikers."

Chad's face paled. "I haven't had a client request that scope." Chad handed the photo back.

Liam wished he had a magnified image with him. "What about the rifle? This is your style, right? That fleur-de-lis checkering with ribbons on the stock."

"Anyone could have done that."

Chad was shutting down on him, but he'd learned a lot, nonetheless. None of the weapons on display had that precise design, but close enough. Yes. Definitely close enough.

"I see my next customer driving up." Chad handed Liam a card. "Make an appointment if you want to get a rifle from me."

Liam scribbled his number on the back of Chad's card and handed it back. "If you remember anything that can help, call me."

Maybe Liam was wrong to spend time canvassing these shops, but a man who was trying to kill the woman his brother cared deeply about — maybe even loved — wasn't someone to sit around and wait on.

Liam thanked Chad and headed to the door. Through the window he could see a stocky man in his fifties approaching. Liam put his hand on the doorknob.

"There was this guy . . ." Chad said.

Liam turned to look at him.

"He was maybe late sixties. He asked a lot of questions. I thought he was going to commission a piece. I told him six, seven months tops. He said he couldn't wait that long."

"Meaning . . ."

"I'm not sure. After he left, I thought to myself that he would try to build his own. He knew enough that he could if he had the right tools."

A ghost gun.

"Got a name?"

Chad crooked his mouth. "John Smith."

CHAPTER FORTY-SIX

Wednesday, 11:47 A.M.
Bridger-Teton National Forest

If this was their man, Heath wanted to look him in the eyes. What kind of monster would do the things he'd done? Heath might even consider doing much more than looking, except he was working for the sheriff's department now, and what he had in mind wouldn't reflect his duties as a deputy.

It might be worth resigning.

Oh yeah, even volunteers could resign.

Heath had been on his way to meet Harper at the sheriff's department when Sheriff Taggart asked him to meet two deputies at Donny Albright's address up Moose Creek Road instead.

Someone had seen Donny in the woods with two hikers, one of whom was Sophie Batterson Osborne. Donny was dressed in hunting gear, carrying a rifle and scope.

None of that meant he was guilty, of course, but it meant they needed to at least question him.

Heath had a bad feeling about this since Taggart was now also heading to Donny's. Heath was halfway there when he found himself following Taggart. He pulled up behind him to park in the drive. The house was old but immaculate. The yard, what there was of it, was mowed and neat before the national forest encroached. And it was located within five miles of where Harper had witnessed the murder. This guy would have moose, elk, bear, and antelope right at his back door. He wouldn't even need a precision long-range hunting rifle of that caliber and price, but need and want were often confused.

Taggart stood at his vehicle, checking his phone.

Heath approached and stood next to him. "What are we doing? Is this our guy?"

"We ran a background check on him but came up empty. I sent Moffett and Shackelford to bring him in voluntarily to answer questions."

The sheriff tucked away his cell, his face twisted with displeasure.

"But now we're here," Heath said. "Why? What happened?"

"Let's go see."

Sheriff Taggart hiked along the side of the house. Heath was confused. Shouldn't they be knocking on the front door? Something had definitely happened.

"Taggart!" Shackelford's voice squawked over the sheriff's radio.

Instead of replying, the sheriff stepped around to the backyard.

Donny Albright sat propped against a tree. A bullet hole in his temple. A pistol near his limp hand. Moffett was taking pictures.

A sour feeling stirred in Heath's gut.

They stood looking over the body. He could hear Harper's voice in his head, complaining about evidence being disturbed. If only Donny's death would mean this was the end of it and Harper was no longer in danger. His death seemed too convenient.

"Well, this is too bad." Taggart crouched to eye level with Donny.

"The county coroner's on the way," Shackelford said. "You got the warrant?"

The sheriff nodded, looking into the woods as if searching. "Get ballistics and make sure his hand fired that weapon and there's gunshot residue on the contact wound. That'll give us the first clue as to whether this was a fake suicide."

"You don't think he killed himself?" Moffett asked.

"I didn't say that. But we'll know soon enough. I want to get on top of this before the state boys get here. If this is the man we're after, then everyone is going to want a piece of him for killing that hiker, especially if he's also the person who killed Arty. But we need to find the murder weapon, the rifle he used, to confirm it." Taggart looked at Heath. "You're with me. Moffett, you too, after you're done with pictures here. Shackelford, you wait for the crew and direct them back here. I don't want too many people in that house yet."

Heath followed Sheriff Taggart into Donny's home. "What do you think happened?"

"He must have known we were coming and he couldn't escape," Taggart said. "But that's only speculation. I wish we could have questioned him."

Inside the man's meticulous house, stuffed, mounted elk and moose heads stared back at them from the walls.

"The warrant is for the rifle, but if you see anything suspicious or that could relate to this crime or another crime, let me know."

In the bedroom, Heath spotted hunting garb on the floor. The clothes he'd worn when he shot Sophie?

Propped in the corner was a rifle. From where he stood, it appeared to be the same rifle that had killed Sophie. Arty too? "Sheriff, in here."

Sheriff Taggart stepped into the room. "Well, now. Just what we were looking for."

Through the bedroom window, Heath could see Donny's body leaning against the tree.

"What are you thinking, McKade?"

"Donny Albright killed a woman, maybe her new husband, for reasons we'll never know. He tried to kill Harper twice, and his second attempt killed Arty. Now he's going to set out the evidence for us and go out back and shoot himself? That's too easy."

"I get that you wanted to have words with him, but sometimes killers come to the end of themselves."

"Do you really believe that's the case here, Taggart?"

"A gunshot wound to the side of the head, the mouth, or the front of the chest usually is a suicide. But let's talk this out. What if he unwillingly shot himself? Was somehow coerced into killing himself? Then our next question is how. What did someone hold over him?"

Queasiness stirred in Heath's gut. "For

that, we'll need to talk to family and friends to find out more about him."

"If this was set up to look like a suicide, that means the real killer wants us to think he's dead so we'll stop looking. If he thinks we stopped looking for him, that's when he gets careless. I might decide to let him think we're done. But honestly, I hope we've found our killer."

CHAPTER FORTY-SEVEN

Wednesday, 12:15 P.M.
Bridger County Sheriff's Office

Harper sat with Meghan to view the images she'd taken, only greatly magnified with special software. Though others had looked at them, crime scene photos were part of her training, and she might as well do something useful. Perhaps she'd spot something unusual or significant that could help them.

But with thoughts of Heath facing off with the person who could be the killer, she struggled to concentrate.

Her cell rang. Emily. Harper stood to stretch her legs. "Hey. How are you feeling?"

"Never better. I slept in. It feels so weird to finally sleep in my own bed." Emily sighed. "Can I just say that despite all this nasty business at the end, I loved the months of camping with you. It was the experience of a lifetime. Like you said, maybe we can do it again one day. That is, when you're finally home."

"About coming home, I have some news on that front. They're checking out someone who could be the killer. If it's him, then it's over, and I can come back."

"Harper, that's great news."

"*If* it's him, it's good news." She held on to that hope.

"What about the two hikers?"

"They haven't found them. At least they haven't told me they have." The image of Sophie's face — eyes vacant, body lifeless — invaded her mind again. A sudden wave of grief washed over her. She kept her emotions at bay, wanting her conversation with Emily to be upbeat.

"Maybe it's premature, but I'm so relieved," Emily said. "I can't wait for you to be safe. I can't wait for you to be back home where you belong."

Harper needed to change the subject. "Please let me know what the neurologist says. Is your appointment tomorrow?" She realized too late that Emily probably didn't want to think about it. Learning about possible seizure issues had to be terrifying. At the same time, it was good the doctors had pinpointed the problem so she could have a thorough examination at home and get the right medications.

"Yeah . . . about that. My appointment isn't until next week."

"Oh?"

"I did have a reason why I needed to get back though. I have to attend a gala at a museum. Along with several other creative types, I'm speaking. My book, *Fire and Ash,* is being featured."

"Oh, Emily, that sounds like a big deal. When is the gala?"

"Saturday night. It's in Dallas."

"What? And you didn't tell me?" So much for them not keeping secrets. Harper would have to get a plane ticket and head home soon — that is, if Emily even wanted her to go. "Why didn't you say something?"

"I'm sorry I didn't tell you, but I didn't want to pressure you into returning before you were ready. I wanted you to come back with me, but not because you felt obligated to attend the gala."

"It sounds like you've known about this for a while."

"Yes. I learned about it when we first started on our tour of national parks. But come on, it's not like you've attended all my events. It's really not a big deal."

Of course it was. "I still think you should

have told me, and we could have headed home together. Maybe you'd still have your Airstream." Harper wished she hadn't brought that up.

Emily sighed. She spoke to someone else, then directed her words to Harper. "Sorry, Michelle is here to pick me up. We're going shopping. I need a new dress for the event. I never mentioned it because you needed time to focus on getting better. I wasn't sure if that meant staying on the road longer than we had planned, so I didn't bring up the gala. Then there wouldn't be any pressure to rush back. I hope you understand that I didn't tell you for your own benefit."

Sometimes Emily amazed her. Her sister was selfless. Emily had practically put aside her life — including any real dating prospects — for a year for Harper. She would have a hard time not carrying a measure of guilt though — her issues had almost kept her sister from this gala and it sounded like Emily was excited to go.

"Thank you, Emily, for being the best kind of person. The best sister. I'm so relieved that you get to attend the gala." Harper chuckled. "And that you finally told me about it. I know they'll love you and your book."

Emily scoffed, teasing Harper. "You

haven't even read the book."

"I'm sorry. I thought you understood why." A smidgeon of guilt pinged her heart. Emily's mysteries involved murder, after all, and Harper had needed a break.

"I do understand. Please don't feel like you have to be there. I'm not going alone."

"So who's the lucky guy?" Harper had a feeling Emily was keeping another secret.

"Excuse me? I didn't say anything about a guy."

"You didn't have to. I figured it out. So who's attending the gala with you?" Harper wished she could be there now.

"My old editor, actually. He's flying into Dallas and will meet me there."

"Your *old* editor?"

Emily laughed. "My *previous* editor. We've known each other a long time, but he took a job with a different publisher. That frees us up to explore a different kind of relationship."

"Wait. He took a different job? Are you saying he did that so that you could date?"

Emily chuckled. "I haven't been home to date, but now instead of talking only about the book, we've been chatting about personal stuff. What we would do when I returned home. Initially, I wasn't sure it would go anywhere, so I didn't tell you that either or else I never would have heard the end of it."

How could Emily have kept this a secret too? When Harper got back, she and Emily would have to have a good, long talk about sisters and secrets. "And you were flirting with Heath."

"Harper!"

Meghan cleared her throat and gestured toward the door. The subject of their conversation had stepped into the room, a mixture of frustration, regret, and relief on his face. How much had he heard?

"Em. I gotta go. Heath is back. I'll call you when I know something." She ended the call.

"Well?" she asked.

"We may have found the killer."

"Oh, thank goodness." Still, he didn't sound completely sure. Trying to read Heath's expression, she eased into the seat next to Meghan.

He pulled up a chair and sat next to Harper. "There's something else."

"Well, what is it?"

"He committed suicide."

"Oh." So they couldn't ask him about the hikers. Where he'd left Sophie's body. Couldn't ask him why. "I had held on to hope that at least Chase was still alive and being kept somewhere and that we could find out where."

"Me too." He released a tenuous breath.

"What aren't you telling me?"

"I don't want to let my guard down until we know for sure."

"Wait, I thought we knew it was him."

"We found the weapon that looks like the one in the image. Ballistics will tell us if it's the one that killed Arty. But not Sophie, because we don't have a body or bullet to compare with. We found clothes. They look like the same ones the hunter was wearing in the pictures you took. They'll have to process the scene to see if the honeymooners were there at his house."

"Then what's bothering you?"

"I don't know, exactly. You took great pictures, Harper, but by those alone, I can't tell if it's Donny or someone else. I know forensics will try to use the images. The state lab probably has software to do that comparison. Still, it seems he went to a lot of trouble to try to kill you. And now it's all too easy. We get a tip, which is hearsay, but we go to follow up and the guy killed himself?"

Easy and convenient. If only her father's murder had been so cut-and-dried. They never found the killer.

She stood up and paced the cubicle. "And what does the sheriff think?"

"He is leaning toward believing all the evidence will show Donny committed the crime. He was seen with the victim hours before her death, though that still needs to be confirmed. He had a rifle that looks exactly like the murder weapon in his possession. He's a hunter and would know how to use that rifle and shoot from a long distance. From that perspective, it all adds up." Heath stood in front of Harper to block her pacing and took her hands in his. "I know you want to go home. You need to get back to your life. You can do that anyway, Harper. And . . . I think you should go."

At his words, truth rose up in her — truth that went against all her resolve. She'd ignored it but had to face it now. Harper wanted this to be over more than anything — not so she could go home but so she and Heath could start something new and fresh without danger shadowing them.

But what did it matter? Heath wanted her to go. She saw the truth in his eyes.

Was he was urging her to go home because he wanted her to be safe? Or because he simply believed she wanted to go and he wanted her to be happy? As far as something between the two of them, Harper certainly hadn't encouraged Heath with the way she'd reacted to his kiss.

So this was it, then . . .

"Okay. I mean, it sounds like they found him, and I only ever wanted to make sure justice was served for Sophie. Besides, I'm worried about Emily."

Harper hoped he didn't see the hurt and confusion in her eyes.

CHAPTER FORTY-EIGHT

Thursday, 12:30 A.M.
Circle S Ranch

Heath ground his teeth and tried to place the cup quietly on the counter. He'd waited up late for Liam, and not because he was trying to act like a father figure. But it sure felt like it. Liam wouldn't like it either.

Liam slipped quietly through the front door and crept across the wood slats, then his eyes found Heath watching him from the kitchen across the expanse. Even in the shadows, Heath couldn't miss Liam's severe frown.

Oh boy.

Just like when they were living at home. Heath said nothing. He waited for Liam to make his way to the kitchen.

"Where have you been?" Heath asked.

"Checking out the custom long-range rifle makers. It takes time to make it around the valley."

Heath checked his anger, his emotion, his pulse. Instead of fisting his hand, he wrapped it around his mug. "You didn't answer my text. There's a killer out there, so I was worried."

"My cell died. Sorry."

"Ever hear of a charger?"

"Why the third degree, Heath? We're not kids anymore."

Heath blew out a breath. "I know. I'm sorry." He was . . . uptight for more reasons than he could count. "What did you find out?"

"The only interesting lead I found belongs to a man by the name of John Smith."

Heath choked on his drink. He composed himself. "You're kidding."

"No." Liam told him about meeting Chad at Curt's Custom Rifles. "And we know that if the guy is wanted anywhere or has felony convictions, he can't buy a gun, even custom-made. But he sure learned a lot from the man who makes them. I suspect that's all he wanted. I also suspect he already knows enough of what he's doing and is set up to make his own ammo. He must have had a few questions about the precision in long-distance shots. These guys specialize in that. So John Smith led Chad on that he was commissioning the rifle. Getting as much as he could out of him."

Rubbing his chin, Heath thought about Liam's words. "Can you go back tomorrow?"

"Why?"

"We got a tip today that led us to the man supposedly responsible for killing Sophie." Heath explained about the house and finding the suspect dead. "Taggart called me an hour ago. Because Arty was killed, the state lab got right on it. Ballistics is back. The rifle is the same one used to shoot and kill Arty. Deputy Custer."

Liam's expression didn't change. "But you're not buying it."

"It seems . . . convenient. Donny had some animals on the wall, but the only expensive weapon he had was the one. How hard would it be to plant the rifle on a guy like Donny? An anonymous tip led us to at least look into him. And then he was dead. The gun was there. The clothes in the picture. Nothing else but what was in Harper's pictures."

That could mean the shooter had taken her camera, after all. His skin prickled at the thought.

After helping himself to a bottled water from the fridge, Liam slid onto a stool. "I get it. You don't want to let your guard down. This is about protecting Harper."

"Yes." Heath had resolved that he would get it right this time. He couldn't afford even one more fail.

Especially when this was about Harper.

And that was a problem in itself. Could two people fall in love more easily if they already had a connection, as was the case with Heath and Harper? Despite his best efforts to the contrary, his heart held on to her, his mind focused on her.

Whoa, boy. He needed to slow his heart way down.

"Does the rifle have a serial number? I could find out if Chad made the gun in question while I'm there."

"Nope. What we want to know from Chad is if Donny Albright and John Smith are the same man."

"Will Taggart let you share the guy's picture with me?"

"I didn't bother asking in case he decided to say no. Didn't want him berating me or firing me from my volunteer job."

Liam spewed his water. "You're a *volunteer*?"

"Oh, yeah. Didn't I tell you that?"

"How does that even work?" Liam wiped away his mess with a paper towel.

"I'll explain later. Check your email. I sent

370

you an image I scraped from the internet. Drive back up there during business hours and show this picture to the gunmaker. See if this is the same guy. Find out if Donny Albright is John Smith. Oh, and take a charger this time."

Yawning, Liam stretched. He grinned. "Not sure I want to take orders from a volunteer."

Heath was still processing a decent response when Liam rose from the seat, then hung his head. When he lifted his chin, he said, "Sorry, bro. Seriously, anyone who would do what you're doing for free, not even on the payroll, is a hero. You're *my* hero. Keep up the good work, Heath."

Chapter Forty-Nine

Thursday, 7:45 A.M.
Circle S Ranch

Heath hadn't slept a wink.

Why would he have? He was supposed to be keeping Harper safe. Watching out for her.

That job would be over today.

That thought alone had kept him up. Pacing the house. Watching out the windows of this spread that wasn't his own. Staring in the mirror. The sun had already risen, and everyone was up. Danger hadn't snuck up on them during the night. He splashed water on his face. His eyes were bloodshot, and he looked as haggard as he'd ever been. Even counting his time in the army, and last year when he was shot in the gut.

Not surprisingly, his side throbbed at the thought. He grimaced and pressed a hand to his midsection. He thought back to the moment right after he'd been shot. His shooter leaned in, and as if his words would absolve him of his crime, he told Heath that Dad hadn't been drunk in the accident that killed a senator and his family. The accident for which his father had been blamed. That moment ripped through his thoughts, along with anger. With a killer on the loose and the cabin bombing and Harper's reappearance in his life, Heath had been forced to push aside his focus on finding the truth about Dad. But as soon as this was over, he would press Taggart again for answers. Heath could guess that the sheriff hadn't had time to work Dad's case either, like he'd assured Heath that he would.

He shrugged off the multiple issues pressing down on him. He had to finish cleaning up and get back out there.

Face the day.

Face Harper — an act he dreaded for no reason that made any sense. As he'd told her only two nights ago, right before he made the colossal mistake of kissing her, he wanted to be close to her and would have been there beside her through this with or without Taggart's request. He didn't regret sharing his true feelings.

But now Harper was leaving. That was what was best for her. And best for Heath.

He released an easy breath. Got his emotions under control.

He splashed more water on his face, then dried off. After combing his hair, he left the room.

Liam had left early this morning on his mission to discover the truth about John Smith. Heath hoped John and Donny were the same man, and then he could feel more confident that this case was closed.

Walking down the hall, he scraped a hand through his hair. Voices in the kitchen drifted toward him. Evelyn spoke. "My boy's coming home soon."

"That's wonderful news, Evelyn," Harper said. "I couldn't be more thrilled for all of you."

Should he tell Harper about John Smith?

Before he reached the kitchen, he hung back and lingered in the hallway to listen to the happy lilt to Harper's voice. Telling her now would make her fearful again. Plus, it could keep her from leaving. It was better to let her believe the evidence was lining up to close the case so she would feel free to let it go. Even if he planned to dig deeper after she left.

He would wait to see what Liam found out. No sense in telling her until then. Maybe it was their man, after all. Heath would be glad for that. Except . . .

He didn't want her to leave. But did he want her to stay?

Even if Heath truly wanted her to stay and could convince her to, she'd made it clear that she didn't want a relationship with him, and that thought brought all the sensations of their kiss rushing at him. He gritted his teeth and forced the overpowering feelings back into the shadows of his mind.

The timing couldn't have been worse. Someone was coming around the corner, and he couldn't exactly hightail it back to his room.

Harper ran right into him. She'd been caught off guard, and he gripped her arms to steady her.

"Oh, Heath. I'm so sorry. What are —"

"I was on my way to the kitchen." He smiled down at her, hoping to cover the truth.

That he'd been dreading facing her.

"Are you . . . all right?" She gazed up at him, and he could swear he saw that same longing in her eyes. That she had a thing for him too, despite her reaction to his kiss.

"Sure, I'm fine. Are you almost ready?" He would take her to talk to Sheriff Taggart like she'd insisted. She wanted to confirm the news that the killer had been found. Then on to the airport.

Harper would exit from his life forever. Because what were the chances she'd come back again and he'd run into her?

"Yes. Let me grab my things."

She rushed by him, leaving him wrapped in her citrusy scent.

He sauntered into the kitchen to grab coffee as if he hadn't drunk ten gallons of it during the night.

Evelyn's eyes sprang to life when she saw him. "Heath, I've got good news. Leroy's coming home tomorrow."

Lori turned from the stove where she was scrambling eggs and gave him her beautiful smile. "I've assured Evelyn that I can make accommodations for Leroy here. Anything you need from me, anything I can do, you let me know." Her deep Texas accent was thicker this morning. "Y'all are welcome to stay as long as you want. You don't have to leave simply because Harper's out of danger now."

She patted Evelyn's hand. "I know you two need to talk about what you're going to do. I'll give you some privacy. I need to talk to my assistant anyway." Lori turned off the stove and placed a lid over the pan. "The eggs will stay warm. Help yourself."

"Thanks, Lori." He poured his coffee as she left.

Evelyn sucked in a breath.

Heath cut her off. "I know what you're going to say."

"You do?"

"Of course." Unfortunately, he hadn't forgotten her words. Any of them. *"A beautiful woman out there is missing the chance to be loved by you. Please don't deprive her of that."* And *"You need to let the good Lord give you someone special, to have and to hold. To love."*

He slurped up the darkest coffee he'd ever tasted and thanked the good Lord that Lori knew how to make the brew. And that wasn't her only great quality. But no matter how kind or skilled Lori was, he couldn't make himself return her affection.

"You're going to tell me to pay attention to Lori. That she's been more than generous to us."

She nodded. "She has been, but that's not what I was going to say."

Befuddled, he angled his head and shook it. "Then what?"

"Lori is a good woman. I don't think you would be disappointed if you let yourself love her, true. Kindness runs to her bones, but she's smart enough to see that you only have eyes for Harper. Smart enough she doesn't want second best. And the rest of it is that we're not going to stay here one more day than necessary."

"Good. I'm glad you agree. I need to get back to my ranch. My home. Besides, I know the man for Lori." Sheriff Taggart. He had made that crazy trip out here to bring Liam when he could have sent a deputy. Lori hadn't been up at that hour though. Heath smiled to himself. He should have seen it before.

"That still doesn't fix your problem, Heath."

"I have a problem?"

"Sure you do. You can't let Harper leave."

CHAPTER FIFTY

Harper had come in to tell the sheriff goodbye and to see if he needed anything more from her before she left. Sitting here in his office now, she realized that stopping here on the way to the airport had simply been her way of stalling the inevitable.

I'm leaving Jackson Hole, never to return.

Because really, she couldn't see herself ever coming back to this place that held so many bad memories. Except not all of them were bad. Some memories included Heath, the sentinel who stood against the wall in the sheriff's office, arms crossed. Noble and strong. Trustworthy. A defender. Protector. Brilliant, soul-piercing blue eyes in an epic fantasy-hero face.

Her heart wouldn't be the same without him in her life.

Liam slipped into the office and stood

next to Heath. "I have some news you're going to want to hear."

Sheriff Taggart stood from his desk. "Well, let's have it."

"I don't think this is a good time, Liam," Heath said.

Harper stiffened. Heath didn't want her to hear what Liam had to say? Too late now.

"Sorry, bro," Liam said. "She's part of this."

Heath pursed his lips.

"I took the picture of Donny Albright to Chad. He said he doesn't think Donny is John Smith."

"John who?" She wasn't technically part of the official investigation team, but she tensed at the realization that she'd been left out of so much.

"I found a custom rifle maker who says someone was asking him questions about making the rifle in question with that particular scope. He told me the guy's name was John Smith. When I went back to talk to him this morning, he suddenly got his memory back. He'd made that rifle, after all."

The sheriff shook his head as if unconvinced. "There wasn't a registration number. If Chad made it, there should have been."

Liam crossed his arms just like Heath always did. "At first he insisted someone could have made it on his own. True enough. But Chad said that's his signature — that checkering. I admit that I let him think we knew he'd made it, so finally he confessed."

Pacing behind his desk, the sheriff was a man with too many people playing dirty in his sandbox. "You went back to see the gunmaker with Donny's picture without asking for the go-ahead."

"I didn't think I needed one. I don't work for you. And Heath is only —"

Heath's eyes grew wide and he subtly shook his head at Liam. "I apologize for my brother, Sheriff."

"Look, Taggart," Liam said. "The bottom line is that Chad made that rifle. And he didn't recognize Donny. Didn't think he was John Smith."

"Well, which is it? Surely he knows if it was Donny or not," Taggart said.

"Bring Chad in for a photo lineup, then." Liam paced Sheriff Taggart's office. "Or have him look at the body in the morgue. What about Harper? Has she been given the chance to confirm that Donny was the man she saw shoot the hiker?"

Harper covered her face. She couldn't

believe any of this.

"Since she didn't get a good look at him, I'm not sure it would make any difference. We have the images she took and we're analyzing those.

Heath had known about John Smith, and he'd kept that from her. He'd wanted her to go home to Missouri believing that they'd closed the case and that Donny was Sophie's killer, though he'd expressed his concerns.

"Let's have Chad confirm that the rifle we found at Donny's is the one he made for John Smith," Heath said.

The sheriff nodded. "That would be a step in the right direction. I'd like to know why Chad refrained from placing a serial number on one of his rifles for sale. He knows that's illegal."

"Uh . . . I believe that's why Chad wasn't initially forthcoming. He didn't engrave the required identifying information on the weapon, claiming he delivered it with an unfinished lower receiver. The client added the remaining parts, conveniently leaving off any identifying information. That's how these guys get around the law."

Sheriff Taggart swiped a hand down his face. "Let's get him to confirm the weapon, if he will."

"Did you find evidence that Sophie or her

husband, Chase, were ever inside Donny's cabin?" Heath asked.

"Nothing yet. Techs are still going over the house. It's clear we still have a lot of pieces to both find and fit together."

"True," Heath muttered.

Nausea swirled in her stomach. The shooter could still be out there somewhere. She'd wanted this to be over.

She glanced at Heath, unsure if she should be angry with him for keeping so much from her or understanding that he simply wanted her to go somewhere safe. He knew she wouldn't leave if she learned about John Smith. Now she better understood why he'd pressed her to go home.

"For now, Donny Albright is our *main* suspect. He had the weapon that shot and killed Arty in his possession. We'll either confirm he's our man or we won't."

"You mean you'll confirm he's your man with additional evidence beyond him possessing the weapon, right?" Heath cocked a brow.

"Don't worry, McKade, we'll tie it all together before it's over. A deputy's dead, remember? A woman's been murdered, and probably her new husband as well. We want the right guy to pay for his crimes." Sheriff Taggart's attention turned to Harper. She could almost shrivel at the look he gave her. What was that about? "This could take a long time. It's probably good that you're leaving today."

"I might hang around here, after all." There. She'd said what was really on her mind and in her heart. Not the way she'd intended, but it was out there. Heath's brow furrowed slightly.

"Well, you're free to go, if you so choose. We can contact you if we need you."

The sheriff clearly hoped to put this case behind him so he could work on solving who was behind the bombings. The state's findings had agreed with the fire chief's — the incident at Emerald M was created by an explosive device.

"I have an idea, Sheriff," she said.

"I'm not sure I want to hear it."

"It's easy to see you're shorthanded and you'd prefer if I headed home, far away from Wyoming. So here's my proposal. I'm going to stay. Heath doesn't need to watch me anymore. I don't believe that I'm in danger now. The guy is either dead or he's gone to a lot of trouble to make it look like someone else killed the honeymooners, meaning he doesn't want to draw unwanted attention by targeting me again. Besides, I'm no longer a threat to him. There's no reason for him, if he's still alive, to expose himself and commit another murder. If he does that, then he's setting himself up to be hunted again."

"Good point," Taggart said.

"Now wait a minute." Heath stepped between Harper and the sheriff.

"I heard you don't have a dedicated evidence photographer. How about I work for you as a crime scene photographer — any kind of crimes? I could work with Moffett. I could . . . freelance. Or maybe even *volunteer*?" She used her most lighthearted, cheerful voice.

What am I doing?

She'd been all set to go home today. She could even attend the gala Saturday night with Emily. Instead, she was asking for a job so she could stay? And for some reason . . . that decision felt like the right one.

"I'll keep that in mind." Taggart's cell rang and he glanced at the screen. He gestured for them to leave. "We're done here for now. Please stay out of trouble."

Great. She left the office with Heath and Liam with more questions than answers.

She strolled in silence with the two through the sheriff's office and out the front doors. Outside, they approached Heath's truck. Liam had parked across the street.

Clouds gathered to the northwest, dark and furious, forewarning of a violent thunderstorm. In contrast to the approaching storm, the sun blazed down on them from the southwest.

"Now what?" Heath stared at her, confusion apparent in his eyes.

Liam leaned against Heath's truck.

"I don't know," she said. She'd known exactly what she was doing this morning, and now?

"I was supposed to take you to the airport. Are you staying or are you going?"

"Well, Liam's news kind of changed all that. We don't know if Donny Albright or John Smith are one and the same. We don't know who killed Sophie. So . . . I'm staying."

"You could still go home, Harper. There's no reason for you to stay. You don't need me to watch over you. You made that case to the sheriff. You going home won't put Emily in danger. So why stay?"

Thick emotion edged his question. She tried to read his eyes, though they were hidden behind sunglasses. What did Heath want? Why was she so willing to change all her plans? Was it truly because of this new information?

I want to stay and see if we could have

something together. She'd been bold enough with her announcement that she wanted to work for the sheriff, but opening up to reveal the raw truth of her reasons wasn't easy.

"Okay. This is my cue to leave." Liam winked. "You two need to figure this out. In the meantime, I'm getting my gear from Circle S and heading home."

"Home?" Heath asked.

"Yep. Emerald M, here I come."

Heath visibly relaxed. He was worried about his brother and needed more time with him. She understood that. She remained concerned about Emily, but as her sister revealed, she had plenty of friends to help her. Harper felt certain Emily would encourage her to stay, just as she'd already done.

She drew closer to Heath. Breathed in the scent of woods and mountains that clung to him. Arms crossed, he raised a hand to lift his sunglasses. So he could study her better? And she looked into his eyes for an answer. For . . . something. She felt like an idiot now.

"When I first came here, I was still a mess," she said.

Heath grinned. She thought he might actually laugh. She gave him a friendly punch. "Listen, I'm being serious. I was on the last leg of this long trip to somehow get better." Afraid to see his reaction, she averted her gaze.

"And now?"

"The survivor's guilt that I couldn't seem to shake. The severe depression. It all stemmed from my inability to act when it was most needed. I see that now and I think I'm getting better."

"From where I'm standing, I would have to agree. You've even offered up your skills as a crime scene photographer to Taggart." That grin again. "I'm so impressed, so proud of you."

Oh. She could so stay here if he would give her a reason, despite the fact that she'd pushed him away. Told him that she couldn't be in a relationship. There was still that risk that Harper would end up alone, but the reasons for her resolve no longer seemed valid. Heath had protected her through this, and he was still alive and well. Still here to prove to her that her fears were unfounded.

Heath pressed his hand against the truck for support and leaned in close. Much too close. "But I need to know the *real* reason you're considering staying." His voice had a husky tone. The emotion coming off him rushed through her. "Is it because of us?"

She slowly nodded, but the words wouldn't come.

"With the way you reacted to my kiss, I didn't think there was a chance for us. At the time, I thought you were right to walk away. I've let too many people down. When I've tried to help people . . . let's just say it never ends well."

"But don't you see, Heath? I don't need your help. I need —" She stopped right there.

"What, Harper? What do you need?"

An explosion ripped the air.

Shook the ground.

Reverberated through Harper's bones.

Then . . . a *whoosh.*

Chapter Fifty-One

Harper's heart pounded. Her eardrums throbbed. Fear would choke her to death.

Heath's body pressed over her, protecting her as glass and debris showered them. The throbbing turned to sharp ringing in her ears and seemed to circle her whole head.

She couldn't move. Was it dead weight? Was Heath —

Oh, Lord, please . . . no . . .

Pressing her palms against the rough concrete, she pushed, but he was immovable.

"Harper, wait." His voice was raspy. Was he hurt? "Stuff is still coming down."

As if on cue, a chunk of wood slammed onto the pavement next to them.

Harper screamed.

Squeezing her eyes shut, she sent up a hundred desperate prayers for safety and protection. Several more seconds passed before Heath moved from his sheltering position, then assisted her to sit. No standing for either of them yet.

Waves of dizziness washed over her. Over and over. Comprehension eluded her. What? How?

"Are you okay?" Heath's words broke through her confusion, his tone gentle, raw. "Hurt anywhere?"

"No. Are you?"

He shook his head as he looked her up and down.

"Heath. Someone could need help. Others must be hurt." From between the two trucks, she couldn't see where the blast had occurred.

Sirens screamed. He hauled her to her feet. How come the blast hadn't seemed to affect him as much? Dizziness swept over her as she leaned against his truck.

"Are you guys okay?" Liam rushed up to them.

"I think so." Heath looked Liam over. "You?"

"Only because I hadn't gotten into my truck yet."

Harper glanced across the street. A large, flaming chunk of metal had crushed the cab of Heath's extra truck that Liam had been using.

"I'm going to see what I can do to help."

Liam took off.

Heath grabbed Harper and urged her toward the sheriff's department building. "I need to get you somewhere safe."

She resisted. Down at the end of the block, flames devoured what was left of the old train depot. "Heath, that building was locked up and empty, wasn't it?" Empty like Heath's cabin, though not nearly as remote. "So that would mean no one was inside during the blast. No one was hurt." She hoped and prayed that was the case.

"People who were standing anywhere nearby could be injured. The shockwave or shrapnel could have hurt them. We need to get checked out too."

"They need our help though."

The same crippling anguish she felt was reflected in his face. "Promise me you'll stay here."

He didn't wait for an answer but rushed off to assist a woman limping in the parking lot, tugging along her crying little boy.

Harper hurried to aid a man in his sixties who stood over a woman sprawled on the ground. A gash in her forehead oozed blood. Harper leaned over to assist. "Let's get you out of here. Away from the building."

"No, I'm okay."

With the man's help, the woman rose to her feet and leaned into him. "We're okay," he said to Harper. "I'll get her to the hospital. Don't worry about us."

Harper rushed to help anyone she could find. A crying woman. Two teenagers sitting stunned on the ground. She could do nothing more than make sure they weren't seriously injured, and reassure them.

She let her eyes scan the scene. The glass windows in the closest vehicles were shattered. Bystanders sat next to each other holding hands. Law enforcement and staff exited the sheriff's department building. People poured out of the burger grill across the street. Someone handed out plastic gloves to protect against glass. Employees from the local hotel only two blocks away were wrapping blankets around people. Volunteer fire trucks approached and emergency crews arrived.

A little girl cried. "My mommy. I can't find my mommy!" Harper lifted the girl into her arms. "Shh. It'll be okay. We'll find your mom."

Her heart pounded in rhythm with the girl's sobs.

She searched the tragic scene for a young mother. Harper spotted a woman lying next to a vehicle across the street. Unconscious?

Not wanting to scare the little girl, she approached the woman cautiously. What if she was dead? Holding the child, Harper crouched at the same moment the woman moaned and opened her eyes.

"Mommy!" The girl scrambled from Harper's arms.

"Careful now. I'm guessing your mommy has a concussion." Harper waited with them until a paramedic rushed forward to assist.

Harper made sure the woman was gripping the child's hand before she retreated to give the paramedic space to work.

Black smoke obscured the sky as a fire raged at the depot, joining the darkening clouds of the impending storm.

Huffing, Sheriff Taggart stepped in her path. "Harper, get your camera. Take as many pictures as you can. Take pictures of everything. The building, the flames, and the smoke. Everything. The people. Understand?"

"But I can't be impartial. I was near the blast."

"You're pulling that *now*? Come on, we were all near the blast in a manner of speaking. Everyone is going to be taking pictures, but I want the professional shots. It'll be hours before other agencies get here. Maybe not until tomorrow. I've contacted ATF as well as the Cody Bomb Squad, which is much closer. They're part of Wyoming Homeland Security Regional Response."

"What if it was only a gas leak or something?" she asked. He was scaring her.

"I wish I could believe that. In the meantime, we have work to do. Now I have to get busy setting up a command center. It's going to rain soon, so you'd better get busy. Are you with me?" Fury and desperation twisted his expression.

"Yes."

Shame at making him waste time infused her. She shook off the emotions, jogged over to Heath's truck and opened the door to grab her camera.

Harper came around the truck and began snapping pictures. She started by photographing the people, which she usually did last. Those helping and those injured. Those who were merely spectators. Sometimes the criminal returned to the scene of the crime, more often in arson cases, so the perp could be in the crowd. Did an explosion that ended in fire have the same dynamics as arson?

Had this been caused by a firebomb? Flames continued to raze the building as firefighters exited empty-handed.

Through her camera lens she could also

search for Heath. Where was he? What was he doing?

Was he okay?

Liam jogged up to her, breathless.

"I don't know where Heath is," she said. "He was helping people, but now I don't see him."

Harper pulled her gaze from the viewfinder to look at Liam.

Soot covered his face. "Heath. He's inside," he said. "He went inside the building to search. Someone told us they'd seen a woman go into the building to search for her child. I went in after him and tried to find him." He leaned over his thighs to catch his breath. "A fireman pulled me out."

Of course Heath would be driven more than most to save someone trapped in a fire. Harper almost crumpled at the news.

Instead, she propelled herself toward the building.

Chapter Fifty-Two

Flames licked the walls around Heath. He had precious minutes, if not seconds, left. The heat and toxic smoke could kill them both if he didn't get her out of here. They'd survived a second explosion near the front of the structure, but who knew if something else in this death trap would explode?

"I got you. You're okay." Heath hefted her up, bolstering her with his arm. She collapsed against him. He lifted her up over his shoulders like a firefighter is trained to carry survivors. Like Dad had shown them when they were kids.

The way he'd entered the burning structure was now an inferno. He'd have to exit the building through the back. He took the path of least resistance, praying this wasn't the road to death.

Images of the day a fire had razed his

childhood home and taken his mother from him fought for space in his mind. He couldn't let those memories shut him down, paralyze him, or he wouldn't make it out. This injured woman depended on him.

Lord, please let her live. Please let it not be for nothing. Please let us escape!

A door hung open at the back of the building. A break in the smoke gave him a window, literally. He could see through the window. Grass. Sky.

Freedom.

He felt a rumble in his legs. A portion of the ceiling collapsed, blocking his way.

CHAPTER FIFTY-THREE

Thursday, 10:44 A.M.
Downtown Grayback

"Heath!" Harper couldn't escape Liam's strong arms. "Let me go. What are you doing? That's your brother in there."

"Stop, Harper. I can't let you go inside."

"Don't you care about him?"

"He's my blood! Of course I care. But he would kick me to the other side of the state if I let you go in after him. You watch. Heath will be okay. He always is."

How could Liam believe his own words? How could he be so convinced as he said them? Her body refused to cooperate with her mind and her limbs went limp against him.

She couldn't help but think of the story Heath had told her about how he'd tried to go in to save their mother, but his father had prevented him.

Heath. There was so much she had yet to

say to him. She'd been about to lay it all out there when the explosion had changed all their lives forever.

While some firefighters held on to hoses and doused the flames, four others rushed from behind the depot, giving it a wide berth. Two carried a woman. Two practically dragged a coughing Heath.

Liam released her, and they both ran across the parking lot toward Heath. She could feel the heat from the flames. The men ushered Heath and the woman to an ambulance waiting nearby, and Harper and Liam followed.

Heath shrugged free and stood on his own. A fireman pressed an oxygen mask against his face. Heath sat on the edge of a gurney.

Heart pounding, Harper slowly approached. She wanted to berate him. To flail her fists at him. What had he been thinking, running into that burning building?

From the gurney where she lay, the woman he'd pulled from the burning building turned her head, her eyes blinking at Heath. Gratitude filled them.

A man approached, holding a child. The child she'd been looking for?

Harper ran her hand through Heath's soot-covered hair. She finger-combed it, black dust flaking onto his shoulders. Much too personal, but affection for him brimmed inside and it needed to go somewhere. His eyes smiled up at her.

"You're some kind of crazy," she said. *A hero.*

Liam — the one who had proclaimed that Heath would always be okay — stared at his brother as if contemplating the grief he would have experienced if Heath had not escaped. Her eyes burned with unshed tears.

"Harper!" Taggart called her name.

She turned to find him rushing toward her. "Glad to see Heath's okay. Now I need those pictures."

A raindrop plopped on her forehead. "Right."

The rain would help the firefighters as they battled what burned like it must have been napalm or an incendiary type of bomb. But the rain could be destructive to evidence, how well she knew.

Concern for Heath had distracted her, but now she had to leave him. "I have to get back to work." Harper leaned over and planted a kiss on Heath's forehead, then backed away. Behind the mask he protested her move to leave — he didn't want her to get hurt, she was sure. Maybe if he wasn't wearing the oxygen mask, she'd full-on kiss him in front of God and everyone.

She walked away and forced herself to focus. The scene was chaos at the moment. She knew how things went down. The sheriff's department would secure the scene. Scour the area for fragments. They would mark the fragments with numbered evidence markers. All of them working together, not just one or two techs. All this they would do while they waited for the ATF or the bomb squad or even the FBI if their involvement was warranted.

In the meantime, Harper would give her best. Her all. She hoped her photographs could be used to find the person behind this and convict them in a court of law.

Another drop plopped on her head, and then another, until the rain beat the pavement and sounded like sizzling bacon.

Again, she took photographs of the crowds. Despite the storm, few had left the scene — other than to be herded back as crime scene tape was put in place. The raw grit of destruction hit her in waves, but she remained strong, as if an invisible force stood with her.

She photographed the sheer relief and joy, capturing the emotion on camera. Her heart skipped a beat. That she was emotionally compromised would be all over these photographs. Harper hoped her photographic documentation would remain admissible in court.

In her peripheral vision, Harper caught a man laughing with tears of joy as he squeezed his teenage son to him, so she swung the camera to capture them. She needed the reminder that life existed everywhere around her too. Not only death and destruction. She'd come full circle in her journey to free herself from survivor's guilt. She had survived again. And that left her to pick up the pieces.

But this time, she wouldn't run away. She wouldn't turn away. She would embrace being a survivor because she could make a difference for the victims.

CHAPTER FIFTY-FOUR

All right, already.

He could breathe fine now. Heath shoved the mask away and sat up on the gurney. They'd pushed him inside the ambulance when the rain had started, but he wouldn't allow them to take him to the hospital. He needed to stay there.

"Thanks for your help. I'm good now. You guys go on and assist someone else." Heath read the EMT's name tag. Vince Saunders.

"The injured have already been assisted." Vince took the mask. "Most are on their way to the hospital or already there."

"Good. That's good. What about . . . did anyone . . . ?"

"So far, no one has died as a result of the blast."

"Also good." Relief rushed through Heath. He was proud to be part of this community that had responded so quickly and efficiently.

"You should see the doctor later," Vince said. "Get your lungs checked. Your ears too. I didn't see anything, but I'm no otorhinolaryngologist."

Heath stared at the man. "That's an awfully big word for this rancher deputy."

"Ear, nose, and throat doctor. The shock wave could have caused damage."

"I feel fine." He breathed in a pungent odor. "I smell like soot and ash. I can hear just fine now too, but I'll keep that in mind."

He hadn't been as close to the explosion as others. He would make sure Harper got checked out too. He left the ambulance to find the rain had paused, but thunder still rumbled as the storm moved through. He made his way to stand outside of the crime scene tape, letting his gaze roam the tragic scene. Where was Harper?

There. He spotted her. She was standing inside the tape taking pictures, her camera now on a tripod. They'd marked off an entire block. Maybe they should tape off the entire town.

He glanced up as a bolt of lightning struck a mountain peak in the distance as if cracking open the sky. A mere two seconds later, thunder confirmed the crack. Much too close for comfort. The storm wasn't done with them yet.

And the criminal behind the bombs? Was he done?

The abandoned building had been an eyesore. The Grayback town council had argued over repurposing it or establishing it as a historical site.

A chill crawled over him.

If the criminal responsible had truly been aiming to kill, he would have targeted a busy building. Why had he taken out the old depot?

What was happening to his town? To this valley? Acid could have burned a hole through his gut. He wanted to find whoever was behind this, but he'd have to get in line behind a lot of people, including Taggart.

He worried about Harper taking pictures. What if another explosive device was set to go off?

And Liam. Where was he? Heath figured he was assisting law enforcement or searching for answers in his own way.

Heath found his way to the command center set up beneath a big canopy where Taggart was in a heated discussion with a couple of deputies and first responders. Detective Moffett stood next to him. Grayback contracted with the sheriff's department for a dedicated law enforcement presence rather than allocating funds for a police department.

Taggart noticed him approaching. "What are you doing? You need to go to the hospital."

"They took care of me already. I'm good. What happens next?"

"We're going to tag evidence while we wait for the ATF. Nobody touches or moves anything. The FBI is watching. They may show up too. It's going to take them time to assemble and haul their mobile units to this valley. It's my job to contain the scene until the feds get here and decide it's their problem."

"You sound confident it will be," Moffett said.

"I have no theories right now. The fire chief is in charge of putting out the fire. Everyone has their jobs. Now get out there and photograph everything, video if you think it's important. Interview witnesses. Get to work."

Heath listened to Taggart rattle off instructions — this was every town's nightmare. Every county sheriff's worst-case scenario.

He once again spotted Harper in the distance, taking pictures. She wiped at her eyes.

His heart reached out as if he could pull her back to him. She was so beautiful. In her element. Doing what she was meant to do. But he worried about her — this woman he was falling for.

"If the feds are coming, and everyone is taking pictures, what is Harper doing out there?"

The sheriff leveled his gaze at Heath and put a hand on his shoulder. "I'm betting you and I are on the same page. I want the person responsible in a bad way. I won't be pushed out of the loop on the investigation. Harper is getting the images she can and giving them to me. I'll share them with other agencies, but I want them first."

"What you need is inside that burning building. Most of the evidence was probably destroyed in the fire."

"You never know what can be recovered. What the blast pattern can tell us. There's plenty laying around in the street and parking lot. We'll do what we've been trained to do, even though we hope to never have to use the training."

A few raindrops gave them warning. A guy rushed up with an umbrella to shield Harper's camera, then the rain started coming down in sheets. The wind whipped around and nearly took the canopy away. Harper headed over, covering the camera as she jogged.

Heath wanted to pull her into his arms.

Soaked, her hair was plastered to her head, and droplets ran down her face. He thought some of them might have been tears. Heath grabbed a towel some thoughtful volunteer had stacked on a table and handed it to her. She traded the camera for the towel, her sad amber eyes boring into Heath.

"Thanks." She wiped her face, dried her hair, then hung the towel around her neck. Her gaze shifted to Taggart, who studied her. "I need to go into that building when it's safe."

He nodded. "And I'd like you to do that. I doubt it will be safe enough for that to happen before other agencies get here. I'll see what I can do to get you in."

Moffett had lingered while others had gone to work. The detective's face remained passive, but perhaps she thought Harper was encroaching onto her turf. She usually took the evidence photographs for Taggart. Or maybe she would be happy to have someone with Harper's skills assist. Heath wished he could read her.

Harper gave a half smile. "Okay. Let me know if and when I can get inside. I missed my flight today, so I'm staying."

Taggart nodded. "We'll talk later about

your proposition."

Heath wrapped a blanket around her.

"Do you want the memory card now? I haven't had a chance to document the images in a photo log yet, which would be important if you intend to use them as evidence later."

"Keep the memory card safe and with you. Do what you need to do. If you get to take more pictures later, they'll be together. I'll be in touch to look at them later this evening. Understand?"

She nodded, a look of satisfaction on her face.

"You did good work, Harper," the sheriff said.

"How do you know? You haven't seen my pictures yet."

"Oh, I've seen your pictures, all right." The sheriff answered his cell, his brow furrowing.

Heath kissed the top of Harper's wet head. He couldn't help himself. As tragic as this was, at least there was something, some light to shine in the darkness.

CHAPTER FIFTY-FIVE

Thursday, 9:02 P.M.
Circle S Ranch

What seemed like a lifetime later had been only a few hours. The sheriff asked that anyone who didn't have to be out in public, remain at home. Law enforcement guarded the crime scene. The face of the small town of Grayback, the town Harper had known as a child growing up, had been changed forever.

With what had happened, everyone staying at Circle S Ranch had not made the move back to Emerald M yet. Liam had borrowed Heath's truck and hadn't returned with it, so Lori had brought Heath and Harper back to her ranch.

Just as well. With the day she'd had, Harper felt comfortable sleeping in the familiar bed in Lori's guest room. After she washed away the grime and dressed in sweats and a hoodie, she stared in the mirror. Exhaustion closed in on her from all sides. She hadn't been able to get rid of the tears or the anguish. A few bruises formed along her back and legs, adding to those still healing after her fall from the camper. At least she'd gotten the stitches removed. But all her injuries were a small nuisance compared to what she'd faced, what Grayback had faced today.

And Heath . . . Her heart bumped around inside her chest . . . Heath had been a defensive barrier, almost crushing her even as he saved her.

A memory, a brief moment destroyed by the explosion, coursed over the chaotic images pressing in on her.

"But don't you see, Heath? I don't need your help. I need —"

"What, Harper? What do you need?"

She'd been about to tell him what she needed.

And for the life of her, at this moment she couldn't remember what she'd intended to say. She really was shell-shocked. She sat on the edge of the bed, her hands clasped in her lap.

If only she could quiet her mind and think of something peaceful, like the national park pictures she'd taken, and let them replace the blast of images from today that still tormented her. And that was just it — Harper always let the images of crime get to her.

Her earlier conversation with Heath hardly mattered in the face of the explosion, but she wanted to remember what she would have said to him, given the chance.

Harper pressed her fingers to her temples. Heath.

Had she really decided to stick around for him? All her life she'd been too broken, too afraid to put her heart out there, but for the first time she thought she might be willing to take a risk with someone — not just anyone, but Heath McKade.

Harper shouldn't be thinking about that right now when people had been hurt and her thoughts and prayers needed to be with them.

But Heath could have been hurt too. He'd run into that burning building to save someone and could have died inside.

She had decided, despite it all, that she could risk loving him, but raw fear wouldn't so easily let go and now Harper second-guessed her decision to take that risk. Her hands shook. She couldn't get control of her breathing or her thoughts. Maybe it was simply the trauma of what she'd experienced today. Over the last several days.

A soft knock came at the door. "Harper? You okay in there?"

She lifted her head and walked to the door, the emotional pain so heavy, it felt physical. Rubbing her palms against her pants, she braced herself to face him. Opening the door, she looked into his concerned face. "I'll survive."

I usually do.

He frowned down at her as if trying to decipher her mood. Good luck with that. She wasn't even sure about it. But he said nothing. Awkward. "Heath, I —"

"Sheriff Taggart is sending Detective Moffett out here to see the images you took so far."

"All the way out here. Why don't we —"

"I don't know. And there's something else."

"What is it?"

"Evelyn is worried about you. Are you okay to come out to the kitchen and get something to eat? She and Lori made elk stew."

Her stomach was queasy at the moment. Could she even pretend to eat it? "It's kind of late. I'm not hungry, but I'll come out so Evelyn will know I'm okay. What about Leroy? I thought he was coming home today."

"Turns out he's going to stay with his daughter in North Dakota until he's completely recovered."

"Is Evelyn going too?"

"She was going to go for a few days to get him settled, but with what's happened, she wants to stay. Feels she needs to take care of us."

"She doesn't have to do that." Harper shut the door behind her and slogged down the hall after Heath. The aches were starting to get to her.

"She considers us family too."

Us? "Heath," she said softly.

He turned before the hallway opened up to the great room.

"Do you hurt anywhere? You went into that burning building. Did you get bruised or injured? How did you keep from getting burned?"

"Don't worry. I've been looked over by paramedics. I was in and out quickly and skirted the flames." He stepped closer, an unreadable emotion in his eyes. "I could have lost someone today. Like Liam. I could have lost you."

He held her gaze, a question in his eyes. Her brain still swam around in her head, unsettled and chaotic. She had no answers to his unspoken question.

The doorbell rang. "That would be the detective. I'll go let her in."

"I'll get the camera." Harper headed back to the guest room, where she grabbed the camera case and her laptop.

In the kitchen, she booted up her laptop. Detective Moffett looked rough around the edges like they all did. Only Harper and Heath remained in the room with her. Evelyn's stew warmed in the slow cooker.

"I told the sheriff I need to create the photo log. I usually do that at the scene and take my time," Harper said, "but the situation didn't allow for it."

"I'm sure that's fine. You know your stuff."

Harper waited while the images loaded, but she would keep them on the memory card too because that's what she would hand over along with the photo log.

"Where's your brother?" Harper asked Heath.

"I haven't seen him. He isn't answering his phone again either."

"Are you concerned?"

"I'm trying not to be. This is what he does. He could be following a lead and doesn't want to talk about it yet." Heath shrugged.

The memory card file came up. She clicked on the icon to open the file and let

Moffett view the images on her laptop. The trauma of the day washed over her in the emotions on the faces of the men, women, and children of Grayback.

Moffett blew out a breath. "It's going to take a long time to sort through it all. Too long."

"What about security cameras?" Harper said. "They could reveal who was coming and going."

"This isn't Boston or New York."

"So, what? You've got nothing?"

"I didn't say that. A fed is already here looking at whatever footage he can get. My hands are kind of tied right now."

"Is that why Taggart wanted you to look at the images here?"

Moffett nodded. "I'm going to need to take the memory card with me."

"First, I need to document the images. I'll work through them tonight. But Taggart wanted me to keep the card in case I'm allowed to take more pictures. He wants them all in one place."

Heath edged closer behind her. "It's true. I heard him."

Moffett shrugged. "Make me a copy, then."

Harper dug inside her gear bag, but this was her last memory card out of her camera pack. "I don't have another memory card. I'll come in tomorrow. Don't worry, you'll get the images."

After Moffett was long gone, Harper clicked on the images and enlarged each one of them, reliving all of it as she worked on the photo log, wishing she could have taken her time. But then, she would still be there at the scene taking pictures and documenting them. On the other hand, many of the images were time sensitive. The fire and smoke. The people.

Heath paced back and forth in the kitchen, drinking coffee and calling his brother.

"Are you going to torture yourself all night with that?" Heath's voice so near jarred her.

"Yes. I don't know why I do it. I relive the pain. I need to feel it again. Have you heard anything about anyone who was injured?"

He nodded. "Sure. Lori went up to the hospital. She's a volunteer. She texted me about the injured. It could have been so much worse. She took Evelyn with her to see Leroy."

That reminded her that Emily had texted a few times. Harper had sent her sister a quick text letting her know she was okay and would call later. Emily would be worried until she did. But she had to finish the log. It seemed strange that she needed to call Emily when she was supposed to have been heading back home today.

With today's incident, indecision paralyzed her. Now she wasn't sure what she wanted to do — stay or go. And if she left, she wasn't sure she would ever come back. She wanted to have made her decision before she talked to Emily, but she grabbed her phone and texted that she was all right. That she had taken pictures and would call later.

"I think I'll have some stew, after all. I need fuel to get me through this." When Harper settled back at the table with a bowl of stew, she focused on documenting the best she could while she ate. The stew was rich and warmed her insides, even after she finished.

Heath pulled out the chair next to her, sat, then urged it closer. He grabbed her hands and held them between his bigger, callused ones. "I'm worried about you."

She tried to gently free her hands, but he wouldn't let go. And maybe his holding on was what she needed at the moment. She was floating around and needed Heath to ground her.

One of the images caught her attention, drawing her thoughts away from Heath. She freed herself from him to focus on her laptop.

"What is it?"

"I don't know," she said, magnifying the image. "Some of the photos remind me of my mother."

"What? How so?"

"She kept articles on a bomb. I think it killed someone close to her. Right before Dad died, they fought about it. Mom was upset. We were kids, and the only thing that bothered me was their fighting. I didn't even think about the bomb. But now I see how devastating this is to a community. Even if no one dies." She looked at Heath. "He's going to do it again, isn't he?"

CHAPTER FIFTY-SIX

Friday, 1:30 A.M.
Circle S Ranch

Driving Heath's truck, Liam parked in front of Lori's chalet — the only way Liam could think of it — and tried to slip inside without disturbing anyone. His boots — yeah, he'd given in and gotten a pair to replace his sneakers so he could fit in — creaked across the wooden slats of the porch. Something caught the corner of his vision.

Heath was sitting on the front porch.

In the dark.

Rocking.

Liam chuckled. "You really should get married and have kids." He sat in the rocking chair next to Heath and rocked too. Good memories flooded him for a change. He'd always loved rockers when he was a kid. "That way, you'll have someone else to sit up and wait for instead of me."

His brother released a heavy sigh. "There

was a bomb today. You disappeared. Can't blame me for being worried, can you? And what do you think they make cell phones for? Why do you even carry one if you're not going to answer it?"

"I was in the hospital. The signs say not to use your cell." It was a good enough excuse.

"What? Why were you there?"

"Well, first, I was checking the perimeter of the bomb scene with other deputies. They shooed me away — official business and all that — but I canvassed the area. Looking. Watching. Sometimes those responsible will hang around to watch."

"See anyone suspicious?"

"Not that I noticed, but I did see Pete in the hospital. He was being treated for an injury related to the bomb."

"What? Why didn't you call me? I would have come up to see him."

"I offered, but he didn't want me to call anyone. Besides, I was sitting in the truck when I saw him leave the hospital. He isn't there anymore. We should head back to Emerald M as soon as possible."

"I don't know. The state came back to look more closely before the bomb in Grayback, and now the feds are going to want to look at my cabin."

"How's Harper?" He was surprised she wasn't up with Heath, still looking at the images she'd taken. Or maybe she had already handed those over to the sheriff.

"Exhausted. She finally went to bed a few minutes ago. She's been up working on documenting the images from today."

"So what happens now, Heath? She was taking pictures today. Offered to stay and work as a crime scene photographer. Kind of eerie that all that happened right before the bomb."

He scowled. "Make your point."

"I thought she was leaving. Is she staying or going?"

"I'm not exactly sure what's going on in her head."

"What do *you* want, Heath? Do you want to make a life with her?"

"I thought I wanted her to stay, which, on the one hand, is selfish of me. She acted like she wanted to stay . . . for us. But that was before the bomb today. And I think she let the pictures get to her, so I don't know where her head is. Or her heart." Heath sighed. "She's a natural, Liam. You should have seen the pictures she took."

"Did you?"

"Yeah. Moffett came out to look at them. It's too chaotic out there now, and Taggart wants to hold these close for some reason. But Harper" — Heath stared off in the distance and shook his head — "she kept looking at pictures. She let the scenes, the tragedy, get to her. It tore me up seeing her like that."

"Maybe she's too sensitive. Isn't calloused enough for a job like that."

"I understand now why the events of her childhood, along with years on the job, brought her down. If she insists on working as a crime scene photographer, I don't know if I'm the one to ride those waves with her."

And that's exactly why Liam stayed away. He was more like Harper than he wanted to admit. Working for the DEA had hardened him in some ways and left him broken in places he'd prefer remain intact.

"She wants to go back to take more pictures tomorrow," he said.

"That's not happening. I saw the ATF and FBI Mobile Command vans. They're already here. Seems like someone put a rush on it."

"Wow. Didn't take them long to decide this wasn't merely a gas explosion." Heath blew out a long breath again. "In that case, she might very well head back to Missouri. She has some big event she had hoped to attend with Emily. I'll encourage her to go."

"Go with her."

"What? I can't do that. I'm needed here."

"I'm telling you that you should go to the event with her, Heath. Whisk her off her feet. Be her prince charming. I'm the last one to offer romantic advice, but you're my brother. I love you and I want to see you happy. It's . . . I have a feeling about this girl for you. Don't you?"

"Yeah. Yeah, I do."

"So what are you going to do? I recommend surprising her with tickets to the event. Maybe airline tickets too. That way, she can't possibly say no."

Heath arched a brow. "I look forward to hearing about where you learned how to be such a romantic."

Liam wished he hadn't said anything to set off Heath's radar. He pursed his lips, waiting for Heath's response.

"I'll think about it. Satisfied?"

Good. Liam nodded, glad the matter was settled.

"I found something else out today. Something Taggart is going to want to know — but it's not related to the bomb. He's going to be distracted. But maybe you can ask him if you can investigate as long as it doesn't interfere with you attending that event with Harper and making it special."

Heath gave him an odd look as if he didn't know Liam at all. There was much Heath didn't know about him.

"What is it?" Heath asked.

"Chad contacted me. John Smith inadvertently left his address."

Liam dug the paper out of his pocket and handed it over.

Shock rolled through Heath.

CHAPTER FIFTY-SEVEN

Friday, 2:45 A.M.
Circle S Ranch

"I know it's late, and I'm sorry."

Lying in bed, she held the cell away from her while Emily gave her an earful. Harper couldn't blame her sister for being upset. A text wasn't always enough. Harper had been exhausted after a day that included documenting images until well after midnight, and had forgotten to call Emily.

She'd woken up suddenly with the thought. "Are you done yet?"

"No. I could keep going."

"I can only say I'm sorry so many times." Harper shifted her pillow.

"I'm good with you saying you're sorry at least once more. And it's not late, it's early."

"What? Oh, right. I'm sorry I didn't call you back, but I was busy." Harper explained everything that had happened.

Emily gave a heavy sigh. "I wish you

hadn't been there, Harper. I'm so, so sorry you had to go through that. Are you okay?"

"I'm fine. A little scratched is all." She huffed a laugh. "New scratches to add to the old ones. At least I got my stitches out." But Harper understood Emily's question went deeper. "I'm sorry it happened, and yes, I'm fine. Sheriff Taggart asked me to take pictures, and I did my best. It felt good to be back, even though I'm still working through the pain of what happened. But it's late, and I should get some sleep. I might have to take more pictures."

"Okay, but before you go, I need to ask you a favor."

Uh-oh. "What is it?"

"I can't stop thinking about Uncle Jerry."

Harper tensed. She had a feeling she knew where this was going. "And?"

"He told us to come back to see him. You're still there, Harper. Will you please stop by? Try again?"

"If this is so important to you, why didn't you stay?"

Another sigh. "You know why I couldn't. I mean, I didn't know it was going to bother me so much. And now, he could have been in town and gotten hurt in that bomb, Harper. You should check on him. Besides, he's sick. Maybe we can plan a trip back to see him later too."

"Why is it so important to you?" Shame engulfed her. "I'm sorry. I should be more concerned about him." But she'd had a feeling he wasn't part of their lives for good reason, and nothing about that had changed.

"He's our only living relative — at least that we know about. And until this week, we didn't even know he was alive. Why didn't we know that he was alive and living in the old house? Aren't you curious why he and Mom weren't close?"

Harper closed her eyes, exhaustion winning the battle in her mind. "Okay. I'll try. But I can't promise. I don't know if I'll have time. The sheriff could want more pictures, and I want to be there if he does." Images flooded her mind.

Her pictures had captured the unexpected event forever on camera and, unfortunately, in her mind.

CHAPTER FIFTY-EIGHT

Friday, 9:02 A.M.
Bridger County Sheriff's Office

Harper recognized and accepted that she had been shut out of taking part in this bomb investigation since all manner of federal and state law enforcement had arrived. Fine by her. She definitely didn't want to be in the middle when it hadn't even been decided who would lead the investigation.

"Taggart's not here," Heath said. "We'll have to see if we can catch up to him at the scene."

"That won't be easy," Liam said.

"I want to go ahead and give the memory card to Meghan, if I can find her." Harper left the men and pressed her way down the hallway and into the cubicle area, searching for Meghan. She found her in the back corner.

Meghan blinked up at her. "Harper. Hey."

430

She held out her hand. "Do you have it?"

Harper nodded and handed over the memory card.

"Thanks. You can have a seat here next to me. I'll download these to a hard drive and make a backup copy. What we need is an audit log system so we can track what happens to the images, but we're not there yet."

"I emailed you my log to go with the photographs."

"Thanks. I got it."

"I did my best to make sure they could be used as evidence documentation, if needed. What I really need is to get back out there today. Yesterday was chaotic. I was rushed."

Meghan smiled, then lowered her voice and looked over her shoulder. "I know he was glad to have someone with your skill level available for the pictures."

Then she pulled up the images on her computer as she downloaded. "This is much more than crime scene photography." Tears choked Meghan's words.

"How could I be impartial?" The scene was still playing out. People were still suffering.

"You're truly gifted. You captured the emotions too. I . . ." Meghan's eyes teared up. "I wasn't there. I didn't realize . . ."

Harper understood the deep emotional

impact the pictures had on Meghan. This was her town, after all, and someone had committed the worst kind of crime against it.

"Oh, Harper." She pressed a hand against her arm. "And you were out there when the bomb went off, but you weren't hurt?"

Unable to speak, she shook her head. *Heath protected me.* What if he had died and she had survived? Those words remained at the edge of her mind and heart. "I'm okay."

Heath found her in the cubicle. "Sheriff Taggart called and asked me to look into something. Are you okay to stay here for a while?"

She nodded. "Sure, Meghan and I can work on this."

His features grim, he nodded and left her. She watched Heath — part rancher, cowboy, and deputy — head out. Would Sheriff Taggart offer her a job and give her a legitimate reason to stay? He'd asked her to take these photographs and she wasn't entirely sure if she was getting paid, but she would have taken them anyway.

She zeroed in on Meghan's computer.

Once the images from Harper's camera were downloaded, Meghan skimmed through other pictures to file away. Images that others had taken.

"These are from everyone else who was out tagging evidence, scraps, things to identify the explosion pattern. So much to look at, and it's going to take a lot of people. They've set up in the conference room to start, but they're going to be moving everything to the high school gym."

"What do they know so far?"

Meghan shrugged. "They don't tell me anything. I don't think the state or the feds are going to share with Sheriff Taggart either, even though they claim to want to work together."

"That's why he wanted me to grab as many pictures as I could. He doesn't want to be out of the loop. Wait." Harper leaned in. "Can you magnify that fragmented piece of pipe?"

Meghan nodded. "Okay, it's magnified. What are you looking at?"

"Are those . . . initials carved into it?"

"I don't know. It looks like P. L." Meghan gasped. "I stayed up late last night researching bombings. Domestic terrorists. I hope that's not what this is. One guy supposedly put what authorities believed were initials in his bombs. They called him the Firebomber. Sometimes he purposefully misled them with false clues, so they never caught him. This could be nothing, but I need to tell the sheriff."

Harper knew a P. L. — Pete Langford. But it couldn't be Pete. She wouldn't let herself believe that. She would mention it to Heath — he was a deputy, after all.

To warn him.

"Meghan." A woman approached the cubicle. "The fingerprint reader is broken. And Moffett's two-way radio is only one way."

Meghan nodded. "Okay, I'll be right there." With a resigned sigh, she handed over Harper's memory card. "Listen, I have a ton of work to do. I wish I could let you help, but beyond what you've already done for us, there's nothing I can have you do unless the sheriff okays it."

"I understand." Harper wished she was officially hired so she could be working too. At the moment, she felt completely useless. "Thanks."

"I'm one of only two IT people here at the department, which means I get to work on anything with an electronic pulse, including radios and fingerprint readers. I'd say you could wait here, but you're not an employee, so . . ."

"It's okay."

"But I'm sure you're fine to hang out in the kitchen. Get some coffee." Her eyes lit up. "And maybe some donuts."

"I'll be fine." She followed Meghan out into the hallway, then stopped at the kitchen, where Meghan left her. She'd have to wait to mention what she'd seen to Heath. He might not like her suggestion that Pete had anything to do with the bombs. All she needed now was a task to keep her from going crazy. Harper knew just the thing, though she dreaded going back.

Chapter Fifty-Nine

Friday, 10:45 A.M.
Uncle Jerry's House

Heath steered all the way up the drive this time. His gut tensed. "What is Lori's SUV doing here?"

Liam unbuckled. "I guess you could ask her."

Lori and Harper stood on the porch. Lori waved and smiled.

Heath's gut soured. He didn't like this. Not one bit.

He'd intentionally left Harper in the dark about their visit to her uncle while they followed up on this lead. The sheriff had given him the go-ahead to question the man about the rifle. Heath suspected he was quick to agree in order to get Heath off his back as he prepared for a press conference. All eyes were on the small town now. Heath was happy to be out of that circle and out of the spotlight should someone try to ask him about his cabin.

The old red truck that had been here last time was gone. Heath climbed out as Harper and Lori stepped from the porch. Heath contained his anger. "What are you doing here? I left you with Meghan at the sheriff's office. You said you were okay to stay there for a while."

"You're not officially protecting me anymore, remember? And I thought you were going to check on something for Sheriff Taggart. I didn't think you'd mind."

He eyed the house. "So is he home?"

"Nobody answered. His truck isn't here. I can only assume he's gone. What are *you* doing here?"

Should he tell her the truth? He hadn't wanted to share the news until they knew if there was an actual connection. If it even mattered. Heath drew in a breath.

Liam stole the words. "The custom rifle maker gave us this address for John Smith." He hesitated, then said, "Your uncle could be John Smith."

Harper frowned. She took in Liam's words as if he spoke in a different language, and then her eyes moved to Heath. "What is he saying?"

"You heard him. I didn't tell you because I wanted to check it out first." He hadn't been concerned that she would come back. She'd seemed so dead set against it.

She crossed her arms. "My uncle is not this John Smith guy you think could be the killer. I don't believe that."

"Well, let's prove that you're right." He loathed putting that hurt in her eyes. Though she hadn't known her uncle growing up, no one liked to think a relative would try to murder them.

"Even though he isn't here, we could still look around the place," Liam said.

"We stopped by to ask him some questions," Heath said. "We can't illegally enter the yard looking for evidence."

"No, but those woods surrounding the house are public lands. National forest," Liam said.

"How do you know?" Heath asked.

"The private property signs for one thing," Liam said.

"He's right." Harper's frown had deepened.

"We can walk all the way around the house in the woods and look for evidence. Maybe we'll see something in plain view that will give us probable cause. I really think we should have tried for a warrant." Liam left them to explore the woods near the house.

"I'll get my camera," Harper said.

Heath wasn't sure that was a good idea. This guy was a relative. Add to that, her father had been murdered on this property. She probably wasn't the best person to take pictures. There wasn't any way she could be impartial, but he also understood her need to take them. No matter what. And he wouldn't stand in her way.

"If y'all don't mind," Lori said, "I'm going to wait in the Navigator, where it's cooler and possibly safer."

"I'll bring Harper, Lori. You can go on home."

Lori eyed Harper. "I'm happy to wait for you."

Harper shook her head. "It's okay. Thank you for bringing me out here."

Lori winked, waved, and climbed into her vehicle. Then she started it and drove away.

Harper hiked next to Heath. He wished she would have gone with Lori.

"So, what if he is John Smith?" she asked. "That doesn't mean he killed Sophie. I can't believe it. That would mean he tried to kill me too."

Exactly what he was thinking.

"It doesn't make sense."

Heath understood why she refused to believe her uncle had anything to do with

439

the crimes. He was still her mother's brother, albeit a man her mother clearly hadn't gotten along with.

From the woods behind the house, Harper peered through her camera. "I told myself I would never come back here. That I would look at those pictures I took if I thought I wanted to come back."

"So why *did* you come back?"

"Emily asked me to. She felt guilty about leaving, I guess. And I felt guilty about not being concerned about our uncle. I knew she wouldn't leave it alone, so when I was cut loose from Meghan, I called Lori. She's always there to help."

Yep. That was Lori.

"Even so, you don't have to be here now. You don't have to take pictures. He's not home. You can tell Emily you tried."

"It's okay." She lifted her chin.

"I wish he were home. Questioning him would be better than slinking around in the woods behind his house." Images remained fresh in his mind — Heath, Harper, and Arty hiking in the woods.

Arty in a pool of blood.

Heath concentrated on the woods around them.

"We could wait on him," Harper said. "He mentioned he wasn't feeling well. I got the

440

impression he was sick. I mean, really sick. He probably won't be gone long."

Heath stuck close to Harper as they roamed the woods near the house. The man hadn't kept the place up. This home was nothing like Donny Albright's.

"I don't think the house has been painted since we lived here," she said.

"Hey, you two, over here," Liam called from closer behind the house.

Crouching, he studied the ground.

Next to him, Harper took more pictures. "Shells. So what?"

"This cartridge is specifically designed for a Remington 7mm Magnum rifle," Liam said.

"So?" Heath asked. "How many people shoot that same kind of rifle?"

"I'm not sure what the percentages are, but considering this is John Smith, we need to go with this. I know you don't want to —"

"It could be a coincidence," Harper said.

"Or this could be our guy," Heath said. "There has to be a target out there somewhere. Let's see if we can find bullets. We can let ballistics figure this out."

"How about a warrant to go into the house?" Liam asked.

Heath frowned. "The sheriff has his hands

full. They all do. I want to bag those shells for evidence, but not until they're photographed as such. So we touch nothing. Hear me? This is all in plain view, so there's nothing illegal about finding this evidence."

Heath glanced at Harper, hating what this was doing to her. "You okay?"

She nodded. He didn't believe her.

"He's an old, sick guy. He couldn't have done any of it."

"You can't see him in the hat, holding the weapon? Killing her?" Liam leveled his gaze. "Or you don't want to see it."

"Liam. Enough!"

Her mouth formed an "O" as she blew out a steady breath. "I want to take pictures, but I'm not working for Sheriff Taggart. Not officially. And it's not a crime scene yet, but you think it will be?"

"I think we have enough to get a warrant." Liam crossed his arms. "But I'm like Harper. I don't work for the sheriff's department either, except, as he loosely termed it, as a law enforcement consultant. So what do you want to do, Heath?"

Heath only shrugged. He got that Liam had a feeling about her uncle. He could be wrong. Let him be wrong.

"I'm worried about him, Heath," she said. "He was sick the other day. Wasn't feeling well. Maybe he's hurt or too sick to answer the door."

"His truck is gone. He's not here."

"You can't know that," she said.

"I'm thinking exigent circumstances," Liam said. "If he is the murderer, he could be out there killing someone else at this very moment — the public could be in danger. So there. Exigent circumstances."

Heath eyed his brother. "Done this often, have you?"

Liam shrugged. "You can call someone to get us a warrant. As for me? I don't like to think a murderer is running around loose, believing that he framed some other guy and we bought it. I mean, the sheriff bought it."

"Look," said Harper, "I can't believe Uncle Jerry is the shooter. Just like you're not going to believe it when you hear that Pete Langford could be the bomber."

CHAPTER SIXTY

Friday, 11:45 A.M.
Uncle Jerry's House

Sitting on the porch of the home where she grew up, Harper could feel the national forest seemingly close in on her. Locusts buzzed, oblivious to her presence. Heath hadn't appreciated that her mind had immediately gone to Pete when she'd seen those initials in the pipe. But she knew he would talk to the sheriff about that too. What would happen? Was the law coming down on his ranch right now in search of Pete? She couldn't be the only one to think of him, what with that bomb at the ranch. At least they weren't there at the moment.

No. They were at her old house. She wished she hadn't come back today, after all.

She shouldn't be sitting there if Uncle Jerry was a murderer because she could potentially destroy evidence. But this wasn't an official crime scene. So she was going to sit on the porch if she wanted to, because . . . no.

Just, no. He wasn't.

How many times had she lounged on this porch growing up? Listening to the sounds of the woods? Unaware that her familiar home and the life she'd known would be ripped out from under her in one fateful moment.

All the energy had long ago drained from Harper. What were they even doing here, looking at her old house like it could be a crime scene?

They couldn't wait here forever for a warrant to come through, or for Jerry Johnson to show up. *Where are you, Uncle Jerry?*

She leaned back on her elbows on the edge of the porch, her feet on the steps, and heard a creak behind her. Harper peered over her shoulder.

Hmm. The door had cracked open — a shift in the wind? Pressure on the porch enough to ease it open? Before Heath had driven up and drawn her attention away from the house, she'd rung the doorbell but hadn't actually knocked. Maybe it hadn't been closed all the way to begin with? Harper stood and approached. She glanced at the others. Heath was on the phone trying to get someone onboard for a warrant to search the house. Liam was casing the forest, looking for those bullets shot from the rifle.

Everyone was preoccupied. Too much was happening all at once, and now she wished she'd gone with Lori.

What if Uncle Jerry was hurt? His truck could be in the shop, for all she knew. Gently, she stood up, pushed open the door, and stepped inside.

"Uncle Jerry?"

She was his niece, after all. She was worried about him, truly she was.

Once she was inside the home, there was no turning back. Memories flooded her. The good ones and the bad ones. Momma and Emily. Daddy sitting in his recliner after work, watching the news.

Mom and Dad fighting. They loved each other — Harper knew that — but they argued more often than not. An old musty smell accosted her, that and too many dirty clothes and dishes. She crept forward across the creaking, scratched wood floor.

She shouldn't be in the house. Harper knew that she shouldn't be intruding, but an invisible force was compelling her forward in search of Uncle Jerry. Or . . . . truth.

"Uncle Jerry?" Now that she was inside,

the house had an empty feeling. She sensed that she was alone. That he wasn't lying on the floor unconscious or injured.

What if he came home and found her here? Would her presence in his home affect any evidence against him if he was the killer?

Why was he living here? Why did Mom tell them she had sold the place without any mention of him? Or had he bought it from someone else? She crept forward, a force driving her as if she were Emily the mystery writer in search of answers about what had happened that night. In search of answers about who had killed her father. But she wouldn't find them here and now.

If only she had looked to see who had shot her father before she'd hidden away. But maybe it was like Heath said, and she would have been killed too if she had seen the person who killed her father.

Since the incident that night long ago, Harper had so many unanswered questions. Too many fuzzy memories. At the end of the hallway, a door was closed.

Her old room where she'd hidden and cowered under the bed as she stifled her sobs for fear the shooter would come for her too.

If she opened it and went inside, would the memories drive her to her knees in anguish? Would being in her room serve as a traumatic stressor and send her back to the place she'd fought to escape? Or maybe she would remember something she'd forgotten that night — a memory she'd shoved deep inside.

Despite the dread creeping up her spine, Harper continued forward down the narrow hallway. No family photos remained on the walls, though now that she thought about it, she distinctly remembered that her mother had left pictures on the walls the day they'd moved.

Harper had never once wondered what had happened to the things they had left behind. She had assumed that, somehow, her mother had taken care of it all.

At the door, she pressed her hand against the old, splintered wood. She gasped as a memory flooded her mind. Daddy's words that night. *"I know what you did."*

A lump filled her throat. All she had ever remembered was the shot fired and her father dropping to the ground. Never the words — until this moment.

And if she entered the room, would she remember more?

Harper pushed the door open and stepped into a room that looked nothing like her old bedroom. Workbenches and machines took up the space. Rifles and gun barrels. Black powder. Supplies for making bullets.

Harper covered her mouth. *So he's a hunter. He makes his own rifles. So what?*

Heath stepped up behind her. "We have a warrant. Taggart told us to go in. I think you found what we came for." He turned her to face him and gently gripped her shoulders. "This doesn't mean he's the killer, Harper."

"But" — she pointed to a hiker's pink backpack — "it's not looking good."

"I don't think the sheriff wants you in here. The truth is, I don't want you here either. You're too close to this. Detective Moffett is on her way."

She nodded in full agreement. "This used to be my room."

"You shouldn't have come inside. I'll escort you back to the truck. I could sit with you until Moffett arrives and then I'll take you back."

"No, it's okay." She handed the camera over. "You take a few for me."

Nausea erupted, and Harper fled the room. She wished now that she'd gone back with Emily. This was too much. Before exiting the house, she hesitated. She had to see Mom and Dad's old room. A quick peek. Had to be Uncle Jerry's room now.

She made her way down another short hallway and stepped through the open door.

Liam stood in the middle of the room. Arms crossed, he stared at the walls, which were covered in diagrams and newspaper clippings. In addition, supplies were scattered on a table at the far end. Pipes. Gunpowder. Fuses.

Liam looked at the walls. "What *is* this?"

"I know exactly what it is. My mother has some of the same clippings in a shoebox. This bombing happened right before Daddy was killed. I never understood why they argued about it, but it tore them apart, I think."

Harper took a closer look. Bomb-making instructions were spread out on another table. "What — is he trying to become some kind of copycat of the Firebomber in targeting the train depot and Heath's cabin?"

"Could he actually *be* the Firebomber?" Liam asked. "As far as I know, the FBI never found him."

She eyed photographs of selected parts and supplies that presumably were used to make a bomb. "I think we should get out of here. He's gone. Maybe it's a trap. He'd wanted us to come back to see him." What kind of sick psychopath was her uncle?

"You're right. We'll let the powers that be

know about what we found. The only thing missing is the man behind the bombs." Liam followed Harper out of the room, down the hallway, out the door, and onto the porch. Harper kept going. Marching. Hiking. She had to get as far away as she could.

Uncle Jerry had not only tried to kill her, but it looked like he was a domestic terrorist. And he'd been using her old house as his command center. On his cell, Liam stopped next to Heath's truck. Heath jogged toward her. She stopped where the drive met the road.

Heath's boots crunched as he jogged, and then he slowed and stepped up behind her. "They had actually taken Pete in for questioning, but I told them what we found. They'll be here soon, Harper. Let's get you away from this before they get here. I know they'll want to question you since he's your uncle, but that can come later."

"It all makes sense now," she whispered to herself.

"I'm so sorry."

"That night, Dad said, 'I know what you did.' And someone killed him. Momma took us away, and she was devastated about Dad's death, but her friend . . . the one who died from a bomb blast. Maybe it wasn't a friend, but instead it was her brother, Jerry, who had died to her, though he was still very much alive. Maybe she had discovered her brother was the Firebomber and Dad had confronted him and was murdered for it."

"Come here." Heath turned her to face him, then pulled her to him.

"But this. Those walls in the bedroom. It's like a memorial to the Firebomber."

"I think it's more than a memorial, Harper. It's a game plan."

CHAPTER SIXTY-ONE

Friday, 5:25 P.M.
New Base of Operation

The judge's timetable had been shredded, but he was nothing if not flexible, and his plans were coming together regardless. Knowing this was the end, knowing he'd never have to feel this sick again, gave him the strength to finish. To follow through with his big plans. Some practice had been in order.

The mailboxes. The irony — he'd gotten the idea to die on his own terms from those kids who'd blown up his mailbox.

Then he'd needed something bigger — that cabin belonging to McKade, then the train depot.

He would push through to the finish. This would be like old times. They hadn't stopped him before, and they wouldn't stop him now.

He would go out with a bang, and they

would pay with their lives this time.

He had a long night ahead of him, if he was going to keep his schedule. Nothing like a big event to go out in glory. He'd collected everything he needed months ago. Working in the shadows with only a flashlight, he kept up the pace, ignored the pain. It wouldn't last forever, and he'd made it this far.

As he prepared his work of art, he thought back to that moment he opened the door to see the photographer standing on his porch.

There she stood — she and her sister, claiming he was their uncle. He hadn't realized the photographer was one of Leslie's girls when he'd tried to silence her. He should have seen the resemblance sooner.

He'd told them he wasn't feeling well, and at the realization of who the photographer was, he'd gotten sicker than ever. He wasn't sure what he thought about the fact that he had any feelings at all. Emotions. Remorse. Regret.

Those could destroy his mission. His cause. He'd let his cause languish as he laid low for far too long.

And now thanks to what he'd discovered in the camper while it was still in one piece, it was as if Providence had shined down on him and he'd found a fitting place to make his last stand.

CHAPTER SIXTY-TWO

Friday, 6:37 P.M.
Circle S Ranch

Harper hardly cared that the man who had tried to kill her was still alive. Heath claimed she could still be in danger, but Uncle Jerry had framed someone else to take the blame as soon as he learned Harper was his niece. With the shooter identified, Uncle Jerry would have no need to take Harper out. Case closed. Harper believed that to her core. Her dad's murder, however, happened under a different set of circumstances, and she suspected her uncle was responsible for that as well. Regardless, she was but one person in danger of losing their life at his hands.

Dazed and wrapped in a western-styled quilt, Harper nestled on the sofa and curled her hands around a hot mug of chamomile tea, compliments of Lori.

"I know you can't wait to get home and

feel safe. Put this nasty business behind you." Lori offered her a concerned, genuine smile.

When Harper didn't reply, Lori continued. "Do you need anything else, hon?"

"I'm good." Harper didn't want or need the pampering, but Lori was a nurturer and needed to give Harper attention.

"Okay, then. I'll give you some time and space. I'll be close if you need me."

Harper held the pain at bay, enough so that she could offer Lori a soft, reassuring smile to ensure that the woman would, in fact, give her time and space. Lori walked away, leaving Harper in peace and quiet. In grief and shock.

A contingent of law enforcement — state and federal — had taken over the home where she grew up. They had also seized her camera to be returned at a later date. Or never. The FBI had arrived in full force to evaluate the explosion in Grayback and at Heath's ranch too. This domestic terrorist — the Firebomber — had eluded them years ago by planting fake clues, like he'd done when he left Pete's initials behind. The feds would not be denied this unexpected chance to finally capture him. And this time was different — they had a name.

Because she was his niece, Harper had

been interviewed in a way that had the earmarks of an interrogation. Would they eventually interrogate Emily too?

But Harper had a few questions of her own about her uncle. How had he become this person? She couldn't fathom her mother's brother doing any of it, but now she completely understood their estrangement. Uncle Jerry was some kind of crazy, but there was much more to it, she'd been told. Psychologists, profilers, authorities — the experts hadn't discovered the reasons why someone would turn to violence in this way. Domestic terrorists — as Uncle Jerry had been labeled — came from all kinds of backgrounds. They were college graduates, military servicemen, rich, poor. It didn't matter.

The FBI investigator had told her that her uncle had been an economics professor at the University of Colorado.

Names had been given as examples. Timothy McVeigh. Ted Kaczynski, otherwise known as the Unabomber. Uncle Jerry, known to the world as the Firebomber, had historically been included in a list of notorious domestic terrorists. He'd also been a member of a terrorist group who called themselves Freedom Force, but the members were either dead or incarcerated, all except for her uncle, who liked to call himself "the judge." Now he operated as a lone wolf, but he connected with like minds on the internet, where his radical ideology was fueled.

Her head throbbed. The rest of her had grown numb.

Looking out the panoramic window, Harper stared at the woods and mountains beyond, but her mind was far from the serene, picturesque view. She was glad they hadn't moved from Lori's to Emerald M yet, or they would be moving right back to Lori's, since the bombed cabin at Heath's ranch was once again in the limelight as the FBI worked to connect that bombing to the one in Grayback. Connect them both to Uncle Jerry.

I should go home now. Go back to Missouri.

Before the bomb in Grayback, she'd been considering staying and working for Sheriff Taggart, if he ever made an official offer, and exploring a relationship with Heath. The thought of actually letting Heath into her heart, risking love, had felt right.

But her intended words to him had been obliterated. She never got to speak them, and now she wasn't sure if she ever would.

Everything . . . *everything* had changed now.

She had answers to questions she hadn't even asked, and those answers left her gutted. Broken again.

Authorities were holding the news close for now, because they didn't want their fugitive to escape them again. Harper suspected it wouldn't be long before someone leaked the discovery to the news stations and national news would be all over it.

The Firebomber, now identified as Gerald Henry Johnson, brother to Leslie Johnson Larrabee, a.k.a. Leslie Reynolds, had been living for two decades in Jackson Hole. Unfortunately, he had eluded capture again and was many steps ahead of them. Uncle Jerry had been making plans for another big bomb. Authorities were hoping to thwart his plans, except they didn't know what structure he would target next. They had determined that his next bomb would definitely be his last because he was reportedly in the end stages of lung cancer.

Uncle Jerry probably thought of it as a last big hurrah, and he might even prefer going out with the bomb instead of from cancer.

Harper sipped the chamomile tea, now tepid instead of hot. Tears had dried on her cheeks. She hadn't bothered wiping them away. She hoped and prayed, once the news was made public, that her and Emily's names weren't released as being connected to the man in any way. They didn't share his last name, but a curious reporter could easily make the connection. Would that information harm Emily's career as a mystery writer, even though she used a pen name? The future seemed muddied at best.

Harper better understood her mother's actions now — why she quickly moved them and changed their names. Mom hadn't lost a friend in a bomb. She'd lost her brother to a crazed, domestic-terrorist mind-set. Harper didn't get why her mother hadn't turned Uncle Jerry in to the authorities back then. After all, he'd murdered her husband. Perhaps he'd threatened their lives too? She could have feared reprisal from the other members of Freedom Force, and that was the reason she fled. That would make the most sense.

Now it was time for Harper to get her act together.

Her hands shook as she gripped the cell phone and stared at Emily's image. She needed to call her sister.

Tomorrow was Emily's big night. Her book was being featured. She was giving a speech.

Harper hesitated. The news that their

461

uncle was the worst kind of criminal would be devastating and could ruin the gala for Emily. Affect her ability to speak to the crowd.

But if Harper didn't tell her, and Emily heard from someone else — such as a news station that had gotten the story early — that could be more devastating.

Releasing a sigh, she set the cell aside.

Lord, I don't know what to do. Do I tell her or do I keep it to myself for now?

Even if she called Emily, she didn't have the words. How did she tell her what had happened?

Harper sensed the moment someone entered the room. Though he crept forward as if trying to surprise her, his cologne let her know it was Heath approaching. His reflection appeared in the window when he stood behind her.

"Trying to sneak up on me?"

He came around the large sofa to sit next to her, his bright blue eyes turning dark with concern. His expression remained warm, gentle even, despite the lines etched in his forehead. "I was never good at sneaking up on you. Or surprising you. But no. I was checking on you and didn't want to disturb you."

"Have you heard something else?" She

wasn't sure how much more she could take.

"Nothing related to the Firebomber. I don't think the feds are going to share anything with us. It's out of the hands of local law enforcement, in spite of Sheriff Taggart's efforts to stay in the loop."

She wasn't sure she could take his intensity at the moment. "I'm sorry." What else could she say?

Heath's smile turned tenuous. "He's still out there, Harper. The man who tried to kill you. I know it's more than that now, but you're in danger — you *personally* are a target — until this is over. I was again tasked with keeping you safe. Taggart suggested I take you away, if I thought it was a good idea. Well, I do think it's a good idea. Taggart doesn't need me." Heath scooted closer and took her hand. "But you do."

She didn't want to need him. She'd tried, really tried, to let herself be free to explore a relationship with this man. But even those words she would have spoken to him about staying had been stolen from her with the blast. As he squeezed her hand, his touch nearly took her breath away. She felt the strength there, the calluses from his work at the ranch, and his complete devotion, the effort he took in caring for the task to which he'd committed himself — or in this case, the person. Harper.

She wanted to ignore the warm thrumming sensations he stirred in her. Because, right now, pain was all around her — the bombing and the house where she'd grown up, still full of death.

An empathetic person, she needed to feel the pain crashing down on her and process through it. She freed her hand from Heath's and hugged herself.

"I'm not going to watch you do this to yourself. Harper" — he turned her to face him — "after what you've just been through, you should know that life's a gift. It shouldn't be wasted or spent on purgatory, or some sort of mental anguish you think is necessary. I won't let you do this to yourself." His eyes crinkled around the edges. He hung his head as if to work up his nerve, then lifted his face again and said, "I have a surprise for you, so maybe I *can* surprise you, after all." A nervous chuckle.

From his pocket he pulled out a printout of two airline tickets.

Sitting forward, she stared at them. "What's going on?" Harper glanced up at him, eyes locking with his. "I don't understand."

"Would you like to attend the Metcalfe Honors and Benefit Gala with me? You can be there with Emily when she is honored and gives her speech."

Her words caught in her throat. Heath — this man — he'd been listening.

He winked, his eyes pleading with her to put this behind them. At least for the gala.

Only Heath could make her smile, albeit a tenuous smile, during this crisis in her life. She hadn't thought of him as a romantic, but this might change her mind. His thoughtfulness could undo her.

Except, well, if only the timing wasn't all wrong.

A wry grin twisted his lips. "I can see huge wind turbines spinning in your head. Look, I know this isn't exactly the perfect time. But there's never going to be a perfect time. You need this for a thousand reasons, and it would mean a lot to your sister too. So, let's get away together. Let's go somewhere safe."

CHAPTER SIXTY-THREE

Saturday, 5:30 P.M.
Dallas, Texas

Harper stared at the long mirror in the hotel room she shared with Emily.

She had hoped she'd be staring at a changed version of herself by the time she'd finished photographing the national parks. Well, there was at least one small change. She had a scar at her hairline. Now she wished she had opted to get bangs. Too late for tonight's event. But the changes she had hoped to see went much deeper than her skin. Admittedly, it was clear she'd held on to a lot of false hopes.

For one, she had hoped to be well and free of the past. She'd tried, believing the therapist's suggestion that focusing on beauty instead of death and murder would help her. But instead of healing from the past, more baggage than she'd known existed had followed, and it was as if she'd come full circle, gathering painful thorns as she walked through a harsh wilderness she'd never meant to travel. She had no control over what had happened, over what her uncle had done.

She never should have gone back.

Emily hummed in the bathroom, pulling Harper's attention back to the moment. Permanent worry lines had taken over her brow and she worked to soften the look. Take the edge off.

Tonight was for Emily, and Harper wanted to focus on her sister, especially after she'd almost lost her to that maniac. Maybe tonight was for Harper too, if only a little.

And Heath?

He could have stayed in Wyoming close to his ranch and his friends. His family — Liam was there, and Heath should spend time with him, catching up. But he had surprised her with plane tickets for two to Dallas. A romantic overture? To some extent that confused her — was he here out of a sense of responsibility that Taggart had assigned him or that he'd assigned himself? Or was it something more? And if his being with her was about exploring a future together, was Harper truly ready to take that risk? Even if she was, Heath might run away when he saw how broken she remained inside.

Regardless, she didn't dare to hope. Not yet. Not until this was over once and for all. Not until Uncle Jerry was behind bars. Shock rolled through her again. She supported herself against the vanity. Squeezed her eyes. She could make it through this night. She *would* make it through this.

God, please let them catch him before he hurts or kills anyone else.

Emily rushed out of the bathroom and headed to the closet for her shoes. "You have five minutes."

On the outside, Harper was ready. On the inside, she was a work in progress who had taken a huge detour and gotten lost. She had done her best to smile and not let on that she carried new burdens. If anything, Emily suspected the pain in Harper's eyes was due to the bomb in Grayback. That was part of it, sure, but maybe the least of it.

How and when should she share the news about their uncle with Emily?

Blinking back tears, she drew in a steadying breath and scrutinized the black dress Emily had let her borrow. Time to focus on the present.

Flashing a brilliant smile, Emily stepped up behind her.

"I know that's not for me." Harper could almost be swept up in Emily's ability to put aside the gloom for an evening.

"Of course it's for you. You look marvelous, darling."

"Thanks."

Maybe Emily had sensed Harper's less-than-enthusiastic response because she immediately hugged Harper long and hard. "I'm so glad you're okay. The last few weeks have been so trying. But we're here together. You couldn't have surprised me more." Emily released her, then added, "And maybe you don't feel it, but on the inside, you're amazing and beautiful. I've been so jealous of you for so long."

"What? Why?"

"Because, Harper . . . you're stronger than anyone I've ever known. I've been thinking a lot about this since I came home. What you've thought of as a weakness, a defect, is actually a strength. You *are* a survivor, and there's nothing wrong with that. I'm sorry for what I said to you before, and that I blamed you for not looking that night when Dad was shot. If you had, you could have been killed too. Instead, you're alive and show me every day, through your determination, how I can be strong too. I know Mom and Dad would be so proud of you. I can only write about detectives and crime scene photographers, but you? You put yourself in the middle for others. Please don't ever change."

Harper wanted more than anything to absorb Emily's words as truth. She didn't want to see herself as broken, as someone who would fail others when it counted most. And maybe she didn't have to.

"When we were still living in Jackson Hole," she said, "we'd see Grand Teton all the time, especially if we had to drive into town. That mountain is so big, and as a kid anyway, it made me think of God. And I used to think if I was that mountain, nothing could move me or scare me. Nothing could hurt me. Now I think I'm finally getting it. God is like that mountain for us and we can hold on to him."

"And no matter what happens in this life, nothing can take us away from him." Emily looked at the mirror. "Oh, look. You've made me cry and now I have to go fix my makeup."

Emily dabbed at her eyes, then glanced at Harper in the mirror and smiled. "That's much better. I do believe that little black dress has found a home. You are now the rightful owner."

Laughter bubbled up inside. Harper released it. For Emily, but for herself too. "Seriously? I look homely in this compared to you and your cobalt blue sparkles."

"When do I get to dress like this? Since I get to walk up on that stage to be honored in this way and give a speech, I want to dazzle them with more than words." She leaned in close, her face next to Harper's, and lifted her cell phone. "Selfie time." Emily snapped the picture.

Harper hadn't been ready. "Give me some warning next time."

"Okay, I'm going to warn you about Heath. He's downstairs and he looks gorgeous." The mischief in Emily's eyes sparkled as much as her dress.

"How do you know?"

"James just texted me a selfie they took in the lobby."

Harper had met James — Emily's previous editor — when she'd first arrived in Dallas.

"Let me see it!"

Emily held back her cell. "That would spoil the surprise. Heath needs to see your reaction."

Okay, now she was nervous. She found a towel and wiped her hands. Emily's teasing grin said she saw more than Harper was ready to reveal.

"What's that look for?" she asked. "It's not like a date or anything."

Emily nodded, but her expression shouted loud and clear that she didn't believe it.

"What about *your* date?"

"What about him? I'm fine admitting that it's a date. Well, sort of. James was having some issues finding a babysitter for his four-year-old and had to bring him on this trip. His son will be attending the gala with us. He's a handful. But you know what? That's fine. Dawson's adorable. I think I might be in love."

"With James or Dawson?"

Her eyes shining, Emily pursed her lips. "We need to get going."

CHAPTER SIXTY-FOUR

Saturday, 6:30 P.M.
Trinity History Theater and Museum
Dallas, Texas

Harper and Heath stood in the lavish foyer of Trinity History Theater and Museum with hundreds of others. Emily and James held hands. Dawson stood close and held his father's other hand as they slowly made their way inside the theater. The place reminded Harper of a cathedral, with its vaulted, arched ceilings. Intricate plaster and elaborate murals depicted images from history.

Harper took Heath's proffered elbow, a flurry of emotions leading her heart in too many directions. For too long she'd been camping, taking pictures, and then hunted by a killer, and now in this elegant setting, she felt like she was in an alternate universe.

Heath grinned down at her as though he was perfectly comfortable in his black suit.

473

His bright blue eyes had lost the shadows. He was clean-shaven, and he'd trimmed his hair. She tried not to think about the kiss they'd shared, but memories and sensations hit her like a straight-line wind. Her legs shaky, she was glad to hold on to his arm. As good as he looked, she wouldn't tell him that she preferred his scruffy cowboy look. Still, Heath looked good no matter what he was wearing, and she breathed in his subtle musky cologne. He was a good man, through and through.

"Have I told you lately how beautiful you look?" With the open admiration in his eyes, she had to wonder if Heath viewed this as a date.

"Not in the last fifteen minutes, but I'm good with that." Maybe she should view it as a date too. "Heath, is this? Are we on a —"

"In all my life, I never dreamed I'd be at a fancy gala with the most beautiful woman in the world on my arm."

He'd cut her off before she finished her question. On purpose? She shouldn't have asked. Of course this wasn't a date. Heath was here because Taggart had instructed him to take her far away from Grayback and protect her. But — the most beautiful woman in the world?

He stepped around in front of her. "I understand better than you know how much caring about someone costs. I'm willing to take that risk with you, Harper. I care deeply about you." The emotion in his searching blue eyes confirmed his words. "But there's time for exploring that when this is over. Not before. I need to stay focused. Are you with me?"

She nodded. "I think so."

She longed for her uncle to be taken down, then she and Heath would have a chance to explore a future together.

Heath and Harper followed Emily and James as he carried Dawson, who was trying to escape, to a row reserved for honorees and their guests. Emily was right about Dawson. He was a cutie and could have the potential to be a heartbreaker one day. She hoped for Emily's sake that his dad wouldn't break Emily's. Her sister was clearly smitten. Harper couldn't have been happier for her.

After a company of actors and artistic dancers performed, the emcee officially opened the event honoring several artists for showcasing the museum and also bringing attention to the Holocaust. The next hour was filled with short documentaries about both the museum and the Holocaust, and in between, the honored guests spoke.

Finally, Emily's moment to address those gathered at the event had arrived.

The presenter read Emily's bio. "We'd like to honor Emily Reynolds, aka L. E. Harper, for her latest work, *Fire and Ash.*"

"Congratulations, Em," Harper said. "You deserve this."

As the crowd applauded, Emily rose from her seat. She looked graceful and polished as she sparkled blue all the way up to the stage, an iPad containing her speech in hand.

The audience couldn't have known what Emily had endured in recent days, nor would she have wanted them to.

"I couldn't be more proud of her," Harper said. Heath nodded, an appreciative grin on his face, but he seemed on edge.

Anxiety pinged through her.

Please . . . Harper needed to stay in this world for a few minutes more.

On stage, Emily tapped the iPad screen and began to read her acceptance speech. "It's such an honor to be here in the midst of those who have received lifetime achievement awards" — she smiled and nodded at another artist honored there tonight — "and I'm truly humbled that you chose *Fire and Ash* — a mystery about a woman who sets out to solve a murder related to the bombing that happened here twenty-three years ago this week. Through her research, she learns of her family's experience in the Holocaust. I love to uncover the truth about history, even as my protagonists solve murders wrapped up in lies. I'm often asked how I come up with story ideas." Emily stared down at her iPad, pausing as if to gather her composure.

Then she lifted her head with a tenuous smile. "But this story is more personal to me."

Harper stiffened and sat taller. Lightheadedness wrapped around her.

"You see, twenty-three years ago this week, my mother lost a dear friend when this museum was destroyed, as you already know, by someone the authorities believed was a Holocaust denier and part of an anti-government domestic terrorist group." Emily gestured at the theater. "But it's been rebuilt into something much bigger, much grander. They did a great job, don't you think?" Like a pro, Emily waited as if she expected applause, and she received it as the audience took in the surroundings.

"Mom died three years ago, and as I was going through her things, I came across a shoebox with articles about the bombing. I had all but forgotten about it. After reading the articles, I knew I had to write this story as a memorial to those who died here and the millions who died in the Holocaust. I'm not going to give the story away, in case you haven't read it, but in real life, things don't always end so well. Still, there's always hope. There can still be redemption. Second chances. This building got a second chance . . ." Emily continued, but Harper couldn't listen.

Emily's words were like thick, hardening cement. Harper barely pulled her gaze away to look at Heath as he listened intently to Emily.

How could I have missed that?

Emily had written a mystery based on the articles Mom had kept about the bomb. Harper hadn't read the book, of course, because she'd been trying to escape death and crime. This was the last place the Fire-bomber had bombed.

CHAPTER SIXTY-FIVE

Uneasiness gnawed at Heath. Emily's speech was a reminder of what they'd been trying to escape. Harper had chosen to wait until after the gala to tell her sister about their uncle, but now he thought that might have been a big mistake.

He reached for Harper's hand, hoping to squeeze it before he lost his nerve, but she stood suddenly and made her way down the row of theater seats and out one of the side doors. He waited a moment for her to return. When she didn't, Heath winked at little Dawson, who squirmed in his father's lap. He feared the boy would eventually escape. Heath eased from his seat, then whispered an apology to James before sliding by people in the row and following Harper through the door. A hallway stretched

479

in both directions, and across the way was a large atrium with chairs. But no Harper.

Hands on his hips, he turned in a circle and then he spotted her. At the end of the hall toward the foyer, she paced. He jogged forward and caught her arms. "What are you doing?"

Tears surged in her eyes. She blinked them back. "Didn't you listen to Emily's speech? The Firebomber. It's here. Tonight. This . . . this is the anniversary of his last bomb. He bombed this place twenty-three years ago. We have to warn them. We have to get people out of here."

"Whoa, whoa. Slow down. What makes you think that? The feds are already on this. They're looking for him and will stop him before his next bomb."

"Like they did last time? They're not moving fast enough. Call it a hunch if you want, but think about it, Heath. We know Uncle Jerry has plans for another bomb. This is the last building he bombed as the Firebomber. Emily and I are here. He could have figured out that Emily would be here. He could have looked inside the camper when we weren't there to get more information about us. Maybe he found out she was an author and that she was being honored here tonight. To a crazy person — that

480

would be the perfect ending to his life. He's sick and dying, we know that. What better way for him to go out? I was wrong to think that he had stopped trying to kill me. I'm still the witness to his crime. Make that, crimes. He killed my father." Hands shaking, she pulled out her cell.

Heath urged her against the wall. He had to think. If she was right, time was against them. It could already be too late. Reporting a bomb if there wasn't one would ruin the evening and make a lot of people angry, not to mention possibly result in prison time for them, depending on how the call was seen. But people's lives could be at stake. He studied Harper. She seemed convinced. He wished he could look around for something suspicious, but that would waste time.

"There's security here for this event. Let's alert them first." He started off to find someone.

"I already told one of them. He left to call someone." Harper lifted her cell to her ear.

"Then that's all we can do," he said.

"Is it? I can't be sure he took me seriously." Harper spoke into her cell, explaining her concerns. "I don't know where it's located. Yes, I told a security guard here, but I don't know what he's doing about it."

She continued to pace, frowning. "No idea

481

when it's going to go off or what it looks like. No, I didn't place the bomb. Please send someone to get these people out of here."

Harper hung up. "I think they're going to send the police, because what else can they do when someone calls in a bomb threat? But what if I'm wrong?"

Heath also pulled out his cell to call Taggart, Moffett, and Liam, because they understood the Firebomber and could take action and get things moving. Heath left voice mails with all three. Time. It all took too much time. He called the local FBI office. Getting through to someone who could make this happen and fast was . . . infuriating.

He should simply pull the fire alarm. That would be faster.

"Special Agent DeSanto speaking."

"Deputy Heath McKade speaking. I think the Firebomber could target Trinity History Theater and Museum tonight during the Metcalfe Gala on the anniversary of the bombing twenty-three years ago. It's packed with people. Should I pull the fire alarm?" That would get them moving.

"Do not activate the alarm. That would incite a panic. People could die as they fled. Someone has already called. We're sending police to assess the situation. They'll make the decision. Let them prepare the building for evacuation and secure the facility. Stand down, Deputy McKade."

Heath ended the call. To assess the situation? To prepare for evacuation? Would they make it in time? "Why couldn't the feds in Wyoming have figured this out from all the information that the bomber left them?"

"Meghan told me something. She said that, in the past, he often left clues to purposefully mislead the authorities. That's one reason they never caught him. Maybe that's what he's done again."

"Let's get your sister and do what we can to save everyone we can."

They rushed back into the theater and stood against the wall. Emily remained on the stage amid laughter and applause, though she glanced offstage as if distracted.

Harper's eyes riveted to her sister. "Oh, hurry, Em. Hurry up, please," she whispered.

"You get out of here. I'll get Emily, James, and Dawson."

"I don't see James. Maybe he took Dawson to the little boys' room. Oh, Heath, what are we going to do?"

"You're leaving the building, Harper. But stay close to law enforcement if possible until I get them out." Heath had committed himself to watching over Harper. Part of him wanted to carry her out of here and away, but she would never forgive him if others were hurt. He would never forgive himself, period.

Heart pounding, he pressed toward disaster.

God, why am I in this situation when you know I never should have been the one to protect Harper? It was my idea to bring her here — and now look! No matter how hard I try, I make things worse!

"I'm not going anywhere without you or my sister." Harper followed him along the far wall where they expected Emily to step from the stage and they could rush her out.

Lord, please let the police get here in time.

He really hoped Harper was wrong about the bomb.

His cell buzzed with a text. He should ignore it. But he'd called several people. He quickly glanced at his phone.

Liam.

Get out! The FBI believes Jerry's going to bomb the Trinity History Museum. Isn't that where you are?

The feds had figured it out. But fast

enough to save people?

Agent DeSanto had told Heath to stand down. But he was here and could do something. He made his way toward the alarm, though he would ask everyone to leave calmly first.

Emily ended her speech. Something offstage drew her attention, and instead of coming toward them, she twisted and walked the other way, then disappeared backstage.

"Oh no, Heath. We have to get her."

With a deafening beep, the fire alarm sounded. Heath shared a look with Harper. He hadn't pulled it.

Someone shouted. "Get out now!"

What?

At that moment, officers rushed in as waves of bodies hurried by them and over them and through them.

Heath reached for Harper and grabbed empty space.

She was gone.

CHAPTER SIXTY-SIX

Harper ran up the steps near the empty orchestra pit. Only the podium remained on the stage.

Heath had been behind Harper as she'd headed to the stage, or so she'd thought, but she'd lost him. She glanced over her shoulder at the escaping vortex of bodies. There was no finding him, or even getting to him, in the panicked crowd as it bottlenecked at the exits. He could take care of himself. He wasn't likely to fall and get trampled.

"Emily!" The alarm still blaring, Harper crept into the shadows backstage. Though growing distant, the cacophony of those fleeing the building still resounded in her ears. Massive curtains and a myriad of props crowded the space. Above her was a catwalk and the fly system of ropes, counterweights, and pulleys, accessed via an opening above. The fly tower. She knew it from her theater days in school.

The complicated maze of rooms backstage was perfect for hiding a bomb. Fear corded her throat.

"Emily! Please, we have to get out of here now. Where are you?"

What if she didn't find her sister in time? Why had she exited the stage on this side? Maybe Emily was simply using a different exit and was already outside.

Harper hurried past dressing rooms with big mirrors. A plethora of costumes. Finally, the crossover. The hallway behind the stage that led to the other side. She ran past more rooms — storage areas for props.

"Emily!"

From beneath her, she heard a voice, but it sounded distant and muffled. Emily? "Please keep talking so I can find you."

Was Emily in the trap room beneath the stage?

"Emily, there's probably a bomb here," Harper shouted. "Meet me halfway. We need to get out of here."

Terror could paralyze her if she let it. She hurried around the corner. Still no Emily. "Where are you? Come on, let's go. Emily, there's a bomb."

Harper found a stairwell and clanked down the studded metal until she stood in the empty space below the stage. The trap room. Stage lift equipment. Boxes. Props. But no Emily.

Emily's scream was muted and came from beneath her yet again.

"Emily!" The hair on the back of Harper's neck stood up as she found yet another stairwell. Her rapidly descending footsteps echoed eerily against the walls. At the bottom of the steps, she entered another doorway and pushed through a heavy curtain. Crates cluttered the place. Another storage space beneath the trap room.

"Emily?"

"I'm here!"

Harper continued past the crates to find her sister.

Emily held Dawson to her as she crouched on the floor. "It's James. He's unconscious."

"Why is he even down here?"

"Maybe to find Dawson? I saw him wander off while I was making my speech." Her words thick with emotion, she stood with the boy. "It looks like James fell and hit his head."

Harper rushed to her sister. "Let's go. I'll get James. We have to get out of here."

Dawson lifted his face from Emily's shoulder and pointed. "That man. He hit my daddy."

Emily stared at the child. "What man? I don't see anyone."

Fear slithered up Harper's spine as she glanced around the space filled with shadows and dark corners and more stage props.

Her limbs shaking as she stood, Harper blinked back the surging tears. What looked to be a timer was attached to a stack of crates labeled COSTUMES.

Five minutes and thirty-three seconds.

Thirty-two.

Thirty-one.

Emily's eyes widened. "Is that what I think it is?"

Harper stumbled. The previous bombs in Grayback were only practice for this one big event. She guessed this would be a much bigger bomb — a highly explosive device joined with incendiary material to create a fire. In other words, whatever wasn't obliterated by the explosion would be consumed by fire.

Her knees almost gave out. No tears came this time. Only hopeless determination to save her sister, James, and Dawson. "Yes" — her words were barely a whisper now — "we have to get away."

"It's too late," Emily said. "We won't make it."

"Of course we will. We'll get away." She

489

tugged out her cell to call the authorities but got no signal beneath the stage. In her limited knowledge, if they could disengage the detonator, he couldn't still activate the bomb. But Harper didn't have a clue how to do that. What did it matter?

"Come on, we're going to be okay." She urged her sister forward and through the heavy curtain. "Go ahead. I'll carry James."

"What? He's too heavy. You can't. And I can't leave him to die!"

Harper frowned. "No, of course you can't. But he would want you to save his son. I'm the strongest between us. I'll carry him fireman-style. Even small women can carry big men like that." Or try to. "No time to argue, now run!"

Emily shifted Dawson in her arms, then entered the stairwell.

Harper focused on James. "I don't suppose you could wake up and run out, could you?"

She tried to lift the man over her shoulder. He had a stocky frame. Many pounds of pure muscle. But she wasn't going to beat that ticking bomb with him on her back. She wasn't going to be able to climb those stairs.

God, do you hear me? Please help me!

James grunted. Was he finally coming to?

She urged him to his feet. Relief rushed through her as she assisted his stumbling form forward. Adrenaline, an answer to her prayer, empowered her to hike the steps with him, but he was still much too slow.

And leaning awkwardly to the side. She shifted him against her.

Her heart hammered as tears choked her. Time was not on their side.

They made it to the second landing. She gasped.

If only she could make it through that door. Then she would have to find her way out of the maze of curtains and props to exit the building. "Come on, James. We can do this."

She gasped her way up the next flight, her muscles straining under his dead weight. He'd passed out again.

No, no, no, no . . .

She let his body slide to the floor, wedged against the door, then plopped next to him to catch her breath. She would have to reposition him. "James, if you don't wake up, neither of us is going to make it out of here."

She wouldn't be able to live with herself if she left him to die, so that wasn't an option.

Why am I so weak? I thought I was stronger than this! Not me, but God. God is stronger.

Help me, Lord. Help us!

"The name of the Lord is a strong tower; The righteous runs into it and is safe." She forced the Scripture out in between her gasps for breath. Squeezed her eyes shut and pictured that unmovable mountain as tears leaked out.

Harper thought of her mother crying over the bombing. She'd been crying over her brother who'd turned into a monster bomber.

And unless the police were searching the place. The bomb squad. SWAT. Someone. She and James were going to die.

CHAPTER SIXTY-SEVEN

"Harper!" Heath yelled as he was forced to exit the theater with the rush of the crowd. He could only hope that Harper had found Emily and made it out.

Once he was outside, he moved out of the tidal wave of bodies. Police officers stood at the exit, herding terrified people away from the building. No way would they allow anyone back in. But if Harper was still inside, that's exactly where he had to go.

"Harper!" He tried again.

Officers directed people as far as a block away. His heart sank. He didn't think she was in this crowd, but how could he know? He kept searching and calling her name. She would be with Emily if she was here.

"Heath!"

Relief surged as he turned. Emily rushed forward, holding Dawson. "I think she's still inside. James was injured, and she was going to help him out. But I don't think she came out. She didn't follow me out like she said she would."

He gripped her arms. "Where is she?"

"She was making her way from a room beneath the stage where the bomb is. I can show you, but I need someone to watch Dawson."

"That's not happening. You take Dawson away and keep him safe."

A few stragglers exited the theater. Law enforcement was creating a barrier — far from the potential explosion. The bomb squad was probably on the way, but they often didn't make it before a bomb detonated. Heath fisted his hands. The bomb squad, law enforcement, they all did their best, but they were only human.

Heath was only human too, but he'd been through this scenario — losing someone he loved — and he wasn't going to stand by and do nothing. He'd told Harper that the price for caring was high. And that he was willing to pay.

Maybe he was insane.

A woman stumbled at the side exit, and an officer assisted her. Heath rushed past, ignoring the officer calling after him.

He ran up the steps of the stage. "Harper! Where are you?"

He got lost in a maze of rooms and hallways. He didn't know where he was. Emily had mentioned it was beneath the stage. How did he get there?

CHAPTER SIXTY-EIGHT

"You shouldn't have come here, girl." The voice was familiar. Menacing.

She stared at Uncle Jerry as he crept up the stairwell. No, she wouldn't even think of him as her uncle. She wouldn't call him uncle. It was too hard. "Why are you doing this?"

"If you're here, you know enough to know why."

"You're insane, that's why."

"The government always covers up the truth. Creates their own lies about our history so they can direct the future."

"But none of that makes any sense now. Blowing up a building filled with people isn't the way to make your point."

"No one listens unless you make them listen. But it doesn't matter. I'm dying, and I found that I can make my point while I go out on my own terms."

"But I'm not dying. I have my full life

ahead of me, if you don't take it from me tonight." And Heath. Harper wanted that chance with him. Even a few moments of gain were worth the risk of loss. How had she ever doubted that before? "Think of your sister, Leslie. She wouldn't want you to kill her daughters too like you killed her husband."

"So you know about your dad." His frown deepened. "I didn't know that was you with the camera, or I wouldn't have tried to kill you. I would have tried to silence you another way."

A lot of comfort that was, coming from a killer. He was too cold to help.

"Is that your idea of an apology? It's too late. People are already dead. More people are going to die."

"They're all gone. I pulled the fire alarm and got them out. All except for you."

Wha— her breath left her. "You?" Hope surged. Harper got to her feet and pulled on James. "You set that off? But why?"

"Your sister. Her speech . . . the book she wrote." He gasped between each word. Planning all this, putting the bomb in place had probably taxed the last of his energy. That and the cancer eating him alive. "I sat on the catwalk and listened. People were mesmerized by her words." He leaned against the wall. "I'm dying. I can't make a difference after I'm gone. I'm the last one of us in our fight for truth and freedom from lies the government perpetuates so they can control us. But Emily needs to live to get the word out." He dragged in a breath and coughed.

"The word out. What are you talking about? What lies?" Her heart twisted in a thousand knots at his complete paranoia.

"To explain it all, I wrote a letter to the *New York Times.* They should receive it tomorrow. Tell her to read that and she'll understand why she needs to look deeper into history and find the truth. I know she'll see it for herself. Then she can write about it and more people will hear."

Emily didn't see history the way Uncle Jerry did or deny that the Holocaust happened. Emily wasn't an extremist either. But Harper wouldn't waste her breath. He wouldn't listen. No. Because he wasn't done talking.

"I know she was meant to carry on the fight for truth in history. It's in her DNA, after all. So I have to let her live. After listening to her speech, I now have peace in knowing that I made the right choices. That Emily will continue my cause, whether she knows it now or not."

Waves of nausea rolled through Harper at his words. The man actually believed he was doing the right thing. She could tell by his labored breathing that he would die soon whether or not the bomb took him. She thought about Emily's acceptance speech and how it had affected Uncle Jerry. He missed one thing.

"Emily talked about second chances, Uncle Jerry. You can have that second chance."

"To do what? It's too late."

How did a person get to the place in life where they believed they didn't deserve a second chance? Harper had lived in that place for far too long. She would forgive herself for her mistakes. For letting Daddy down.

But she couldn't wait for Uncle Jerry to have his come-to-Jesus moment, if he ever did. She tried to heft James up onto her shoulder. He moaned. Was he waking up? Was there enough time left for them to get out?

"It's odd," Uncle Jerry continued. "There's a kind of euphoria knowing that I'm going out with a bomb. I'll leave behind a legacy."

"A legacy of death and destruction." Maybe she could take him out, and then what? The bomb was still counting down. "Help me. Please stop the bomb. I'm not ready to die. Are you?"

"I'm ready, yes. And on my own terms. But even if I wanted to, I can't stop the bomb. No one can."

CHAPTER SIXTY-NINE

Heath found a door to a stairwell and ran down the steps.

"Harper!" He rushed through a heavy curtain and found a big, spacious room. A small red light caught his attention.

Counting down.

18 seconds.

The oxygen was sucked from him. "Harper, where are you?"

Fear gutted him.

Liam would be absolutely furious with him if he got himself killed. He'd be furious with himself if he let anything happen to Harper. Wasn't this how it all worked out though?

Didn't it always end this way? He'd brought her there. Him. He was responsible. And this time, he would lose the woman he loved even if he found her in the next few seconds, because there wasn't time to get out of the building.

He found him then.

Jerry. The man stared at Heath, his eyes glazed.

"Where is she? What did you do with her?" Heath demanded.

"This way." Uncle Jerry started walking.

"Wait. Where are we going? Why should I trust you?"

"You have ten seconds to decide." Jerry kept walking.

"Harper!" Heath called as he followed her uncle. This was nuts.

God, help me. Should I be following this killer?

But he had no idea where to search for Harper. Was she even still in the building?

Jerry took him down a tunnel, then pointed at a blast door. "She's in there."

He pounded on the door. "Opening up!" Without waiting for a response, he shoved a lever upward, then pulled the door open.

Harper gasped when she saw Heath and pulled him inside.

"Lock it now!" Jerry shouted as he shut them all in.

Wait!" Heath should open the door and pull Jerry in with them, but it was too late.

A thunderous rumble resounded. He pulled Harper down to sit on the ground and wrapped his arms around her. *Oh, Lord, please let us survive.*

She pressed her face into his shoulder. The structure felt as if it moved a few centimeters. Harper's fingernails cut into him.

If the shelter didn't protect them against the shock wave, they were all dead anyway. Their survival depended on what size bomb Jerry had built and if the shelter had been built to withstand it.

But there was something else.

The incendiary effect. How long could they reasonably stay in there?

Would it outlast a prolonged fire that would suck up all the oxygen? He hoped adequate ventilation had been installed.

After a few seconds, the rumbling died down.

Harper flicked on a flashlight. A wide-eyed James sat on a beanbag in the corner holding a flashlight too, a purple lump on his head. Seeing James there surprised Heath.

"Emily should already be safe. She took Dawson out." Harper spoke as if to reassure herself as much as James.

"You're right," Heath said. "She told me you were still inside, so I came to find you. And that's when I ran into your uncle."

"He was the one who set off the fire alarm. He couldn't stop the bomb. But he could save me. Save us" — she looked at

James, then back to Heath — "and now you. After the building was destroyed the last time, the architects put in a bomb shelter when it was rebuilt. Uncle Jerry said it was the only way to survive."

"Your uncle couldn't have survived the bomb blast."

"No. He wanted to die in the bomb instead of from cancer. But he had one last redemptive act, Heath."

As though that could repair all the damage. The lives he took in the past and more recently. But if that's what Harper needed to believe, he would give her that.

After a few seconds, he relaxed, if only a little.

"Do you think it's over?" she asked. "Is it safe to go out now?"

He released her and stood on shaky legs. "I think it's over. I hope it's over. But if we open that door, it could be dangerous. The place could be up in flames."

"He told me that he didn't have enough time or money to gather the incendiary materials. I think because he was dying and because we were closing in on him. Weird to think he was disappointed about that."

James cleared his throat. "But there could be secondary fires."

Heath agreed. "We could have a window

of opportunity to get out of here before the building crashes completely down on us, if it's not already too late. But maybe we should wait for emergency response teams."

"No," Harper said. "They won't even know that we survived unless they know about this blast shelter, and even then, they could take too long. I'm for opening the door."

"I'm with her," James said. "I need to make sure Dawson is all right. I don't want him to think I'm gone. He already lost his mother."

Heath unlatched the blast door and shoved. It wouldn't budge.

CHAPTER SEVENTY

"We have to keep trying." Harper paced the small space that seemed to grow smaller by the second. This was just great. They were trapped. It was hot and stuffy.

I have to get out of here.

Heath and James grunted, pushing, shoving with their brute strength against the door. At least James had recovered enough to help.

Harper wanted to help, but there wasn't room. "I don't think they're supposed to be that hard to open."

"Unless something on the other side is preventing it." James gave up. "Isn't there another way out? Another exit in here?"

She didn't see one. "Why did they build it this way so that the door opens out? That seems like a bad idea."

"The hinges," Heath said. "The blast could blow the door inward, otherwise."

Heath continued his efforts. The blast

506

door gave an inch. Dust rushed in. A crack. It was something. He put his face up close to the space and looked out. "No fire. Let's keep working on this door. Maybe someone can squeeze out and go for help."

Harper took James's place and shoved against the door. "We can yell for help too."

"We're too far down," James said. "They're never going to hear us down here. We have to get out before more of the building collapses. It makes sense to put the shelter deeper in the basement, but then living through a bomb means also having to survive the rubble as you get out."

Sweat dripped down her back and beaded across her brow and upper lip. The door moved another few inches. "Only a little more and I can fit through. I can go for help."

Heath gasped for breath. "I don't know. You could get hurt. It could be dangerous. The building is unstable."

"What did you think was going to happen when we opened the door? It's our only chance." James's voice gave away his desperation. "What's the matter with you?"

And he was right. No good options were available.

"Maybe I can move what's blocking the door," she said. "Don't worry, Heath. I have to do this. You know I do."

Heath and James gave it another push and she squeezed through, ignoring the flitting image of the door slamming and crushing her. On the other side, she sucked in a breath.

"Okay, I'm out." As if they didn't know. She flicked on the flashlight and stayed near the blast shelter that was all but buried.

Sparks and a buzz drew her attention up to where the entire left side of the ceiling had collapsed. The flashlight revealed much. Jumbled rebar dangled. Concrete, drywall, and steel — it was all twisted together. Pure rubble.

They were on the bottom floor.

Any hope she had quickly fled. Thick emotion filled her throat. So what if the blast shelter had safeguarded them? They would never get out.

No. She couldn't think like that.

She wouldn't let go of hope, no matter how small.

We're going to get out of here.

She turned her attention to a chunk of concrete blocking the blast door. How had they opened the door at all? Moving that would take muscles. The kind she didn't have. But maybe she could use leverage. She searched for something — anything. A rumble shuddered through the building. Dust trickled.

She tried not to think about the tons of building materials pressing in on them.

"What's going on, Harper?" Heath's voice sounded muffled.

Disheartened, she didn't want to answer him. She glanced up at the ceiling and the beams barely hanging. The electrical wires. Lines sparking.

"I'm trying to move concrete out of the way. I need leverage. Hold on."

A severed steel rod would work. She propped it under a piece of concrete that was shaped like the state of Florida wedged against the blast door.

She thrust the rod under Florida, then leaned on it. Nothing. Put her full body weight on it. Nothing.

God, have you really brought me through all this only to die here and now?

She tried again.

The Florida Panhandle broke away.

"Yes!" She pumped her fist and called out to Heath, "Okay, try the door now."

The men groaned inside as they pushed on the blast door. It budged, but not much. That rumble again.

"Guys!" She peered inside. "Squeeze out.

The ceiling isn't going to last. It's now or never."

"Just one more push," Heath said. "James can't make it through this."

"Okay, let me see if I can move more of Florida."

"What?"

She ignored his question and worked her magic lever again. It was no use.

"Heath, it's not going to work. Please come out so you can do it."

Heath squeezed out, then turned toward the opening and spoke to James. "Come on, you can do it."

James tried, but his thickset form wouldn't let him through.

Heath looked at Florida. "Let me try."

He took the steel rod and pressed down. Groaned and shoved. The chunk of debris fell away from the blast door. Along with the ceiling on the far side of the building. Dust filled the air, choking them. More chunks began falling. They were running out of time.

Heath pulled the blast door all the way open and reached inside to yank James forward. "Come on!"

Flashlights lighting the way, they scrambled over chunks of concrete and obliterated building materials. Their progress was much too slow to outrun the massive cave-in. Harper wasn't sure where they were going as they pressed forward. Heath pulled her into a partially intact stairwell. James was on their heels. He shoved the dented door that hung from one hinge into what remained of the doorframe.

"How —"

The crashing ceiling cut off her words. She pressed her face into Heath's chest.

Was this the end? Was she going to die in his arms?

Dust billowed into the stairwell. Harper coughed, along with Heath and James. The ceiling had collapsed inward like a bowl, leaving the stairwell undisturbed. Good. This was good, wasn't it?

He released her and peered upward. Though the stairwell hadn't crumbled with the rest of the building, the stairs no longer looked like stairs but instead were a mass of twisted metal that was torn apart near the next floor.

"That?" James asked. "You want us to go up that?"

"That's our only way out, man."

"It will probably come down on our heads."

"It might. We'll climb one stair at a time." Heath glanced at James. "Harper is going first. You can go next, my friend."

Harper didn't like this. She didn't want to leave either of them behind, but she wouldn't save Heath by wasting time arguing with him. Her only choice was to climb carefully and quickly up what was left of the stairs.

Heath helped her gain purchase. When she gripped the rail and placed her knees on that first clump of steel, she looked down at him.

"Don't worry." He winked. "I plan to make it out alive tonight too. Now go. Make it out and find your sister."

Was this the last time she'd see him?

CHAPTER SEVENTY-ONE

The building shuddered again. Heart pounding, she gripped the next step and crawled forward. The walls had crumbled and bent in places, so she couldn't stand up. Instead, she had to keep crawling like she was in the ever-shrinking tunnel of an underground cavern. She didn't dare look down or she might lose her nerve.

"You're doing great, Harper." Heath's words echoed through the stairwell. If only he could have made this climb along with her.

Just a little farther and then she should be at ground level. That didn't mean she could get out. She risked a glance down and couldn't even see Heath or James. Harper slid beneath splintered drywall to continue on the path, only to find the stairs didn't go all the way.

They had torn away from the wall and what might have been a door.

Her flashlight flickered and went out.

Oh no. Her heart tumbled.

Above her, voices sounded. And through an opening in the wall, light. Hope surged.

Could she make the jump from her perch on the twisted metal stairs to the railing next to the wall? She sucked in a few breaths, then propelled herself forward. She grabbed the rail, but her palms were moist and she started to slip.

"Help!"

Strong arms reached toward her. "I got you." Hands gripped hers and pulled her through the opening. People cheered as a man lifted her to her feet.

She sucked in a breath as she wiped sweat and grime from her eyes. "There are two men down there. Heath and James."

"Harper!" Emily cried out from across the street where onlookers watched.

The man who had pulled her from the building handed her off to another guy — a firefighter? He urged her away from the building toward a waiting ambulance.

"No, I'm staying. I have to wait for Heath!" *He has to make it out.* "Will you please let my sister over? James was her date tonight. He's down there too. He should be coming out."

Her bones ached. Her limbs screamed.

And her heart pounded. *Come on, come on . . .*

Emily ran across the street and hugged her. She cried in her arms. "I thought I'd lost you. I never would have left you behind if —"

"It's okay. You had Dawson. Where is he?"

"A policewoman is watching him for me. He's sitting in the car with her. But what happened? How could you survive?"

Harper's mind felt like it would collapse in on itself before this was over. "Uncle Jerry saved me. Showed me to a blast shelter. After the last bomb, the owners had insisted on building a safe room in case of a terror attack. The problem was that we were almost trapped in there."

A man assisted James from the building, drawing Harper and Emily's attention. The crowd cheered.

James bent over his thighs to catch his breath and pointed at the building. "He's still down there." James shook his head. "The stairs collapsed, so I don't know how he can get out."

"What?" Harper grabbed his collar and shook him. "And you left him down there?"

"There was nothing I could do. I didn't see him behind me when it collapsed. I just had to crawl out as fast as I could."

Emily pulled Harper to her and hugged her. "It's going to be okay."

"It's not. It's not going to be okay." Harper sobbed into Emily's beautiful sequined dress.

All because of Uncle Jerry. But Emily's speech had somehow turned him. He'd saved the people he'd initially planned to kill. He'd saved Harper and James and . . .

Emily gently turned Harper and pointed. "Look."

Harper was afraid to look. She was afraid to hope. Finally, she glanced to the opening as Heath climbed out. Clanking and crumbling resounded as a plume of dust rose from what had been the stairwell. There must have been enough material left that Heath had been able to climb out. The building wasn't done collapsing though.

"Back. Everyone stand back!" Firefighters pushed Emily and Harper away from the building. Screams resounded.

Harper didn't want to leave Heath again. She turned to run toward the building. A cloud of dust rose to the sky like a miniature mushroom cloud.

A man caught her up in his arms and carried her away.

Heath!

Once they stood at a safe distance, Harper spotted her sister and James. Everyone except her uncle was out now — and safe, though maybe not sound.

She leaned into Heath. "I thought I'd lost you."

He hugged her long and hard. She never wanted to let go. "I'm so sorry, Harper."

But she did let go so she could face him. "What are you talking about? What are you sorry for?"

His eyes glistened with pain. "I did this. Every time I try to fix things, I make them worse. I thought things could be different, but I see now that nothing has changed. I brought you here so we could get away from what had happened. But I brought you right into the thick of it. You almost died."

Oh, Heath. "You have it all wrong, Heath. First, you got me those tickets to see Emily — that meant everything to me. You listened to my heart. You knew what I wanted. It was . . . so romantic, even though I'm not sure you meant it that way." Harper seriously wanted to kiss the guy, but she had to finish so he would understand. Harper knew his insecurities all went back to his mother — if he hadn't begged her to come back, she wouldn't have died in the fire. Or so Heath believed.

"You brought me to the right place at the

right time," she said. "I was able to help Emily. To save her life and get her out. I wasn't the only survivor. And something else. I was able to talk to my uncle and hear his last words. He was a sick man. Sick in the head and sick in his body. And then you came for me — you risked your life and came in search of me . . ." Tears choked her next words. "I told myself I was too broken to love. People die and leave loved ones behind to suffer with the loss. All I could think about when I thought I would die in that bomb was how much I wanted a chance with you, Heath McKade."

He lifted her face. Dirt and grime smudged his skin. She doubted she looked any different. Bright blue eyes stared out from behind his dirt-covered face.

"What are you saying, Harper?"

She couldn't answer him. Why had she said any of it?

He peered into her eyes like he would comb through her mind and heart until he found the answer.

"It's okay," he said. "I know you're still afraid. I was wary too. But I'm not anymore. I'm done holding back. Harper, I don't want to scare you off before we've even had a chance, but I could love you, if I don't already. We can take it slow though — that is, if you want to take that chance with me."

She didn't want her decision, her words, to be the result of the traumatic series of events that had brought them together. But as he said, they could take their time.

"I already told you I want that chance, Heath, but how *can* we explore this? You live in Grayback. I live in Missouri."

"For now." He eased her chin up and planted his lips against hers, gently, but with the promise of so much more. She had no physical or emotional energy left to fight what had grown between them, and that was probably a good thing.

CHAPTER SEVENTY-TWO

Few places in this world are more dangerous than home. Fear not, therefore, to try
the mountain passes. They will kill care,
save you from deadly apathy, set you free,
and call forth every faculty into vigorous,
enthusiastic action.

John Muir

Three Months Later
Emerald M Guest Ranch

Heath took in the newly finished cabin that
replaced the one Jerry had bombed. Heath
had lost too much time already to this
bombing business. He was more than ready
to move on with the next chapter of his life.
Thank goodness guests were scheduled to
start arriving again next week, though the
season would soon be over.

Leroy stood next to him, using a cane to
support his injured leg. "It's going to take
time, Heath, but you'll get back into the

swing of things."

If a year hadn't been enough for him to get over the pain of his gunshot wound, even psychologically, he had no idea how long recovering from the trauma of recent events was going to take. Maybe a lifetime. But Leroy was referring to the guest ranch business.

Not Heath personally.

Leroy had suffered much more. He'd finally recovered enough to join Heath back at the Emerald M a few days ago.

Heath clapped him on the shoulder, but not too hard. "I'm glad to have you back."

"But you're going to need someone to replace me. I can't do for you what I did before."

"I'm not going to replace you, Leroy. You're family now. You and Evelyn. Don't ever forget that. I'll pick up the slack. Liam's here too. He can help with the horses. He's gifted with them."

Liam was down by the barn in the corral working with Amber, Charlie's favorite horse. She was making plans to bring Amber down to Texas. Heath looked forward to seeing her soon.

As he watched Liam, Heath tried to wrap his thoughts around how much had changed over a few weeks' time. Liam was back, and

Harper Reynolds had come back into his life and left again. She was still in Missouri helping her sister sell her house and plan a big wedding. Yep. James had proposed a month ago. Heath figured the near-death experience had expedited the timeline for James and Emily's relationship. They'd known each other long enough to know, Harper said.

For his part, Heath struggled to hang on to the hope that he and Harper could spend enough time together that he could propose and she wouldn't run scared. Granted, they hadn't known each other that long — as adults — and they'd gone through a lot of turmoil, but Heath wasn't the kind of man to waste time.

He knew she was what he wanted.

The daily texts, nightly phone calls, and weekly video chats would only work so long. It would only take them so far.

He couldn't seem to get the chance to convince her that he was the guy she wanted. He hoped, how he hoped, they could make a future together and put all this behind them. That was his heart turning the rational part of his brain to a bowl of soggy breakfast cereal.

They might have too much baggage with everything that had happened. Harper wasn't likely to forget. He couldn't make her forget, but could he help her put it behind her and forge a new life and future?

That might not be so easily done in Grayback.

And Heath couldn't exactly give up his ranch and horses, his lifeblood, his home . . . or could he?

He hiked back to the main house and clomped up the porch in time to see Lori Somerall driving up in her Navigator. Oh, great. She smiled and waved. She had a passenger too.

He crossed his arms and waited for her to get out. She'd stopped by a few times. Brought a meal now and then as if she didn't have her own guest ranch to run. She stayed for the meals too. But this had to end.

How could he let her down gently?

Lori got out on her side, and another woman got out from the passenger side.

Harper.

Heath stumbled. Caught himself on the post. Harper's grin stretched across her face, and Lori laughed as she walked with Harper to his porch.

"She had me watch out for you, Heath. Make sure you and yours were okay. I don't think she took your word for it."

Harper took a step up onto the porch, a question in her eyes. *Do you want me here?*

"Come here, you." He pulled her to him and kissed her. He never wanted to let her go, but he was afraid to hold her too close.

When he released her, she laughed. "Lori can keep a secret. Actually, she was the one who convinced me to come. She said you were pining away for me."

He arched a brow. "Pining away?"

"Her term, not mine. Well? Were you?"

"I *was* pining away, yes." Was that all she wanted from him?

Lori smiled. "I'm heading out to get ready for my big date with Jud."

"Jud?" Heath knew that name.

"Sheriff Taggart. You know *him*, right?" She waved and climbed into her vehicle.

As Lori drove away, Heath pulled Harper close again. How did he keep her here this time?

"Heath, I'm sorry it's taken me so long. It wasn't on purpose, I promise."

"You don't owe me an explanation. The fact is, I live here. This is my home. I told you we would make it work."

"It can only work if I live in Jackson Hole too, Heath. I know you can't move, and I would never ask you to do that. I had planned to stay before the bomb, but every-

524

thing got messed up. I'm here now. In fact, I talked to Sheriff Taggart this week. His offer is still on the table if I want it. And . . . I do."

Heath wanted to hug her. "Are you sure about this?"

"I'm sure about us, Heath. I already told him I'm interested, and Lori is letting me stay with her until I can find a place of my own."

He drew her close again and pressed his forehead against hers. Tucked her hands in his against his chest. "I missed you, Harper. I love you. I know all I need to know. Marry me."

He cringed inside. Had he scared her off?

Harper lifted her face and kissed him, sending tendrils of warmth through him. "I've only known you for more than twenty years, Heath. I thought you'd never ask."

ACKNOWLEDGMENTS

Writing a novel requires not only an author but also a team of encouragers and experts, as well as the patience of family and friends.

My heartfelt gratitude goes to Jeff and Tina Moyers, my brother and sister-in-law, for your encouragement through the years. And as RV campers and dwellers, thank you for offering your expertise and your ideas to make my scenes ring true.

Richard Mabry, MD — I always appreciate your willingness to assist when I have a medical crisis in a book! You're always eager to answer my questions and even rewrite scenes if necessary.

Susan Sleeman — you're such a treasure. A gem. A wealth of information. And you have so much patience with my many lengthy emails. You've been such a great friend to me personally, and to my writing career as a whole. I can't thank you enough for being quick to answer my questions about technical issues, police procedures, or scenes in general.

Retired Undersheriff Roger Harrison — for answering my many questions about police and crime scene procedures in rural areas. I appreciate your patience with my "crazy imagination," as you put it!

Wesley Harris (http://writecrimeright.blog spot.com) — for your input about every aspect of police procedures and crime scenes.

Judy Melinek, MD, forensic pathologist — for the time you took to detail what happens to a body when a bullet of a certain caliber enters. It's important to know what characters will truly see when someone is shot — as opposed to what television and movies might show us.

Martin Roy Hill — once again, you've come to the rescue! Sure, a person can learn how to make a bomb on the internet, but it's much more complicated than I could ever understand. Thank you for setting me on the right path.

Crime scene writers' group — to the many technical voices within the crime scene writers' group for always stepping up to answer my countless questions.

Tari Faris and Susan May Warren (Novel Academy) — for setting me straight on my characters and helping me understand the numerous layers of their dark-moment stories!

Sharon Hinck — there are no adequate words to describe how much your help has meant to me. You have such a deep love for the Lord and encourage my heart so much. Your eye for great writing and storytelling is exceptional. Thank you for taking the time to read my story, for not being afraid to tell me when I missed the mark and where the story didn't work for you, and for offering suggestions in countless brainstorming emails.

Lynne Gentry — for your insights into the characters' motivation. You have an eye for details no one else catches.

Lisa Harris — what a journey this has been! I don't know what I would have done on this writing road without your encouragement.

Proofreader (and my amazing daughter) Rachel Goddard — for reading the manuscript for inconsistencies, weird sentence structures, and plot holes. I loved reading your comments that made me laugh so hard (freaky Leroy)! You have such a great sense of humor, which made working through your critique so much more fun. I love you!

Ellen Tarver — once again, you've helped

me strengthen the story and showed me where you weren't "buying it"! Your expertise has been invaluable.

The Revell team — Lonnie Hull DuPont, once again, thank you for believing in me. Amy Ballor, your patience with me and attention to details are exceptional. Karen Steele — you make my books sound so good. To the art department — thank you for the effort you put into the cover and interior designs. I love how you seem to get into an author's head and know exactly the "look" that will convey the story best.

My agent, Steve Laube — I'm so glad you saw something in me eight years ago when you signed me. It has been an amazing ride!

My husband and children — Dan, I couldn't have seen my dreams come true without your continued encouragement and patience with me as I traveled to conferences every year and wrote books instead of earning a decent income at a regular job. I love you! Rachel, Christopher, Jonathan, and Andrew — thank you for inspiring this crazy writing momma!

Jesus — it's all about YOU.

ABOUT THE AUTHOR

Elizabeth Goddard is the award-winning author of more than forty romance novels and counting, including the romantic mystery *The Camera Never Lies* — a 2011 Carol Award winner. She is a Daphne du Maurier Award for Excellence in Mystery and Suspense finalist for her Mountain Cove series — *Buried, Backfire,* and *Deception* — and a Carol Award finalist for *Submerged.* When she's not writing, she loves spending time with her family, traveling to find inspiration for her next book, and serving with her husband in ministry. For more information about her books, visit her website at www .ElizabethGoddard.com.

The employees of Thorndike Press hope you have enjoyed this Large Print book. All our Thorndike, Wheeler, and Kennebec Large Print titles are designed for easy reading, and all our books are made to last. Other Thorndike Press Large Print books are available at your library, through selected bookstores, or directly from us.

For information about titles, please call:
(800) 223-1244

or visit our website at:
gale.com/thorndike

To share your comments, please write:

Publisher
Thorndike Press
10 Water St., Suite 310
Waterville, ME 04901